Waiting i

Keith A Pearson

Inchgate Publishing

Copyright © 2021 by Keith A Pearson

All rights reserved.

No portion of this book may be reproduced in any form without written permission from the publisher or author, except as permitted by UK and international copyright law.

Chapter 1

"Would you like to live somewhere else, or would you prefer to be euthanised?"

He doesn't reply, and his expression remains neutral.

"I'm assured the procedure is painless if that's your concern. I'd imagine it's like falling asleep."

Still no reaction.

"Come on, Merle," I urge. "You must have a preference: new home, or death? Which is it to be?"

He blinks slowly, twice, and then saunters back across the kitchen towards the hallway.

"Shall I take that as a maybe for euthanasia?" I call after him. He doesn't look back.

Merle and I have lived together for fourteen years. It was Mother who invited him into our home but she's no longer here, so there's just the two of us now, rattling around the house. I, too, will soon be gone and despite his independent nature, Merle can't stay here alone. If he doesn't make a decision himself, I'll have no option but to make it for him, and I'm leaning towards a trip to the vet.

"Stubborn feline," I mumble.

I return to my list and ink a question mark next to Merle's name. There are sixty-two other items on the list and nearly all are ticked. I am almost ready.

Turning the page, I return to my notes. When the time of departure is upon me, my final act will be to complete a tribute letter to Mother, and my notes will ensure I cover the most pertinent points in that final correspondence. It is the least I can do for the woman who has dedicated almost thirty years of her life to my well-being.

Merle returns to the kitchen. He jumps up to the table and makes himself comfortable.

"Have you reached a decision?"

He yawns and then proceeds to groom his sleek black fur using his right paw as a brush. We don't have much in common — Merle being a cat and me being, well, a species other than a cat — but I do admire his obsessive cleanliness.

"I understand the magnitude of your decision, so take your time to consider both options. I will need to know soon, though."

Despite their obvious intelligence, it is disappointing cats are unable to communicate verbally. I suspect they'd make much better conversationalists than many humans. Alas, I don't have time for evolution to address my disappointment, so I'll have to keep an eye out for a physical indicator of Merle's preference in the coming days.

It is not the only sign I'm waiting on.

I close the notebook and open a leather-bound day planner. A4 size, it was a Christmas present from Mother, although I don't think she popped out herself to buy it or had any say in the decision because it's unlikely Mother even knows what year it is. The last time she entered a shop on her own, the police were called. It was a spherical-headed police officer who, during a quiet conversation in this very kitchen, first suggested Mother might be losing her faculties. Up until the intervention of PC Folkes, I presumed Mother's errant behaviour was merely a symptom of old age, an eccentricity.

We paid a visit to Dr Nash, and Mother underwent several tests before the dementia diagnosis finally arrived, delivered sombrely by Dr Nash in person. The decision was made, and with confused reluctance, Mother moved to a care home. That was a good day; not for her, obviously, but for me as I knew Helen Armstrong's needs would be catered for after my departure. Her condition is now at the stage where she no longer recognises me as her son, so it's unlikely I'll be missed — another plus.

As always, *They* were looking out for me, removing all barriers to my return.

Of course, Mother is not my mother in the biological sense. There was a time I believed her to be, but four months after my sixteenth birthday, I discovered the truth. Most adolescents would be devastated to overhear an argument between their mother and father — an argument in which the father loudly proclaims his deep regret at their decision to adopt — but it was a seminal moment for the young Simon Armstrong. Everything suddenly made sense.

I notice Merle is now staring at me in the way he sometimes does.

"Yes?"

His shamrock-green eyes narrow.

"I know what you're thinking, Merle, but it's not an option. You cannot live with Mother."

He tilts his head just a fraction to the right.

"And, no. You definitely cannot come with me."

If he feels rejected, the long, lazy yawn seems an inappropriate response. In truth, I'm also tired — tired of waiting.

I know with absolute certainty I will be leaving Earth on the thirtieth day of this month, September, for it is my thirtieth birthday. That is only nine days from now, and *They* have yet to confirm the place, time, or method of my departure. I have faith those questions will be answered soon, but I'm not blessed with eternal patience, as Mother used to say.

Perhaps my impatience is down to living on my own. Ever since Mother departed for Elmwood Care Home, the days have felt longer. I try to keep busy, and I have forged new routines to replace those Mother kept so religiously, but it's not the same.

Merle is incapable of playing chess, and he steadfastly refuses to engage in debate as we watch *Question Time*.

I glance at my watch. It's almost time to leave.

"I must be on my way, Merle. Mother will be … I'm due at the care home at two."

Closing the day planner, I gather it up with the notepad and return both to a drawer in a pine dresser older than I am. I pause for a moment and survey the kitchen: the quarry-tiled floor, the Belfast sink beneath a window framed with cornflower-blue curtains, and the chunky oak table we used to congregate around as a family unit. And then there's the odour. I couldn't begin to isolate the numerous constituent scents, but it's an odour as unique as DNA.

There is no logical reason I should want to remember this room or indeed this house, but having lived amongst humans for so long, perhaps it was inevitable I'd succumb to some of their peculiar traits. Nostalgia, I'm told, blossoms with age. Maybe one day I'll recollect this kitchen in my mind's eye, and I'll experience the supposed cosy glow of memories, as relentlessly purported by those of advanced years I meet in the Post Office. It sounds like a favourable state of mind but not one I can envisage. I have no affection for the past, only the future.

I nod at Merle and head upstairs.

Being an only child, I've never had to share a bedroom with a sibling. At the age of ten, I said goodbye to my first bedroom in a semi-detached house eighty miles east of here. Until that point in my life, I had no idea who I was or why my parents had decided to up sticks and move from suburban Surrey to rural Wiltshire. They never consulted me, but even before I knew the truth, I knew I preferred it here; the open fields and vast skies preferable to the brick and tarmac of Surbiton.

I strip naked and pad back along the landing to the bathroom for my second shower of the day. I'll shower again before retiring at 11:00 pm. Three showers, every day without fail, although not for reasons of vanity. It is part of the ongoing battle to ensure my human body remains free from bacteria or infection, and for twenty-nine years, eleven months, and twenty-one days, my strategy has paid dividends. Not once have I visited a doctor's surgery or hospital.

It is imperative I maintain this body after *They* engineered a vessel robust enough to carry me through to the mission's end. Cleverly designed, it is not so extraordinary it might attract unwanted attention, but it performs significantly better than the average Earth-dweller's body. Consequently, I possess the physique of an athlete, the mind of a scientist, and the immune system of a Komodo dragon. I am the best of humans, but I am no human and never will be.

Showered, I return to the bedroom and open the wardrobe door. Like the pine dresser downstairs, the wardrobe is several decades old and manufactured in an era when furniture was built to last. The same cannot be said of the desk Mr Choudhary expects me to work from. I will not miss that desk one iota.

The selection of garments on the rail represents my apathy towards fashion. Ordered by type and limited to a palette of dark shades, I purchased each garment solely for function and value for money. After trials, I established denim jeans are a comfortable fit and hard-wearing. For the same reason, I favour polycotton sweatshirts over woollen jumpers. Underpants, socks, and vests are all from Marks & Spencer. The suit I wore to Father's funeral was the right size at the time, but I experienced a growth spurt in the months afterwards. With Martin Armstrong's corpse still relatively fresh in the ground, the ill-fitting suit found its way to a charity shop. I've never had reason to replace it.

I dress.

A set of keys, a wallet, and a mobile telephone are lined up side-by-side atop the chest of drawers. I slip into a lightweight waterproof jacket and transfer each of the items to its designated pocket. Zippers securely fastened, I then tap each pocket to be certain everything is present and correct.

I'm ready to leave, but the futility weighs particularly heavy today. I've visited Mother every single day for eleven months, and every day I come away with the same question: why do I bother? She hasn't said an intelligible word to me in months, and there's no longer any flicker of recognition in her eyes. She is now but a husk of a human. I fully comprehend the degenerative nature of her condition, but what I don't understand is my compulsion to visit.

A distraction comes as an electronic tone chimes from the corner of the room. I turn to the desk where a personal computer waits on constant standby; a glowing blue icon displayed on the screen. The icon signifies a new message from the only person on this planet who knows my true identity. His codename: The Shepherd.

Message 2806

Priority Level 4 | Encrypted @ 13:22

From: TheShepherd82

To: Epsilon30

Message Begins ...

Ĝojan novaĵon, frato Epsilon,

Apologies for the delay in today's communication. Many issues to contend with my end.

I assume you have heard nothing since yesterday?

The Shepherd

Message 2807

Priority Level 4 | Encrypted @ 13:24

From: Epsilon30

To: TheShepherd81

Message Begins ...

Ĝojan novaĵon, frato The Shepherd,

Nothing significant to report as yet. I will brief you fully later.

Epsilon

Chapter 2

The distance between 30 Bulford Hill and Mother's care home is exactly one mile. Walking briskly, I complete the journey on foot within fourteen minutes; my heart rate never exceeding sixty beats per minute. Fit as I might be, there's little I can do to combat either basic human physiology or the warmth of the autumn sun. Consequently, I pass through the open gates of Elmwood Care Home with a moist forehead. Unpleasant.

I approach the main door and press the intercom button. A shrill voice responds with the same well-worn statement and question delivered on every visit.

"Elmwood House. May I take your name and confirm the nature of your visit?"

"Simon Armstrong to see Helen Armstrong."

A buzzer sounds above the door as the locking mechanism disengages. I tug the handle and brace for the first assault to my senses.

I've never acclimatised to the air in Elmwood House. The stench is different on every visit as the faux-pine musk of disinfectant battles against the lingering aroma of boiled vegetables. They have fish every Friday. It is the worst day to visit.

Breathing through my mouth, I approach the reception desk.

"Good afternoon, Simon."

Elaine is one of two receptionists, working a rota so haphazardly contrived I've yet to crack the methodology behind it. Today, I expected Susan.

"Good afternoon."

I couldn't venture a guess at Elaine's age because of her obesity and the thick rolls of fat occupying the space where her neck should be. Despite the obvious risks to her health, I have resisted warning Elaine about her weight because, as a child, Mother said people don't always like to hear the truth and I should bite my tongue. This advice was first administered after I informed a woman at the bus stop her breath smelt like a bin. I bit my tongue hard, and it bled profusely. We never made it into town.

I fill in the visitor card, which Elaine signs with a pudgy hand. The card is then placed in a transparent sleeve and attached to a blue lanyard.

"Has there been any change in Mother's condition?" I ask.

"No worse, no better," Elaine replies, bowing her head forward and accentuating the collar of fat.

I avert my gaze.

"Is she in the lounge?"

"She is, yes."

I thank Elaine and make my way through a set of double doors and along a wide corridor with panelled mahogany walls and floral-patterned paper. I understand Elmwood House was constructed in the mid-nineteenth century as a family home, although not in the way 30 Bulford Hill was once a family home. The Elmwood clan must have been many in number to need so much space.

There's an archway at the end of the corridor leading into the communal lounge. Not only is the room larger than any lounge needs to be, but there are six windows taller than the average male. The windows fill the space with an excessive amount of natural light, and while most humans crave natural light, I do not.

Of the many armchairs lined up around the room, approximately half are occupied. I can still vividly recall the moment I first entered this room, and my abject horror upon seeing the sick and the senile, all silently lined up as if waiting their turn in line for the mythical Reaper. What life is this for any species? I thought. The daily visits have desensitised my reaction — I no longer want to turn and run.

I scan the room. Mother is seated alone with both adjacent armchairs empty, her gaze fixed upon the stone fireplace on the opposite wall. She must like that fireplace tremendously as it attracts much of her waking attention.

As I approach, her gaze doesn't shift.

"Hello, Mother."

Nothing.

I perch on the arm of the chair to her right, so I'm looking down on Mother from the side. On previous visits, I have tried sitting directly in her line of sight, but it seems to unsettle her almost as much as it unsettles me. It is best we avoid direct eye contact.

We sit in silence as I appraise her physical condition, looking for any further signs of deterioration. Mother has always maintained a slim physique, but now she is near emaciated. It shows in her face the most. Her skin, once luminous, now hangs from her cheekbones like empty saddlebags. Her eyes seem to sink deeper into her skull with every passing visit, and her once lustrous mane of coppery hair is now a thin patchwork of translucent threads.

I've known for a long time this woman is not my biological mother, but now she's no longer my mother in any sense of the word. That woman is no more because her mind is no more. Witnessing its tortuous departure has not been a pleasant experience, best explained by a simple analogy. Helen Armstrong's mind was once like freshly fallen snow: crisp and bright and occasionally dazzling. But, as the snow inevitably melts, her mind has also dissolved to a mushy grey pulp.

And yet, I still come.

"How are you feeling today?"

She draws a long, wheezy breath.

As recently as last month, I'd ask Mother a question, and she'd tense her shoulders, or a sudden crease would form across her forehead. I initially thought it might be a physical response, but I've since witnessed too many involuntary movements to conclude her reaction was anything other than coincidence. There is no return now, and if her health continues to decline at the present rate, it will soon be Mother's turn to feel a tap on the shoulder.

Still, it is for the best.

A member of staff approaches. She smiles at Mother and then turns the smile in my direction.

"How's she doing?"

I know most of the staff by name, but this interloper is new.

"She is dying. That's how she's doing."

The woman's cheeks redden.

"Sorry. I, um, I meant … is she comfortable?"

"Even if she wasn't, how would we know? She's not muttered an intelligible sentence since July."

"I'm new. I'm just trying to get to know the residents."

"There is nothing to know. My mother is all but a vegetable."

The female's lips part, but no words follow. Humiliation? Embarrassment? I don't know, but an uncomfortable silence ensues.

"Are you Helen's son?" she then asks. A safer question.

"Yes."

"I'm Rosie," she declares, thrusting out a hand. "I started yesterday."

I don't much care who the female is, but if Mother were here, mentally that is, she'd tell me to mind my manners.

Reluctantly, I stand up. The difference in height between us becomes apparent, although it is not significant at around eleven centimetres. Mother, if she were able, would scowl and convert my measurement to imperial — the female being four inches shorter than my six feet and one inch. I've never understood why humans on the island of Great Britain cannot agree on a single form of measurement. Then, I don't necessarily understand much about humans, wherever they reside.

I glare at the female's outstretched hand with appropriate disdain.

"I'm Simon Armstrong, but I don't shake hands. It's a grossly unhygienic custom."

"I suppose it is when you think about it," she replies, lowering her hand. "But it's nice to meet you, anyhow."

"Is it?"

"Is it what?"

"Nice? This situation doesn't tally with my understanding of the word nice."

"I'm just trying to be pleasant. Sorry."

She shuffles awkwardly and twiddles a strand of hair. The colour is not wildly dissimilar to that of my mother's two decades ago, although this woman's locks shine with a hint of brass over copper, and they're curlier. She is not obese.

"Can you go and be pleasant elsewhere? I'd like to be alone with my mother."

I fix her with a firm stare. It's usually enough to deter strangers from unwanted chatter, and on this occasion, it works as I intended. She nods once and hurries away. I return to my perch.

"Apologies for the interruption, Mother."

Slowly, her head turns in my direction, but she doesn't lift her chin. Her gaze rests on my chest and stays there as if I'm invisible, and she's inspecting the view from the window behind me. Maybe I am invisible because her expression is as cheerless as the car park beyond the glass.

I release an involuntary sigh.

"This is futile, isn't it?"

Seconds pass, and she returns her gaze to the fireplace.

Seamlessly, we slip into the same routine. Mother stares straight ahead, silent and still, while I count the swirls on the patterned carpet until the clock on the wall confirms thirty minutes have passed — never twenty-nine, never thirty-one.

I stand up.

"I'll see you tomorrow, Mother. That's assuming I'm still here."

My thoughts turn to the letter I'm yet to compose — to be read at her funeral. There was a time, not so long ago, when Mother would have understood at least some of my parting words, but that time has passed. As illogical as it is, I must commit her memory to paper because no one else will — a token gesture, but a gesture nonetheless.

"Goodbye, Mother."

Not so much as a twitch.

I return to the reception desk and hand the lanyard back to Elaine. She knows better than to ask how my visit went.

The walk home takes precisely fourteen minutes. I return to the kitchen and sit at the table, but Merle is nowhere to be seen. Breathing slow breaths, I close my eyes and let the silence wash over me. My body might be human, but the energy within is not. It requires constant regulation, particularly after interacting with the unfamiliar. It is what sets me apart, what has always set me apart.

I once overheard Father talking about me on the telephone. It was a long time ago, but his words remain ingrained in my mind: *There's something not quite right about Simon. He's a troubled soul, alright.*

Later that same day, with Father making his regular evening visit to the public house near our home, I asked Mother what a soul was. She has always been a fanatical follower of the Christian religion and explained the soul is like a jar, containing all the ingredients of who we are.

Some years later, as I came to understand my true identity, I realised the significance of Mother's words. Because I am not human, I have no soul, and therefore there is no jar to contain my essence. If there were such a jar, metaphoric or otherwise, it would need to be constructed of material from a planet other than Earth because the energy within me pulses with the heat of a white dwarf star.

At times it is a challenge keeping that heat to a low simmer. The moment when I'm finally able to release it and escape this fleshy cage cannot come soon enough.

Message 2808

Priority Level 4 | Encrypted @ 13:39

From: TheShepherd82

To: Epsilon30

Message Begins ...

Ĝojan novaĵon, frato Epsilon,

I presume no contact or signs since your last message?

With eight days remaining, I would not be too concerned, but I do understand your growing impatience now the mission is complete. With every additional revolution of this planet, and every unnecessary interaction with these damned humans, you have every right to feel frustration. My own tolerance is at breaking point. I will not burden you with today's events but suffice to say, I too cannot wait for the day when we can leave this Godforsaken rock.

We must trust in those who know best. The time will come, and we will finally meet as brothers of Andromeda.

Remain strong. Remain vigilant. They will come for us soon — I know it.

The Shepherd

Chapter 3

I cannot abide many facets of human life, but it's the general lack of organisation that ranks highest.

I wake at 6:44 am. It takes nine minutes to defecate, brush my teeth, and shower. I then get dressed and descend the stairs to the kitchen, arriving at 6:55 am. Merle is equally punctual, always waiting by the table for his breakfast. I fill the kettle with three hundred millilitres of water and switch it on. I then place two slices of wholemeal bread in the toaster, and in the ninety-three seconds required to brown that bread to the desired colour, I open a tin of cat food and fork it into a bowl for Merle.

Once the toaster pops, I place both slices of toast on a plate and set a timer for sixty-six seconds. That time allows the toast to cool to my preferred temperature. The kettle boils, and I pour water into a cup and insert a bag of Twinings breakfast tea. The timer buzzes, and I apply sunflower spread to the toast before cutting each slice exactly in half. Finally, I remove the teabag from the cup and transfer it to the table, along with my plate.

I switch the radio on and sit down just as the 7:00 am news bulletin is about to start. The pips coincide with the first mouthful of toast, which I chew thirty-two times.

My morning, every morning: organised and efficient.

I listen intently as the newsreader churns through the headlines. Inevitably, those headlines include a sombre statement about some random human killing another human, a political figure preaching a controversial view, and a so-called celebrity breaching a moral code set by a committee of unknowns.

Nothing I could remotely interpret as a sign.

They remain silent.

I allow my mind to drift away from the newsreader's voice to The Shepherd's last message: *Remain strong. Remain vigilant.* Wise advice, but I expected no less from my comrade.

The Shepherd is as close to being a friend as anyone in my life — not that there's a long list of other candidates. I wouldn't go so far as to call him a friend, though. Protocols insist we never disclose personal information beyond the mission remit, and humans base friendships on the amount of personal information they're willing to share. The closer the friend, the more they like to trouble one another with their petty problems.

The Shepherd and I have never met. I don't know his earthly name, his address, or even his age. All that connects us is our situation — we are both Andromedan Starseeds.

Our first connection took place six years ago, and only a human would put the crossing of our paths down to fate. The odds of two genuine Starseeds connecting were so unfeasibly small; only *They* could have orchestrated it. In the hours after that first conversation with The Shepherd, I struggled to maintain my equilibrium; such was the magnitude of our connection.

I had to share my news with someone.

To his credit, Merle patiently listened as I added context to the circumstances leading up to my first shared words with The Shepherd — back story, I believe it's called.

I first heard the term *Starseed* while watching a documentary on the Discovery Channel, only days after my twenty-first birthday. At that point, I'd already begun to question my role on this planet. I looked like a human, but hidden behind that facade lurked a being unlike any human I'd ever encountered. For as long as I could remember, I'd been plagued by an unanswerable question: why was I so different?

That first brief mention of a Starseed fuelled my research. I spent seven hours locked away in my bedroom, my eyes never leaving the computer screen, my fingers tapping relentlessly at the keyboard, stopping only to make notes. Slowly, website by website, I unlocked the truth.

I discovered Starseeds are highly intelligent individuals whose origins lie not on the Earth plane but far-distant planets. We all share a common sense of misplacement; literal aliens dropped on Earth without a compass. We know we don't belong here.

Further research confirmed Starseeds are typically oblivious to their true identity or purpose until the moment of awakening.

In the months after that initial discovery, I continued to research Starseeds in the hope my moment of awakening would soon follow. My life, however, continued on the exact same trajectory it always had. Every day, I completed the same routines while awaiting my celestial epiphany. Months turned to years, but I never lost faith.

Then, three years after I first watched that documentary, I received a notification on my personal computer. I'd set up an alert system to activate whenever a new web page mentioning Starseeds appeared on the internet. Until that moment, every notification only confirmed the launch of a page with rehashed information or wild conspiracy theories.

With minimal expectation, I opened the notification and clicked on the newly discovered link. What I found was not a typical website but a forum named StarseedsUK.com.

At the time, there were only sixty-one members but the conversations, or threads, were plentiful. One had to sign-up for membership before reading the threads or contributing, so I duly did. After completing the process, a new thread appeared at the top of the page, welcoming the latest forum members. There were two: Me, Epsilon30, and TheShepherd82.

I clicked on the link to TheShepherd82's profile to discover we'd both found the forum and signed up within thirty seconds of one another, and we both resided in the county of Wiltshire. A minute later, I received that seminal first message: *Our arrival at this forum cannot be a coincidence. We should talk.*

My awakening had finally arrived.

I do recall Merle's eyes narrowing when I first told him I'd made contact with my earthly handler — a sign of his scepticism. I understood because I'd complained to him relentlessly about the deranged and deluded humans I'd encountered while researching Starseeds. The internet is awash with humans who think they're different, unique, and indeed, I have grave reservations about the claims made by every member of the StarseedsUK.com community. Without exception, they've all misinterpreted or misrepresented their circumstances to fit the narrative. True Starseeds like The Shepherd and I are rarer than Kashmir sapphires. Together, we have waited almost six years for our time: the moment we leave this planet and return home. Our relationship is one born of mutual understanding and allegiance to the mission. In that sense, perhaps we might be considered friends.

My thoughts are interrupted by an overly excited travel reporter on the radio. My plate empty, I drink the remains of my breakfast tea and then wash up. Merle, his hunger now sated, disappears through the cat flap into the rear garden. It is unlikely he will return before I leave for work.

I hurry up to my bedroom, put on a lightweight waterproof coat, and place my keys, wallet, and mobile telephone in their respective pockets. Because I'm venturing onto the bus, I also take a pocket radio with headphones. A check of the bedside clock confirms what I already know — I am due at the bus stop in six minutes.

The journey from Durrington to the town of Amesbury takes approximately nineteen minutes on the bus. I know this because I record the duration of every journey and calculate the average time. Once, Salisbury Road was closed without notice — a water leak, the bus company confirmed in response to my letter of complaint — and the journey took twenty-eight minutes with the diversion. I was late. I try not to think about that day or my consequent reaction to the delayed start of the working day.

After checking the front door is securely locked, I begin the two-minute walk to the bus stop.

Bulford Hill forms the southern boundary of the village of Durrington. Our house backs onto farmland with the River Avon some two hundred metres beyond. The hill itself is a moderately busy route during peak times because humans are fundamentally lazy and selfish. Mr Talbot, who lives at number nineteen, utilises a large, four-wheel-drive vehicle for his daily commute to the college, which is only just under one mile away — well within walking distance. Mrs Talbot's vehicle is smaller, but she could commute to Amesbury by bus, as I do.

Most mornings, I'm able to observe their departure. They leave the house together and stand on the driveway for a few seconds. They then kiss, which is a gesture every bit as disgusting as shaking hands, before taking to their respective vehicles. Mr Talbot usually leaves first and turns up the hill. Mrs Talbot turns left, passing the bus stop. I'm confident she must know I'm waiting for the Amesbury bus, but not once has she ever stopped to ask if I might like to journey with her, even during spells of heavy rain.

Selfish. Lazy. That is the Talbots. That is humans.

Of course, if Mrs Talbot were ever to stop and ask if I'd like to journey with her, I'd vehemently decline. The thought of spending time trapped in a confined space with a relative stranger makes my blood run cold, metaphorically. Even so, the point of objection remains valid.

The bus arrives.

I first started working for Mr Choudhary eight years ago, and for the first eighteen months of employment, I'd either walk to Amesbury or Mother would offer a lift in her motor car. I tried the bus once, but it was so filthy I vowed never to use public transport again. Then, the company who operated the service lost their contract. A different company subsequently replaced them, and they deployed brand new buses with acceptable standards of cleanliness.

Less can be said of their passengers.

There was once a middle-aged man who travelled on the bus every day. He reeked of stale sweat and attempted to mask his foul odour by applying enough cologne to generate his own atmosphere. One day I pointed this out to him. His face flushed red, and after mumbling a series of expletive-ridden insults, he got off at the next stop. I haven't seen him since.

Fortunately, today there are only two other passengers, and neither smells offensive. There's also enough room we can sit comfortably apart.

Once seated, I turn on the pocket radio and place a small rubber bud in each ear. Every morning, I spend my journey scanning the radio waves just in case *They* are broadcasting a message. I begin with the FM band and slowly turn the dial to move through the frequencies. Some months back, I heard an unusual series of repeated beeps, and I felt sure it was a signal transmitted in binary. My initial hopes were dashed after The Shepherd suggested the tones were more likely a broadcasting test. Besides the noise of radio stations, the airwaves this morning are full of the usual static and nothing else — always preferable to the intolerable chatter from my fellow passengers.

We arrive at Amesbury after nineteen minutes and forty-four seconds. I thank the driver for his punctuality as I disembark, and ninety-seven seconds later, I'm at the rear door of Mr Choudhary's business premises. I press the button, and it activates a bell within.

Seconds pass. The door opens.

Mohamed Choudhary is a stout man of Indian heritage; approximately sixty years of age. He smiles far more than he frowns, and even during the warmest days of summer, he wears a woollen cardigan.

"Good morning, young Simon. How are we today?"

I'm greeted by the exact same question every day. There was a time, in the first few weeks of my employment, I answered honestly: I'm tired, I'm cold, I'm irritable, I'm flatulent. I asked Mother if Mr Choudhary's repeated question was a condition of my employment, and she attempted to stifle her laughter. How was I to know humans ask certain questions without the expectation of an honest answer?

"I'm fine, thank you."

"Good, good. Come in."

My Choudhary runs a chain of dry cleaners; six branches, including the one here in Amesbury. My job is to correlate the daily figures from all six branches and enter the information into a spreadsheet. I then break the data down and calculate profitability, efficiency, and other metrics my employer deems useful. I've repeatedly suggested it would be more efficient to use a cloud-based system and each branch to input their own data, but Mr Choudhary prefers to pore over my printed spreadsheets at the end of each three-hour shift.

I've worked here so long we now have an established routine. I enter the small office and switch the personal computer on while Mr Choudhary makes us both a cup of tea. Once the tea arrives at my desk, I'm then left to my own devices and rarely ever disturbed by the staff who work in the dry cleaners. Apart from the occasional hello, I've managed to avoid engaging any of them in conversation, and that suits me.

I get on with my work, transferring a list of numbers to a field of individual cells, one by one: slowly, methodically, accurately. Most humans would find the work monotonous, but I do not. The three hours always seem to pass by quickly, although I'm aware it's simply a trick of the mind as time is constant, never changing. Three hours is three hours, whether you're inputting data into a spreadsheet or ironing underpants.

As is customary, Mr Choudhary appears just as the printer begins to churn out the fruits of my labour.

"All done?"

"Yes,"

"Excellent."

I nod.

"How is your mother?"

Not content with asking about my wellbeing at the start of my shift, Mr Choudhary always asks after Mother before I depart.

"There's been no change in her condition."

"Oh dear," he sighs, shaking his head. "Such a lovely woman, too."

It was Mother who secured my job with Mr Choudhary. She came home from the shops one day and said we needed a chat; Mother's code word for a conversation. She then admitted her concerns about how much time I spent alone in the house and suggested I might like a part-time job helping Mr Choudhary with his books. There was no reason for me to seek employment as Father made adequate financial provisions in his will, but Mother did seem keen. Patently she had no idea of my mission, and not wanting to raise suspicion, I accepted the offer of employment.

I put my jacket on. Usually, Mr Choudhary wishes me a good day and then sees me to the rear door. Today, he hesitates by the desk.

"I need to have a quick word, Simon."

I glance at my watch.

"Will it take long? The bus leaves in eleven minutes."

"No, not at all. Would you like to sit down?"

"I'll remain standing if it's all the same."

"Fair enough," he replies, his smile withering.

He then rests his buttocks on the edge of the desk and folds his arms.

"There's no easy way to say this, Simon, but I've just agreed to sell the business."

Unsure why this news is of significance to me, I return a blank stare.

"The thing is," he continues. "The new owners already have staff who look after their books."

"And this information is relevant, how?"

"I tried my best to convince them of your value, but … they don't need an employee who does what you currently do."

"I see."

He adopts a pained expression. It's the kind humans utilise when sharing news they'd rather not.

"Do you understand?" he asks, misinterpreting my inertia as a sign of confusion.

"Yes, I understand."

"Are you okay?"

"I'm thinking."

I've nothing more to say, but humans cannot cope with prolonged periods of silence during a conversation. Mr Choudhary unfolds his arms and places his hands together as if offering a prayer.

"Won't you please consider a position up front?" he pleads, not for the first time.

"Serving members of the public?"

"Yes."

"Absolutely not."

"The pay is better, and the new owners have agreed to retain all the frontline staff. Your job will be safe."

"I cannot work with … people."

"I understand, but wouldn't you at least like to try?"

"No."

He emits a long sigh.

"Very well. I don't really have any other choice, then."

He withdraws an envelope from his pocket and hands it to me.

"There's a cheque in there," he says. "Severance pay. It's more than I'm legally bound to pay, but you've been a good and loyal employee."

"Thank you."

I glance at my watch again.

"Will I be required for work tomorrow?"

"That's entirely up to you. You can work as little or as much notice as you like, up until the new owners take over."

"I will work tomorrow. Goodbye, Mr Choudhary."

I nod once as a mark of courtesy, and leave.

Chapter 4

As the bus pulls away, I open the envelope and examine the cheque for £1,500. I won't cash it because, unbeknown to Mr Choudhary, I intended to resign tomorrow as per the terms of my employment contract. The fact he pre-empted my resignation must be another celestial omen — *They* are assembling the final plans for my departure. My employment was the only remaining chain tethering me to this life. I am now wholly unshackled.

As I let the realisation settle, my brain releases a dose of dopamine, and a tingly sensation fizzes in my stomach. Not unpleasant, I am experiencing what humans call excitement.

Eight days. I am going home.

Such is the power of dopamine, I barely notice the nineteen minutes pass by. Before I know it, the bus is travelling up Bulford Hill. I disembark and hurry back to the house. I'm keen to share my news with The Shepherd, but not so much I'm willing to break my routine.

In the kitchen, I measure out forty-five grams of organic muesli and deposit it into a bowl. I then add two hundred millilitres of soy milk. Unlike humans, I derive no pleasure from food. If I could survive without eating, I would, but this cursed body requires a thrice daily injection of fuel and nutrients. Eating is an arduous task at the best of times, but today it's made worse by the latent fizz in my stomach.

Lunch consumed, I wash up and return to my bedroom. There, I sit down at the desk and begin compiling a message to The Shepherd, précising this morning's events.

After our initial communications via the StarseedsUK.com website, we decided the risk of sharing information on a public forum was too great. It was The Shepherd who suggested we use an encrypted and now-obsolete messaging program. To add an extra layer of security, we initially sent every message in the constructed language Esperanto, as few humans understand it. Unfortunately, neither do The Shepherd or I, and the translation to and from English impeded our communication. We both agreed that the encryption alone was probably sufficient, although we retained the opening greeting as a safety net: *Ĝojan novaĵon, frato* — Glad tidings, brother.

I'm about to send the message when I consider the priority level. We've been at level four since *They* put Mother in a care home, having remained at level five for far too long. Does the termination of my employment constitute a level three message? We've only been at level three once, and that was in the days after Mother's diagnosis when the messages flowed with unprecedented regularity.

I decide to stick at level four for now. If events continue to escalate as I presume they will, we'll be sending priority one messages soon enough. I click the mouse button to send the message.

I'm about to undress and take my second shower of the day when the doorbell rings. Immediately, my inner energy pulses at the interruption to my routine. My first thought is to ignore it, but I'm expecting a delivery of antibacterial shower gel. I thud back down the stairs and open the front door. It's not a delivery driver.

"Afternoon, Simon."

"Hello, Father Paul."

"If you've got a minute, may I come in?"

Why do humans insist on lying about the time they require from you? It's rarely ever just a minute and never close to only a sec. And, I know from his previous unwelcome visits, Father Paul is incapable of keeping his word.

"I have three minutes available. Maximum."

The priest steps into the hallway and wipes his feet on the mat. Four seconds gone already, and he's yet to disclose the purpose of his visit.

After the fifth wipe of each shoe, he looks up from the mat and smiles. I don't know why but there's something about his perfectly circular face and hairless head I find unsettling. Then again, it could be his cavernous nostrils or bulbous goat-like eyes.

"What do you want?" I ask.

"One of the parishioners gave me this," he replies, pulling a small blue box from his coat pocket. "For your mother."

"What is it?"

"It's a pendant featuring St Christopher."

He opens the box to reveal a silver disc on a chain, about the size of a ten pence piece.

"What possible use would my mother have for this or any other trinket? She can't even put her own clothes on, let alone jewellery."

"It's symbolic. St Christopher is the patron saint of travellers."

"I don't think Mother is likely to be embarking on any travels in her condition, do you?"

He adopts a similar expression to that of Mr Choudhary earlier. I would describe it as solemn.

"We're all destined to take that final journey one day, Simon. I know your mother will take great comfort knowing she's not alone when the time comes."

"What time?"

"The time of her passing."

"Her death, you mean?"

He nods.

"She'll be dead," I state. "She won't feel comfort or any other sensation, and she certainly wouldn't want this round her neck, rusting away in the ground with her corpse."

Just for a fraction of a second, the priest closes his eyes.

"I know you're not a man of faith, Simon, but your mother is. Please respect her beliefs."

He moves a hand in my direction with the box resting in his palm, inviting me to take it.

I've never understood Mother's obsession with religion, or religion itself. When I was an adolescent, she attempted to inflict her strange beliefs on me by including religious studies in my home-schooling curriculum. Her attempt proved futile as I asked questions she could never satisfactorily answer, and I was so vehement in my questioning she eventually shed tears. We agreed it would be for the best if we never discussed religion again.

"Please," Father Paul prompts. "For her."

I look at the priest and then at the box.

"Very well."

I pluck it from his palm, careful not to touch his leathery skin.

"Thank you. It'll mean a lot to Helen, even if remains in the box in her pocket."

I check my watch. I've established there's no better way to indicate I no longer want my time wasted besides telling the person guilty of said wasting.

"I'll be off then."

"Goodbye, Father Paul."

He nods and opens the front door.

Just as he steps onto the path, the opportunity to avoid any further unwelcome visits presents itself. I call the priest's name, and he turns around.

"I'm in the process of preparing for a journey of my own, and I won't have time for interruptions over the next eight days."

"Really? Where are you going?"

"That is none of your business."

"How long will you be away for?"

"I refer you to my previous answer."

"What about your mother?"

"What about her?"

"Who'll be visiting her while you're away?"

"No one, I should expect."

"You haven't asked anyone to cover for you?"

"No."

"I'll schedule a few extra visits, then."

"It doesn't matter if no one turns up as she's oblivious, but if you wish to waste your time, I cannot stop you."

"I don't consider visiting a dear friend and one of my most loyal parishioners a waste of time."

"As you wish. Goodbye."

I close the door and recheck my watch. Two minutes and fifty-one seconds wasted — cursed priest.

There is no force greater than my inner energy, and it will not let me cut corners in my hygiene routine, no matter how hard I try to resist. I attempt to make up the lost time by dressing at speed, but I'm still seventy-seven seconds behind schedule when I lock the front door.

Walking at a quicker pace than usual, I'm able to offset the time deficit, and I arrive at Elmwood Care Home at precisely 2:00 pm. I'm warmer than is comfortable, but at least my inner energy has returned to a manageable hum.

I press the doorbell and prepare to deliver the same answers to the daily questions. I gain entry.

To my surprise, Elaine is at the reception desk again.

"Good afternoon, Simon."

"Good afternoon."

I notice a plate next to her keyboard, containing a half-eaten slice of brown cake and a fork.

"Would you like a slice?" Elaine asks, as she follows my eyes to the plate. "It's Trisha's birthday today."

"Do you know how many grams of sugar are in a typical slice of cake?"

"Do I look like I know?" she replies with a snort of laughter.

"The equivalent of eighteen teaspoons."

"Really? That much?" she replies, slack-jawed.

"Yes. And for that reason, I would not like a slice."

Elaine's cheeks flush pink, and she hands over a lanyard while avoiding eye contact.

"Have a good visit."

I half nod and leave Elaine to her cake.

The scene in the residents' lounge is slightly different to yesterday. Outside, the sky is overcast, so the light is more to my liking. Mother is seated in the same armchair, staring at the same fireplace. I can't remember if she's wearing the same clothes, but I doubt she cares.

I cross the carpet and perch in the same position I occupy every day.

"Hello, Mother."

No response.

"How are you today?"

My question fails to prompt any kind of response. Asking her again would be futile, so I fold my arms and begin counting down the first of the thirty minutes I feel obligated to give Mother. She remains the only constant throughout the three decades I've resided on this planet, and if I'm in the right frame of mind, I occasionally like to reflect on our shared experiences.

I don't know why, but I have few memories of my early years. Perhaps *They* deemed such memories superfluous and wiped them. One surviving memory, and possibly the earliest, is of Christmas some twenty-five years ago. That Christmas, and indeed every subsequent one throughout my early childhood years, our home in Surbiton changed beyond all recognition.

Father would venture up into the loft and return with a number of dusty boxes. Those dull brown boxes contained an array of decorations that my parents would distribute around the house. The trip into the loft would coincide with the arrival of an evergreen conifer twice my height, and Mother encouraged me to assist her in the decorating process.

We'd spend an age fixing shiny glass balls to the branches, along with a rope of coloured lights. Then, Mother would layer lengths of gold polyvinyl tinsel from tip to trunk, a task I was too short to conduct. However, there was one task my parents always delegated to me — the placing of a silver-painted wooden star on the top. I would stand on a dining chair and take my time, ensuring the star was perfectly positioned.

The dusty boxes spent their first December in the loft last year, being Mother wasn't at home to oversee their removal. Because I am no longer an ignorant child, I understand the religious connotations behind the festive celebrations. As a point of principle, I cannot actively participate in the annual rituals of Christmas. For that reason, I wasn't inclined to decorate an evergreen conifer myself. In hindsight, I regret not doing so, being my last Christmas on Earth.

The only other memory I vividly recall from my formative years is the first day I attended school. Mother was highly emotional, but I cannot say I felt anything as I glanced back towards the school gates, where she stood amongst a group of equally tearful parents.

All I learnt on that first day is how much I detested humans. I didn't understand why at the time, but at the end of the school day, I couldn't wait to get home and scrub myself clean in the shower. I also recall my reluctance to return on the second day, and the third. Then, on the fourth day, *They* must have intervened because my mind-set changed.

Mid-morning, the female teacher, Miss Woodrow, would lead the class out to an area of grey tarmac and instructed us to play for fifteen minutes. Rather than participate, I would stand on my own and observe the other children. Over those fifteen minutes, a conclusion formed in my fledgling mind: the other children were nothing like me. They were loud and erratic while I was quiet and calm. They would whine or cry for no good reason while I remained steadfastly stoic. It also became clear I was blessed with superior intellect and motor skills. I excelled in Miss Woodrow's lessons, and if it were not for Mother's intervention, I am certain the school would have fast-tracked my progress through the education system. I later realised *They* must have somehow influenced events because I left school for good at the age of ten. Mother then assumed the role of teacher after we moved to Wiltshire.

As for the small humans, they quickly realised I was not like them, and they kept their distance. Mostly.

I glance up at the clock on the wall: thirteen minutes and Mother hasn't moved. Instinctively, I check she's still breathing. She is. Endorphins flow.

I return my attention to the patterned carpet and count down the remaining minutes.

Once it is time to depart, I stand up in preparation. I can't abide physical contact with humans as a rule, but I've learnt to tolerate Mother's tactile behaviour over the years. She is no longer in a position to place her hand on my arm or press her lips to my cheek, and I've never been willing to instigate such gestures myself. That hasn't changed.

"Goodbye, Mother."

I pause for a moment, and just as I'm about to turn and leave, Mother lifts her chin a fraction. Her lips slowly part, allowing a long raspy breath to escape. Then, to my surprise, she looks straight up at me, her brow deeply furrowed.

"Prim … Primrose. H … H … Hill …"

"What?" I respond, squatting down, so our faces are level. "Primrose Hill? Did you say Primrose Hill?"

Her chin drops, and Mother's focus returns to the fireplace beyond my right shoulder.

"Mother? Can you hear me?"

Glazed eyes, no sign of recognition. One fleeting moment of near lucidity, over before it even began.

I remain in the same position until my thigh muscles ache — long enough to establish Mother's state of permanent silence has resumed. She is now silent, but my mind is not. I repeat my goodbye and hurry back to the reception.

Elaine is ending a phone call as I approach the desk.

"Mother spoke," I state. "Please ensure she is closely monitored for the next twenty-four hours in case she speaks again."

"What did she say?"

"Is that relevant to my request?"

"Possibly."

"She said, Primrose Hill."

"As in, Primrose Hill in London?"

"I do not know. Is there such a place?"

"Don't quote me on this, but I think it's well known as a film location because you can see most of the city from the top. Never been there myself."

"Interesting," I remark, unintentionally.

"Can you think of any reason she'd mention it?" Elaine asks.

"No."

"There's no connection to friends or family … or perhaps it was a place special to your mother?"

"To the best of my recollection, she has never mentioned the place in any context."

"In which case, I'm afraid it was probably just a verbal tic. You might want to speak to Nurse Clifton, but I think it's common amongst residents in the latter stages of dementia. I'm sorry."

I do not want to speak with Nurse Clifton because I doubt she would understand the possible significance of Mother's words.

"I must go."

Handing over the lanyard, I repeat my request that I want Mother closely monitored. However, even if she never utters another word, my alien instincts tell me she's already said what I've waited so long to hear.

Chapter 5

When humans say their mind is elsewhere, they are not talking in a literal sense — that would be ridiculous. But I am not human, so I'm able to detach my mind and leave my body to its own devices. Fourteen minutes after leaving Elmwood Care Home, I arrived home with no recollection of the journey. As my legs managed the navigation, my mind was free to focus on two words: Primrose Hill.

My mind and body reunite as I unlock the front door.

On weekdays, I have a two-hour window before preparing the day's final meal at 5:30 pm. I typically use those two hours to progress my research into humanity, the core purpose of my mission on Earth. Mother always said I had an unusually inquisitive mind, and during a lesson on modern history, I asked her a question she was unable to answer: do humans deserve this planet? To this day, I have no idea where that question came from or my motivation for asking it. I can only assume *They* seeded it in my young mind. That question formed the basis of my thirty-year mission, and I believe I'm on the cusp of answering it.

Today, though, I have more pressing research to conduct.

At my desk, I confirm there are no new messages from The Shepherd. I'm tempted to send a report on this morning's developments, but it would be premature. Not so long ago, Mother went through a phase of spouting utter gibberish, including random names, places, and most bizarrely, references to the Crossroads Motel. I happened to mention this to Father Paul, hoping he might know the relevance or location of the motel. He confirmed it was a fictional establishment from a television programme Mother once enjoyed.

I will not make the same mistake again.

My research begins with an internet search. I quickly establish Primrose Hill is indeed in London, as Elaine suggested. The name refers to a hill within Regent's Park and a wider district within the London Borough of Camden. Again, I try to recollect if Mother has ever mentioned it. After investing fifteen minutes' thought, I conclude she has not.

It would be easy to dismiss Mother's words as just splutter from a dying mind before it finally closes, but she hasn't muttered a word for months. The fact she mentioned a geographical location is a good enough reason to be diligent. I'm awaiting a sign, and this could be it.

I read several articles about the area's history and study photographs captured from the top of the hill. Almost every photograph portrays the same vista, that of a distant London skyline with many notable landmarks in view, including The Shard and the dome of St Paul's Cathedral. The only difference between each of the photographs is the colour of the backdrop. One features the view against slate-grey clouds, another beneath a vibrant blue sky. One photograph shows the city shrouded in a silvery mist, and then there are many captured at night with light pollution smudging the silhouetted structures.

Did Mother ever stand atop the hill and look out across London? Did she visit on a cloudy day or when the sky was at its bluest? Did she visit at night and behold all those twinkling lights, like those around our Christmas conifer? These are questions I've no hope of ever answering. Pointless to ask, really.

I return to the page of websites mentioning Primrose Hill. There are sixteen million more. Assuming it will take five seconds to scan each page of results, checking them all will take ninety-two days if I never leave my desk. Allowing for sleep, food consumption, hygiene breaks, and my other commitments, I can probably double that time. It equates to roughly six months. With only eight days at my disposal, this is a problem.

I can only have faith *They* will intervene if I'm on the wrong path. With that, I begin the task.

Fifty seconds, ten pages, and all the links relate to historical and visitor information, properties for sale or rent, or businesses operating in the area. The subsequent hundred links could all fit in one of those three categories, as do the next hundred and the hundred after that.

The deeper into the search results I dig, the more tenuous the links become. There are minutes from council meetings, notices relating to school events, and various medical practitioners offering all manner of treatments.

Another page. And another, and another.

The futility of the task suddenly hits, as if the weight of gravity has somehow tripled. I close the internet browser and open a message window. At times like this, I'm grateful I can call upon another mind.

I compile a report to The Shepherd outlining the apparent significance of Mr Choudhary terminating my employment and Mother's cryptic words. Knowing he possesses a broader range of general knowledge than I do, I'm sure he'll either validate my interest in Primrose Hill or dismiss it. As it stands, we have nothing else to go on.

As I lean forward and turn off the computer monitor, I catch a flash of blue in the corner of my eye — the box Father Paul insisted I give to Mother is still on the chest of drawers. In my rush to make up for the time he wasted, I inadvertently left it behind. He'd be none the wiser if I tossed it in the bin, and it's not as though he can ask Mother if I gave it to her. Well, he can ask her, I suppose.

I stand up and step over to the chest of drawers. Without consciously instructing it to do so, my hand reaches out and picks up the box. The wastepaper basket sits next to the chest of drawers, and the effort involved in moving my arm and dropping the box into the basket would be negligible.

For some reason, I choose not to.

I've become increasingly conscious that some of my decisions since Mother's internment at Elmwood are not grounded in logic. There is no logic, for example, in keeping Merle alive. There's the cost of purchasing his food and replacing his flea collar every four weeks, and he contributes nothing to the upkeep of the house. If anything, that cat is a liability. Why is he still here?

I open the box and remove the silver disc and chain. Constructed from low-cost alloy metal, there is no weight to the trinket. If I were so inclined, I could easily fold the disc in half and snap the chain with just my fingers. It's of little value in a monetary sense, but I suspect that's not where the value lies. Mother, and her beliefs.

I return the disc and chain to the box, placing it back on the chest of drawers.

With twenty-seven minutes remaining until food preparations, I ponder the list of tasks I must complete before my departure. There is one I've perhaps avoided, and it relates to this house and the contents. When Mother and I are both gone, I presume the house and contents will be sold. I don't know who will oversee the sale or benefit financially, as Mother managed the household admin. Before her mind went, she did tell me never to worry about the bills because Father's investments would cover all our utility bills and upkeep of the house. Seeing as the lights still work, and water still flows from the taps, her arrangement must still be in force.

I don't much care what happens to the house itself, but I am curious what will happen to the chattels within. Humans have a propensity to hoard, and Mother was no exception. Our home is full of pointless paraphernalia, and the most pointless of all are the scores of framed photographs dotted around every room except my bedroom. I don't know if there are any on display in Mother's room as I haven't stepped foot in there in almost nineteen years after Father made me vow I'd never enter without seeking permission first.

He was quite insistent about that if I recall.

I awoke one night with a question, and my curiosity would not let me rest until I'd answered it. In the darkness, I crept out of bed and made my way along the landing to my parents' room to seek their input. As I reached my destination, I remember the door being slightly ajar and, with a dim light leaking out, I concluded one or both parents must have still been awake, reading probably. I nudged the door open.

They were not reading.

I stood in the doorway and, gripped by a morbid fascination, stared at the strange scene before me. Mother was lying on her back, legs apart, and Father was lying on top of her with his upper body at such an angle I couldn't see Mother's face. In my head, I counted along with the rhythm of Father's buttocks as he moved his pelvis back and forth with the precision of a Swiss watch. One up, two down. One up, two down. This continued for another seventy beats until his body stiffened, and he emitted a long yawn-like growl.

Without notice, he then suddenly rolled off Mother, flopping onto his back next to her. Both facing the door, it would have been impossible for either parent to miss their eleven-year-old son standing in the doorway. Panic ensued as Mother scrambled to pull her nightdress down, and Father wrestled his underpants up from his knees, yelling at me to get out. The following morning he made me solemnly promise I would never enter their bedroom again. I've kept that promise.

As for the photographs, I'm ambivalent to their presence, but I admire the way Mother organised their display, chronologically, starting in the hallway and running around all four walls of the lounge.

It is possible to chart the lives of Martin and Helen Armstrong by walking from the front door to the fireplace in the lounge. The earliest photographs are in the hallway and feature deceased relatives I never met or can't remember. As they're not biological relatives and human, I have no interest in who they were. Then, there are photographs of Helen Rudge and Martin Armstrong on their wedding day.

After my parents married, little happened in their life, if the photographic timeline is any barometer. There are a few shots of beach scenes and coastal views at the end of the hallway, but no other humans.

Upon entering the lounge, the first photograph on display is of a tiny infant lying on a bed. Mother insists it is a photo of her newly-adopted son — that, being me — at ten months. I cannot see any resemblance. There are more photographs that almost exclusively capture my development from baby to toddler, child to adolescent.

One frame, however, is different from the others because it contains a cutting from a local newspaper.

At the age of thirteen, I reluctantly attended the Durrington Village Fete with Mother. In the corner of the green, an elderly female was seated behind a table, displaying a huge glass jar full of jelly beans. Mother handed the female a twenty pence piece and asked me to estimate how many jelly beans were in the jar. I spent nineteen minutes calculating a number, which the elderly female eventually wrote down. An hour later, a male with a low voice announced over the public address system that Simon Armstrong had won the jar of jelly beans, not simply by guessing the nearest number of beans in the jar but by guessing the exact number: 1630. This was seen as such a remarkable achievement, much fuss ensured, culminating in a man with a camera capturing a photograph of me holding the jar. A week later — much to Mother's excitement — my achievement appeared in the Avon Advertiser newspaper.

There are few photographs of me after the press cutting because I refused to have my photograph captured once I reached puberty. The final photograph, taken not long after Father died, is of a melancholy teenager who looks nothing like either parent or the man I am today. For that reason, I agreed Mother could keep it on display.

My tour ends to the right of the fireplace. On the wall is not a picture but a framed cricket bat signed by members of the English team. Protected behind a glass window, the bat belonged to Father, although I couldn't say when it came into his possession. Whenever guests entered the house for the first time, he would invite the males to view his bat, and it was the only time I ever recall him smiling in this house. It was also the only time I think he ever displayed any pride.

I haven't considered it until now, but I wonder if I should destroy all the photographs of Simon Armstrong before I depart. Would it be wrong to leave a trace of my existence on Earth? I have so far kept the lowest of profiles, limiting my exposure to just a small number of individuals. None of those humans knows me well enough to question my impending disappearance, with perhaps the exception of Father Paul. Thanks to my mother, he has been a constant in our lives ever since we moved to Wiltshire, but if he proves problematic once I've departed, I presume *They* will deal with him, as they did Mother.

I check my wristwatch. Even if I were so inclined, there is insufficient time to remove all the photographs and destroy them before dinner.

Message 2809

Priority Level 3 | Encrypted @ 18:44

From: TheShepherd82

To: Epsilon30

Message Begins ...

Ĝojan novaĵon, frato Epsilon,

I note the termination of your employment. I concur it is of significance, but it pales compared to the news of your Earth-parent.

Are you 100% certain she said 'Primrose Hill'? I have no reason to doubt your word, but it could be a critical moment in our mission, and therefore clarity is everything.

Assuming you are correct, I would draw your attention to the novel. 'War of The Worlds' by HG Wells. If you have yet to read it, I would strongly recommend you do as it centres on an alien invasion of Earth, and the final battle is fought in London where the alien forces stockade … at Primrose Hill!

It cannot be a mere coincidence the only words your Earth-parent has muttered in an age relate to an area synonymous with alien activity. It is the most subtle of clues, but They must be passing on an instruction. If you have time, read the novel, and we can discuss it during tomorrow's communication.

Bearing in mind the significance of this development, I have raised the priority level to three. I would hope you agree it is an appropriate response.

The Shepherd

Message 2810

Priority Level 3 | Encrypted @ 19:24

From: Epsilon30

To: TheShepherd82

Message Begins...

Ĝojan novajon, frato The Shepherd,

I am writing these words with an approximation of human excitement. Yes, I am as certain as I can be my Earth-parent said Primrose Hill. I have never read the novel you reference, so I would never have made the connection between our mission and Primrose Hill. As always, your input has proven invaluable — They will be most pleased.

I have ordered a copy of War of The Worlds from an internet book retailer, and they claim it will be delivered by 1:00 pm tomorrow. I will endeavour to read it in full before we communicate again approximately 24 hours from now.

I agree with the change in priority level — They are coming, and we must be ready.

Epsilon

Chapter 6

The bus arrived in Amesbury four minutes late. Unacceptable, and I told the driver as much.

I complete the final leg of my journey to Mr Choudhary's premises and ring the doorbell. The door opens, and we repeat the same familiar routine up until a cup of tea arrives. My employer then loiters.

"I've been thinking, Simon, about our conversation yesterday."

Conscious of making an error, I keep my eyes on the computer monitor.

"What are you going to do?" he asks.

"Do?"

"For a job."

"I have plans."

"Really? May I ask what those plans are?"

"You may ask, but don't expect an answer."

He moves over to the desk and sits on the edge, close to the boundary of my personal space. I sense a prickling sensation across my shoulders and shrink into the chair.

"I only ask because I worry about you," he continues.

Mr Choudhary, like many humans, worries far too much — to the point where it could be considered a pastime. Whenever his mind is idle, he loves nothing more than fretting over issues that are either beyond his control or no concern of his: the state of the economy, the weather, the batting order of the Indian cricket team, and my wellbeing.

"I note your concern, Mr Choudhary, but it is without foundation."

"My wife says I'm a born worrier. I can't help it."

"In my case, there really is no need."

"Maybe, but knowing your mother isn't well, I do worry who's looking out for you."

"Looking out for me?"

"You've no family, have you?"

"No."

"Friends?"

"Friendship is an overrated concept in my experience."

"Do you not consider me your friend?"

I cease work momentarily to consider his question.

"I consider you my employer."

His shoulders slump.

"Listen, Simon," he says in a level voice. "From the moment I first met your mother, I knew we'd be friends … good friends … and it pains me to think of her in that home. There's nothing I can do for Helen besides keep an eye out for you."

I pause again.

"I'm sure Mother would appreciate your goodwill, but really, I am fine."

"You won't reconsider working in the shop?"

"No."

"Well, if you change your mind, you only have to ask. There's a job waiting for you."

I nod, and it's enough for him to withdraw from the desk.

"I'll leave you to it."

I get on with my job, although it is difficult today. I cannot ignore the knowledge of a paperback book en-route to Bulford Hill and what implications might lie within its pages. I have only ever read sixteen works of fiction, and I'm not conversant with HG Wells or his *War of The Worlds*. I did conduct some rudimentary research yesterday evening, and as The Shepherd suggested, there is a link to Primrose Hill.

It cannot be a coincidence, and I am keen to know the whole story.

My three hours of work finally come to an end, and I depart before Mr Choudhary shares any additional worries.

The bus on the return journey to Durrington is more punctual than the outgoing one, and I reach the front gate of our home precisely on schedule. As I open the door, a brown package reveals itself on the mat.

"Excellent!"

I snatch it up and continue on my path to the kitchen. I'm suddenly torn. Part of me wants to open the package and begin reading, but the urge to stick to my routine is overbearing. I place the package on the table and start measuring out muesli.

Merle appears at my feet.

"Yes?"

He looks up at me but offers no response.

"I'm a little busy at the moment. If you want something, it'll have to wait."

Ignoring my feline housemate, I measure out soy milk and tip it into the bowl. As I sit down to eat, Merle jumps up onto the table. There, he sits quietly, watching my every move.

"I don't suppose you've read anything by HG Wells?" I ask.

Apparently not.

"I understand several of his novels have been adapted into motion pictures. We could watch one this evening if you like?"

His eyes narrow.

"We are in agreement. Let's convene in the lounge at 7:00 pm."

Having suffered an interrogation into my plans this morning, I decide not to question Merle's. I'm sure he'll let me know his intentions before long.

Once I've finished eating and washed up, I open the package and extract my copy of *The War of The Worlds*. The front cover contains an artist's impression of a machine in two parts, with the Palace of Westminster silhouetted in the background.

I read the synopsis on the back cover.

There is a reason I have little interest in science-fiction, and that's down to the fictional element. As long as humans have been concocting tales about extra-terrestrials, they've portrayed aliens in a negative light, with perhaps a few exceptions. Typically, those tales centre on a battle of good against evil, with humanity always taking the role of the good. Has it never crossed the mind of an author or screenwriter that perhaps their casting is flawed? My research has found ample evidence of how evil humans can be, and that evidence stretches back to the dawn of their existence.

I am right, beyond doubt, because I've experienced it first-hand.

As for the science part of sci-fi, it too leaves a lot to be desired. I have discussed this with The Shepherd, and we both agree it is ridiculous that humans consider their science worthy of the name. There are civilisations dotted across the galaxies with technology so far in advance of what humans have developed, the best scientists on this planet might as well be throwing spears at one another and howling at the moon. The Earth is an insignificant grain of sand on a beach too large for any human to comprehend.

It is I who now bear the responsibility of reporting humankind's failings. Those I tell will decide the fate of humanity.

Not before I've had a shower, though.

Without Father Paul to interrupt, I leave the house on schedule. I will use the time with Mother to read *The War of The Worlds*. Other visitors read to residents, although, much to my annoyance, they read out loud. I will not. I'll then use the remainder of my time this afternoon to complete the book before communicating with The Shepherd at 6:30 pm. There will be much to discuss.

I arrive at the reception desk of Elmwood Care Home to find Susan on duty. Older than her colleague but at less risk of type-two diabetes, she has the facial features of a crow: a long beak-like nose, dark eyes, and hair unnaturally black for a woman her age.

"Hello, Simon," she squawks. "How are you today?"

"Fine, thank you."

"Are you here to see your mother?"

"What other reason would I be here for?"

Judging by the look on her face, I think Susan has just caught wind of the same obnoxious odour currently filling my nostrils — stewed broccoli, I'd venture. She signs the visitor card and hands it to me with no further comment.

Mother is in her regular chair, as I prefer her to be. I don't know if it would be her choice, but it does offer the best view of the fireplace.

"Hello, Mother."

Experience has taught me that there is no logic in waiting for a reply, and usually, I don't. Today, however, I'm minded to examine Mother more carefully after she broke her vow of silence yesterday. I study her face intently and count to sixty. There is no change in her expression from the first second to the last, so I perch on the adjacent armchair and open the book.

Eight pages in, I'm interrupted.

"Hello, Simon."

The new member of staff approaches.

"Hello."

She comes to a standstill two metres away. I wonder if she's learnt from our previous encounter.

"I'm sorry about yesterday," she says, almost as if she possesses the ability to mind read. "Sometimes I try too hard, you know, to make a good impression."

"Apology accepted."

"Elaine explained you prefer to sit quietly with your mum."

"She is not my mum. She is my mother."

"Sorry … again."

"Accepted."

She looks at her feet and flicks a strand of hair from her forehead.

"I'll leave you in peace. I think Derek needs me."

"Who?"

"The gentlemen in the corner," she replies, turning her head slightly.

"Right."

I look across towards the old male. Our eyes meet for a fraction of a second, and he waves at me. Inexplicably, I feel compelled to wave back.

Returning my attention to the female, her expression is not as tense as before.

"Enjoy your book," she says, glancing towards my lap where the book is resting. "No spoilers, but the aliens are arseholes."

With a parting smile the female returns to her duties, and I return to the fictional world of HG Wells.

The clock on the wall continues to tick, but I'm so engrossed in the story, I barely notice the time. By good fortune alone, I happen to glance up one minute before my designated departure time. I tuck the book under my arm, stand up, and count down the final minute.

"Goodbye, Mother."

I watch her for ten full seconds, then turn and walk away.

Keen to get home and continue reading, I move at pace along the corridor towards the reception area whilst simultaneously removing the lanyard up and over my head. The book slips from under my arm and lands on the carpet. I stop to pick it up.

"That's a cracking read," a voice remarks.

I look up. Father Paul is standing at the end of the corridor, three metres away. He is a distraction I can do without.

"How is your mother today?" he asks, still eyeing the book.

"I assume you're here to visit her?"

"Of course."

"I'll let you make your own judgement, then."

He takes a step forward.

"*War of The Worlds*? I didn't know you were a fan of sci-fi."

"I'm not. This book is for research purposes."

"Oh, really? What are you researching?"

"I need to go," I reply, glancing at my wristwatch. "I have a lot to do this afternoon."

"Before you shoot off, I wanted to talk to you about Helen."

"What about her?"

"I'd rather not discuss it in a corridor. Can you spare five minutes?"

"As I've already …"

"Simon," the priest forcibly interrupts. "We *really* do need to talk."

"I'm a busy man."

"So am I, but I always find time for what's important."

"What is it that's so important you're delaying my departure?"

"You mentioned you were going away yesterday, on holiday."

"It's not a holiday."

He closes his eyes and exhales a long breath through his nose. It's a common occurrence during our conversations.

"Five minutes," he then repeats. "That's all I'm asking for."

If I were due home to consume food or shower, I wouldn't even consider his request, but I have no fixed agenda for the next two hours besides reading. Perhaps it would be prudent to hear what the priest has to say now if it means he won't turn up at the house unannounced.

"Five minutes."

"Thank you. We can talk in the prayer room."

"The what?"

"Just follow me."

He leads me to a nondescript room with beige walls and a threadbare carpet. Eight chairs are lined-up in two rows, facing a wall with a wooden cross in the centre. There's also a table with five blue bibles stacked on top.

Father Paul grabs the nearest chair, spins it around, and drags it two metres from the others.

"Take a seat," he says, pointing to a chair at the nearest end of the row.

I sit down. We're facing one another but not quite head-on. I check the time.

"I'll get straight to it," he begins. "Before your mother's condition deteriorated, we had a long conversation about her health, her fears, and her funeral."

"So?"

"At the end of that conversation, Helen said she'd like to remove the burden from you."

"What burden?"

"Arranging her funeral."

"If I'm still around, I'm sure I can …"

"Wait," he interrupts. "What do you mean still around? You're not planning anything stupid, are you?"

"Define stupid?"

"Like … you're okay, in yourself, mentally?"

"I have no issue with my mental faculties."

"That's good to hear, but if you ever do need to talk, you know my door is always open."

I don't reply.

"Getting back to the point," he continues. "Helen said she would write a list of her wishes for the funeral while she was still capable."

"What does it matter? She'll be dead."

"I'm not having this debate with you again, Simon. It matters to your mother, and therefore it should matter to you. Okay?"

"Your agitation is unsettling."

He raises both hands, palms out.

"I apologise."

"Four minutes."

"She told me it's in a box in her wardrobe, and if you can retrieve it, I'll handle everything as per Helen's wishes."

"Correct me if I'm wrong, Father Paul, but isn't it customary to wait until someone is dead before planning their funeral?"

"And what if the next of kin isn't around when a loved one passes? You said you're going away soon."

"Yes, I am."

"So, what happens if, God-forbid, Helen passes while you're away? Who will ensure her last wishes are fulfilled if we don't know what they are?"

"Is that what you want? A letter from Mother's bedroom?"

"In short, yes. And before you go away, please."

"Why the urgency?"

For a human who appears to enjoy the sound of his own voice, his silence is telling.

"I spoke to the resident nurse after my visit yesterday," he replies in a tone close to a whisper. "And she fears Helen might not have long to go now."

"How long?"

"A few weeks, but possibly just days."

I digest the priest's revelation. It tallies perfectly with what I presumed *They* had planned. I return home, and then Helen Armstrong dies shortly after, ensuring a clean end to my time on Earth. A satisfactory plan from my perspective. The added benefit is I don't have to break my vow. Once I'm gone, Father Paul can root around Mother's bedroom to his heart's content. I just need to avoid him for the next seven days.

"I understand," I confirm. "I'll retrieve the list and drop it off at the church."

"Thank you."

The priest nods and then squeezes his features into an expression I can't decipher. We both stand up.

With nothing of significance left to discuss, Father Paul turns to the method of filling time that humans seem to favour: small talk.

"How far have you read?" he asks, pointing to the book in my hand.

"Not nearly far enough."

"I read it a few years back, and I've seen both the movie and TV adaptation. Perhaps I can help with your research."

"Unless you possess intimate knowledge of the area known as Primrose Hill, I doubt your insights will be of much use to me."

His facial features morph once more as his bulbous eyes widen.

"Why are you researching Primrose Hill?"

"Is that any of your business?"

"Probably not, but what's the harm in telling me?"

"If you must know, it's a place Mother mentioned yesterday."

"But … I thought …"

"It came as a surprise, yes. Those are the only words Mother has uttered in months, and I'd like to know what significance they hold."

"And, um, how is that research going?"

"I've only just started. Why are you so interested?"

"Er, no reason. Anyway, I'm sure you want to get on."

Some humans are better liars than others. In my limited experience, men of the cloth are the worst.

"Judging by your obvious anxiety, I'd say there is a reason. What are you not telling me?"

"I … um, it's not important," he mumbles, checking his own wristwatch. "Gosh, is that the time?"

He takes three steps forward. I take two steps to my right, blocking his path.

"I strongly suggest you tell me what you know, Father Paul. Resistance may have implications for us both, and in your case, I cannot guarantee those implications will be favourable."

"Please don't threaten me, Simon. Your mother would disapprove of your tone."

I move closer to the obstinate priest than I would usually consider comfortable.

"I won't ask again. What is it you know about Primrose Hill?"

Once more, he draws air in through his nostrils, although his eyes remain focused on the carpet.

After a moment, he replies.

"You'd better sit back down."

Chapter 7

I remain standing until Father Paul steps back towards his chair. When he eventually sits down, with obvious reluctance, I return to my seat.

"Well?"

He clears his throat twice.

"Your mother and I have been friends for a long time; you know that?"

"Yes."

"But I'm not just her friend; I'm her priest, her confidant."

"Your point being?"

"Over the years, Helen chose to share many parts of her life with me, but she did so in the knowledge I would never betray her confidence, either as a friend or a man of God."

"That woman is gone. She will never know."

He leans forward and rests his elbows on his thighs.

"I cannot, in all good faith, justify breaking your mother's confidence. Not now, not ever."

"Then what is the purpose of this conversation?"

"You asked about the relevance of Primrose Hill. I can't tell you anything."

"You can, and you will."

"I'm sorry, but I won't. However, I can suggest you look into your adoption."

"Why would I do that?"

"Because you might find answers from those who are in a position to give them. I'm not."

"What does my adoption have to do with Primrose Hill?"

"Please, Simon," he pleads. "You can ask a thousand times, but you'll find I take my vows seriously. I won't betray Helen."

With that, he gets to his feet.

"I really do need to go see her now," he says. "And, please don't forget that list."

He strides away while I remain rooted in my chair, the inner energy still humming in my chest.

I could follow him and use my superior strength to beat a confession, but that would make me worse than a human. Threats might provide a solution to a problem, but violence never does. And yet, a need for answers is clouding my otherwise impeccable judgement.

The musty atmosphere in the room soon weighs heavy. I don't like it, or being alone in a place where humans seek hope from a fictional deity. It patently did Mother no good when *They* decided her fate, nor will it help the next fool who looks up at the cross and prays for a miracle.

I get up and leave.

The walk back to Bulford Hill offers an opportunity to collate my thoughts, of which there are many. The urgency to read *War of The Worlds* has been surpassed by a greater need: to follow Father Paul's advice. Clearly, he knows there is a connection between my arrival on earth and Primrose Hill, and I need to establish what that connection is.

After I discovered I was adopted, neither of my parents were keen to discuss the matter. The information they relayed was scant, but they did confess to adopting me as a nine-month-old infant. I should have pressed for more information, but my human body was transforming at the time, my veins coursing with a chaotic mix of hormones. Consequently, I lacked focus and never asked the questions I should have. Where was I before they selected me? What happened to me in those months? Why Martin and Helen Armstrong? I have concluded there might be some tenuous link between the surname of my adopted parents and that of the first human to set foot on an extra-terrestrial body. As a single piece of data, it might be considered a coincidence, but when added to the litany of facts about my true being, I concluded *They* had a hand in selecting my earthly guardians.

Over the years, I have continued to ask the same questions, but being the highly-strung human she is, or was, Mother always met those attempts with the same tearful statement: my past didn't matter because no one could love me more than her. It now seems that while she was reluctant to share such information with her adopted son, she was more than willing to confide in Father Paul.

Now she is no fit state to confide in anyone. For reasons I am still unsure of, it is down to me to unveil the secrets she has kept hidden. Whatever those reasons are, there must be some relevance to my departure. The facts fit, at least those I know.

I arrive home and bound up the stairs, almost tripping over Merle as he lies near the top step.

"Foolish cat," I scold. "How many times have I told you not to sleep on the stairs?"

He looks up at me, yawns, and then promptly returns to his state of slumber.

I pass by Mother's room, the door still firmly shut after she closed it for the final time. Two thoughts occur: did she know she was closing it for the final time, and what plans did she make for her funeral? Neither question is worthy of my attention at this moment. I quickly dismiss both and continue to my bedroom.

Sitting down at the desk, I check the time. I left the care home seventeen minutes later than I usually do; a dent in the two hours I had at my disposal this afternoon. There is no sense in reading a book now, but I can begin piecing together my own story. It's likely to be of much greater significance than the fiction of HG Wells.

With my fingers hovering over the keyboard, I consider the best place to start. I then type a question into the search field: *how do I establish information about my adoption?*

Much like my search for Primrose Hill, there are many results. I click the first link, and a website page loads.

There are ten paragraphs of text on the page, plus a series of bullet points. I begin reading and try not to skim the overly long sentences peppered with acronyms. It is not an article designed to stoke hope or offer solace — more of a warning about the pitfalls of researching one's adoption. At the beginning of the third paragraph, there's a link to an organisation named Family Connect. The article confirms their role is to help adopted adults find answers to questions about their origins.

Their use of the word origins is an interesting choice. Whoever this organisation are, it's unlikely they'll have answers relating to my true origins. I click the link.

The difference between the two websites is stark; the Family Connect website utilising bright colours and photographs of seemingly cheerful humans to convey positivity. Their navigation system is also clear and concise, and I click the prominent link to confirm I am adopted. The next page offers six navigational options. I select the obvious: *getting started*.

I'm met by a page of warnings, thinly veiled as important questions to consider. Have I fully considered the implications of researching my adoption? Yes. Do I have a support network to help me through the process? No, nor do I need one. Is this the right time to seek answers? Definitely, yes.

I retreat and select the second navigational option: *accessing records.*

The first snippet of information relates to birth certificates. Without reading a single word, I know this section is unlikely to be of use because Mother lost mine many years ago. When I was old enough to open a bank account, the application form cited a birth certificate as an acceptable form of identification. Mother spent an entire day in her bedroom searching for it but to no avail. I used a National Insurance card and a letter from HM Revenue & Customs in the end.

Neither will help me with this quest.

I backtrack and click another option relating to adoption records. Within the first three paragraphs, it becomes clear how many levels of bureaucracy I must navigate. First, I need to establish the name of the adoption agency. Helpfully, the website suggests I contact the local authority where the adoption took place. I open another browser tab, and a quick search confirms the local authority covering Surbiton is Kingston Council. Five more clicks, and I arrive at the website page with information relating to social services. There is scant information about adoption, but there is a link to another website.

There is a well-worn adage humans use a lot — third time lucky. Unsure if there is any scientific basis behind it, I click the link to a third website.

After two more clicks, I finally unearth a telephone number. I activate my mobile telephone and input the eleven digits.

A female answers, and she then asks the nature of my enquiry. I offer a vague outline, confirming I need information about my adoption. She requests I hold the line while my call is transferred to the appropriate department.

"Good afternoon, this is Cindy Akinyemi."

"Hello. I need to access my adoption records."

"Okay. Can I start by taking your full name?"

"It's Simon Armstrong."

"Your date of birth and address?"

I relay the requested information.

"Thank you. So, Simon, how can I help you today?"

"As I've already stated, I need access to my adoption records."

"Understood. There is a process we need to go through. Would you like me to talk you through it?"

"If you must."

"Firstly, have you considered the implications of what your adoption records might reveal?"

I refer to the page of notes I made not fifteen minutes ago.

"Yes, I've fully considered the implications of researching my adoption. No, I do not have a support network to help me through the process, nor do I need one. And yes, this is the right time."

"Oh, I gather you've already conducted some research."

"A minimal amount, but I cannot proceed until I have access to my adoption records. I would like you to post them to my address."

"I'm afraid it doesn't work like that. There are protocols to follow, safeguarding checks to make, and we strongly advise all adults seeking information on their adoption consult with a counsellor first."

"For what purpose?"

"It's a life-changing decision, Simon, and once you've made it, there's no going back. Our job is to support you through the process and ensure your best interests are met."

"I do not require your support, and surely it is up to me to determine what is in my best interests, is it not?"

"Well, yes, but we have a duty of care. Whether you like it or not, we can't just hand over files willy nilly and leave you to get on with it. That would be grossly irresponsible."

"What is grossly irresponsible is a government-sponsored service preventing me from accessing information I have every right to see. So, I'll ask you again – can you send a copy of my adoption record to my home address?"

"Sorry, but we can't give you access to your records until you've spoken to a counsellor."

My inner energy begins to thrum as my grip on the mobile telephone tightens.

"Listen to me," I demand. "I don't have time to speak with your counsellor."

"The sessions only take an hour or so. Would you like me to schedule an appointment?"

Her offer does little to quell the heat rising in my chest, burning the back of my throat.

"No, I would not. My time on Earth is nearly at an end, and your bureaucracy is preventing me from finding answers. Do you not understand … I need to know."

Within a second of finishing my sentence, I wish I could retract it. I allowed the inner energy to cloud my thoughts to such an extent I relayed information of the most sensitive nature. *They* will not be pleased.

Judging by the silence on the line, it seems the woman is just as displeased by my outburst.

"Hello?"

"Sorry, Simon. I'm still here."

Her tone of voice is surprisingly soft, which I did not expect. On the odd occasion I raised my voice with Mother, her reaction was always negative. Unsure how to proceed, I remain silent.

"Um, did I hear you correctly?" she asks. "You said your time on Earth is nearly at an end?"

"Yes. I have a matter of days."

"I'm so sorry to hear that."

I do not understand her apology or sudden change in demeanour. She continues with another question.

"Is that why you're so keen to find out about your adoption?"

"Correct," I reply, as the heat in my chest dissipates a fraction. "There are questions I must answer, and your organisation is the only way I'll find those answers."

"Can you bear with me for a minute? I just need to speak to my line manager."

"I will."

I remain on hold for nine minutes, not one; Cindy Akinyemi making the same deceitful assurances as Father Paul.

"Are you still there, Simon?"

"Yes."

"I've had a long chat with my line manager, Vicky, and we think, considering your circumstances, we might be able to circumnavigate some of the safeguarding measures."

"In what way?"

"We'll allow you to see your records without speaking to a counsellor."

"Thank you."

"Are you well enough to travel?"

"I am. Why?"

"I appreciate the urgency here so I can clear a slot for you on Monday morning if that works?"

It's not ideal, but I am at her mercy.

"Monday morning will suffice. Where am I expected to travel to?"

"You'll need to get yourself to our office. I can email you directions, but it's not far from London Bridge Station."

"In London?"

"That's right."

"What time?"

"Does nine-thirty work for you?"

There are many reasons I do not wish to travel to London, not least because it will significantly impact my routines, but what choice do I have? There is, however, a reasonable chance I can return in time for my daily visit to Mother.

"I will be there at nine-thirty."

"Great. And just to let you know, we will ask you to sign a disclaimer to confirm you've waived our offers of support. You'll also need to bring three forms of identification. Is that okay?"

I confirm it is, but that is not the end of this ordeal. In order to retrieve my records, I must first endure a lengthy telephone interrogation relating to my history and that of my adopted parents. It takes thirty-eight minutes to conclude.

Finally, she requests my email address. Cindy Akinyemi then ends the call with another unnecessary apology and a quote from The Bible.

I could remain on this planet for a thousand years, and I'll never understand humans.

Message 2811

Priority Level 3 | Encrypted @ 19:27

From: TheShepherd82

To: Epsilon30

Message Begins ...

Ĝojan novajôn, frato Epsilon,

The magnitude of your last message was not lost on me. I read it three times to be certain.

It is a pity we cannot interrogate the priest to ascertain what he knows, and you are forced to travel on Monday. I believe, together, we could break his silence and discover what information your Earth-parent shared with him. Are you certain that is not a course of action you wish to pursue? I have contacts on Earth who would be willing to assist in an interrogation, should you change your mind.

It is now clear that Primrose Hill is the key to your arrival on this planet, and your departure. It is also clear there are powers working against us, and I implore you to take the utmost care in the coming days. Our mission is close to completion, and we cannot risk it being undermined at this late stage.

Be assured, They will be monitoring developments carefully, to ensure your safe passage.

Remain strong. Remain vigilant.

The Shepherd

Chapter 8

"Please, Simon. At least consider it."

"I'm not interested."

Mr Choudhary throws his arms in the air.

"It's a great opportunity for a smart young man like you."

"I have other plans, and they don't involve working for your cousin."

I'd barely taken my first sip of tea when Mr Choudhary revealed his news. He'd had a conversation with his cousin, also Mr Choudhary, regarding a role in his accountancy practice. The work is similar to what I do now, apparently.

"The pay is better, and you could even work from home if you wanted. It's the perfect position for you."

"That's as maybe, but once I have completed my notice here, I won't be available for work."

"Why not?"

"That is my business."

"You can be infuriating sometimes," he says with a heavy sigh. "You know that?"

"I only know it because Mother used to tell me. I disagreed with her, and I disagree with you."

"Won't you at least think about it?"

I know if I agree, he will likely end the conversation.

"I will think about it."

"Thank you. I'll let you get on."

I allocate ten seconds of thought over the ensuing three hours of work. It doesn't alter my earlier decision, not that it matters as

Mr Choudhary doesn't mention it again before bidding me a good weekend.

I have the opportunity to think freely on the bus journey home, but my brain is unwilling to entertain any thoughts other than Monday's trip to London. Whilst I'm willing to suffer local buses, I don't like trains, and I really don't like the humans who use them. And, although I've never been to London, I have grave doubts I'm going to like it much either. From what I've seen on television, it seems crowded and chaotic; the antipathy of my structured existence in Durrington.

Perhaps I could ask The Shepherd if he would join me. His knowledge of humanity would be of benefit on such a journey into the unknown.

By the time the bus pulls up on Bulford Hill, I have made a decision. I will ask The Shepherd to accompany me to London. It is a break in protocol, but we are so close to completing the mission, I'm sure he and *They*, will understand. My course of action confirmed, I'm able to dislodge further thoughts on the matter, although I sense they may return as I attempt to sleep tonight.

At home, I have lunch and then shower. The weather forecast predicted spells of rain this afternoon, but I distrust The Meteorological Office almost as much as I distrust humans who ask for trust. Erring on the side of caution, I put on my waterproof jacket.

Halfway to Elmwood Care Home, a light drizzle develops. I up my pace and arrive a minute earlier than I usually would. I dislike arriving early, so I seek cover beneath a tree in the car park before completing the entry process at 2:00 pm.

With so much of my attention focused on more important matters, I neglected to consider the day. Being a Friday, the stench of cooked fish arrives like a slap to my cheeks. I hurry to the reception desk where Susan is on duty.

"Hello, Simon. Punctual as always, I see."

"Good afternoon, Susan."

"Are you okay? You look a bit peaky."

"Fish," I reply, gulping hard. "I find the odour nauseating."

"Oh, I am sorry."

I don't think she is sorry at all.

"Your mother is in her room today."

"Why?"

"If you go through, I'll ask Nurse Clifford to pop in and have a chat."

She fills out the visitor card with no further comment and then hands it to me with a strained smile.

"Thank you."

I set off on a different route, through a door to the left of the reception desk and along a corridor with white doors on either side, interspersed with framed pictures depicting rural scenes. I come to a stop outside number eight, turn the handle, and enter.

Some months ago, in a conversation with Father Paul, he complained that Mother's room wasn't particularly homely. He then suggested I should bring in some of the framed photographs and a few of Mother's favourite ornaments to brighten it up. I complied on his third time of asking, purely to prevent a fourth. Personally, I preferred it before: uncluttered and utilitarian.

Unlike her bedroom at Bulford Hill, this is a room I've had cause to enter several times over the last eleven months. On such occasions, Mother has not been deemed well enough to sit in the residents' lounge. On this day, I would concur with such an assessment.

I take a seat on the plastic chair next to the bed.

"Hello, Mother."

I visually examine her, not for signs of recognition, but with Father Paul's statement yesterday still fresh. There are no obvious clues to her impending death, but I am perhaps not best placed to notice. If I hadn't seen her in months, maybe the withering of her frame or the greyness of her skin would be striking, but does she look any different today to how she looked yesterday or last week? I don't think so. In Mother's case, death is creeping within her, like corrosion on the inside of an iron drainpipe. It has already eaten away at her mind, and if the nurse's assessment is correct, it is now feasting on what little remains.

There's a knock on the door, and a middle-aged woman in a blue tunic enters.

"Hello again, Simon."

I don't much care for Nurse Clifford. We've only conversed four times, and there is something about her inquisitive nature I find unsettling. Almost certainly without foundation, it's as if she can see what lies beneath this human facade.

"Hello."

She steps across the room and gently takes Mother's limp hand in hers. Seconds pass, and then she carefully returns that hand to its prior position. The nurse then turns to me.

"I understand you had a chat with Father Paul yesterday."

"Yes."

"He updated you on your mother's condition?"

"Correct."

"I know you don't like talking about it, so I won't go over what we discussed in detail. But you do understand where we are?"

I nod.

"If there are any family members or friends who'd like to drop by and … to say goodbye to Helen, I'd suggest you ask them sooner rather than later. You know why, don't you?"

Again, I nod.

"Is there anything you need from me?"

"Such as?"

"Anything at all. I don't want you to think you're on your own, okay? There are lots of people who want to help if you're willing to let them."

"Can any of them prevent Mother's death?"

"Sadly, not, but I wasn't referring to your mother. It's you who might need support."

"Your concern is misplaced but noted. I have all the support I need."

"You might think that now, but no matter how strong we think we are, there are times in life we need help. We're all human, Simon."

As much as I'd like to correct her, I remain silent. Nurse Clifton appears to deflate.

"Alright," she says wearily. "I'll leave you in peace. I'll be in my office if you need me … today, or at any time. Understood?"

"Understood. Goodbye."

She departs.

The Shepherd referenced certain powers working against us, and Nurse Clifford is unlike most other humans I know, making her a potential antagonist. I do sense a level of malevolence lurking behind her grey eyes, and whenever she speaks to me, her tone of voice infers a deep-seated need to control. I will endeavour to avoid her on future visits, and I certainly won't be dropping by her office.

I check on Mother. She appears to be lost in a place somewhere between sleep and semi-consciousness, her breathing shallow, her eyelids flickering occasionally.

"Not long now, Mother."

I sit back in the chair. With no other way to occupy my mind, I begin counting the slats in the horizontal blind covering the room's only window. There are thirty — a number of great significance to me.

During my early research into Starseeds, I discovered an article relating to number frequency. That article suggested one of the critical signs that an individual is indeed a true Starseed is the common recurrence of a particular number in one's life. In my case, that number is thirty. I arrived on this planet on the thirtieth day of September, and ever since that same number has cropped up on too many occasions to be a coincidence. My father died on the thirtieth day of March, and the doctor delivered Mother's diagnosis on the thirtieth day of January. When we moved from Surbiton, it was to 30 Bulford Hill.

In between all the significant events, I've noticed the number thirty has appeared countless times in many places. Before the current bus company lost their contract, the bus to Amesbury was the number thirty. The telephone number allocated to our home address is 01980 65 30 30. My payroll code in Mr Choudhary's business is SAA30. The list goes on and on, which is why I am certain I will leave this planet on the anniversary of my thirtieth birthday, on the thirtieth of September — exactly one week today.

There's another knock on the door.

"I'm not disturbing you, am I?"

I look up. The member of staff, Rosie, steps through the doorway.

Like all the staff here, except Elaine and Susan, and Nurse Clifford, she is wearing black trousers and a greenish-coloured tunic with 'Elmwood' embroidered in white letters on the front. The uniform appears a better fit than it does on other members of staff.

"What is it you want, Miss?"

"My name is Rosie, remember?"

"I am aware of your name. Would you prefer I use it?"

"Yes, I would."

"As you wish."

My eyes dwell on the grey, block-shaped item in her right hand.

"It's a Bluetooth speaker," she says.

"For what purpose?"

"Music. I wanted to run an idea by you if that's okay?"

"Go ahead."

She takes four steps forward, coming to a stop at the end of Mother's bed.

"Have you ever heard of music therapy?"

"No."

"It's been proven to be of real benefit to people with dementia. They say it helps to reduce anxiety and lower blood pressure."

"Your point being?"

"I was wondering if we could perhaps give it a try with your mum … sorry, mother."

"If what you claim is true, why has no one suggested such treatment before?"

She reacts with the slightest bow of her head.

"Um, can I be honest?"

"You don't need my permission."

"Between you and me, I was told you don't respond well to new experiences."

"That would be a fair and accurate assessment."

"I just thought maybe … it can't do any harm to try, can it?"

Unlike Nurse Clifton, Rosie's demeanour is conciliatory, verging on benign. Equally, I cannot deny she possesses an agreeable physical presence, unlike most of her colleagues. Her question is also accurate — there's a minimal chance her treatment will harm a woman already close to death.

"You may try your treatment."

"Great," she replies with a broad smile. "What kind of music does your mother like?"

"Kind?"

"Does she have a favourite song or artist, or is there a particular genre of music she likes?"

I consider her question for a moment.

"Merle Haggard."

"Um, who's he?"

"An American performer of country and western music. Mother played his music when preparing meals, along with that of Slim Whitman and Jim Reeves. She named her cat after him, so I suppose he must have been her favourite artist."

"Never heard of him, but let me do a quick search."

She places the grey box at the end of the bed and extracts a mobile telephone from her pocket. I watch on as she taps the screen with remarkable dexterity.

"Right, found him, and … wow. He put out a lot of stuff, didn't he?"

"I don't know, but Mother played his album, *Pride In What I Am* far too much. I specifically remember it as she said I should always take pride in what I am, not what others want me to be."

"Sounds like good advice."

Her fingers return to the screen.

"We're in luck," she then declares. "Shall we play it?"

"If you wish."

A final tap on the screen and she adjusts the position of the grey box, so it faces Mother.

The music plays. It is the track titled, *Take a Lot of Pride in What I Am*.

I've never understood the appeal of popular music, but then I'm not the target audience. It is humans who are susceptible to love, prone to heartbreak, and paranoid about infidelity: the core tenets of popular music from what little I've heard. Saying that, the music currently playing in Mother's room tells the story of a vagrant. There is no mention of love, heartbreak, or infidelity. I think it is a song about loneliness.

With Rosie standing motionless at the end of the bed, I turn to face Mother.

"Is it just me?" Rosie then says in a hushed voice. "Or does she appear to be breathing a little easier?"

"Possibly."

Slowly, Rosie steps around the bed and sits on the edge, uncomfortably close to my chair. I try not to let the discomfort show.

"Watch her chest," she says, nodding towards Mother. "I think the music is having a calming effect."

The rise and fall of Mother's chest is not quite as pronounced. I struggle to understand how my human brain functions most of the time, so I'm not about to guess what's going on in Mother's. But, as Rosie suggested, the music doesn't appear to be doing any harm.

For one whole minute, we sit in silence and watch Mother.

"What kind of music do you like, Simon?" she then asks.

"I rarely listen to music."

"But when you do?"

"Classical music. Holst, Prokofiev, and if the mood takes me, sometimes Stravinsky."

"That's a bit too high-brow for me. Don't you listen to any contemporary music?"

"I find it irritating, and the lyrics make no sense to me."

"What about your mother's music?"

"Background noise; no different from the sound of a vacuum cleaner or washing machine."

"Right."

Merle Haggard's voice drifts away, and it's followed by five seconds of complete silence. The second track then begins.

"Can I get you a coffee, Simon?"

"I don't drink coffee."

"Tea? Water?"

"No … thank you."

"Fair enough."

Without warning Rosie stands, takes two steps in my direction and then leans forwards to take a closer look at Mother. The slight hint of fish in the air clashes with a sweet floral scent. My immediate concern is not the change in odour but my proximity to a human. I lean as far back in the chair as I can until my head touches the wall.

Skin prickling, the familiar urge to flee is almost overwhelming.

I was a young adolescent when I first experienced this condition, and for many years I couldn't understand why I found human contact so detestable. I later realised it must be a safety valve in my alien DNA; there to serve as a warning should I ever get too physically close to the subjects I'm supposed to study. Now, it feels like every strand of that DNA is ablaze.

I'm about to leap from the chair when Rosie retakes her position on the edge of the bed.

"She seems so relaxed."

Mother might be, but I am not. I glance at my Earth-parent and then calculate the distance between Rosie and the wall opposite her. I estimate it to be 120cm — wide enough I can move past with minimal chance of contact.

The urge to flee relents, but not sufficiently. I stand up and stride forward in one swift movement, keeping my left shoulder up against the wall. Only once I've passed the end of the bed do I dare turn around.

"I must go."

"Oh, right. I haven't said anything wrong, have I?"

"No. Goodbye … goodbye, Mother."

I make my escape, but the prickling sensation does not ease until Elmwood Care Home is out of sight.

Message 2812

Priority Level 3 | Encrypted @ 20:21

From: TheShepherd82

To: Epsilon30

Message Begins ...

Ĝojan novaĵon, frato Epsilon,

It is almost as if the humans are conspiring against us. I received your message on Friday evening and due to unforeseen interference, I have only just had the opportunity to respond.

Regretfully, I am unable to accompany you on your quest to London tomorrow. It would have been a moment of great pride to finally join you in person but the circumstances are not favourable. In fact, I am concerned my position might be compromised and it might not be sensible for us to meet until I have established the risk level.

I wish you well, and I will endeavour to rectify the situation my end soon. Report on your progress at the earliest possible opportunity.

Remain strong. Remain vigilant.

The Shepherd

Chapter 9

I'm not sure if it's possible for a cat to look confused, but Merle makes a valiant attempt as he watches me decant his food into a bowl.

"I know we're breaking routine, but my taxi will be here in thirty minutes. You eat now or not at all."

He decides to eat now.

Having my routine commence forty-five minutes earlier than usual, I've had to recalibrate the timing of every task. I check the time twice before sitting down to breakfast.

I have no appetite.

Having messaged The Shepherd on Friday evening, I had to wait almost forty-eight hours for a response. After the first twenty-four, my concern began to mount. When he finally did respond, I struggled to process the associated emotions. I'm sure there was a sense of relief, but that was soon overwhelmed by disappointment when I learnt he would not be joining me today. Within thirty minutes, that disappointment had evolved into an emotion I have yet to decipher, and it's still present this morning.

A lack of sleep did not help.

I spent much of yesterday planning the journey. I calculated the most efficient way of completing each leg, with the least exposure to humans. The taxi will take me to Salisbury train station, some six miles from home, where the direct train to London Waterloo leaves at 7:15 am. I have reserved a seat in the first-class carriage and the adjacent seat to ensure no human can sit next to me. At Waterloo, I will take another taxi to Tooley

Street in London Bridge, and I should arrive there around 9:14 am.

Unfortunately, my need to avoid crowded public transportation resulted in a ticket cost close to £290. If it were not for the fact money will be of no use to me come Friday, I'd be inclined to write a letter of protest about the exorbitant rail fare.

I manage to eat one slice of toast, but I cannot stomach the second. I offer it to Merle, and he turns his nose up at it.

I check, double-check, and triple-check I have all I need for my journey, and then wait on the front doorstep for my taxi. When I booked it, I left the female operator in no doubt how highly I valued punctuality. I stressed I wanted it to arrive at 6:45 am precisely — not a minute earlier or a minute later.

With seconds to spare, it arrives.

I climb in the back seat. For good measure, I conduct another check to ensure I haven't forgotten anything.

"Salisbury station, isn't it, mate?" the driver asks.

"Yes."

Over the years, I have developed an effective strategy for discouraging small talk. So, when the driver asks if I watched a football match yesterday, I reply with a single syllable answer: no. He then asks if I've lived in Durrington long. I reply with a yes, nothing more. The conversation ends there.

We arrive at Salisbury train station at 7:04 am, and I pay the requested fare. Seven minutes later, I am in my reserved seat, next to the window, and with no other seats facing me. I place my satchel on the adjacent seat and take out the pocket radio. I inserted fresh batteries last night to ensure they would last the ninety-four-minute journey to and from Waterloo station.

The train sets off, and I begin a methodical crawl through the FM frequency, lingering on the static whilst skipping past the music and chattering radio presenters. It proves an effective distraction from the disorganised humans who board in vast numbers at each of the six stations the train stops at. Why they subject themselves to such a miserable experience every morning is beyond my understanding. I find the comparatively serene bus journey to Amesbury disagreeable enough, but the scenes beyond this window are my idea of earthly hell.

Finally, we approach Waterloo station.

I found a helpful resource on the internet yesterday — a virtual tour of the station concourse and exit points. Using that tool, I was able to plot my route from the platform to the nearest taxi rank. Having memorised that route, I wait until the platform is clear of commuters and alight the train with a measure of confidence.

With the satchel strapped securely over my shoulder, I head towards the ticket barrier. It takes seventeen seconds to cover the distance, and I arrive at the barrier with my ticket in hand. I slide it into a slot on the exit gate. It opens, allowing access to the main concourse.

Six short steps, but it is akin to entering another dimension. My legs freeze as my eyes try to make sense of the unreal scene. Stony-faced humans in their hundreds swarm like drones; some buzzing past with purpose while others amble, seemingly lost and confused. My sight is not the only sense to experience the tumultuous scene. The noise is unlike anything I've ever heard; the thrum of disembodied human voices layered against a secondary soundtrack of beeps and whistles and electronic chimes.

A command forms in my mind: *abort and return to base!*

I remain frozen, and for possibly the first time in my human life, I don't know what to do. Did *They* send the command, or was it triggered by my own imagination? What of the mission? I am one taxi ride from establishing the truth about my arrival on this planet, and if I turn around now, there will be no second chance. Worst case, inaction could prevent my departure.

I try to seek out my pre-determined exit point beyond the chaos, and when it's finally in my sights, I summon every ounce of resolve, forcing my legs into action.

The short walk in a straight line I anticipated during the planning phase of this operation fails to materialise. I end up weaving left and right whilst continually adjusting my pace to avoid colliding into one drone after another. Despite my erratic movements, no one seems to notice me and even when I leap from the path of a male in a brown overcoat, he keeps his eyes fixed on his route ahead. I have often wondered what it must feel like to be invisible, and my journey across the crowded concourse offers an unexpected hint.

I reach the exit, and the crowd thins sufficiently to continue in a straight line towards a row of black taxis lined up at the kerb. With great relief, I approach the open passenger window of the nearest.

"I would like to go to Tooley Street, in London Bridge."

"Go to the first cab in the line," the driver replies without looking up from the newspaper on his lap.

"Why?"

"Because that's the way the system works."

He presses a button, and the window closes.

Irked, I join a queue behind six humans. Fortunately, the line moves quickly and within seventy-seven seconds I am at the head of the queue. Again, I state my desired destination to the driver.

"No worries," he replies. "Hop in."

I do as instructed.

The design of London taxis is more to my liking than the Ford saloon which transported me to Salisbury station. I am separated from the driver by a transparent polymer panel, and the diesel engine is too noisy for prolonged conversation. I fasten my seat belt.

Having already used an internet planning tool to calculate the route and time required to reach Tooley Street, I check my watch to ensure I am on schedule. Two minutes ahead. My heart rate drops to within a few beats of its resting level as the driver presses a button on a box with an LED display. He pulls away.

I have invested many, many hours researching London, knowing it is a city of some significance to humans. I know more than nine million of them live here, although judging by those I saw on the station concourse, most are unhappy about it. I know it is where the United Kingdom Government is based, as are the monarchy. Opinions on both are mixed, I established. Some of the population detest their government while others voted for them in number. Humans, in general, appear positive about the head of the monarchy, Queen Elizabeth II, although no one voted for her.

I turn my attention to the view from my window and the unfamiliar buildings we pass by. As the train approached Waterloo Station, I caught a glimpse of the London Eye and The Palace of Westminster, but I had hoped to see some of the landmarks in closer detail. Briefly, whilst planning my route yesterday, I did entertain the idea of visiting some of those landmarks after my meeting in Tooley Street, but I know they are likely to be surrounded by crowds of humans. For that reason, I decided against it.

The only significant landmark I've physically visited in my time on Earth is Stonehenge. Only six miles from Durrington, Mother took me there on what she called an educational visit, although I left with more questions than answers. Some years later, my curiosity got the better of me, and I spent one weekend investigating the structure and its history using the internet. I discovered that 4,000 years ago, Stonehenge comprised an outer circle of standing stones, called sarsens — thirty of them. That fact added weight to my theories about why we moved to Wiltshire and my Starseed status.

I've no idea if we're heading in the right direction as the driver takes me on a tour of London's back streets. There is little of interest to see.

One minute ahead of my estimated time of arrival, we come to a stop outside a five-storey brick building with large windows.

"That'll be £11.80, mate."

"We are here?"

"Yeah."

I fish my wallet from the satchel, count out the requested amount, and pay the driver. He checks it and then mumbles a thank you. Satisfied our transaction is complete, I exit the taxi.

This part of London is much busier than Amesbury, but there are far fewer humans than at Waterloo. With fifteen minutes to kill before my meeting, I scan the street, searching for a place to wait where I'm least likely to be mugged, buggered, or murdered — I've read all about London's violent crime statistics. I seek refuge in a doorway three doors down from the building I'm due to visit.

Standing sentry-like, I remain on high alert as I count down the minutes. Many humans pass by but again, I might as well be invisible for all the attention I attract.

I leave my post one minute before the scheduled meeting time and enter the building.

Accustomed as I am to dealing with receptionists, there are two behind the desk, and I don't know which one to approach. I come to a stop two metres away and wait for one of them to acknowledge me. The one on the left looks up.

"Can I help you?"

"I have a nine-thirty meeting with Cindy … please, wait."

I tried to memorise the surname but not well enough, it seems. I'm about to check my notebook when the receptionist intervenes.

"Do you mean Cindy Akinyemi?"

"Yes, I believe that is her."

"Please take a seat. I'll call her down."

I nod, but I don't want to sit down. Having overcome the most challenging obstacle in getting here, why does it feel like my stomach has contracted to a quarter its usual size? I step to the side of the desk and stare out of the window. Seconds drag by as my stomach threatens to turn itself inside out. I know enough about human biology to understand how unlikely that is.

"Simon?"

I turn around to find a squat woman approaching. Her skin is dark, more so than Mr Choudhary's, and her blouse a vivid shade of orange. She raises her right arm and extends a hand.

"I'm Cindy," she then states without waiting for my acknowledgement.

I glance at her hand, hovering in the space between us.

"I am Simon Armstrong, yes. I don't shake hands."

It suddenly occurs my refusal to shake Cindy Akinyemi's hand could be misconstrued. Mr Choudhary once told me some humans are unnecessarily hostile to others purely because their skin is a different shade. He couldn't explain why and despite giving the subject considerable thought, I could not see any logical reason either. In this instance, I do not want Cindy Akinyemi to think I am a prejudiced simpleton, so I offer clarification.

"I never shake hands … with anyone. It's not because of your skin colour, you understand?"

"Err, right. Dare I ask why you don't shake hands?"

"Germs."

"Okaaay. Fair enough."

She briefly turns to the receptionist, and they share a facial expression I cannot interpret. Her attention then returns to me.

"Would you like to follow me, Simon? My office is on the fourth floor."

I nod and follow her across the reception area. She stops at a silver set of doors and presses a button.

"Is that a lift?" I ask.

"Yes, it is."

"I don't trust lifts."

"Oh, boy," she says quietly. "Fine. We'll take the stairs."

I then follow her through a door to a stairwell. There is no small talk, which is just as well as my entire focus is on maintaining a six-step distance between us. As we reach the third floor, it becomes clear why Cindy Akinyemi has remained silent.

"Christ, I'm unfit," she pants, pausing to catch her breath.

"Maybe you should use the stairs more often."

"Maybe you're right."

"And it's wrong to blaspheme, so Mother used to say."

"Sorry. It slipped out."

"Your apology is unnecessary. Mother is not here, and I myself am an atheist."

She responds with just a strange kind of smile and then continues on her way, still panting hard.

From the top of the stairs, we pass through another door and continue silently along a corridor.

"I've booked a private room for our meeting, so we're not disturbed," Cindy Akinyemi says over her shoulder. "It's just through here."

She invites me into a room barely large enough to warrant the name. I'd be inclined to call it a sizable cupboard.

"Grab a seat."

There are four chairs around a circular table, with a single filing cabinet in the corner and a small window behind me. I wait for Cindy Akinyemi to sit and then position the nearest chair as far from hers as possible.

"Um, do you have a problem with confined spaces?" she asks.

"It's not the space, as such. More a proximity issue."

"Is this room too small?"

"As long as we maintain this distance, it is acceptable."

She nods and then leans her elbows on the desk.

"Before we start, I just want to say I'm sorry about your … situation. I can't imagine how hard it must be."

Unsure what situation she's referring to but not wanting to delay the reason I'm here, I thank her.

"How are you coping?"

"I am coping."

"I think you're incredibly brave, and I guess it's a reminder that none of us knows how long we've got."

I consider her statement, and I wonder if she's referring to the situation with Mother. I don't recall mentioning it during our telephone conversation, but governmental departments have access to all manner of information.

"Humans die. It's unavoidable."

"Well, I hope when my time comes, I can be as strong as you."

I don't reply, and she drops her gaze to a folder on the desk.

"Anyway, shall we start with the paperwork?"

"Yes."

The paperwork in question is a nine-page disclaimer which I must read and sign before we can proceed. I then have to prove I am who I say I am. Opening my satchel, I hand Cindy Akinyemi my bank card, a provisional driving licence I secured for this exact purpose, and a letter from the local council.

"I just need to take a copy of these. I'll be a few minutes."

"Understood."

"Can I get you anything while I'm down the hall?"

"Anything?"

"I mean a drink. Tea, coffee, water?"

"No, thank you."

It takes six minutes to complete her task, stretching the definition of 'few' to its limit.

"Right," she says, closing the door to our cupboard. "Now that's all the paperwork out of the way. I'm sure you're keen to discover what you came here for."

"Indeed."

Cindy Akinyemi sits down and straightens her shoulder.

"Listen, Simon. I just want to calibrate your expectations."

"In what way?"

"The reason most adopted adults want to access their records is for one purpose: to ascertain the name or names of their birth parents. I'm sorry to say that in your case, that information simply isn't available."

"Why is it not available?"

"We don't know who your birth parents are."

Chapter 10

Cindy Akinyemi pauses. Perhaps she's looking for signs of disappointment or despair.

"Did you hear me, Simon?"

"Yes, perfectly."

"We don't have any record of who your parents are."

"As I just stated, I heard you."

"I know that must come as a huge disappointment."

"No."

"Oh."

"What other information is in the file?"

"Not much. It's basically a copy of what we gave to your adoptive parents."

"My parents have already seen this information?"

"Yes, it's standard protocol to share all the information we hold on a child, just in case any of it becomes relevant down the line."

"May I see it?"

"It's best if I talk you through what we've got. There's a lot of internal documents which aren't necessarily relevant to your enquiry."

She licks her finger and uses the tip to leaf through the pages. Disgusting.

"Do you know anything about the circumstances surrounding your adoption?"

"Nothing. My parents were reluctant to discuss it."

"How did you discover you were adopted?"

"I overheard a conversation in which Father referred to my adoption. He tended to raise his voice when agitated."

She turns a page.

"Would you like to know the circumstances? Remember what I said on the phone yesterday — there's no way to rewind once you know the truth."

"I want to know."

"Okay."

I watch her orange-painted fingernail run slowly along a line of text as if committing it to memory. From my position, I cannot read it.

"There's no real way to sugar-coat this, so I'll just tell you as it is. You were found abandoned in the Accident and Emergency department of Epsom General Hospital in Surrey."

"Abandoned? As in, left there?"

"Correct."

"Who left me there?"

"No one knows, I'm afraid. The information in the file is scant, but it appears there was an area-wide appeal in the months after your abandonment and no one came forward. That's why we can't tell you who your birth parents are."

I begin processing her revelation. Only five seconds pass before she speaks again.

"Are you okay, Simon?"

"I'm just considering the implications of this new information."

"It's a lot to take in. Take your time."

My mind drifts back to the kitchen table in our house on Bulford Hill, and a story Mother once relayed as part of my history lesson — that of the Trojan Wars. I later discovered those wars were more a myth than historical fact, but I found the story compelling nonetheless. For that reason, it stuck in my memory.

"A Trojan horse," I muse, inadvertently saying the words aloud.

"Pardon?"

"Ignore me. Inner dialogue."

"Right, err, how are you feeling?"

"I am fine."

"Would you like me to continue, or do you need a break?"

"Is there more?"

"Not much. Two days after you were found, the authorities placed you with a foster family. Then, once the appeal ended and the police confirmed there were no further leads regarding your birth parents, the decision was made to put you on the adoption register."

"And that's when Helen and Martin Armstrong came along?"

"Not quite. The adoption process is thorough but slow, hence the nine-month delay before the Armstrongs officially became your parents."

This information is of no significance, and I dismiss it. My mind has greater priorities, working through Cindy Akinyemi's first revelation.

"There is nothing more?" I confirm.

"Um, I don't think so."

To be sure, she thumbs through the ream of pages again.

"No, I think that's … wait. There's one final document."

She then extracts a single page and scrutinises it closely.

"Ah, I don't think it'll be of much use in establishing who your birth parents are."

"What is it?"

"It seems they discovered a note in your Moses basket when they found you at the hospital. But, before you get too excited, it only contained a few scrawled words, and it says here the police discounted its relevance in the search for your biological parents."

To prove her point, she places the page on the table and slides it towards me.

"One of my colleagues copied down what the note said."

She then taps her fingernail against the relevant line on the page.

"As you can see, it's pretty meaningless: *Primrose Hill 29/09.*"

With Cindy Akinyemi's words echoing in my ears, I stare down at the words printed on the page. Such is the magnitude of this discovery, I momentarily forget to breathe.

The words are far from meaningless. They are the key to my departure.

"Simon?"

Her voice jolts my attention back to the room.

"Do those words mean anything to you?"

There must be a temporary malfunction with my saliva glands as my reply comes in the form of a dry croak.

"I must go."

"Are you sure you're okay? You look a bit dazed."

"I am fine. I … train to catch. Goodbye."

Without seeking permission, I snatch the piece of paper from the table and stride towards the door. With her lack of fitness, there's no chance of Cindy Akinyemi catching up as I rush along the corridor and back down the stairs.

I continue through the reception area and out to the street. There, I look left and right in search of a taxi, but there are none. Is this a road where taxis regularly pass by? I don't know, but I feel I should get as far away from this building as I can, as quickly as I can.

I turn right and walk, the piece of paper still clutched in my hand. My mobile telephone rings. Extracting it from my pocket, I note the area code happens to be the area I'm currently trying to escape, so the call is almost certainly from Cindy Akinyemi. I turn the mobile telephone off.

I cannot recall where or when I discovered it, but I was surprised to learn that driving a motor vehicle is considered one of the most neurologically taxing tasks the average human performs on a day-to-day basis. Indeed, I used to watch Mother with mild fascination as she pushed and pulled levers, pressed pedals, and constantly adjusted the steering wheel, all while checking her makeup in the small mirror at the top of the windscreen.

Perhaps my brain is wired differently as I'm having difficulty just putting one foot in front of the other whilst thinking.

"Primrose Hill 29/09," I whisper.

From the moment Mother uttered the words, right up until I left the house this morning, I could never have imagined the true significance of Primrose Hill. All those doubts about making this journey, all the times I told myself it was a waste of energy, it is a miracle I'm here at all. There can be no doubt I made the right decision because I now know why *They* sent me here — to confirm the location and date I will leave Earth. It's one day earlier than I predicted, but this Wednesday, the twenty-ninth day of the ninth month, I am going home, and the extraction point is Primrose Hill, here in London.

My jubilation is tainted, however. If only Helen and Martin Armstrong had been honest, this journey would have been avoidable. I understand why Father never told me — he never told me much about anything — but I cannot understand why Mother kept the note a secret from me. She had to relent in the end, though, and perhaps I should forgive her betrayal. With her mind failing and certain death looming, she somehow managed to spit her secret out. Her last ever words, I suspect.

Unable to focus properly, I stop and lean against the wall of a building. I need to train my energies on piecing together all the information I gleaned in the twenty-four minutes I spent with Cindy Akinyemi.

As the metaphorical clouds begin to part, a ray of light illuminates the answers I've waited a lifetime to understand.

Putting the Primrose Hill revelation to one side, my thoughts turn to the first snippet of information I discovered: my supposed abandonment at Epsom Hospital. Unbeknown to the authorities, I wasn't abandoned at all — I was left there deliberately, like a Trojan horse.

I concentrate hard and focus on what I know about the mythical tale, to be sure I'm not mistaken.

From memory, The Trojans had successfully kept the Greeks out of Troy by fortifying the city with unbreachable walls. For ten long years, the Greek strategists tried and failed to think of a way into the city whilst the Trojans waited for their enemy to admit defeat. Then, the Greek general Odysseus came up with a masterful plan. It was considered customary for an army to admit defeat through a peace offering, so the Greeks constructed such an offering; an enormous wooden effigy of a horse.

Upon construction, the Grecians left the wooden horse at the gates of Troy and retreated. The Trojans — celebrating their long-overdue victory — then dragged the horse into the city. They had no idea a small group of Grecian warriors were hiding inside. That night, under cover of darkness, the warriors silently climbed out of the wooden structure and opened the gates to Troy. Defeat for the Trojans was inevitable, and Troy finally fell.

They might not consider the human race an enemy, but they still deployed a Trojan horse of their own. No human would ever suspect that an abandoned, helpless infant might be from another world, with a mission to complete. *They* implemented the perfect plot in which I was the perfect infiltration tool.

I have never understood art, but I can now understand how an artist must feel when brush strokes finally take form, and a picture emerges. For the first time, I can now see my life on Earth in its fullness, from the arrival to departure, laid out like the landscape paintings on the walls at Elmwood Care Home.

"You got any spare change, mate?"

I turn to my right, to an unkempt human with greasy hair and a matted beard.

"Spare? No monies are spare — they are merely unspent."

"Alright, you got any change?"

"Yes, I do."

"Enough to give me a few quid?"

I look the man up and down just as a sudden gust of wind sweeps past him.

"You smell atrocious. Are you a vagrant?"

"I'm homeless, mate."

I consider his admission.

"I used almost all my change to pay a taxi fare, but I can empathise with your situation. I, too, have wanted to go home for a long time, and I have just discovered I will be returning on Wednesday."

"Good for you."

I withdraw my wallet from the satchel and remove one of the two notes.

"Have this," I say, holding the note at arm's length. "Perhaps it will go some way to addressing your search for a home."

"Twenty quid? Are you sure?"

"Yes."

"That's bloody good of you, mate. Thank you."

"You are welcome, and I would strongly suggest you spend some of it on deodorant."

I bid the vagrant goodbye and continue on my way.

Reaching the end of Tooley Street, the intersecting road appears to be a main thoroughfare, and I'm able to hail a taxi within a minute. On arrival at Waterloo station, I endure another dash across the crowded concourse, although it is not quite as torrid as my earlier experience as there are fewer humans. I'm ahead of schedule, but rather than loiter amongst the gaggle of humans waiting for the train to arrive, I walk to the very far end of the platform.

The train arrives, and I board, taking my reserved seat. There is nothing to do but wait now.

On cue, an alarm sounds and the doors close with a hiss. A whistle then blows, and the train judders the first few metres away from the platform, away from London. When I get back home, I need to purchase another ticket for another journey here. It will be a one-way ticket.

Chapter 11

Merle appears confused.

"I know I said Thursday, but it's now Wednesday. You've got until 10:00 am tomorrow to make up your mind."

He jumps down from the table and disappears through the cat flap, presumably to ponder his options in the garden.

On the journey back to Salisbury, I asked the ticket inspector the time of the last direct train to Waterloo tomorrow evening. He confirmed it to be 9:25 pm. I'm due to depart on Wednesday, but the exact time remains unknown. Therefore, it is imperative I arrive at Primrose Hill before Wednesday officially begins at midnight. I cannot say I relish the prospect of spending the night on a hill in Central London, but *They* could come for me at any point within a twenty-four-hour window, so be there I must.

Despite the enormity of knowing the exact date and location of my departure, the loss of an entire day is unwelcome. My carefully crafted plans must now be brought forward. That task, however, will have to wait until after I've visited Mother.

I leave the house.

The walk, brief as it is, provides time enough to run through a mental checklist. If I were inclined, I would congratulate myself as I can now reap the benefits of living such a peripheral existence. Humans, as they journey through life, amass baggage. Besides the material ties of a home and all the possessions within, there's family, partners, friends, colleagues, and innumerable other connections. I have no such ties to sever. In fact, if not for Mother, I wouldn't have to deal with Mr

Choudhary or Father Paul, or indeed the staff at Elmwood Care Home.

For the penultimate time, I arrive at the reception desk. Elaine is on duty.

"Afternoon, Simon. How are you?"

"I am fine."

"Good, good. Let me get you checked in."

Her demeanour lacks its usual sprightliness.

"Just so you know, your mother is in her room."

Sometimes, it's possible to glean more from the tone of a human voice than the words alone. No doubt Nurse Clifford has updated Elaine on Mother's condition.

"Understood."

Elaine prepares a visitor card while the memory of yesterday's visit resurfaces. I pose a question.

"Is Rosie on duty today?"

"Not till three o'clock."

This is good, as I would rather avoid the possibility of another close interaction. That woman has no concept of personal space.

Elaine places the lanyard on the desk and attempts to make eye contact. I snatch it up, mutter a thank you, and proceed to the door.

The room is empty, bar the barely-living human lying supine on the bed. The scene, and indeed Mother, are unchanged from yesterday. I sit on the plastic chair.

"Hello, Mother."

I'm about to turn and begin counting the horizontal slats in the window blind when a thought strikes. I can now count my remaining words to Mother on just two hands: *hello* once, *Mother* three times, and *goodbye* twice. Even with my mathematical dexterity, I couldn't begin to calculate how many words we've shared since I spluttered my first as an infant. Now, there are just six left to be said.

A sudden spasm tugs the muscles in my lower stomach. It is uncomfortable but quickly passes; probably hunger pangs as I missed lunch. I adjust my position in the chair and begin counting the slats in a slow, methodical manner.

On completion of the fifty-eighth count, I check my wristwatch. It is time to leave.

The two words I say to Mother cut the total remaining by a third. The delivery coincides with another hunger pang.

I return the lanyard to Elaine.

"Thanks, Simon. See you tomorrow."

Typically, I have so little interest in anything Elaine has to say, I've usually forgotten her pleasantries by the time I reach the front gates. Today, however, they strike a chord. As I close the main door behind me, it occurs I will never see Susan again. Yesterday, I said goodbye, unaware it would be the final time.

This fact is of no great significance, but it does remind me of a conversation I had with Mother after Father died.

The day of his death began just like any other. He entered the kitchen at eight o'clock while Mother and I were eating breakfast at the table. I expected him to leave for work as he always did, with a perfunctory goodbye. Instead, he chastised Mother about a stain on his shirt. The conversation quickly escalated, and both parents yelled obscenities at one another until Father stormed out.

He would never return.

Some days later, the doctors confirmed Father died of a heart attack; his high blood pressure a contributory factor. He lived for fifty-four years.

Long after his funeral, Mother continued to rue those final words she yelled at her husband. On one such occasion, I told her there was no logic in regret because no one can undo the past and therefore, it was a waste of time regretting anything. She countered with the same tired argument: *if only I'd known those were the last words we'd ever say to one another*.

The conversation ended after I suggested the only way a human could avoid her mistake would be to never engage in an argument with anyone, ever, but I think we both knew how ridiculous a notion that was. Humans argue. Humans fight. They can't help themselves.

I cross the road and turn right into a street lined with cherry blossom trees and semi-detached houses. I've journeyed the same route so many times, every step and every turn is now instinctive. Ahead, some sixty metres away, a red motor car is parked up against the kerb. Ordinarily, this would not be a scene worthy of my attention, but two humans are standing on the adjacent pavement. Even at this distance, I can clearly hear their heated conversation.

As I get nearer, I recognise one of the humans. Rosie is shouting and pointing at a man who is at least twenty centimetres taller, or eight inches in Mother's vernacular. Judging by the man's scowl, I presume he is unhappy. I consider crossing the road, but just as I'm about to, Rosie turns around. Her expression immediately changes.

"Simon!" she blurts. "I didn't … will you be my witness?"

"A witness to what?"

"This man drove into the back of my car, and now he denies liability for the damage."

"I ain't denying nothing," the man interjects, fixing me with an unwelcome stare. "This crazy bitch slammed her brakes on for no reason, and I tapped the back of her motor. The light was already broken."

"No, it was not."

"Yeah, it fuckin' was."

"Fine. We'll let the police decide, shall we?" Rosie suggests.

"I don't think so."

With that, he turns and takes four steps towards a stationary white van behind the red motor car. Rosie leaps towards him and grabs hold of his coat.

"You're not going anywhere," she yells. "I'm making a citizen's arrest."

I have no interest in this petty dispute and attempt to edge past the arguing humans.

"Get yer hand off me, bitch," the man sneers.

"No."

"I ain't tellin' you again. Let go."

I pause and assess the situation. If I were Rosie, I'd be inclined to let go of the man, being he is larger and likely stronger. She, however, has other ideas. With one hand clamped on the man's arm, Rosie uses the other to extract a mobile telephone from her jacket pocket. As she raises it her ear, the man suddenly lashes out, swatting the telephone to the ground.

I do not like his sudden show of aggression.

"You'll pay for that too," Rosie snaps.

"You reckon?"

He then grabs her wrist and turns it to such a degree, Rosie yelps. Despite the obvious pain he is inflicting, the man seems to be deriving pleasure from his action. I definitely do not like this.

"Let go of her," I demand.

"Jog on, mate. This ain't any of your business."

"You are assaulting her. That is against the law."

"I said, jog on. Are you deaf?"

"No, I have impeccable hearing, but I do wonder if the same could be said of you."

"What?"

"Did you not hear my command? I said, let go of her."

He does let go of her and then takes three steps in my direction.

"You want some, do you?"

"Some what?"

Another step. The male is now dangerously close to breaching the perimeter of my personal space.

Rosie attempts to grab his coat again. This time, the man reacts first and forcibly shoves her to the ground.

"Try that again, and I'll lamp you," he snarls.

Inside my skull, a reaction occurs, akin to the splitting of an atom. It is a sensation I've experienced before, and I know that what is about to happen will be overwhelming. Nerves pulse and muscles twitch as a raging heat seeks an outlet.

I cannot contain it.

There is no method to measure it, but my right arm suddenly swings forward with the kinetic force of a cannonball. I am powerless to stop it. My fist connects with the male human's jaw, but I feel no pain as bone cracks against bone.

The male collapses to the pavement. A sudden sense of calm engulfs me, and an indeterminable period of time elapses before a voice breaks through the serenity.

"Simon! Simon!"

Besides the voice, I can now hear birds twittering and the whine of a combustion engine nearby, possibly a lawnmower.

"Are you okay?"

Rosie steps directly into my line of sight, her facial muscles taut.

"Yes. I am okay."

She turns around and squats down next to the felled human male. Words and muffled grunts are exchanged, and he then slowly clambers to his feet, one hand covering his jaw. On unsteady legs, he then stumbles towards the white van, opens the door, and falls into the driver's seat. Three seconds later, the van screeches away from the scene, leaving behind the scent of burnt rubber and near silence.

Rosie steps closer. Too close.

"It's alright," she says in a soft voice, her hands raised, palms displayed. "I think you broke that idiot's jaw — not that I care — but I want to see if your hand is okay."

"My hand?"

I look down just as a droplet of blood drips from my finger to the paving slab below.

"I've got a first aid kit in the car," she says. "Give me a minute, and I'll fetch it. Don't you dare move."

Rather than move, I assess the pulsing sensation in my hand. Rosie returns with a small green box.

"Come and sit here," she orders, moving towards a waist-height brick wall bordering one of the semi-detached houses. I comply. She then places the green box next to me and opens the lid.

"Let's have a look at that hand, shall we? Don't worry; I'm first-aid trained."

In the same way I had no control over my arm as it swung towards the human male, I cannot override the muscles as they slowly raise my hand. With some caution, Rosie carefully moves her hand into position to gently grip my wrist. The second her skin makes contact with mine, I instinctively flinch.

"Sorry," she blurts. "Did I hurt you?"

Unable to speak, I shake my head. Every fibre of my alien soul wants to withdraw my hand, but there is a force keeping it locked in place — a force I do not understand. Besides my mother, I cannot recall the last time I allowed a human to touch me, and I presumed that situation would remain unchanged for the remainder of my time on this planet. Now, there is seemingly nothing I can do to prevent this human's touch.

"I think it looks worse than it is. I'll clean the blood, and we'll see what's what."

Rosie removes a small packet from the green box and tears it open with her teeth.

"I'm just going to clean the wound with an antiseptic wipe, okay. It might sting a little."

Using her teeth again, she tugs the wipe from the packet and then takes it in her right hand. The clinical odour blends with the same sweet floral scent I breathed in Mother's room yesterday.

Her touch is so slight, I barely notice it. That is until the sting arrives.

"Pain," I hiss.

"Don't be such a wuss," Rosie smiles, keeping her attention fixed on my hand. "Be thankful you're not that other bloke because I'm sure he's suffering a lot worse than a mild sting."

"He was badly injured?"

"He'll live, but I don't think he'll be chewing gum for a while."

I don't understand her reference and say nothing in reply.

"Thank you, by the way," she continues. "I'm my own worst enemy for getting into scrapes, and I don't know what I'd have done if you hadn't turned up."

"Your actions were foolhardy. That male could have severely injured you."

"True, but he was an arsehole, and I can't stand arseholes. I kinda saw red for a minute."

"Red?"

"You know, like a red mist when you're angry."

"I have never experienced such a mist."

She looks up, her eyebrows arched.

"Really?"

I look away, and Rosie continues to clean my wound. I am sixteen seconds into a count when she speaks again.

"It's just a slight cut on your knuckle. A sticky plaster will stop the bleeding."

She releases her grip on my wrist and delves into the green box again. A beige-coloured patch is then applied to the wound.

"There we are," she declares. "Good as new."

I examine my hand. It is not as good as new, but the plaster appears to be serving its purpose.

"I am grateful for the medical attention."

"You're welcome, and I'm grateful you've got such a potent punch. Have you ever taken boxing lessons?"

"No."

"But I'm guessing you work out?"

"Work out? Work what out?"

"No, I mean … you're obviously fit, and I thought, what with the buzz cut, you were into boxing or martial arts or something."

"I do not understand. What is a buzz cut?"

"Your hair — shaved close to the scalp."

"I don't like barbershops. Mother used to cut my hair but when she became incapable I purchased clippers from an internet retailer and now shave it myself."

"It suits you."

"In what way?"

"I don't know; it just does. Take the compliment, eh?"

Rosie then closes the lid of the green box and returns to her car. After shutting the boot lid, she stands back and examines the alleged point of impact again.

"A garage will charge a small fortune to fix this," she complains. "What do you think?"

I'm not qualified to offer an opinion, but I feel obligated to look. I stand up and cross the pavement. The damage is minimal.

"It's just a cracked light lens," I confirm. "Easily replaced."

"Is it?"

"Mother once reversed her motor car into a concrete post on the driveway. She purchased a replacement lens from an automotive retailer in Amesbury, and I fitted it."

"You're obviously a man of many hidden talents."

Hidden to disguise my true being, I reflect. I don't share that thought with Rosie.

"I know it's a cheeky question, Simon, but if I get a new lens, would you fit it for me?"

Her request is unexpected.

"I … I will be leaving Durrington tomorrow evening."

"But you're popping in to see your mother tomorrow afternoon, as usual, right?"

"Yes."

"Perfect. I'm working tomorrow afternoon so you could fit it after your visit, couldn't you? You did say it's easily replaced, so it won't take long, no?"

"Nineteen minutes."

Her expression implies surprise.

"Are you always so precise with time, Simon?"

"Surely it is preferable to lying or guessing?"

"Definitely."

"Then, what is your point?"

"Um, I don't know." She then laughs. I have no idea why.

"Anyway, would you help me out, please? I've got a toolkit in the boot."

My brain immediately formulates an answer and sends instructions to my mouth. At some point between the two, the answer becomes corrupted. The word 'yes' leaves my mouth when I intended to say 'no'.

"You're a star! Thank you so much."

Before I can backtrack, Rosie checks the time.

"Oh, my God! I'm so late for work … gotta rush!"

She then yells a goodbye over her shoulder before jumping into the motor car. Much like the injured male, her exit is swift and decisive.

As I watch the red motor car speed away, I question how I allowed events to escalate, how I let a female human manipulate me so easily.

Even though I give both questions my entire focus all the way home, answers remain elusive.

Message 2813

Priority Level 1 | Encrypted @ 19:11

From: TheShepherd82

To: Epsilon30

Message Begins ...

Ĝojan novaĵon, frato Epsilon,

I am almost speechless.

I knew our paths were due to separate soon but your news of today's events has shocked me to the core. It is a mark of how despicable the humans are that your Earth-parents hid such a secret from you. To think, you might have missed your departure date because of their deceit.

It proves that humans can never be trusted. Never.

It was always my hope that we might finally meet before your departure but with so little time left, that cannot be. I admit, I am envious you will soon be leaving this awful place but They have decided I must remain and continue my work here on Earth. We have been on quite the journey, and whatever mission I am given next, and whichever Starseed I am set to assist, it is unlikely we will share the same bond you and I have.

I shall miss you greatly, my friend.

Travel far, travel well.

The Shepherd

Chapter 12

"Father Paul."

Merle tilts his head.

"I don't have time to take you to the vet, so euthanasia is no longer an option. I'm sorry, but planning takes time, and time takes planning."

After reading The Shepherd's message yesterday evening, I turned my attention to the plans for my final day in Durrington. It proved difficult as I struggled to purge his words from my mind. I concluded the heaviness I felt was down to an infection. Thirty years is a long time to live amongst humans, and despite my best efforts, their emotions have infiltrated my alien soul like a disease. It would explain why I took pity on Rosie and agreed to repair the damage to her motor car.

Acceptance proved key to moving my thoughts away from The Shepherd and the end of our friendship. Only then could I turn my attention to the problem of Merle.

"He will feed you, and eventually, once he realises I will not be returning, he will find alternative accommodation for you."

No response.

"I know he is human, and an irksome one at that, but who else can I ask?"

Merle commences his ablutions which I take as a positive response. Now I have the unenviable task of telephoning Father Paul.

The telephone rings.

"Father Paul."

"This is Simon Armstrong."

"Oh, Simon. It's … early."

"I have much to do today. Are you available at 12:20 pm?"

"Possibly. What for?"

"I need you to come to the house."

"Why?"

"I don't have time to discuss it in detail now. Should I expect you at 12:20 pm?"

"Um, yes, I suppose …"

"Goodbye."

I terminate the call and return the mobile telephone to my pocket.

"Did you hear that, Merle? I'll formally introduce you to Father Paul later."

Total disinterest.

"Ungrateful feline."

I rush upstairs and get ready to leave the house. As I slip on a coat, I'm careful not to dislodge the plaster I applied earlier. I had no idea Mother kept a green box of her own in the understairs cupboard. Until I found it, I had to improvise a wound covering using toilet paper and Sellotape, which was less than ideal.

The plaster serves as an unwelcome reminder of my obligation to Rosie later. Without consciously requesting it, my mind then conjures up a picture of her face. It is not a particularly unusual face, but her green eyes are, I suppose, uncommon. And, I would admit, her pale skin is not as flawed as that of most humans I come into regular contact with. Besides those features, she is extraordinarily ordinary, like the other eight billion humans on this planet.

I cast the image from my mind and leave the house.

At the bus stop, I watch the Talbots go through their departure ritual. For the briefest of moments, I consider crossing the road and asking Mr Talbot why he drives such a short distance to work and Mrs Talbot why she has never offered anyone at the bus stop a lift. They both depart, as does my final chance to ask. In the scheme of great unknowns, neither are questions I'll likely dwell on for too long.

My final journey to Amesbury is uneventful, although the bus does arrive at my destination within twenty-eight seconds of the nineteen quoted on the timetable. I thank the driver.

Mr Choudhary greets me with his usual enthusiasm, and once I settle behind the desk, he brings in the tea. He then lingers.

"I don't wish to press you, Simon, but have you given any thought to our conversation last week?"

"Regarding your cousin's employment opportunity?"

"Yes."

"I have."

"And what have you decided?"

"My position remains unchanged. I do not require a job."

"But, how are you going to pay your bills?"

"All in hand."

"Are you sure?"

"Yes, and while we're on the subject of decisions, today will be my final day in your employment."

"Oh, that's a bit sudden."

"You said I could choose the period of my notice, and I have. Is that a problem?"

"Not at all, it's just … well, I wanted to get you a gift as a thank you for all your hard work."

Humans are so obsessed with the giving and receiving of gifts, they'll use even the most tenuous of reasons to indulge that obsession. Early in my employment, Mr Choudhary asked if I would like to contribute to the cost of a gift for one of my fellow employees. The reason: she was still alive after fifty years. I argued her not dying was surely reward enough. She did not invite me to her party.

"A gift would be a waste of money."

"Not at all. I'll pop out to the shops now."

"I would rather you didn't."

The conversation ends as Mr Choudhary slops tea on his cardigan and departs with no further word on the gift.

As I get on with my work, I try to maintain my usual focus, but my insufferable human brain has other ideas. Today is a day of lasts, each one a cause for positivity. After today, there will be no more bus journeys, no more number-crunching for Mr Choudhary, no more visits to Elmwood Care Home, and no more Father Paul. And, there will be no more Mother, no more Merle, no more Elaine or Susan or Rosie.

There will be no more of anything familiar. Definitely a positive, I think.

I return my focus to the numbers, and time passes in the same way it always does. With only minutes remaining, Mr Choudhary reappears in the doorway.

"Surprise!" he sings while holding out a box wrapped in shiny paper.

"If that is a gift, it is not a surprise. We discussed the subject barely three hours ago."

"Ahh, but you don't know what's in the box, do you, young Simon?"

"No, I do not."

"Well then — that is the surprise."

I can almost hear Father's voice in my head: *at least appear grateful, boy.*

"Thank you, Mr Choudhary."

Brimming with excitement, he skips over to the desk and places the box in front of me.

"Go on then. Open it."

I nod.

"You're a tough one to buy for," Mr Choudhary says. "I mean, what do you buy a man who has zero interest in anything?"

"Nothing?" I suggest.

My remark seems to amuse my employer, and he chuckles away while I remove the wrapping paper.

With the paper removed, I'm left with a brown cardboard box, roughly thirty centimetres square. Urged on by Mr Choudhary, I use a pair of scissors to cut the tape keeping the two flaps on top together. I then open the flaps to reveal a thick layer of polystyrene.

"It's fragile."

"Clearly," I reply, removing the polystyrene.

At first glance, it appears my gift is a glass orb roughly the size of a cabbage.

"Take it out so you can see it properly."

After removing yet more polystyrene, I'm able to free the glass orb and a cylindrical block of polished wood beneath.

"There's a switch on the bottom of the stand. Here, let me show you."

Mr Choudhary takes the block of wood from my hand and turns it upside down. He fiddles with it for a few seconds until a bright white light shines from the top. He places it on the desk, takes the glass orb from my left hand, and carefully rests it on top of the cylinder.

The previously transparent glass orb is now alight with a number of spherical objects of differing sizes.

"It's the solar system," Mr Choudhary confirms. "Natty, eh?"

I lean forward to take a closer look. At the very centre of the orb, the brightest spherical object is patently a representation of the Sun, and around it are the eight planets of this Solar System, crudely in scale.

Mr Choudhary steps away from the desk and switches off the light. The darkness creates an optical illusion as if each celestial body is no longer entombed in the glass but floating in space.

"I hope you like it, Simon. I got the idea from your mother."

"Mother?" I reply, my eyes still locked on the orb.

"Yes, she once told me you loved sitting in the garden, staring up at the night sky. And, you have a telescope, do you not?"

"I do. I mean, I did."

My fascination with the night sky only began after we moved from Surbiton. Prior to living in Durrington, there was little of the night sky to see; such was the level of light pollution in suburban Surrey. The first time I stood in our current garden at night, it was akin to seeing the sky for the first time, a vast black canvas dotted with countless silvery specks of light. I stared up into the void, mesmerised, and then I spotted the faint wispy outline of the Andromeda galaxy. I didn't know it was the Andromeda galaxy at the time, but I still felt its pull. Even then, I think I knew it was my real home.

Mother, noting my obsession with the night sky, later purchased a Celestron Newtonian Telescope for my seventeenth birthday. It was too cumbersome to move in and out of the house, so I improvised a solution. I cut a square metre aperture in the roof of Father's beloved garden shed, using his electric jigsaw. He didn't object on account he was dead. Using more of his tools, I fashioned a viewing platform from a workbench and a removable, weatherproof cover to place over the aperture. The position was not ideal, and it lacked basic utilities, but I spent many, many contented hours in my makeshift observatory.

Two years ago, it was struck by a lightning bolt and burnt to the ground, telescope and all.

"So? Do you like it, Simon?"

"It is … it is a nice gift. Thank you."

"You're most welcome."

He switches the light back on, and I carefully return the orb and stand to the box.

"I was thinking," Mr Choudhary then says. "Would you like to meet up for a coffee next week? I'd like us to stay in touch."

"I don't like coffee."

"A nice cup of tea then?"

"I'll think about it."

"You have my phone number. Don't be afraid to use it, eh?"

"Understood."

I put my coat on and pick up the box. My employer knows me well enough I don't have to endure a goodbye handshake.

"Thank you for all you've done, Simon," he says. "I will miss you."

"You are welcome. I ... my bus."

"Yes, yes. Off you go."

He stands aside and waves my path to the back door. I hurry past and don't look back.

The bus on my final journey from Amesbury travels at a much slower speed than usual, I'm certain. It arrives in Durrington, and I check my wristwatch. Twenty minutes but I estimated twenty-six. I put the miscalculation down to a lack of sleep; my usually reliable perception of time compromised.

I arrive home and place the box on the kitchen table. There it will stay until someone — I've no idea who — is hired to clear the contents of the house. I'm sure they will make good use of the glass orb, unlike all the framed photographs and Mother's ornaments.

With no appetite, I munch through a bowl of muesli. I'm about to wash the bowl up when the doorbell rings at 12:14 pm.

"Unbelievable," I sigh, sharing a frown with Merle. "Six minutes before the agreed time."

I wonder if all priests are so shoddy with their time-keeping. Would they ever agree on a time for a wedding ceremony and then leave the bride and groom waiting at the altar for ten minutes? Do they ever commence a funeral service while the emotionally feeble humans are still weeping their way towards the vestry?

I suppose I'll never know.

"Afternoon, Simon."

"Father Paul."

I usher him into the kitchen. Merle looks up at the priest, but his interest is minimal.

"So, what can I do for you?" he asks.

"For me, nothing. It is Merle who requires your assistance."

"Does he?"

"Yes. He's an intelligent animal, but he cannot open tins."

"Right, and ... sorry, you've lost me."

"As I told you, I am going away, and Merle requires feeding twice a day. Can I trust you to take on that task?"

Without being invited, he pulls out one of the chairs and sits down. Merle eyes him suspiciously.

"I thought you asked me here to discuss your adoption."

"Why would you think that?"

"We haven't spoken since our chat last week, and it's been playing on my mind. I didn't mean to fob you off like that. It was wrong."

"Your guilt is unnecessary. I took your advice, and I now know about the note and the relevance of Primrose Hill."

"What relevance?"

"Seeing as you've been as duplicitous as my parents in hiding the truth from me, I'm not inclined to share that information with you."

"Be fair, Simon. Your mother chose not to tell you about the note because there was nothing to tell. As I understand it, both the police and Social Services agreed it was meaningless."

"If that were the case, why didn't you tell me last week?"

"Because it wasn't my place to tell you. As I said, Helen told me in confidence."

"What is the point in protecting an inconsequential confidence? It is illogical."

"Illogical or not, it would have been wrong for me to say anything."

"Is there anything else you're not telling me?"

He turns his attention to the clock on the wall.

"I haven't got long. Can we get back to the point of you summoning me? Where are you going?"

"That is not relevant to my request."

"Why the secrecy?"

"Why not? I'm not obligated to tell anyone my plans."

"If you say so. How long will you be away for?"

"I don't know."

"You must have a vague idea. A few days? A few weeks?"

"I don't know. What was the third question?"

"When are you going?"

"I'm leaving this evening."

"Seriously? Thanks for the notice."

"It can't be helped. Can I rely upon you to feed Merle? Yes, or no?"

"I do have a fourth question. Have you forgotten your manners?"

"I do not understand."

"Your manners, Simon. When you're asking a favour of someone, it's customary to say please. And, it would be nice if you framed your questions so they don't come across as an order."

I can't read Merle's mind, but I have a fair idea what he's thinking: *Yes, he is just as irksome as you implied.*

"Father Paul, will you please ensure Merle is fed twice a day from tomorrow morning?"

"Yes, I suppose so," he replies, rolling his eyes.

"His first feed is at 6:58 am and the second at 5:58 pm."

"That's very specific."

"He's a creature of habit. Mother would have told you as much."

"Well, he'll have to adjust his schedule to fit in with mine. That's the best I can do."

With so little time to explore other options, it'll have to suffice.

"Thank you. I'll get you a key."

"No need. I already have one."

"You do? Why?"

"Helen gave me one, just in case of emergencies."

"She never told me."

"There's a lot your mother never told you, Simon, most of it for your own good."

"Such as?"

The priest closes his eyes and bites his bottom lip. I reach a count of four before he opens his eyes again.

"Ignore me," he says, getting to his feet. "It's been a long day, and it's far from over. I'd better get on."

Part of me wants to press him for an answer, but I also have much to do. I follow him to the front door.

"I'll pop by and see Helen later," he says.

"Understood."

"Are you?"

"I'll be visiting her as usual at 2:00 pm."

The priest then searches his jacket pockets. He locates a set of keys but doesn't leave.

"You've chosen the worst possible time to go away, Simon — you do know that?"

"It is beyond my control."

"Can I give you a word of advice, then?"

"If you must."

"Whatever you need to say to your mother, say it today."

Chapter 13

Father Paul's statement lingered in my head long after he departed. Even now, as I approach Elmwood Care Home, I am trying to make sense of it. What does he think I should say to Mother, and more importantly, what is the point?

I should have asked, but he hurried away before I had the chance. Typical, as I usually struggle to get rid of the man.

Elaine, as she confirmed yesterday, is on duty at the reception desk when I arrive. We go through the same greeting ritual before she prepares my visitor's card. A second member of staff then joins us.

"You're keen," Elaine says to Rosie as she approaches the desk. "Your shift doesn't start for another hour."

"Simon has kindly agreed to fit a new light lens on my car, haven't you, Simon?"

"I suppose I did."

"And, he assures me it'll only take nineteen minutes, so I'm going to grab a coffee while he sees his mother and then we'll convene in the car park just after two-thirty."

"2:32 pm?" Elaine suggests.

"Exactly."

The two females swap smiles, and Elaine then hands over my lanyard.

"See you at 2:32 pm then, Simon," Rosie says.

"Yes. Goodbye."

On the way to Mother's room, I catch the sound of laughter echoing from the reception area. Even if I were party to their joke, I'm not sure I'd understand it — in all my time on Earth, I've never fully grasped humour.

For the third time in the last three days, and the final time, I take a seat in the plastic chair.

"Hello, Mother."

Two-thirds of my final six words spent. One-third remain.

I begin counting the blind slats, but as I reach the end of the fifth count, Father Paul's words return once more, breaking my concentration. An internal dispute ensues as rigid alien logic clashes with illogical human emotion. To no great surprise, logic wins the argument — what is the point of saying anything to an unconscious, near-dead human?

However, human emotion isn't willing to give up without a fight and poses a question: why do I always say hello, and goodbye?

Further thought tips the balance in favour of logic. Every hello and goodbye is no more than a verbal cue to signify the beginning and end of each visit.

Satisfied with my answer, I continue counting the slats.

At 2:29 pm, I terminate the count and stand up. Looking down on Mother, I'm about to say my final goodbye, but a sudden build-up of mucus in the back of my throat requires clearing. I cough twice.

"Goodbye, Mother."

Even to my own ear, the slight rasp is discernible. I cough again, and for no more than a second, I consider placing my hand on Mother's as a final parting gesture. The urge passes, and I stride purposefully away in case it should return.

At the reception desk, Elaine is on the telephone. I remove the lanyard and place it on the desk. She looks up and mouths three words: *see you tomorrow.*

Unsure how else to respond, I nod, but I will not be seeing Elaine tomorrow.

Despite the significance, the final walk to the main entrance is no different to all the other times I've completed it. Then, at precisely 2:32 pm, I turn the corner towards the car park. In the third bay on my right, there's a now-familiar red motor car with an equally familiar human in the driver's seat. The door opens.

"Bang on time," Rosie says, getting out of the motor car. "I wish all men were as punctual as you, Simon."

"And I wish all humans were as punctual, irrespective of gender, but wishing is a futile gesture."

"Tell me about it," she huffs.

We convene at the rear of the car, where Rosie opens the boot lid and removes a box.

"The guy in the parts shop said this is the right lens."

She hands it to me.

"And I've got the toolkit ready. Anything else you need?"

I open the box and examine the replacement lens. Although the car model is different to Mother's, I would estimate it to be of a similar age; at least twenty years have elapsed since its production. Consequently, it not as over-engineered as most modern motor vehicles.

"No. I only require a screwdriver."

"Great. I'll let you get on with it, then."

I nod, expecting her to wait in the car, or return to the building. Instead, she leans up against the rear wing.

"I hope you don't mind me watching? It'll be good to learn, just in case another moron hits me up the arse."

"You may observe, but small talk is not welcome. I cannot abide pointless chatter."

"Fair enough. Am I allowed to ask questions if they're not pointless?"

I squat down and remove the first screw from the damaged light lens.

"I suppose."

"Okay. Let me think … what hobbies do you have?"

"What do I do with unallocated time?"

"Yes."

"Primarily, I spend my unallocated time conducting research."

"And what do you research?"

"Humanity."

"Cool. Are you doing a degree or something?"

"No."

"So, you're just interested in people?"

"In a broad sense."

I begin removing the second screw.

"People are fascinating, aren't they?"

"Individually, no."

"Do you genuinely believe that?"

"Why else would I have said it if it wasn't what I believed?"

My question goes unanswered, and I'm able to focus on the third screw.

"Do you think I'm interesting?" Rosie then asks. "I mean, I know I'm not interesting like David Attenborough or the Dalai Lama, but I reckon there's one thing about me you'll find interesting."

"Tell me if you must."

She shuffles half a metre closer.

"I once met George Takei, in Las Vegas. I got a photo and his autograph."

"That is not interesting on account I do not know who George Takei is."

"You've got to be kidding me," she replies indignantly. "He played Sulu in Star Trek?"

"The television programme?"

"Yes, the television programme and film franchise. It's the greatest sci-fi show ever made."

"I've never watched Star Trek, so I hold no opinion of my own."

"Good God, I can't believe you're not a fan. I would have bet my last tenner on you being a Trekkie."

"And you would have lost that bet because I don't even know what a Trekkie is."

"What about Star Wars? Surely you've watched at least one of the movies?"

"No."

"Battlestar Galactica?"

"No."

"Stargate SG-1?"

"No."

"Red Dwarf?"

"Again, no. I don't watch science fiction programmes or films because they're all fantasy. Puerile make-believe."

I remove the fourth screw and use another screwdriver to prise the damaged lens from its mount.

"Yes, I know they're not real, but sci-fi gives you a glimpse at the endless possibilities out there."

"Out where?"

"In the universe: extra-terrestrial life, alien planets, hyper-advanced technologies. You can't deny it's not a fascinating subject."

The weather report on the radio this morning predicted the temperature to be eighteen degrees centigrade today. As I remove the new lens from the polythene wrapper, I conclude the forecast was wrong as it feels decidedly warmer.

"Well?" Rosie presses. "Is that not a fascinating topic of conversation? I could talk about my holiday, or the new shoes I bought yesterday if you prefer?"

"It is fascinating, yes."

She squats down and watches me position the new lens.

"Ahh, so there is something that gets your juices flowing. I knew it!"

The shrill ring of a mobile telephone cuts through my silence. Rosie withdraws her telephone from a pocket and frowns at the screen.

"Bugger. Better get this."

She wanders over to the opposite side of the car park.

Freed from distraction, it takes only five minutes to fit the new lens. I then return both screwdrivers to the toolkit and the packaging to the boot of the car. Now behind schedule, I need to return home as soon as possible.

As I make my way towards the gates, Rosie catches my departure. With the mobile telephone still pressed to her ear, she intersects my path.

"Give me a sec," she says to whoever is on the other end of the line.

I pause.

"I hope you weren't planning on walking off without saying goodbye."

"You are on the telephone."

"Um, yes, I am. Anyway, thank you so much for doing that for me, Simon. I really appreciate it."

"You are welcome. Goodbye."

I take six steps towards the gate when she calls after me.

"Maybe we can continue our chat tomorrow?"

"Yes, maybe," I reply.

I pass through the gates, knowing I did not technically lie, the word 'maybe' inferring no commitment on my part. I will never see her again, or Elmwood Care Home.

As I walk, I reflect on my conversation with Rosie and her presumptions regarding life beyond this insignificant planet. During my many years of research, I've studied numerous humans who also believe in extra-terrestrial life. The likes of Carl Sagan and Seth Shostak offered theories, but it was the renowned theoretical physicist, Professor Stephen Hawking, who added legitimacy to the argument.

I watched a documentary in which Hawking stated that, based on the sheer number of planets scientists know about, it would be ridiculous to assume humans are the only life-form in the universe. There are billions and billions of stars in the Milky Way galaxy alone, and therefore it is reasonable to assume an even greater number of planets orbiting them. In conclusion, Hawking said it is not unreasonable to presume the existence of alien life, and for some of that alien life to be intelligent and capable of interstellar communication.

To date, I have watched that documentary thirty-one times. It is the ideal antidote to the small-minded, cynical voices who are foolish enough to believe humans, and indeed the planet they occupy, are somehow unique. Then again, perhaps humans are unique in that they're the only civilisation naive enough to believe the preposterous tales Father Paul spins from his pulpit. Many, including Mother, prefer fantasy over science.

I will leave this planet with no regrets, but as I unlock the front door, I wonder how events might have evolved differently if I'd met Rosie a year ago. I have invested an inordinate amount of time in research but I have never discussed my findings with anyone, apart from The Shepherd. And, overlooking her weakness for science fiction, perhaps Rosie and I might have engaged in meaningful conversation; something I have not been able to do with any human.

By the time I reach the kitchen, I've already dismissed the very notion. *They* would not be pleased if I were to even hint at my true origin, theoretically or otherwise.

I telephone the same taxi company I used yesterday and book one for 9:00 pm. That done, I have five hours and thirty-one minutes to prepare.

Those preparations begin upstairs.

When I was thirteen, Mother enrolled me into the local Scout group. Being home-schooled, she was concerned about my lack of socialisation. Despite my protestations and reluctance, I attended one meeting. I returned home, clear in my determination never to go back. Unbeknown to me, Mother had already purchased equipment for a camping trip the group had planned the following weekend. I refused to go, and the equipment eventually found its way up to the loft, where it has remained ever since. Today is the first time it will serve a purpose, but not for rambling across Salisbury Plain with a group of pre-pubescent males.

I pull down the loft ladder, check it is stable, and climb up to the hatch. There, I switch on the light before carefully stepping onto the boarded floor.

Considering Mother's propensity for hoarding, the loft is remarkably clear of junk. Nearest the hatch are four boxes which contain the Christmas decorations, and there are three suitcases which, to the best of my knowledge, haven't been used since Father died. There is, however, a stack of boxes tightly packed into the eaves. Beside those boxes are a red, sixty-five-litre rucksack, a fold-up chair, and a pair of walking boots which are almost certainly five sizes too small for me. The boots are an irrelevance, but the rucksack and chair will prove useful for my trip to Primrose Hill.

Ducking down, I step across the floorboards and grab the chair and the rucksack. As I'm about to turn around, my attention is snagged by one of the boxes squeezed into the eaves. I place the rucksack on the floor and pick up the pale blue box.

"Oh."

Staring up at me from behind the transparent cellophane window is a plastic model of Buzz Lightyear — a toy I recall being particularly fond of in my early childhood. Whilst I remember the toy itself, I have no recollection of the moment it no longer featured in my life. Presumably, I must have outgrown it, and it would therefore have remained in my toy cupboard, untouched and unused. Did Mother retrieve it and place it up here? If so, why?

I check the next box in the stack. It contains another toy I haven't seen in many years: a caricature of a bear with beige fur and large almond-shaped eyes.

"Oscar," I whisper, though why I felt compelled to utter the name I once bestowed upon this inanimate object is beyond me.

I place the bear back in the box and check the next one.

Fourteen boxes later, I have no desire to continue as it is already clear Mother kept many of my childhood toys, and for reasons I do not understand, she kept them hidden away up here.

Perhaps her dementia began much earlier than the doctors estimated. It is the only explanation that makes sense.

I replace the last box and pick the rucksack up. Like my general understanding of human behaviour, I suppose Mother's motives will remain a mystery.

I put the fold-up chair in the rucksack, sling it over my shoulder, and exit the loft.

Returning to my bedroom, I open the desk drawer and remove three hefty ring binders. Each binder contains over five hundred pages of notes — the total of my research over the last decade. The notes, although comprehensive, are merely a snapshot of what I've learnt about humanity; the rest stored in my head.

I place the binders in the rucksack.

Over the next hour, I collate everything I'll likely need while I wait on Primrose Hill, including a torch, two litres of water, a packet of nuts, and my pocket radio. I check the contents against a list three times and then securely fasten the rucksack. The forecast for tonight is clear skies and a low of eight degrees centigrade. I will dress appropriately when I conduct my final preparations later.

My next task is to eat, and then I must complete the one task I've put off — Mother's letter.

The reason I've yet to complete the letter is that I'm not entirely sure there's a point to it. I'm confident Father Paul will have plenty of material for Mother's funeral, and I cannot compete with his sentimentality. By comparison, anything I have to say will come across as cold and uncaring.

I consider abandoning the idea until a seed of an idea germinates. I let that seed grow while I eat dinner. Then, I return to the loft.

Thirty-one minutes later, I am back at the kitchen table. In front of me is a piece of paper containing just a few hand-written sentences, together with a caricature of a bear with beige fur and large almond-shaped eyes. I re-read my words again; more a note than a letter …

This is Oscar.

My Mother, Helen Armstrong, gifted him to me when I was a young child. He was my best friend, my only friend.

It is only right Oscar remains with Mother. For a time, they both mattered a great deal to me.

Simon Armstrong

Satisfied with my work, I fold the note into an envelope and place it on the table next to the stuffed bear. Father Paul will find it in the morning when he feeds Merle, and although he might not open the envelope tomorrow, he will once he realises I'm not coming back. He is nothing if not nosy.

On cue, Merle jumps up to the table and shows an immediate interest in Oscar. That interest begins and ends with a few cautious sniffs.

"The bear will be here for a while, Merle. I, on the other hand, will be leaving tonight."

I fork out his food and watch him eat. Despite his inability to converse, Merle has proven a reliable companion in Mother's absence. It is a shame I can't take him with me, but the practicalities of transporting a cat on the train are too numerous, and interstellar travel would likely prove terminal for a feline his age.

He departs through the cat flap whilst I am washing up. I don't know if he'll return before I leave but, like me, he's probably not one for long, sentimental goodbyes.

"Farewell, Merle," I say, hopeful his superior hearing picks up my voice. "It has been an honour."

Chapter 14

The last direct train to London Waterloo departs Salisbury train station, and I make myself comfortable. The view in the window is that of a first-class carriage, reflected back. Beyond the mirror-like glass is a landscape of dark monotone shapes interspersed with the occasional speck of light. I have the carriage to myself, so the pocket radio remains in a zipped compartment in the rucksack occupying the seat next to me.

There is nothing to do other than wait and wonder.

Inevitably, my mind drifts towards the humans I will never see again. They are few in number, which is probably why my mind settles on a human I haven't seen in fourteen years: Martin Armstrong.

Mother, although not my biological parent, earned the title — Martin did not. It was he who insisted I call him Father, never Dad and never Daddy. My early memories of him are few and far between, but I know he worked long hours, and when he wasn't at work, he would visit the local public house or spend all day playing golf or tending to the plants in the garden. Even at a relatively young age, I realised my father would rather be anywhere else but the house he paid for, or with the family he funded.

Then, after we moved to Wiltshire, he changed. I remember wishing he'd spend more time at work or playing golf or tending plants in the garden. Anywhere but home. In the ensuing months and years after our move, he only ever displayed three emotions, and they were all toxic. When Mother informed me of his death, I didn't feel what they say a human should feel — unsurprising, considering what I would later discover. There was no grief, no shock, not even sadness. I responded to Mother's tearful announcement by asking what we were having for dinner.

To me, Father never died because he never really existed.

The train stops twice, but there is limited movement on the platforms. As we depart Andover and the carriage settles back into its repetitive rocking motion, I allow my eyes to close. I have no idea when I'll be able to sleep again, and in truth, I'd rather spend the rest of the journey unconscious than thinking about Martin Armstrong.

I awake when the train comes to a juddering halt. Squinting at the relative brightness, I look out of the window to ascertain where we are. The graffiti-stained pillars of a bridge suggest we must be close to Central London. Just as abruptly as it stopped, the train lurches into motion again.

Six minutes later, Waterloo. The time is 11:13 pm.

Having already calculated the journey time to Primrose Hill, I am in no rush. I swing the rucksack onto my back and ensure the straps are secure. Then, I complete the long march down the platform to the ticket barrier, where my one-way ticket is swallowed at the gate. The barriers swing open, and I step out onto the station concourse. The impact is minimal on this occasion; the crowd thin and the noise subdued.

Three minutes later, I am in the back seat of a taxi. Having confirmed my destination, the driver — the same driver as yesterday for all I know — presses buttons next to an illuminated display and pulls away from the rank.

The journey yesterday, to London Bridge, was in an easterly direction. This evening, my destination is north, across the River Thames. We pass over Westminster Bridge, towards the Houses of Parliament and the iconic Elizabeth Tower, typically and wrongly referred to as Big Ben. To my right, visible through the rear window is The London Eye, lit up in red, white, and blue lights. I have seen countless images of these landmarks, so the sudden rush of endorphins is unexpected.

The driver then takes a right turn, and we pass The Cenotaph. Once a year, Mother would sit in front of the television to watch a memorial service held on this very road. Dignitaries from far and wide gather here to commemorate the vast number of humans killed by other humans in the name of peace. Mother would always shed a tear when the lone bugler played *The Last Post*.

At the end of Whitehall, our route takes us past Trafalgar Square. Again, I have seen the famous column many times on the television and the internet, but still, I find myself staring up at the statue of Horatio Nelson.

As Trafalgar Square disappears from view, my attention turns to the streets; still crowded as tourists spill out from restaurants, theatres, and public houses. I would not like to be amongst them but it is fascinating to see so much human activity at this late hour. In Durrington, the entire village is asleep by 11:00 pm.

Another familiar scene comes into view as we approach Piccadilly Circus. I have no idea how the driver maintains his concentration as a million pixels of light in a never-ending rainbow of colours sweep across the surrounding buildings.

I check the time and close my eyes. In part, it is to prevent a sensory overload but also to reduce the rapid beat of my heart. In twenty-nine minutes, it will be midnight, and the twenty-ninth day of September will begin. My time on Earth is nearly at an end.

The taxi slows to a standstill.

"This do you?" the driver asks.

I open my eyes and assess the view from the window.

"This is Albert Terrace?" I confirm.

"It is."

I pay the fare and exit the taxi, the driver pulling away before my rucksack touches the pavement.

Scanning the area, I confirm there are no pedestrians in close proximity. When planning this leg of the journey, I assessed various access points to the grounds of Primrose Hill. I determined Albert Terrace to be the best option, being a relatively quiet residential street. Avoiding pedestrians is crucial because I am about to break the law.

The mount known as Primrose Hill is in the centre of Regent's Park, and my research revealed the gates to the park are locked at 8:00 pm in September. At first, I considered this a significant obstacle as the only other way into the park would be to climb over the railings, which stretch around the entire perimeter. Then it dawned on me — with the park closed, there can be no witnesses to my departure.

Once again, *They* have covered every possible base.

I grab the rucksack and double-check no one is watching. Confident, I approach a wooden bench next to the railings and step onto the slatted seating area. From there, it's a simple task to drop the rucksack into the park grounds and then follow it with an easy vault.

Once I'm on the other side of the railings, I grab the rucksack and check again for possible witnesses. Now I am trespassing I need to move quickly away from the streets which surround the park.

There is enough light to identify the long stretch of tarmac leading from the entrance gates into the dim distance. I cross the grass and move at pace along the path until the sound of motor vehicles on the main road is but a background hum. The urban soundtrack gives way to the steady but pronounced thumping of my heart.

The scenery, albeit bathed in darkness, is not as claustrophobic as I imagined. Despite the Central London location, the view ahead is no different to the open parkland in Durrington. I can almost make out the point where the path ends and the sky begins. The tension in my calf muscles confirms I'm on a steepening upward incline.

Then, the tension begins to ease as the black silhouette of a tree creeps above the horizon. Four more follow until the path levels out and I can see a wide vista laid out before me.

I continue along the path until it ends at a large, oval-shaped area of hard standing. It is the spot where humans gather to appreciate the view of London — the highest point of Primrose Hill.

Having reached my ultimate destination, I turn around.

On my taxi journey here, I realised there's a world of difference between a static photograph and a first-hand view of London's famous landmarks. As mesmerising as those sights were, they were scant preparation for the view before me.

I need to check the time, but I'm unable to pull my gaze from the view of London in its near entirety, stretching across much of the horizon. Only now, standing here, am I able to witness what no photograph could ever convey — the sense of constant motion, the radiating aura of energy, and the sheer scale of the structures. It is unlike anything I have ever seen.

"Incredible."

Seconds tick by until an invisible force draws my wrist up towards my face, blocking the view. My watch confirms the time as 11:55 pm. I must prepare.

I place the rucksack down, unzip it, and remove the fold-up chair. It takes almost a minute to erect and a further half-minute to decide where I should place it. I settle on a spot at the rear boundary of the oval.

I take my seat and ensure the rucksack is safely stowed beneath. Then, with only a minute remaining, I begin the countdown.

Fifty-nine.
Fifty-eight.
Fifty-seven.

Chapter 15

Merle has no idea the average lifespan of a domestic cat is fifteen years. In fact, Merle has no concept of what a year is, so fifteen years has no more meaning to him than fifteen weeks, fifteen hours, or fifteen elephants. Time is, after all, a construct created by humans, for humans.

That is why, one hour and nine minutes into my wait, I am not concerned. It is, comparatively speaking, a single atom of a molecule of water in an ocean spanning the surface of Jupiter. In other words, one hour and nine minutes of human time are pitifully insignificant in the grand scale of the universe. *They* will come.

The view of London has edged from stupefying to merely transfixing. It is a shame the sky above the city is a soup of nothingness. There are a few pinpricks of light, but the stars I can clearly see from our garden in Durrington are patently shyer in the city.

Another hour passes.

At 2:19 am, I pull the rucksack out and retrieve a thermal blanket. I dressed appropriately for the forecasted temperature, but I underestimated the chill factor from the wind whipping across an exposed hilltop. Mother used to say the February winds were the cruellest, and they'd chill her to the very bone. Biology was never her strong point.

I continue to wait, watch, and question if this city has ever been truly silent. There must have been a time, once, before the first Roman settlements on the banks of the Thames. Two thousand years of evolution and two thousand years of man-made disruption to the once peaceful land. It is difficult to see how the next two thousand years will be different, but in the unlikely event London should ever fall silent, I will not be around to witness it. Then again, silence would imply humans themselves are no longer around. Would that be so terrible for this planet?

My thoughts turn to more relevant matters and my imminent departure. This is a topic I have discussed at length with The Shepherd as we speculated how *They* would extract one lone faux-human from this world. Unlike me, The Shepherd studied science fiction in-depth, although he readily mocked the idea of flying saucers and little green men. In his view, the only viable method of transporting a being from one galaxy to another is teleportation.

If The Shepherd is correct, time is running out. Regent's Park re-opens to the public at 5:00 am, and I cannot see how *They* would risk teleportation with humans around to witness it. Then again, perhaps *They* have another plan beyond any theoretical notion The Shepherd or I considered. We have no more information at our disposal than what is available to the humans, and their knowledge of the universe currently rests between nothing and negligible. Trying to second-guess an advanced alien race is as futile as seeking Merle's opinion of his namesake's music — incomprehensible on every level.

With little else to occupy my mind, I look up to the limited range of stars visible in the pre-dawn sky. My attention settles on the brightest: Capella, in the Auriga constellation. Gazing up, I know the light particles hitting the back of my eye began their journey thirteen years before I arrived on Earth. A forty-three-year journey is a relative hop compared to the light particles emitted from other visible stars. As a child, I couldn't quite believe the light particles landing in our garden from the star Betelgeuse, in the constellation Orion, began their journey just as the Black Death started its journey across fourteenth-century Europe.

My neck stiffening, I check the time: 3:55 am. The minutes continue to tick by, and the scene before me doesn't alter, but I suddenly become conscious of a dull ache emanating from my lower abdomen. I adjust my position, and the ache eases a fraction, only to return within a minute. I move again, but the dullness becomes more pointed.

I need to urinate.

With reluctance, I remove the thermal blanket and stand up. Scanning my immediate surroundings, the only option appears to be an oak tree some forty metres away. I then conclude modesty is not a priority as I'm alone on a hilltop, in the dark — where I choose to urinate is academic. I take twenty steps away from the chair and stand with my back to the London skyline. The relief is welcome, but the thought I could be teleported away with my genitalia exposed is unwelcome.

My concerns prove unfounded. With an empty bladder, I return to the chair, unteleported.

Time ticks on, and 5:00 am arrives. It is still dark, but I know the gates to Regent's Park are now open. This is not an insignificant concern. Humans will soon be wandering around the park, and I am now five hours into the 29th of September. I didn't anticipate waiting quite so long.

Unable to control my thoughts, I begin to question if I've followed the right path. What if my original instinct was correct, and departure day is tomorrow, the 30th?

I try to shake the doubts away. There are still nineteen hours remaining.

One hour into those nineteen, the first yellowish smudge of light creeps up behind the buildings littering the horizon. Not long after, the first human appears on the path some eighty metres from my vantage point.

With the Earth turning slowly on its axis, the Sun comes into full view. The dawn chorus begins with the rising rumble of combustion engines drifting in from every direction. From my elevated vantage point, I'm able to watch the flow of humans scurrying across the park, like worker ants: some running, some walking, and several accompanied by canines. All too soon, some of the humans arrive at the oval viewing platform, undermining the solitude I've enjoyed all night. Pausing briefly to take in the view, they show little interest in the waiting alien.

At 7:00 am, my stomach provides an update on the time. My digestive system is sensitive to change, and even though I hoped not to be here at breakfast time, I had to plan for all eventualities. With that, I chew on a handful of mixed nuts and try to ignore the thought I might be dining from this bag once or even twice more today.

Another two hours pass and the ant-like humans give way to a plodding variety who arrive at the viewing platform in small groups. They all linger to chat with one another and take photographs — many, many photographs. A few use binoculars to stare at the city they could easily see close up if they so bothered.

They remain elusive.

By mid-morning, it's warm enough I can return the thermal blanket to the rucksack. The chill breeze has diminished, and the sun has warmed the air to a comfortable level. There is little the sun can do about the toxicity of the air, and I can almost taste the pollutants. The view of London loses clarity as a thin haze blurs the edges.

Tiredness, like the smog, steadily builds.

Some respite arrives in the form of an inquisitive canine. The chocolate-brown hound pads over and sniffs my shins before a rotund female calls him away. Several more dogs follow the same routine. None of the accompanying humans attempt to engage in small talk. Only one apologises.

I consume five handfuls of mixed nuts and five gulps of water for lunch. The calories provide a temporary boost to my energy levels, but within an hour, the urge to sleep returns. I clamber out of the chair and walk laps of the oval to stave off the tiredness. It is a strategy I repeat every thirty minutes until it is time for a dinner of more mixed nuts at 5:00 pm.

By 6:00 pm, I can feel my mind approaching a mush similar to Mother's. It is not helped by a growing sense *They* are displeased with me, and I am being punished. Only six hours of the 29th remain. Why am I still here?

To make matters worse, I urgently need to defecate. I have already packed up the chair and carried the rucksack to the public toilets twice, and the sign next to the door stated the toilets close at 7:00 pm. I go now or not at all, and not at all is not an option.

Wearily, I pack the chair away and trudge down the hill.

There are three cubicles in the toilets, and they're all disgusting. I select the furthest one from the door and invest five minutes cleaning the seat with an antibacterial solution I always keep on my person. The urge to evacuate my bowels reaches a critical level.

One minute later, I'm almost overwhelmed with the sense of relief and the stench. Surely it is a major design flaw that humans convert food into such a foul-smelling stodge. Despite the stench, I don't have the energy to get up. Instead, I flush the waste and suffer the smell in lieu of a few minutes of additional rest. Apart from the rhythmic drip of a tap, it is quiet, almost peaceful by comparison to the park itself.

Drip. Drip. Drip.

On the fourth drip, a snippet of information flashes through my mind. At first, I struggle to decipher the relevance but piece by piece, a conclusion forms: I am intoxicated, drunk.

No. That is ridiculous. I cannot be intoxicated because I have never consumed alcohol, let alone this afternoon. And yet, I have read about the symptoms, and from memory, they are remarkably similar to the symptoms I am now suffering. I can think of no reason why I'm so light-headed or why I feel dizzy. Of more significant concern, why does it feel like I now exist outside my own body?

Outside my own body.

Outside my own body.

Outside my own body.

"Of course!"

How could I have not realised? *They* are coming for me, but they're not coming for this bag of human flesh. It is my mind that is alien, and it alone will travel across time and space. This body has served its purpose, but it is human, and it will remain on Earth.

I'm about to stand up and adjust my attire, but suddenly, the cubicle walls close in. A faint sense of nausea arrives, and with it, dizziness. I close my eyes and prepare for the extraction.

For the last time ever, I send a blanket instruction to every muscle: disengage. Cut loose, the process begins, and my mind pulls away.

This is it. I am going home.

Chapter 16

All five human senses are redundant. In this place, wherever this place is, there is nothing: no light, no sound, no odour. If there is anything to touch in the black void, I wouldn't know because I cannot feel my limbs, let alone instruct them to reach out. Am I standing? I can't tell. If there is anything to taste, I don't know if I still own a mouth.

I am nothing in a world of nothing.

"Welcome, Brother Epsilon."

I did hear that I think.

"Can you hear us, Brother Epsilon?"

I understood the words. The voice is synthetic, genderless.

I should respond, but am I capable of speech? I compose a sentence and process it, in the same way I would on Earth.

"Yes. I hear you."

The voice I've employed for decades now sounds unfamiliar.

"You have travelled far, but your true journey has only just begun."

"My true journey?"

"To enlightenment, for we are They."

If I still possessed a human heart, it would now be pounding.

"I ... I have arrived? I am home?"

"Yes, Brother Epsilon. The planet Earth is your history, and we must look to the future."

"I am ready."

"Then let the procedure commence. Open the door."

There is no physical door, and in my detached state, no means to open it. They must be referring to a metaphoric door.

"How?"

"Open the door!"

Confused, my mind stumbles over itself.

"I don't …"

"Open the bloody door!"

Suddenly, I am aware of my body, and the dull ache of muscles jarred into action. Dry lips smack together as sour-tasting saliva scorches the back of my throat. My eyes flicker open. It's dark but not the absolute darkness I just experienced.

"Oi! Sleepyhead. You alright?"

I slowly raise my head. My neck clicks in protest.

The voice belongs to a head with thin hair and puffy features, its chin resting on the top edge of a door … a door with an aluminium coat peg and locking mechanism attached. Resting up against the lower quarter is a red rucksack.

"No," I rasp. "This cannot be. I'm … no. I'm not meant to be here."

"No sunshine, you're not. Do you want to pull your kecks up and unlock the door?"

"Kecks?"

"Trousers. You know, the pair around your ankles."

The light is dim, but as my eyes adjust, the scene eases into focus. I am in the toilet cubicle I visited … when?

"What time is it?"

"Just gone five."

"In the afternoon?"

"The morning."

"Of the 30th?"

"Yes, and I've got a lot to do, so can you stop asking questions and get your backside out of there."

"Who are you?"

"Bob, the park warden. Now, I don't want to be a jobsworth, but if you're still here when the cleaners arrive, I'll have to call the police. Got it?"

I nod, and the head vanishes. Mumbled words follow footsteps as they echo away.

It is silent again, almost.

Drip. Drip. Drip.

There is so much data to process, but my immediate concern is the cold, and my naked lower body. I attempt to stand up. My usually reliable human body objects in every conceivable way, but I manage to stand upright and tug my trousers up. Dignity restored, I lift the rucksack from the floor and open the door.

The air outside the toilet block is frigid, but a vast improvement over the air I've been breathing for … I don't know how long. Dizziness strikes. I lean against the wall and wait for it to pass before assessing my options. A wooden bench opposite is the closest sanctuary. I need to sit down and think.

My backside has barely touched the wooden slats when the enormity of the situation lands. Today is the 30th of September, my human birthday.

There will be no celebration. I should not be here.

My brain is capable of asking questions, but it's in no state to answer them. I commence a diagnostic checklist: dehydration, fatigue, hunger, discomfort. Addressing the discomfort of the cold first, I remove the thermal blanket from the rucksack and drape it across my shoulders. Then, I finish the last of the mixed nuts and empty the bottle of water. I feel fractionally better, in a physical sense, at least.

The fatigue, I concede, is linked to my emotional state. Is this how grief feels? A sense of overwhelming loss, of helplessness? The dream — if it was a dream — tallied with the reality I expected, and now it is gone. One moment I am on the cusp of fulfilling my destiny, and the next, I'm in a toilet cubicle in pre-dawn London.

Something must have gone terribly wrong. *They* would not leave me here like this, surely?

An icy blast of wind cuts straight through the thermal blanket. I cannot remain here, but I never considered the need for a contingency plan. There is only one realistic option: I must return to base and contact The Shepherd. It is his role to guide me, and I've never needed his guidance more than now.

I pack the blanket away and stretch out the stiffness in my limbs. A time check confirms thirty hours have elapsed since I first stepped foot in Regent's Park.

Rather than vault the railings, I'm able to depart via the open gates. I follow the sound of traffic towards a main road, and after four minutes, a taxi pulls over. The warmth is welcome, but I battle against sleep all the way to Waterloo station.

On arrival, I locate the ticket office and purchase two first-class seats on the first available train to Salisbury. The attendant confirms the train won't be departing for some time.

Some time is a seventy-minute wait, followed by a journey of one hour and forty-two minutes. A total of three hours and twelve minutes I might have put to good use. Instead, I spent the time drifting between consciousness and semi-sleep. When I finally pass through the ticket barrier at Salisbury station, I consider turning around and leaping in front of the next passing train. How is it possible a human body can descend from peak perfection to the depths of wretchedness in such a short space of time?

There is no improvement in my condition over the final leg of the journey. Such is the deterioration in body and mind, I hand the driver a note and exit the taxi without waiting for change.

I then go through a series of mundane tasks I've performed thousands of times without thought: opening the gate, unlocking the front door, and kicking my shoes off in the hallway. I assumed such tasks were part of my human history, but here I am again. And so is Merle.

Exhausted, I flop down on a chair at the table, and he pads towards me.

"I wouldn't approach if I were you, Merle. I haven't showered since Tuesday, and London is filthy."

Ignoring my warning, he presses his forehead against mine. I close my eyes as his purr reverberates across my skull. I've no evidence cats are therapeutic, but the headache I've endured since waking up in the toilet cubicles eases slightly.

The problem with Merle, and cats in general, is their low boredom threshold. He retreats, and I open my eyes to find him sitting down, staring at me.

"Has the priest fed you this morning?"

He licks his lips.

"Unfortunately, he's not the most reliable of humans."

Merle isn't the only one in need of food.

"Give me four minutes, and I'll fix us both some breakfast."

I attend to Merle first because there's plenty of cat food in the cupboard. My options are limited because I cleared all the perishable foods before I left. I settle on a bowl of muesli with tap water.

With breakfast addressed, I'm about to take a much-needed shower when my mobile telephone rings. I recognise the number as that of Cindy Akinyemi from the local authority in London. She's probably calling about the document I snatched from her desk as I left our meeting on Monday. I have neither the time nor patience to deal with her bureaucratic box-ticking, so I ignore the call and head upstairs.

I spend nine minutes in the shower, although nine hours would not be enough to scrub away the lingering stench of the toilet cubicle.

Hunger sated and ablutions complete, I put on clean clothes. If there is any irony in my actions, it's the reward of feeling human again. But feeling human and being human are not the same; I now find myself trapped between those two states. What is my next move?

I open the desk drawer and retrieve the piece of paper I took from Cindy Akinyemi's office. There, in black and white, is the line which prompted my trip, my hopes: *Primrose Hill 29/09.*

No matter how many times I read it, I cannot establish any other inference. By waiting on Primrose Hill on the twenty-ninth day of the ninth month, I did what was asked of me. Why did *They* not come?

I invest thirty minutes turning that question over before conceding there is only one person on this planet who might provide an answer. The Shepherd is my only hope, but if we are to plan our next move, I must first lay the foundations. I must research.

Message 2814

Priority Level 1 | Encrypted @ 9:53

From: Epsilon30

To: TheShepherd82

Message Begins ...

Ĝojan novaĵon, frato The Shepherd,

By virtue of the fact you are reading this message, it is clear I have not left Earth. I waited on Primrose Hill for every second of the twenty-four hours of the twenty-ninth day. They did not come.

It is now clear the mission is in peril. For that reason, it is imperative we meet to assess all available data and consider a strategy.

I concede this is a significant break from protocol, but in your last message, you did imply regret at having never met. The circumstances now dictate we must put our minds together. This is our time, Brother. We have no other choice.

Having identified the following rendezvous point as suitable, I propose we meet at 10.00am tomorrow.

Station Cafe, Salisbury Railway Station, South Western Road, Salisbury SP2 7RS

Confirm at your earliest opportunity.

Epsilon

Chapter 17

Four hours and two minutes is a long time to do nothing. And by nothing, I would include sitting and staring at a computer screen.

By 1:45 pm, The Shepherd had not responded, and the lure of my previous daily routine proved too strong. That is why I am now on my way to Elmwood Care Home, to sit with an unconscious woman for thirty minutes.

I arrive to find Susan on reception duty.

"Ahh, Simon," she says without the usual greeting. "You're back already."

"Back?"

"You didn't show up yesterday. We were worried, so we called Father Paul."

"Why would my whereabouts worry you?"

"Because you've popped in every single day since your mother arrived."

I did contemplate telling the staff I would not be returning, but it would have led to questions I had no appetite to answer.

"I don't wish to sound like a drama queen," she continues. "But considering your mother's situation, you really should have told us. It's not the parish priest's job to inform us a resident's only next of kin is on holiday."

"No, I concur, but he does like to interfere."

"That's not what I mean. You should have informed us you were going away."

"Your point is noted. I assume Mother is still in her room?"

"Yes."

"May I have a visitor's card?"

Susan opens a drawer and her mouth at the same time.

"Why are you back so soon?" she asks. "Father Paul thought you'd be away for at least a week."

"Father Paul was wrong. There was a significant glitch in my plans."

"Sorry to hear that. Dougie and I had a glitch with our holiday last year."

"Who?"

"Dougie, my husband. We'd booked a fortnight in Majorca, but the travel company went bust a few days before we were due to fly out."

There is a good reason why I avoid conversing with humans. They are adept at turning even the most innocuous question into an inane conversation, as Susan had just demonstrated.

She places the visitor's card on the desk. Despite my silence, she continues.

"It was awful, Simon. The only holiday we could afford at such short notice was a caravan park in Bridlington. And, it took four months to get our money back."

"Is that the end of your story?"

"Well, yes."

"I must go."

"But, hold on. I need to …"

I grab the lanyard and proceed hastily towards Mother's room.

The scene is not quite the same as it was on Tuesday. The room is no different, but Mother now has an oxygen mask strapped across her mouth. It can only mean her life force has deteriorated further.

I sit down on the plastic chair.

"Hello, Mother."

As little as I want to, I find myself examining the face I never thought I'd see again. I wonder how Mother would react if she were capable of looking in a mirror and comprehending her reflection. To me, there's enough of her former features to remain recognisable, but how would she react to seeing the skeletal face and sunken eyes peering back at her? Although she wasn't a vain woman, Mother took a great deal of pride in her appearance, particularly on Sundays when she attended church.

I try to recall the last time I watched Mother ready herself in the hallway mirror. More than a year but less than two, I think. It must have been cold and windy because she wore a mushroom-brown overcoat and a satin headscarf patterned with yellow flowers. And yes, there was a gold brooch fixed to her lapel. I remember she told me the brooch once belonged to her mother, who I never met. Her father died in a military conflict when Mother was a teenager, and Father's parents were killed in a car accident before I was able to forge any lasting memories.

It is probably just as well I am not a biological member of the Armstrong family. They all died prematurely through bad choices or bad genetics, and Mother will be the last to carry the Armstrong name. That assumes I'm able to escape this world before she does.

I turn to the window and begin counting the slats in the blind.

After the forty-ninth count, I get up and say goodbye to Mother. Perhaps a sign of sleep deprivation, but I feel compelled to say more than is logical.

"In the highly unlikely event you can hear these words, Mother, I would be grateful if you could wait until I've left before you … before you pass. I'm confident it won't be long so, just … just hold on a bit longer, please."

No more than five seconds pass before I accept the absurdity of my own words. Tutting under my breath, I turn away and depart.

I make it as far as the main gates before my journey is interrupted by a male voice, shouting my name. I'm confident I know who it belongs to.

I turn around to find Father Paul approaching from the direction of the car park.

"I thought it was you," he says, coming to a standstill.

"You were correct."

"That was a short break. You've only been gone a day."

"A glitch in my plans."

"I'm sorry to hear that, but perhaps it's no bad thing, considering the circumstances."

"I would say it was a very bad thing indeed, but here I am."

"Well, seeing as you are here, I can wish you a happy birthday."

"Thank you."

"If you give me a moment, I'll go fetch your cards. They're in my briefcase, in the car."

"Cards?"

"Yes, birthday cards. I meant to give them to you before you left, but it slipped my mind."

"You said cards, as in plural."

"One from me and one from your mother. I'll be two ticks."

Before I can argue, he jogs over to his motor car. As I wait, I consider two questions: one, what is the point of birthday cards, and two, how could Mother have possibly purchased a card for my birthday?

The priest returns with two envelopes, one yellow and the other bright blue.

"I was going to buy you a gift," he says, handing me the cards. "But you're not the easiest man to buy for, so you'll have to settle for a book token."

"Thank you, but I have told you before I consider gifts a waste of money."

"That depends on the sentiment behind it. Perhaps you can buy yourself a cookery book; expand your culinary skills."

This conversation is veering too close to small talk.

"I will consider it."

"Good, oh, and before I forget, did you manage to dig out that list?"

"List?"

"Your mother's list, for her funeral service. The one we discussed, remember?"

"You have a key to the house. Why didn't you look for it yourself?"

"Simon, Helen is your mother, and it's not my place to rummage around her bedroom."

"I will see to it."

"I trust you will, and soon. You've been to see Helen, I presume?"

"Again, you are correct."

"Can I also presume my cat-feeding services are no longer required?"

"For the time being, yes."

He nods and then takes another step closer.

"What about Oscar? I presume you'd like me to keep hold of him for the meantime?"

With the priest's question still hanging, I curse my weakness. I'd forgotten all about the stuffed bear and accompanying note.

"Um, do with it as you wish."

"I haven't embarrassed you, have I?"

I focus on a blue van parked thirty metres away.

"Simon?"

"No," I reply, my voice quieter than anticipated.

"I hope not, because that note was … well, I thought the message was beautiful. It genuinely touched my soul."

I don't know what to say in response.

"I need to go."

"Righto. I'll see you soon … and don't forget that list."

"Goodbye."

As I walk away, one of my alien senses kicks in. Without looking, I know the priest's gaze is following my every step beyond the gates. I can tell because all the nerve endings from the back of my skull to the base of my spine are twitching. That, and my hot skin. I'm only able to terminate the discomfort by counting the vehicles I pass on the way home.

Although my conversation with Father Paul proved brief, I'm a full twenty-two minutes behind my usual schedule by the time I unlock the front door, having also stopped off at Tesco Express for provisions. After unpacking the groceries, I dash up to my room to check if The Shepherd has responded. He has not.

I return to the kitchen, and the same state of limbo I hoped to have escaped by now. What am I to do?

The only task that comes to mind is retrieving the list Father Paul wants so urgently.

It is a ridiculous notion, but as I make my way up the stairs, I can hear my father's voice booming in the back of my head. By the time I reach the landing, it's almost as if an unknown force is pressing against my chest. Mother believed in an afterlife but I've always treated her assertions with the contempt they deserve. There are no ghosts or spirits, only the responses of a confused brain, seeing what it wants to see, believing what it wants to believe.

I reach the door to Mother's bedroom and place my hand on the doorknob. Instructions are sent, but my wrist refuses to turn. Again and again, I will my muscles to engage, but to no avail. Perhaps *They* don't want me to enter Mother's room. I don't know why but it would explain my flawed motor functions.

I release my grip on the doorknob. If the priest wants the list so badly, he'll have to retrieve it himself.

Returning to my bedroom, I consider emptying the rucksack and putting it back in the loft. However, it would almost be an admission of failure, and I cannot think that way. Instead, I sit down at the desk and switch the computer monitor on. Only six minutes have elapsed since I last checked so it's no surprise my message to The Shepherd remains unanswered.

Having already tested my patience to the limit this morning, I cannot sit idle and stare at the screen. With no expectation, I open an internet browser and type 'Primrose Hill 29/09' into the input field. One strike of the enter key delivers 56,900 results, ordered by relevance. I scan the first page and links to community associations and planning applications. Even with the date added, the results are no more meaningful than the first time I searched Primrose Hill.

I delete the words 'Primrose' and 'Hill', and strike the enter key again. A page from an online encyclopaedia appears at the top of the results. The chances of discovering any useful or relevant information are almost nil, but with time to kill, I click the link.

I learn that September 29th is the 272nd day of the year, except in leap years. Below that nugget of useless information, there are three lists relating to the 29th September: events that occurred, and notable humans who were born or died on that day. I scan all three lists. Most of the events and names I recognise, but it's all meaningless trivia.

Sitting back in the chair, my attention returns to the rucksack and the birthday cards inside. It's a near-certainty that Father Paul purchased both cards and penned the messages inside. Well-intentioned, he would argue. Others might say insensitive. I get up, retrieve the cards, and return to the desk.

My Christian name is written in the same handwriting on both envelopes, thus validating my assumption they were both purchased by Father Paul. For no reason, I choose to open the pale blue envelope first. It is from the priest and contains a generic birthday greeting and a £10 book token I'll likely never spend.

I toss the card to one side and tear open the yellow envelope.

The image on the front of the card is of a purple-blue sky, dotted with gold stars and a representation of a full moon, decorated in silver glitter. The text in the centre, also in gold, reads: *My Darling Son — I Love You to The Moon and Back — Happy Birthday.*

No one has ever accused me of being overly sensitive, or sensitive at all for that matter, but the priest's choice of card is wholly inappropriate.

I open it up.

The handwriting inside is different to that on the envelope. It is a shaky variation of a style I recognise. I can only conclude Mother wrote it before her condition deteriorated — possibly not long after my last birthday — knowing she would be in no fit state to write a card ever again.

I eye the lines of spidery text without reading them. Do I want to read them? I suppose they must have been challenging to write, physically and emotionally, and therefore worthy of three or four seconds of my time.

My dearest Simon

I may not be with you today in mind, or possibly in body, but I will always be with you in spirit. Have a wonderful 30th birthday, sweetheart.

Sending you all my love on this special day, and every day – Mum xxxx

This human brain must have an unknown fault as I must consciously gulp air to avoid suffocation. As I do, the air sticks in my throat, like I am choking. The malfunction continues, and I need to reset it. I focus on the list of names on the screen and begin reading them out loud.

"1240 – Margaret of England, Queen consort of Scots."

Breathe.

"1276 – Christopher II of Denmark."

Breathe.

"1373 – Margaret of Bohemia, Burgravine of Nuremberg."

Breathe.

"1402 – Fernando, the Saint Prince, of Portugal."

Breathe.

I continue through the list until my breathing is close to normal. Not wanting to risk another episode, I open the desk drawer, place both birthday cards inside, and slam it shut.

If only it were so easy to slam Mother's words from my mind.

Message 2815

Priority Level 1 | Encrypted @ 17:41

From: TheShepherd82

To: Epsilon30

Message Begins ...

Ĝojan novaĵon, frato Epsilon,

It is with much regret I write these words, for I thought we would never have reason to communicate again. That regret is only matched by my concern for the mission — you should no longer be here. I fear the humans are getting ever closer to knowing our true identities, and it is not inconceivable They deemed your departure too risky. We must be careful.

I am now under heavy surveillance and it is therefore impossible to meet with you tomorrow. It will be some days before the risk reaches an acceptable level so I propose we meet next Tuesday, 5th October, at the place and time you suggested. Confirm at your earliest convenience.

In the meantime, I will give further thought to the Primrose Hill conundrum.

Remain vigilant, Brother.

The Shepherd

Chapter 18

As I step out of the shower, the same cursed question repeats for possibly the thousandth time: five days — then what?

That question haunted my thoughts as I tried to sleep last night, along with one other significant concern: human emotions. The reason, I suspect, is because I'm no longer supposed to be here. Could it be that thirty years is all any Starseed can tolerate before our alien protection mechanisms falter? I have researched rudimentary human psychology, and it is not uncommon for a captive to adopt their captor's mind-set after a prolonged period of isolation. Is it the same for my kind? Will I eventually succumb to emotions and then embrace small talk, and religion, the giving of gifts, and every other intolerable human trait?

I cannot become one of them. But, unless I leave, and leave soon, I am fearful that fate will be mine.

Fearful.

Fate.

These are not concepts I accept, and yet, they have found their way into my subconscious thoughts — human emotions at play, not logic. I have resisted for thirty years, but after I've met The Shepherd, what will become of me? I can only hope he will propose a suitable course of action when we meet.

Yes, hope.

I get dressed and arrive in the kitchen at 6:55 am.

"Good morning, Merle. You'll be glad to know we're back to our usual routine today."

He does appear glad if his purring is anything to go by.

We eat breakfast, and I return to my room to get ready. At 7:22 am, I leave the house.

Having sampled London, I get on the bus with a new perspective. Five passengers are tolerable by comparison to the chaos I experienced at Waterloo station. The seats, although not spotless, are cleaner than those on the train.

I arrive in Amesbury twenty minutes later. An acceptable journey time.

At 7:54 am, I ring the doorbell at the rear of Mr Choudhary's premises. He is his usual disorganised self and takes almost forty seconds to open the door.

"Simon? What are you doing here?"

"It's a weekday. I'm here for work."

Unusually, he doesn't smile or wave me inside.

"But … you don't work here anymore. Your last day was Tuesday."

"I changed my mind. I thought I might be going away, but there's been a delay."

"That's as maybe, but I've sold the business. I did tell you."

"You're still here."

"Um, yes, but only today."

"In which case, I can work for you. I don't require payment."

"You've caught me off guard," he replies, scratching his head. "I suppose I could do with an extra pair of hands. I'm packing up before the new owners take over."

"My hands are available for three hours. Is the kettle on?"

Belatedly, he finds his smile and waves me in.

I enter the office to find it in utter disarray. The computer has gone, and there are piles of books and folders stacked in its place. The floor space is full of half-empty boxes, and there's a pile of random miscellanea in the corner. I hang my coat on the peg.

"Here we are," Mr Choudhary announces. "One cup of tea."

He places it on the edge of the desk.

"You've seen what a pickle I'm in. I have to pack some of this mess into my car and the rest of it needs to go in the dumpster outside."

"Based upon a lack of any obvious system, would I be right in presuming you've yet to ascertain what's going where?"

"As always, you're one step ahead of me, Simon. Welcome to my messy hell."

"We should make a start, then. Do you have a pair of latex gloves?"

"For?"

"You can't expect me to handle waste without adequate protection. It's a health hazard."

"I'll see if there's a spare set of Marigolds in the kitchen. Give me one minute."

He returns after sixty-six seconds with a pair of pink rubber gloves.

For the next two hours and forty-seven minutes, we meticulously work through the clutter Mr Choudhary has amassed over the two decades he's owned this business. There is little opportunity for small talk but ample opportunity for Mr Choudhary to debate with himself about what he'd like to keep and what should go in the dumpster.

The task ends with us both standing in an empty room.

"I guess that's that," Mr Choudhary says, slowly surveying the scene. "The end of an era."

"You appear sad."

"Yes, I am. A bit."

"Why did you sell the business if sadness was a possible consequence?"

"Time moves on, young Simon, and I don't have the energy for business anymore."

"What are you going to do now?"

"I'm not planning on doing anything. I'm officially retired."

"Mother says it's unhealthy, not having a purpose in life."

"And a very wise woman she is."

"She was wise. Now she's permanently unconscious."

Mr Choudhary scratches his head again; a gesture I've come to understand as a sign he's thinking.

"I'll pop in and see Helen over the weekend if that's okay with you?"

"That is your choice."

Seconds pass without any further words exchanged. I await confirmation we can depart, but Mr Choudhary continues talking.

"And what of you, Simon? What are your plans?"

"They are to be confirmed."

"Do you have a job lined up?"

"No."

"The offer still stands if you want to consider my cousin's position."

I glance at my watch.

"My bus leaves in nine minutes. I must leave now."

"Okay, but let me pay for your time. Forty quid, okay?"

"No, thank you. Payment is not necessary."

"Come on. I insist," he replies, extracting two purple notes from a well-worn wallet.

"Goodbye, Mr Choudhary."

I leave him standing in the empty room.

My routine continues as usual once the bus arrives. I journey home, eat a bowl of muesli, listen to the lunchtime news on the radio, and then shower. I'm in the process of getting dressed when my mobile telephone rings. The number on the screen is familiar — Cindy Akinyemi, again. After ten rings, the telephone falls silent. I'm in the process of tying my shoelaces when the telephone beeps to signal a voicemail message. Irritated, I snatch it up and press the buttons to delete the message. Cindy Akinyemi has become almost as much a nuisance as Father Paul.

At 1:46 pm, I leave the house and arrive at Elmwood Care Home precisely fourteen minutes later.

Once again, my memory fails to remind me of the day. I enter the reception area, and within three steps, I know it is Friday.

"Good afternoon, Simon," Elaine says.

"There is nothing good about an afternoon when it includes the stench of kippers."

"You're not a fan of kippers?"

"I don't eat fish."

"Not even cod and chips?" she asks, her voice shrill. "God, a chippy tea on a Friday is the highlight of my week."

"May I have a visitor's card, please?"

The card is duly processed without another word, and I proceed to Mother's room. I stop dead in my tracks as I pass through the doorway. From Mother's position on the bed to the stillness of the air to the shards of weak sunlight painted on the carpet, it is akin to travelling back in time twenty-four hours. Nothing has changed.

Of course, it is just an illusion.

Humans are obsessed with the concept of time travel. The Shepherd once told me about a movie he watched in which two humans travelled back in time using a DeLorean motor car and a lightning conductor. We spent many hours dissecting the numerous and varied flaws in such a plan. If time travel is possible, it is ridiculous to assume humans would be the first species to manage it.

I sit down on the plastic chair.

"Hello, Mother."

I settle into my slat counting routine.

Time passes without any change until I complete the twenty-sixth count.

"Knock, knock."

Across the room, Rosie is standing half in the room, half behind the partially closed door.

"Why do hu … people do that?" I ask.

"Do what?"

"Say knock, knock? Either knock on the door or offer a standard greeting, like hello."

"Ohh, is someone in a grumpy mood this afternoon?"

She steps over to the foot of Mother's bed.

"Maybe this will cheer you up."

She withdraws a red envelope from behind her back and places it on the edge of the bed.

"What is it?" I ask.

"It's a birthday card. Sorry, it's a day late."

"Who told you it was my birthday yesterday?"

"Um, your priest friend, Father Paul, must have mentioned it. We had a nice chat when he popped in to see your mother."

"Of course. I should have guessed."

"Well? Are you going to open it?"

If there's anything worse than receiving birthday cards, or gifts, it's being in the presence of the giver when opening them. I am no actor, and my attempts to appear grateful lack the required authenticity.

I snatch up the envelope and peel open the flap.

"I hope you like it."

The front of the card is plain white, with blue text. It reads: *Not Everyone Likes Cake on Their Birthday – Some Prefer 3.14159265359.*

"I showed it to Susan," Rosie says. "She didn't get it."

"Some people prefer Pi. It's a play on words, correct?"

"Yep."

"It's clever. I do like it."

"My God," she then blurts. "Are you actually smiling, Simon?"

"If I am, it is an involuntary response."

"All smiles are involuntary, or at least the ones that matter. No one appreciates a fake smile."

"Noted."

I open the card and read the printed message inside. At the bottom, Rosie has added a message of her own in blue ink: *Happy birthday to my knight in shining polyester.* Below that, she's signed her name with a single cross below.

"I don't understand the reference."

"The other day, when you came to my rescue and knocked that moron out. If we were living in medieval times, you'd be my knight in shining armour."

"I see."

She moves a few steps around the bed and sits on the edge.

"So, how did you celebrate your birthday?"

"I didn't."

"Eh? It was your thirtieth, wasn't it?"

"Correct. I presume Father Paul told you that too?"

"Why didn't you celebrate?" she asks, ignoring my question.

Wary of being lured into small talk, I consider my answer for four seconds.

"I live alone. I have no family besides Mother, so there is no one to celebrate with, even if I were minded to, which I wasn't."

"What about friends?"

"What about them?"

"Surely your friends wanted to do something to mark the day?"

"I do not need friendships."

She shakes her head.

"Wow, that is unbelievable."

"It is quite true," I shrug. "I don't approve of lies."

"No, I meant … that's crazy. I'm lost for words."

If only that were true, perhaps she might leave me in peace.

"Tell you what," she then says excitedly. "Why don't you let me take you out for drinks tomorrow evening, as a belated celebration? It's the least I can do after you fixed my car and saw off that bloke."

"Drinks?"

"Yes, a bar or a pub. Pardon the assumption, but I'd guess clubbing isn't your thing."

"I don't drink alcohol."

"Fine. Have juice or Coke, or whatever."

"Water."

"Water it is. Are you up for it?"

"No."

"Why not?"

Two short words, one simple question. And yet, I struggle to compose a cohesive answer.

"I … I just don't want to."

"Fair enough. How about I cook you dinner?"

"I'm particular about the food I eat, the preparation, and the time served."

For some inexplicable reason, she smiles.

"I won't give up, you know," she says with a wink. "How about a movie night, then? No food, no drinks — just you and me and a good film."

I glance across at Mother. I know what she'd say if she were capable of speech. To decline an invitation once is regrettable. Twice is verging on rude. A third refusal is beyond ill-mannered.

"Where would we watch this movie?"

"I don't mind. Your place or mine, but wherever you're comfortable."

"And what movie would we watch?"

"Ahh, great question," she replies, her eyes as green and wide as Merle's. "We can start with the first in the Star Trek series. I've got all of them on DVD."

"I am not good company," I say in a final attempt to dissuade her. "I deplore small talk."

"There will be no small talk, I promise. And don't do yourself down – I'm sure there's a genuinely interesting guy lurking below that cold exterior."

How did I get myself entangled with this bloody-minded female? Most humans are perceptive enough to realise within a few words how little I wish to engage with them, overlooking Father Paul and Mr Choudhary. I can now add this human to that list.

I turn to Mother again. She is of no help.

"7:00 pm," I concede. "I live at 30 Bulford Hill, Durrington."

"Excellent. I'm already looking forward to it."

Rosie stands up and skips away, stopping only to wave goodbye at the door.

"Seeya tomorrow."

Silence returns, but it's then punctuated by a faint, gasping breath — Mother's, not mine.

Chapter 19

If I had to declare which part of a house I prefer the most, it would definitely be the landing. It's not a room as such, but the landing in this house is long enough and uncluttered enough for pacing, so it serves a practical purpose. The etymology is also interesting — a 'flight' of stairs has to end somewhere, so logically that would be a landing. Mother told me that.

This morning, I've been pacing the landing carpet for thirty-one minutes. I've attempted to open the door to Mother's bedroom twice but failed both times.

After returning from Elmwood Care Home yesterday, I focused my attention on the failed departure and the conversation I had with Father Paul the day before I left for Primrose Hill. He knew about the note, yet he failed to share the knowledge of its existence. Therefore, he cannot be trusted any more than my parents after they wilfully withheld information relating to my adoption.

As The Shepherd suggested, the humans do seem to be conspiring against us. If that is so, what other information are they hiding?

There must be a reason why Father forbade me from entering their bedroom, and I now wonder what other secrets are waiting on the other side of the door. Is it possible my parents knew about my alien origins? If so, did they know before they adopted me, or did they discover it later? Perhaps Father found out and considered informing the authorities. It would explain his premature and untimely death — *They* would have intervened. It would also explain why he argued with Mother on the evening I learnt about my adoption. His exact statement has lost clarity over time, but I'm sure I heard the words, *send him back*. Only later did it occur to me that 'back' might relate to my home planet — *send him back where he came from*.

So many questions, too many assumptions. I need facts.

I stop pacing outside Mother's bedroom and grab the doorknob. Almost immediately, my heart begins to beat at an increased rate. I send the instruction to turn the knob and wait for my wrist to respond. It stubbornly refuses to comply.

After another six minutes of pacing, I stop again.

It is not excessively warm on the landing, but both palms are moist with perspiration. I wipe my right palm on my trouser leg and grip the doorknob again.

"Just. Turn. It."

Ever so slowly, my wrist rotates in an anticlockwise motion until the lock mechanism clicks. I just need to push the door open now.

Millimetre by millimetre, a vertical line of greyish light widens at the door's edge: four centimetres, six centimetres, eight centimetres. It reaches ten, and a waft of stale air escapes, carrying with it faint traces of Mother's perfume mixed with a hint of beeswax furniture polish, plus a musky odour I can't quite place.

GET OUT, BOY!

My wrist, having repeatedly ignored previous instructions, reacts of its own accord, and tugs the knob so hard the door slams shut. Heart hammering, I stagger back until my shoulder blades touch the door to the airing cupboard. I don't know what trickery my human brain just enacted, what twisted illusion compelled my arm to react that way, but the resulting discombobulation is not welcome.

I return to my bedroom and count the circular swirls in the ceiling Artex. There are one-hundred and thirty-two, just as there were the first time I counted them as an adolescent.

My heart rate returns to normal, but the episode on the landing has left its mark. I'm certain I've not suffered an aneurysm or a brain haemorrhage, but there's a dull pressure across my cranium like I'm wearing a lead helmet. I'm not overly concerned because I've felt this discomfort many times before. Mother used to say it happens because I think too much, and the brain is just like every other muscle in the human body — put it under too much strain, and it'll ache.

I have been thinking an awful lot of late, and hearing my dead father's voice is likely a symptom of excess stress.

I check the time. It's almost 11:00 am, and eight hours until Rosie arrives. As little as I want to spend an evening in the company of a human, it is, I suppose, an opportunity to focus on trivial tasks and reduce the mental demands on my brain.

I reach a decision — I will put aside all thoughts of Primrose Hill and the conundrum of my departure for today and pick up the quest tomorrow.

Taking into account the time I require for food and visiting Mother this afternoon, six hours should be enough to plan. And, having never entertained a human before, plan I must.

Once a month, Mother used to invite some of her church-going friends to the house. I would retreat to my bedroom for the duration of their visit but on occasion, I would still be in the kitchen as she prepared for the arrival of her delusional guests. Refreshments, I recall, were necessary, although I never understood why. Could these people not eat and drink before leaving home?

I never did establish why the host is obliged to provide food and beverages, but I should follow the same peculiar custom for my guest, I suppose. There is insufficient time for a trip to Tesco Express either side of lunch, so I shall stop by on the way back from Elmwood Care Home.

Mother's second obsession before her guests arrived was the cleanliness of the house. Humans are, to paraphrase my mother, highly judgemental when it comes to hygiene in other people's homes. In my limited experience, they are not so pedantic when it comes to their own homes. So, on top of securing refreshments, I also need to ensure the house is clean. Fortunately, I always allocate four hours every weekend to domestic maintenance, so there will be no significant change of routine today.

The final issue I recall being of importance related to Mother's attire. Once the house was clean and the refreshments prepared, she would spend an inordinate amount of time flitting between the bathroom and her bedroom. Why, I do not know, because she looked no different, despite the obvious stresses of the process. I will shower before Rosie arrives.

Planning complete, I commence with the cleaning.

By 1:46 pm, the house is presentable, and I'm able to leave for Elmwood Care Home with only two tasks on my to-do list. I use the fourteen minutes to contemplate what refreshments I should acquire from Tesco Express, but there is a significant hole in my knowledge base. I will need to seek advice from one of the customer service assistants.

I arrive at the entrance to Elmwood Care Home and press the buzzer.

"How can I help you?"

The tinny voice doesn't belong to either Susan or Elaine or a female.

"I am Simon Armstrong. I'm here to see my mother, Helen Armstrong."

"Can I see some ID, please?"

"What?"

"Identification, Sir."

"Why? I've just told you who I am."

"Yes, but for security purposes, I need to confirm you are who you say you are."

"I don't tell lies."

"I'm sure you don't, but some people do, hence the need to see ID. If you could hold up a driving licence or bank card to the camera, I'll buzz you straight in."

This process has already wasted many seconds, and I cannot afford to waste any more. I extract a bank card from my wallet and hold it up to the fish-eye camera.

"Thank you."

The buzzer sounds.

I hurry through to the reception area, where a male in a white shirt is waiting behind the desk. Approximately forty years of age, the smile belies the ugliness of his weasel-like features.

"Sorry about that, Mr Armstrong," he says, as I approach.

"Why are you here? I was expecting Elaine or Susan."

"It's Susan's day off, and Elaine called in sick. I usually work at Carmella House, but I'm covering today."

"And who are you?"

"Sorry, I'm Dylan."

"Dylan?"

"That's right."

Somewhere in the deep recesses of my brain, a neurotransmitter flares. Why, I do not know, but the male's name appears to have been the trigger. The resulting wave of norepinephrine induces a peculiar sensation in my lower gut. It is unpleasant.

"Are you okay there, Mr Armstrong?"

"Err, yes. Visitor's card, please."

"Sure."

As the male processes my request, I continue to unpick my subconscious mind's reaction to his name. That process takes me back to my time at junior school and one pupil in particular — Dylan Metcalfe. I haven't heard the name for many years or had reason to think about my childhood nemesis until now.

By the age of nine, I had learnt how to hide in plain sight amongst my classmates. I kept myself to myself, and most of the children were ambivalent to my presence — I was merely the odd child who wasn't like them. They rarely spoke to me nor I to them, and that suited both parties. Then, Dylan Metcalfe moved to our school.

It took only a matter of weeks for Dylan to establish himself as the class alpha male. Even at such a young age, his rudimentary grasp of human psychology allowed him to gain popularity amongst his peers using either threats or flattery. If he chose you as one of his allies, it was an honour, but if you shunned his twisted brand of friendship, you were immediately ostracised.

Of course, I made it abundantly clear I had no interest in joining the cult of Dylan, and he took exception to my decision. I became his de facto enemy.

The war raged for seven long months. During that time, not a day went by when I didn't suffer some form of ill-treatment at the hands of Dylan Metcalfe. If I were lucky, the abuse would only extend to taunts and name-calling. Mother had drummed into me that sticks and stones might break my bones, but names would never hurt me. Armed with her advice, the verbal abuse proved futile.

That's when Dylan decided to up his game, and so began a campaign of psychological warfare.

Week after week, I endured everything he could throw at me. His threats were never physical — we were of a similar height and build, so perhaps he feared I might have the beating of him — but he didn't have to touch me to inflict harm. Many a time, I would return home from school with chewing gum embedded in my hair or dry glue on my coat. Too frequently, I had to wipe saliva from the back of my jumper, and on one occasion, I discovered dog faeces in my coat pocket, wrapped in tissue paper. He was relentless.

Then, one day someone tried to trip me up in the corridor on the way to the luncheon canteen. I stumbled and turned around to find Dylan and three of his comrades, smirking like they were innocent bystanders. I refused to be intimidated and told Dylan as much. That's when he first laid a hand on me. It began with a push, then a shove, and finally, he attempted to fix his hand around my throat and pin me to the wall. To use Rosie's term, I experienced a red mist and punched Dylan Metcalfe squarely in the face.

I don't remember a lot about what happened afterwards. There were splatters of blood on the tiled floor, and I vaguely recall Dylan lying in a heap as the three comrades assessed his condition. A teacher appeared, and I then found myself waiting outside the headmistress's office. Mother soon arrived, and within fifteen minutes, we were walking home together.

That was the last time I stepped foot in a school, and soon afterwards, we moved to Wiltshire. I never asked either parent if the two events were connected, but if they were, it might explain why Father resented me. Maybe he never wanted to move from Surbiton. I'll never know for sure, but logic suggests Mother might have decided I would be safe far away from Dylan Metcalfe and the education system in general.

I make my way to her room.

The ensuing visit proves uneventful as Mother is reliably unresponsive, although I noticed the blind slats require a thorough clean. I make a note to mention it to Susan or Elaine.

I depart without saying goodbye to the male at the desk, on account I'm one full minute behind schedule because of him.

Eleven minutes later, I arrive at Tesco Express. The assistant behind the counter is busy with customers, so I search the aisles looking for one of his colleagues. I locate a middle-aged female stacking toilet rolls on a shelf.

"Excuse me."

"Yes, Love?"

"I require assistance."

"Sure. What can I help you with?"

"I am entertaining this evening, and I need to purchase refreshments."

"Refreshments?"

"Yes."

"Can you be a bit more specific?"

"No."

The female steps away from the shelf.

"Are you talking about nibbles?"

"Possibly. What are nibbles?"

"Like, um, party foods. Just something to snack on, like a buffet."

"I think so."

"Okay. We only have a limited range of party snacks, but if you follow me, I'll show you where they are."

Maintaining a safe distance, I follow the female along the aisle and left towards the chiller cabinets. She comes to a stop.

"Here we are."

I eye the shelves laden with unfamiliar products.

"What would you recommend?" I ask.

"Sausage rolls, mini eggs, pork pies, and cocktail sausages are the most popular."

"This is what you call refreshments? Buffet food?"

"Yes. Basically, it's anything you can eat in one hand, you know, bite-size portions."

I lean forward to examine the packaging.

"Is it customary to offer processed pig meat when entertaining?"

"Um, not really."

"Yet, all of these products contain said meat."

"You never said your guests were vegetarian or vegan."

"I did not because I don't know."

"Well, I'll err, leave you to browse. Everything we have is in this cabinet."

The female departs.

I decide against the pig meat products, but now I know the basic requirements of refreshments, I can select appropriate items without assistance. I simply need to purchase small items of food which can be consumed with one hand. I have no idea why a guest would need to keep one hand free, but I assume it's some peculiar human etiquette.

Eleven minutes later, I depart Tesco Express with one bag of Brussels sprouts, a punnet of button mushrooms, and a packet of ready salted crisps. I also purchased a bottle of elderflower cordial because human females like flowers, I understand.

I arrive home and unpack the refreshments. Then, I refer to one of Mother's cookery books for instructions. The Brussels sprouts are to be boiled in water for five minutes and seasoned with salt and pepper, while the button mushrooms require frying in butter or sunflower oil for three minutes. There's no guidance on ready salted crisps.

With nothing left on my to-do list, besides dinner and another shower, I have time to kill before preparing the refreshments. After vacuuming the carpets again, I retire to my bedroom and check if The Shepherd has sent any further messages. He has not. Not wishing to tax my brain, I decide against internet research or reading or any of the usual ways I fill my spare time. Instead, I return to the lounge and place a Merle Haggard record on the stereo system.

Sitting in my preferred armchair, I listen to the album in its entirety. The music itself is inconsequential — I could be listening to the sound of a washing machine on a spin cycle — but there is no denying each of the tracks invokes memories of Mother when she was in good health. If I were to close my eyes, I could probably summon a memory of her singing the words to herself, as she often did while conducting household chores.

The clock on the mantelpiece chimes five times. I put the record back in its sleeve and return it to the shelf, along with the rest of Mother's albums. It is time for my final meal of the day.

As it's Saturday, the meal consists of new potatoes with peas and broccoli. I place a portion of each in a steamer and set it to thirty minutes. Merle is less reliable at this time of day, so he might appear any time between now and 6:00 pm. I prepare his bowl.

One hour later, as I wash up, Merle is watching me from the table, having consumed his food.

"We have company this evening. A human you have not met before."

Indifference.

"I am only warning you as I know you like to sleep in Mother's armchair of an evening. We will be watching a movie in the lounge — Star Trek, apparently."

Merle yawns.

"Quite."

I put the washing up away and check the time. I am on schedule.

"I'm going up for a shower. Please refrain from making any mess in my absence, and by mess, I'm referring specifically to furballs."

As I climb the stairs, I become conscious of an unrecognisable sensation in my chest. Unlike Father, I have no issues with my cardiac system, so the sensation is unlikely to be life-threatening. It's not a pain or an ache, more a quivering. Most likely, it's the acids in my gut, struggling to break down a particularly tough broccoli stalk.

I dismiss it.

Chapter 20

Fresh from a nine-minute shower and dressed in clean clothes, I tip the bag of Brussels sprouts into a pan of boiling water. Two minutes later, I empty the button mushrooms into a preheated pan, together with a teaspoon of sunflower oil. Whilst they cook, I dig out a serving platter and tip the ready salted crisps into a bowl which I place in the centre. Not being creative, the best I can do is serve the refreshments on one single plate.

If my timing is correct and Rosie arrives as agreed, my preparations will be complete six minutes before the doorbell rings, allowing enough time for the sprouts and mushrooms to cool.

The mechanical timer pings. Using a colander, I drain the sprouts, season them with salt and pepper, and tip them onto the serving platter. I decant the mushrooms and stand back to appraise my efforts. It's food on a plate — mission accomplished.

Barely a minute later, the doorbell rings, five minutes before it's supposed to.

I'm tempted to make my guest wait until 7:00 pm before opening the door, but Merle's narrow eyes suggest he disagrees.

"Fine."

I walk down the hallway at a leisurely pace and open the door.

"Evening, Simon."

I've only ever seen Rosie in her utilitarian work attire, and her black and purple patterned dress with ankle boots are a stark contrast. I absorb the view longer than perhaps necessary.

"What's the matter?" she asks. "Have I got toothpaste on my chin?"

"Sorry?"

"You're staring."

"Your appearance is different."

"I would hope so. The Elmwood uniform isn't exactly flattering."

"Indeed. Come in."

She steps into the hallway and sniffs the air.

"What's that smell?"

"I was preparing refreshments. I apologise about the odour."

"What were you preparing? It smells like … cabbage?"

"No. Brussels sprouts."

"Interesting."

"Do you find the odour offensive?"

"I work with old folks, Simon. They expel methane like a herd of flatulent Friesians, so I'm used to it."

"Right. Come this way."

I hurry through to the kitchen and stand by the table, Merle at my side. Rosie enters.

"This is nice," she remarks, turning to inspect the room. "Homely."

Then, she notices my feline companion.

"Aww. He's cute."

She steps across to the table, her hand outstretched. Merle meets her hand with his forehead and purrs loudly.

"Merle is Mother's cat."

"Ahh, right. I remember you saying she named her cat after her favourite singer."

Rosie continues to stroke Merle's fur, seemingly unfazed by the silence in the kitchen. As host, I'm sure there are protocols I must follow.

"May I take your coat?"

"Sure. Thank you."

She slips her coat off and hands it to me.

"And your bag?"

"I'll keep hold of it, thanks."

I take her coat into the hallway and hang it in the understairs cupboard, noting it carries the same sweet floral scent that follows Rosie around.

Back in the kitchen, Merle is proving a more engaging host than I.

"Would you like some refreshments? Nibbles, I think they're called."

"Sure. What have you got?"

I fetch the platter from the side and present it to my guest.

"You weren't joking, were you?"

"Joking?"

"You really have cooked sprouts … oh, and mushrooms."

"I wasn't … I didn't know if you consumed meat."

She plucks a mushroom from the platter and places it in her mouth, whole.

"I do love a mushroom," she says, swallowing it down. "But, can I be honest? I'm not a fan of sprouts."

"I'm sorry. I've never had to serve refreshments before. Do you like ready salted crisps?"

"Who doesn't?" she replies, smiling.

"What about elderflower cordial?"

"I've never tried it."

"Nor I. Would you like a glass?"

"Yeah, go on."

I return the platter to the side and pour two small measures of cordial into glasses before topping up with tap water.

"Here we are."

Rosie takes the glass and then raises it towards me.

"Cheers."

I have seen humans do this before. It is customary to tap my glass against hers before sipping or gulping the fluids.

"Cheers."

We simultaneously sip the elderflower cordial. One sip is enough.

"That is quite vile," I remark.

"Yes, it is," Rosie agrees.

I don't understand why her smile remains broad.

"You find it amusing that I have served such an abhorrent beverage?"

"I'm smiling at your reaction. Why did you buy a drink you've never tried before?"

"Females like flowers. You are a female. This beverage contains elderflower."

"I can't fault your logic, and it was a sweet thought, even if elderflower does taste like donkey piss."

"Donkey's urine?"

"I'm guessing donkey's piss doesn't taste too pleasant either."

"I imagine not. Or any urine."

She chuckles to herself.

"Why are you laughing?"

"Because you make me laugh, in a good way."

"But I have no sense of humour."

"I beg to differ. Your humour is just a bit more deadpan than most."

I nod, unsure how else to respond. The silence lingers.

"Are you ready to take your first step toward becoming a Trekkie, then?"

"The movie?"

"Yes, and I took the liberty of bringing the second in the series too, if you're not completely bored of Star Trek within the first ten minutes."

She removes the large bag from her shoulder and unzips it.

"But let's not get ahead of ourselves," she adds, handing a DVD box to me.

"Thank you."

"Oh, and I also brought some popcorn. It's illegal to watch a movie without popcorn."

"Is it?"

"No, but it should be. Do you have a bowl?"

I search through the cupboard and locate one of Mother's mixing bowls.

"Will this suffice?"

"Perfect. Shall we get started then?"

"Yes."

I wait for further instructions. Rosie looks at me.

"Err, lead on then. I don't know where the lounge is."

"Yes, of course. Shall I bring the platter?"

"Maybe just the crisps, eh?"

We retire to the lounge. I'm sure there is another protocol to enact here.

"Would you care to take a seat?" I ask, casting my hand across the sofa.

"Thank you."

She sits down. I switch the television on and activate the DVD player. After slotting the Star Trek disc in, I press the play button and take a seat in my usual armchair.

"You're sitting over there, are you?"

"This is where I usually sit."

"Wouldn't it be more sociable if we were both on the sofa? We can talk without yelling across the room at each other."

I assess the distance between Rosie and the third seat on the three-seater sofa. It is on the edge of what I consider comfortable, but as a host, I must avoid rudeness. I sit down, pressing my right thigh tight against the armrest.

"Don't panic," she says, placing Mother's bowl on the seat between us. "I don't bite."

The movie begins, although nothing happens for the first two minutes other than a series of names are displayed on the screen over a computer-generated impression of space. I presume the orchestral music score is for the purposes of drama.

Finally, some action as three crude spacecraft drift towards a nebula. The scene then switches to, presumably, the cockpit of the lead craft and its crew of humanoid creatures with bark-like foreheads.

"Who are they?" I ask.

"They're Klingons. They're the bad guys."

"And what year is this supposed to be?"

"2273."

"Really? In two-hundred and fifty years, a race is technologically advanced to conquer interstellar space fight, but the display screens in their spacecraft utilise technology from twentieth-century Earth."

"Eh?"

"Look at the screen they're studying. It's cathode ray technology, like an old television."

"They made this movie in 1979. Try to keep that in mind."

The Shepherd was correct — human science fiction errs on the side of fiction rather than science.

"How am I supposed to believe this is real when the science is so contrary?"

"If you focus on the characters and the story rather than the holes in the science, I promise you'll enjoy it."

"Understood."

With my belief levels suspended, I sit back and do as instructed.

Forty minutes in, there are questions raised in the story which, to my surprise, I would like to know the answer to. Presumably, this is how movies work, by putting characters in a challenging situation and seeing how they escape that situation. It is not as uninteresting as I predicted.

Some of the characters are also intriguing. If I overlook the fact they're not the crew of a starship but actors on a set, they each possess their own distinct personality — a crew of humans, but dramatically different humans. One crew member, in particular, isn't even human.

"Why is Mr Spock different from the other crew?"

Rosie turns to me.

"Shall we take a break, and I'll answer your question? I could murder a cup of tea."

"Would you like me to bring in the refreshments?"

"I'm good, thanks."

I get up and pause the DVD. Rosie then follows me to the kitchen.

"I only have soy milk. Do you take sugar?"

"Soy milk is fine, and one sugar, please."

I put the kettle on and prepare the cups whilst my guest fusses over Merle, still loitering on the table. The last time I opened the sugar canister, it was to make Mother a cup of tea. She claimed to have a sweet tooth, despite my objections that the sense of taste is conveyed by the tongue and not the teeth.

"What do you think of Spock?" Rosie asks.

"It is intriguing the way he reacts logically to the other crew members, rather than emotionally."

"I thought you'd like him. You're very similar."

"He's a fictional character. I am not."

"All characters are based on someone, even those who aren't entirely human."

"What is he supposed to be, if not human?"

"He's part human, part Vulcan."

"Vulcan?"

"From the planet Vulcan."

"There is no such planet, to the best of my knowledge."

"Exactly — to the best of your knowledge. Whether Vulcan exists or not, it's Spock's home planet."

"And now he serves with humans, on a starship."

"Yep, although you probably noticed he has a strained relationship with most of his colleagues."

"Why?"

"Vulcans live by logic and reason, and they see emotion as weakness. But, with Spock, his mother is human, so he suffers this constant battle between his logical Vulcan genes and his emotional humanity."

"Which is why you are attempting to draw a comparison between us?"

She pulls out a chair and sits down, continuing to stroke Merle's chin. He appears appreciative.

"I said you're similar, but you're way more human than Spock."

Her statement stalls my thoughts momentarily, to the point I almost miss the kettle click off. I turn around and pour the water into the cups.

"Sorry, Simon. I haven't offended you, have I?"

"No."

"Oh, good. My granddad used to tell me off for speaking out of turn."

"Your grandfather disapproved of your character?" I ask, unsure why I want to know.

"No, not really. We didn't always see eye-to-eye, but I still loved him to bits. He passed away last autumn."

"And your parents? Do you have a stable relationship with them?"

"I don't have any kind of relationship with them," she replies wistfully. "Mum died when I was fifteen, and my step-dad kicked me out a few months later."

"I am sorry for your loss … and your step-dad."

"Thanks," she shrugs. "But it was a long time ago, and I don't think about them now. I didn't have the happiest of childhoods."

I remove the tea bags and stir both cups. It does not feel appropriate to continue the family-related questions.

"Moving the conversation in a more positive direction," Rosie continues, "You've now got the privilege of watching a whole catalogue of classic sci-fi movies for the first time."

"Indeed."

"When I was a kid, I spent a few months in a foster home, and there was this lad, Danny, a few years older than me. He had a huge collection of sci-fi DVDs and let me borrow them. I barely left the house that summer."

"What is a foster home?"

"It's like a temporary home for kids who are having problems or waiting to be adopted."

"What? You are adopted?"

"No … worst luck," she snorts. "My mum, God rest her, had problems with drugs and alcohol throughout her life. She managed to keep a lid on it most of the time, but there was a period when I was about ten or eleven when she completely went off the rails. Social Services got involved, and within a few days, I was living with some random family."

"But you returned to your family home in the end?"

"Yep, but nothing was ever the same after that. Mum died four years later of an overdose."

"That is … unfortunate."

"That's one way of describing it."

"Is there another?"

"There are plenty, but it's academic now. The damage had already been done by the time Mum died, so perhaps you're right. Maybe it was unfortunate, but for me rather than my mum. I'm not the person I think I was meant to be."

"I do not understand. What kind of person were you meant to be?"

She briefly stares into Merle's eyes, her expression unreadable. I follow her stare but see nothing of note, and then Rosie's demeanour suddenly changes.

"Anyway," she says brightly. "Let's not dwell on that. As granddad used to say: we can't pick our family, so all you can do is make the best of what you've got."

"Quite. Would you prefer to drink tea in here?"

"Suits me."

I take the cups over to the table and place them down before taking a seat opposite my guest.

"Would you like to know more about Spock?" Rosie asks.

"Yes."

"I hope it isn't too much of a spoiler, but he eventually falls in love."

"How can that be if his race places logic above emotion? From what I understand, love is anything but logical."

"You're right, but it's what makes us human, and Spock is part human. If we didn't possess the capacity for love, there wouldn't be a human race."

"But humans also possess the capacity to hate and to destroy."

"Some humans, and thankfully they're a minority. Anyway, I thought you said you studied humanities, so you should know better than me that not all humans are arseholes."

"I have studied humans at length but still struggle to understand them. I think I'd find Vulcans easier to comprehend."

"Ahh, got a soft spot for Vulcans, have we? Let me show you something."

I've noticed Rosie smiles a lot, almost as much as Mr Choudhary. Her smile remains fixed in place as she extracts a mobile telephone from her pocket and repeatedly flicks at the screen.

"What do you think of this?" she then says, holding the screen in my direction.

I am greeted by a photograph of Rosie dressed in a tunic-style dress, the same shade of blue as the one worn by Spock. It also sports the same insignia on the chest and black border around the V-neck collar.

"I was at a Star Trek convention in Bristol a few years back," she confirms. "What do you think?"

"Your hair is a different colour."

"I dyed it black. Can you see my pointy ears sticking out?"

I lean in for a closer look at the photograph.

"Yes, I can."

"I've still got it at home, so if you ever want to go to the pub with a Vulcan, I'm your gal."

"I don't like public houses."

She takes a sip of tea. I know from experience this is often an opportunity for humans to consider what they are going to say next if Mother was any barometer.

"Tell me to mind my own business," Rosie then says. "But, what's the deal with your social life?"

"The deal?"

"You said you don't have any friends."

"I think friendship is overrated, frankly."

"Depends on who your friends are, I guess. And you said you don't have any family? Is that true?"

"I wouldn't have said so if it wasn't."

"I presumed you meant immediate family. Don't you have any uncles, aunts, or cousins?"

"There is just Mother and me. Once she is gone, I will be the sole remaining member of the Armstrong family."

My disclosure provokes a pained expression in my guest.

"Good grief, Simon … don't you get lonely?"

"No. I have Merle and a television. They provide all the company I need."

Perhaps if I were human, I might require companionship from my fellow kind. Mother certainly did, but fortunately, she also understood I preferred my own company. After her failed attempt to enrol me into the local scout group, I think she came to terms with my preference for solitude.

Judging by the look on Rosie's face, she is a long way from Mother's level of understanding.

"But, don't you want to get married one day ... maybe have children?"

"My wants are an irrelevance. My future lies elsewhere."

"Says who?"

This is not an avenue of conversation I wish to pursue.

"Shall we return to the lounge?"

"Are you avoiding the subject?"

"Yes. My life is complicated, and I'd rather not discuss it any further, thank you."

"That's fair enough," she replies apologetically. "I didn't mean to pry."

I nod and stand up.

"Do you wish to continue watching the movie, or not?"

"Yeah, sure."

Her words convey a positive response, but her body language is contrary. Perhaps I have offended her. I do not know, nor do I have the capacity to care.

Humans.

Chapter 21

I determined the landing is my favourite space in the house. I've never held an opinion on the understairs cupboard. Rosie's coat might have gone, but the faintest trace of the sweet floral scent is still present this morning. It is not unpleasant.

I return to the kitchen.

"What?"

Merle looks up at me, eyes like slits.

"You found her company agreeable, did you not?"

After the movie finished, Rosie attempted to lighten the mood after our impasse in the kitchen. We discussed the movie at length, and thirty-nine minutes later, I suggested it was time for her to leave. She obliged without complaint.

Despite the poorly received refreshments and my guest's overly-curious nature, the evening proved to be the banal distraction I sought. That was yesterday, though, and today is today. In exactly forty-eight hours, I am due to meet The Shepherd, and I must prepare.

Whilst showering, it struck me that perhaps *They* did not fail to execute my departure, but I misread the information in the note. I presumed 29/09 is a date, but what if it isn't?

I head up to my bedroom and sit down at the desk. There, I extract a notepad and pen from the drawer, along with a calculator. The first and most obvious calculation

$29 \div 9 = 3.2222222222$ recurring.

I write the number down, but my initial instinct is that it's too vague to be relevant.

$29 \times 9 = 261$.

Opening an internet browser, I search for the meaning of the number 261 and click the first link. The information is too ridiculous to be of use: *the number 261 resonates with a universal view, humanitarianism, and tolerance.*

I click back to the results page and the next link. It contains a list of references to the number 261: the German submarine U-261, the Messerschmitt Me 261 aeroplane, and the KiHa 261 series diesel train. All irrelevant, but the next item on the list piques my interest. 261 is an AM radio frequency but not used by any known station. My pulse quickens as I consider the ramifications. Primrose Hill is one of the highest geographical points in Central London, and therefore ideal for picking up a weak radio signal. Could it be possible I visited Primrose Hill on a specific date when I should have listened to a specific radio frequency while I was there? Perhaps *They* were broadcasting instructions. Perhaps *They* have been broadcasting instructions for years, and because I was unaware of the note, I never knew.

I furiously scribble notes on the pad. It's a tenuous lead, and there are far more questions than answers, but that doesn't mean it's not worthy of further investigation.

Returning to the list of references, there are three items within a sub-category labelled space. Top of that list is 261 Prymno, a minor planet. Again, my pulse rate increases as I click the link but disappointment soon follows on the next page. Prymno 261 is classified as a B-type asteroid, so not a planet at all. I make a note on the pad purely because the information might resonate with The Shepherd.

The second item on the list is Kosmos 261: a Soviet satellite launched in 1968. It's highly unlikely a defunct piece of human space junk is relevant, but I jot the name down. The final item on the list is NGC 261: a diffuse nebula located in the constellation Tucana. Further investigation reveals only scant detail. It could be meaningless, but in my current state of limbo, I cannot afford to disregard anything.

With the lists exhausted, the only remaining link is to a page titled: *facts about the number 261*. That page contains a raft of numerical data, including bases, divisors, factors, and scales. With my calculator for company, I invest a hundred and nine minutes trying to find potential clues in a haystack of permutations until it feels like I'm wearing the lead helmet again.

I turn the computer off and resume my regular routine. It is time for lunch.

As I eat, I try to think of anything but the relevance of what I've unearthed this morning. If I learnt one lesson from all those wasted hours on Primrose Hill, it's not to make assumptions if I want to avoid further mistakes. It is not conducive to optimum brain function either, dwelling on so many possibilities and a multitude of unknowns. Perhaps Mother was right when she used to suggest ill feelings stemmed from ill thoughts. I should park all such thoughts at least until I've met with The Shepherd.

Two hours later, on my walk to Elmwood Care Home, I decide to follow Mother's advice. Rather than think about my departure, I focus on the evening with Rosie yesterday. As an adult, I've never endured the company of a human, besides Mr Choudhary and Mother, for more than short periods. Granted, much of the time Rosie and I were watching a movie, but the discomfort I usually experience never materialised. Perhaps her interest in space means she's more tuned to my wavelength than most humans. I don't know. What I do know is that she suggested we watch another movie next weekend. I intimated I would be amicable to such an arrangement, but I've no idea if I'll still be here next weekend, so I stopped short of committing myself.

I arrive at Elmwood Care Home. I'm about to press the buzzer when thoughts of yesterday's experience with the temporary staff member return. Fortunately, a female voice answers. I'm granted access without showing identification.

At the reception desk, Susan is not seated but standing with a telephone to her ear. She notices my approach and quickly ends the call.

"Hello, Simon," she says.

"Hello, Susan."

She glances towards the door and then the carpet.

"May I have a visitor's pass, please?"

"Um, yes, but … Nurse Clifford needs a quick word with you. She should be down in a mo."

"How am I supposed to maintain a schedule with such vagaries? What exactly is a 'mo'?"

"A minute or so."

"And how long is a quick word?"

"I'm sure she'll explain when … oh, here she is."

Nurse Clifford approaches the desk.

"Hello, Simon."

"Hello."

"Would you like to come up to my office? We need to have a conversation about your mother."

"Can we have the conversation here and now? I'm already one minute into the time I usually spend with Mother."

"Not really. Please, I really do need to talk."

Nurse Clifford remains silent, putting the onus on me to reply.

"Fine, but can we make it quick?"

"Come this way."

Without another word, Nurse Clifford turns on her heels and walks towards the door. I follow her into the corridor and up a flight of stairs. She then turns right and opens the door to her office, waving her hand to intimate I should enter first.

"Take a seat on the couch, Simon."

"I'd rather stand."

"Okay."

I enter the office, and Nurse Clifford follows behind. Rather than sit in the chair behind her desk, she stands next to it. Her face contorts into an anomalous expression.

"I'm afraid I've got some bad news."

"Regarding Mother?"

"Yes."

"Has her condition deteriorated?"

"I'm so sorry, Simon, but your mother passed away half-an-hour ago."

This is unexpected news. I need to process it.

"Simon? Do you understand what I'm saying?"

I understand, but I cannot believe what she's saying. This was not supposed to happen until after my departure.

"She is dead?"

"I'm afraid so."

"You're absolutely certain?"

"The doctor left a few minutes before you arrived. We wouldn't ordinarily break such awful news to a resident's family but ... you're a stickler for punctuality, and we haven't had time to organise."

I don't know what they usually organise, but it strikes me as pointless. Dead is dead, irrespective of how much planning goes into delivering the news.

"May I see her?"

"Of course."

We make the journey back down the stairs to Mother's room. She looks no different to how she did yesterday, apart from the lack of an oxygen mask.

"I'll give you a few minutes alone," Nurse Clifford says, retreating towards the doorway.

"Thirty."

"Sorry? You need thirty minutes?"

"That is how much time I spend with Mother, so yes, I require thirty minutes."

"Right, I'll ... um, leave you in peace."

Nurse Clifford departs. I take a seat in the plastic chair.

"Hello, Mother."

I turn to the blinds and begin counting the slats.

On the fifty-fourth count, the door opens. I'm about to dismiss Nurse Clifford for her premature interruption but as I look across the room, it's a male figure standing in the doorway.

"Is it okay if I come in, Simon?" Father Paul asks.

"I suppose so."

"I'm so terribly sorry for your loss."

"You, and Nurse Clifton. Apologies are of no help to Mother or me, are they?"

He shakes his head and then steps silently across to the other side of Mother's bed where he looks down on her. I want to continue my slat count, but the priest's presence is a distraction.

"Eternal rest grant unto them, O Lord," he then whispers. "And let perpetual light shine upon them. May their souls and the souls of all the faithful departed, through the mercy of God, rest in peace."

Prayer delivered, he takes Mother's right hand in his, kisses it, and then carefully lays it back on the bed.

"I'll miss her enormously, you know."

"Are you speaking to me or your God?"

"I'm not speaking to anyone, Simon; I'm just voicing my thoughts."

His prerogative. I prefer to keep mine locked away.

"How are you holding up?" he then asks. "Perhaps we should go have a chat in the prayer room."

"Chat about what?"

"About you and your state of mind. I've seen enough grief in my life to know it affects different people in different ways, so whilst you might not be feeling anything at the moment, it'll come. Mark my words."

"I'm prepared for all emotional eventualities. I don't need a chat."

"Please, Simon. Don't put up the barriers … not now."

I check the time and stand up.

"I must go now."

"Where?"

"Home."

"Let me drive you."

"I prefer to walk."

"Alright. Can I pop over later?"

"Why?"

"Just to check you're okay. Please?"

"I don't see the point."

The priest beckons me towards the door, so we're no longer talking over Mother's corpse.

"Listen to me," he says in a low voice. "You've just lost your Mother, and whether it's today or tomorrow or next week, you will need support. I guarantee it."

"If I do, I shall let you know."

"You misunderstand. The problem with grief is it sneaks up when you're not expecting it, and in my experience, you need to be prepared for that moment. I think it would be in your best interests if we had a proper talk. That's all."

"Instructions for the recently bereaved?"

"If you want to put it like that, yes. And I promise, there will be no talk of religion."

"It's not necessary."

My first instinct is to turn and walk through the door, but it occurs I will never see Mother again. Of course, I had the same thought five days ago, but on this occasion, I find myself burdened by the certainty of permanence.

Mother is dead. Mother *is* dead.

I knew this moment would arrive, but I hoped … no, I assumed I would be far, far away. Perhaps, at least mentally, far, far away is where I should be. I glance back towards the bed and take one final look at Helen Armstrong's ashen face.

"Good … goodbye, Mother."

The priest speaks again.

"She wouldn't want you to be alone right now," he remarks quietly. "You know that, don't you?"

"No, and we can't ask her, can we?"

"Trust me, Simon. I knew your mother better than anyone, and she'd be mortified to think of you dealing with her passing on your own. Please, don't do this for me, but do it for Helen."

My judgement, no doubt tainted by the emotion of this situation, leads me in an unexpected direction. Would it be such a sacrifice to grant this one final indulgence? Not for my mental wellbeing of course, but as a mark of respect to Mother's legacy.

"Six-thirty," I reply through gritted teeth. "One hour maximum, and don't be late."

Message 2816

Priority Level 1 | Encrypted @ 15:49

From: Epsilon30

To: TheShepherd82

Message Begins ...

Ĝojan novaĵon, frato The Shepherd,

It is with regret I must break protocol with an update not directly relevant to the mission. Helen Armstrong's life force ceased this afternoon — she is dead.

It is now imperative I leave this planet as I am concerned I will succumb to the human emotions if I stay here much longer. Already, I sense an unease in my alien soul and I cannot risk becoming like them. Time is now of the essence.

Accordingly, I spent time this morning investigating alternative theories regarding the Primrose Hill note. There is some evidence my earlier presumption may have been incorrect, which is why I am still here. I will explain more on Tuesday when we meet.

Epsilon

Chapter 22

I've always suspected it, but now I am almost certain — Father Paul McCready is the enemy. I don't know who his paymasters are, but he revealed his true motives during our conversation yesterday evening.

Seven minutes into his sermon, he said I should embrace my emotions because it's not healthy to keep them bottled up. Nor should I be alone, apparently. He then suggested I might want to stay in his spare bedroom for a time. He never confirmed how long that period would be, or the purpose, other than to be in his company. An obvious ruse to keep me under close observation, I figured.

The more he preached, the clearer his agenda became — to break my resistance. He wants me to abandon logic and embrace his God-fearing ways, become one of his flock. It's not a flock, though, it's a tribe, and one thing I've learnt about humans is they'll do anything to ingratiate others into their tribe.

Not this alien, though.

The Shepherd once asked what I considered humanity's most significant flaw, and I answered without hesitation — tribalism. They start young when seedling cliques evolve in the playgrounds of infant schools, encouraged by adult educators. Some tribes form organically, based upon gender or age, whilst others develop through a system of communal selection during a child's formative years. Those adept at playing a sport are invited into a tribe. Those follow a particular brand of popular music or watch mainstream television programmes are invited into a tribe. Those who wear specific clothes or shoes are invited into a tribe.

I was never part of any tribe then, and I will not be part of one now. The priest will not break me.

The bus arrives.

Once I've selected a seat, I don my headphones and tune the pocket radio to 261 on the longwave frequency. There is nothing to hear other than the crackle of static, but it's no less than I expected, considering I'm a long way from Primrose Hill. Depending on what The Shepherd has to say tomorrow, I intend to revisit London on Wednesday to see if there is any foundation to my theory. More than at any point, I need it to be correct.

I arrive in Amesbury three minutes after the time quoted on the bus company's timetable. I do not thank the driver.

The walk to Mr Choudhary's business premises passes without incident. Knowing my former employer will not be inside the building, I ignore the doorbell and sit down on a low brick wall separating the building's parking bays from the access road. I then remove a notepad from my satchel, along with a Thermos flask. Fortunately, Mother used to drink the same brand of tea as Mr Choudhary, and I found a half-empty box of teabags in the kitchen cupboard.

At precisely 8:00 am, I pour tea into a plastic cup and take a sip. It's almost indistinguishable from Mr Choudhary's tea. I then open the notepad and set to work, counting the passing vehicles and placing them into their respective categories using a tally chart. There are four columns: motorcycles, motor cars, commercial vehicles, and public transport vehicles.

There are fewer vehicles than I expected, but enough to keep my pen busy. The wall is not as comfortable as the chair in Mr Choudhary's office, and I'm not as warm as I would like, but those minor issues are cast aside when a particular vehicle passes by. Being a small hatchback, it is clearly a car, but the bodywork sports the logo of a domestic cleaning company. It is a car, but it's also a commercial vehicle. Which column do I add it to?

I add a miscellaneous column and strike a vertical tally line.

At 11:00 am, I close the notepad, put it back in my satchel, and stand up. I'll analyse the data later. I have a bus to catch.

I arrive home on schedule and, upon entering the hallway, I gather up the mail. There are three envelopes, two of which are addressed to Mother and appear to be unsolicited. I drop them into the bin, unopened, and examine the third letter which is in a plain white envelope and marked private and confidential, for my attention. I tear it open and then wish I hadn't wasted the effort. The address at the top is that of a building I visited in London exactly one week ago. Cindy Akinyemi is nothing if not persistent. Having failed to make contact via telephone, she has written to me.

I scan the single paragraph of text.

It appears Ms Akinyemi has located another document relating to my adoption, and I am to contact her at my earliest convenience should I wish to discuss it.

I screw the letter into a ball and drop it into the bin. The letter is more likely a ruse to entrap me, and once I make contact, she'll interrogate me about the document I snatched. Even if that is not the case, there are no facts surrounding my adoption likely to assist my current plight. Besides, I have more pressing issues to attend to. With that, I hurry up to my room to check the computer for messages. There's nothing from The Shepherd, which I take as a positive sign after he declined my original request for a meeting. As Mother used to say, no news is good news.

After lunch, I sit down at the computer and input the data from the tally onto a spreadsheet. In total, I counted 862 vehicles, of which 48.08% were motor cars, 35.89% commercial vehicles, 10.69% public transport vehicles, 5.23% motorcycles, and 0.11% miscellaneous. Further analysis will have to wait.

I take a shower and leave the house at 1:46pm.

Fourteen minutes later, I arrive at Elmwood Care Home. Elaine is at the reception desk and appears surprised to see me.

"Um, Simon. We weren't expecting you today," she says, getting to her feet. "I was so sorry to hear about your mother … such a lovely woman."

"Yes. Thank you."

She responds with an approximation of a smile.

"So, what can we do for you?"

"A visitor's card, please."

"A … oh."

She appears perplexed by my request as if she's forgotten how to do her job.

"Can you give me a moment, please?" she then asks.

"I can give you one minute."

She shuffles away towards the door and disappears. I count the seconds until she returns.

"You want to sit in the lounge, Simon?" she asks, near breathless.

"Yes."

"Okay. I'll sort you out a visitor's card, but Nurse Clifford would like a word before you leave."

"Noted."

She completes the card and hands over a lanyard. Already behind schedule, I snatch it from the desk and hurry to the lounge.

Mother's chair is empty, as is the one I usually perch on. I cross the floor and take up my usual position. Besides not being able to greet Mother, all is as it usually is. I glance at the clock and begin counting the swirls on the carpet. At 2:30 pm, I get up and leave.

Elaine is on the telephone, so I deposit the lanyard on the desk. I have no intention of visiting Nurse Clifford. I'm halfway to the exit when a female voice calls out my name. I turn around. Rosie approaches.

"Hey, how are you doing?" she asks, her expression sad. "I heard about your mother."

"Are you going to apologise?"

"What for?"

"I don't know, but it seems to be the done thing."

"Yeah, I know. It kinda irks after a while, doesn't it?"

"Yes, it does."

"No one ever knows what to say, so they just apologise."

"So it seems."

"How are you holding up?"

"I am coping."

I read somewhere that coping is an integral part of the human bereavement process.

"That's good."

Rosie then glances over her shoulder towards the reception desk, where Elaine is still on the telephone.

"I overheard Elaine talking to Nurse Clifford about your visit today."

"What about it?"

"Listen, I can't talk now as I'm supposed to be in the lounge but … do you fancy meeting up?"

"To watch a movie?"

"If you like, but if you just wanted to talk, that's cool. Maybe we can go for a walk or something."

"When?"

"I'm on lates today, but I'm free tomorrow evening."

"Can I think about it?"

"Of course. You've got my number, so give me a call tomorrow and let me know."

"Noted."

She takes two steps towards me, and before I can react, she reaches out her right arm until her hand touches my upper arm in a conciliatory gesture. My eyes lock on her hand but not with the typical revulsion that comes with human contact, but curiosity. Why has my body failed to react with its usual flinching spasm?

"Hopefully I'll see you tomorrow, then."

My eyes flick between Rosie's face and her hand on my arm. I nod, and with no encouragement from my brain, the edges of my mouth curve upwards a fraction.

She nods back at me, withdraws her hand, and hurries away.

As I depart Elmwood Care Home, Rosie's parting words come with me. She is hopeful of seeing me tomorrow — why? I remember when one of Mother's close friends died four years ago, and I didn't want to be in the same house as her, let alone the same room. I have no understanding of grief or how a non-human should behave towards the bereaved. I found the experience deeply uncomfortable, which is why I cannot understand why Rosie would want to be in my presence, even if my supposed grief is asymptomatic.

If I were to remain on this planet for a hundred lifetimes, I don't think I'll ever understand humans.

I return home and check for messages — still nothing from The Shepherd.

Being the first Monday of the month, the lawn in the rear garden requires mowing. It is not a task I welcome, and I had hoped the cut in September would be my last. The grass is now unkempt, and I can't ignore it. I'm about to pull on my Wellington boots when the doorbell chimes. For once, I'm glad of the interruption, even if it only delays the mowing by a minute or two.

Then I open the front door to Father Paul, and I'm no longer glad.

"Can I come in?" he asks.

"I'm about to mow the lawn. Is it important?"

"We never finished our conversation last night."

"I heard all I wanted to hear, and much I didn't want to hear. What else is there?"

"Your mother's list. Just nip up and fetch it, and I'll be on my way."

"As I said, I'm busy."

"It'll take one minute."

"I don't have one minute to look for the list, and every second I stand here talking to you is one less second available to mow the lawn."

"It's important, Simon."

"I don't even know where it is, so your estimate of one minute is likely inaccurate."

"It's in a filing box in the bottom of her wardrobe."

"How do you know?"

"Helen told me, obviously. Her will is in there too, and you'll need that soon."

"Why?"

"Because … can we just deal with the more pressing issue of the list?"

"If you know where it is, you can fetch it yourself."

He looks up to the sky, closes his eyes. and whispers a short prayer about giving strength.

"Fine," he eventually huffs. "Not that I want to, but you've left me no choice."

I stand aside so he can enter. He steps onto the doormat.

"It's the second door on the right, but remove your shoes first. I scrubbed all the carpets on Saturday."

After kicking his shoes off, he stomps up the stairs. I return to the kitchen to minimise the risk of further conversation. After only nineteen seconds, the same heavy footsteps return. Father Paul then appears in the doorway.

"Got it," he declares.

He steps over to the table and places the metal box down. It's the colour of an old battleship and just as scarred.

"Why did you bring the whole box down?"

"As I said, you'll need Helen's will, and there's probably a heap of other paperwork you'll need in time."

"Why?"

"Probate."

"What is probate?"

"Besides being a bureaucratic pain in the backside, it's the process of dealing with your mother's estate: the house, her car, and pretty much everything she owned."

"I see."

"Now, how do we get this open?" the priest says to himself, examining the front of the box.

From my vantage point, I can see there's a latch tarnished with age, and below that, an equally tarnished frame the size of a business card. There's a piece of beige card inside the frame with a series of typed characters imprinted on the front. The text is too faint to read from four metres away.

The priest clicks the metal catch and then opens the hinged lid, revealing a series of buff-coloured document pockets. He then flicks through the first five pockets, taking a cursory glance in each one.

"Fortunately, it looks like Helen kept everything in this folder. I wasn't sure if you knew what you were looking for so, if you can spare a few minutes, perhaps we can look through it now?"

"As I said, I don't have any spare minutes available this afternoon."

"Fair enough," he sighs. "But we'll have to do it at some point, I'm afraid."

Consigned to defeat, the priest turns his attention back to the filing box and pulls out two white envelopes. He then shows me the handwritten words on the front of both: *Funeral Arrangements,* and *Last Will and Testament.*

"Would you like me to go through these with you?"

"No."

"You're sure?"

"Positive."

"Are you not in the slightest bit interested in your mother's wishes?"

"Only if they directly involve me."

He wobbles his head as if he can't decide between a nod or a shake. The envelope marked *Funeral Arrangements* is transferred to his jacket pocket.

"I'll go through it later," he says. "I'll let you know if there's anything you need to do, okay?"

"Noted."

"This other envelope contains Helen's will. Do you know what a will is?"

"It's a list of who gets what when someone dies."

"More or less, yes. Your mother's solicitor should have a copy but keep this safe."

He closes the filing box and places the will on the dresser.

"Would you like me to take this back up to Helen's room?" he asks.

My first instinct is to say yes, but then my mind races back to Saturday and the aborted attempt to enter Mother's bedroom. If my parents have hidden other information from me, it might be within the battered metal walls of the box.

"No. Leave it."

"Alright, I'll let you get back to your lawn. Bye for now."

I wait until I hear the front door close and approach the table. As I get within a metre, I catch a faint musty odour like the old newspapers Mother kept in the garage for no apparent reason. I sit down and reach for the latch. In the same second my fingertips touch the cold metal, I notice the card below. The text, although faint, reads: *Property of Martin Armstrong — Strictly Private & Confidential.*

DON'T TOUCH WHAT ISN'T YOURS, BOY!

My hand snaps away from the latch as if it were scalding hot. In the same breath, I leap from the chair and stumble backwards, my hasty retreat only arrested by the refrigerator door. There, I attempt to diagnose what just occurred. My reaction can only mean one thing: I've been on this planet too long, and not only is my brain beginning to malfunction but so too is my central nervous system. On this occasion, the filing box proved the catalyst for another misfire.

Why didn't I tell the damn priest to return it?

In lieu of any other solution, I snatch a tablecloth from a drawer and drape it over the filing box. If I can't see it, it isn't there.

That done, I open the door to the rear garden and focus on the overgrown lawn, which I know is fourteen metres wide. The diameter of the lawnmower blade is fifty centimetres, so there will be twenty-eight individual stripes; fifty-six if I mow it twice, eighty-four if I mow it a third time.

I really need to mow the lawn.

Chapter 23

In the United Kingdom, the average human male lives for 79.4 years, although they're unconscious for 26.5 of those years. After millions of years of evolution, humans are required to spend a third of their life asleep. That is a significant design flaw.

Over the last two weeks, I have found it increasingly difficult to engage sleep mode. Last night, I went to bed at ten o'clock as usual, but I was still awake at midnight. I have a theory why. The human body reaches its physical peak at thirty years, so logically, mine must now be in a state of decline. Over time, muscles will waste away, cognitive abilities will fade, and major organs will fail. Eventually, I'll either succumb to a disease that rapidly terminates my life force, or I'll end up wasting away in a place like Elmwood Care Home.

How does any human over the age of thirty cope with this knowledge? How does Mr Choudhary maintain his cheery disposition while his body is falling apart?

I couldn't answer that question last night, and I'm no closer to establishing an answer this morning. Nor do I understand why sleep is such a necessary yet temperamental condition.

"Any ideas, Merle? Why do humans spend a third of their lives asleep?"

My feline housemate is washing his face, post-breakfast, and distracted.

"Mind you, your species is even worse. You spend more than half your day asleep."

He yawns and then jumps down from the table.

"Garden, or lounge?"

I watch him slope off to the lounge; to sleep, no doubt.

The change in schedule this morning means I am in no hurry to wash up. I've two hours until the pre-booked taxi arrives, and I'll be at Salisbury train station at least twenty minutes before the designated meeting time with The Shepherd. He has not messaged since we agreed to this meeting, but it isn't the first time he's remained silent for a prolonged period. As he's warned in the past, there is good reason to be cautious and that sometimes means limiting non-essential communication.

I finish the washing up and then rue having time to do nothing. When there is nothing to do, my mind has developed a worrying habit of wandering off towards issues I'd rather not address and thoughts I don't want to ponder. A point in question is the rectangle box on the table, covered with a red gingham tablecloth.

"Ignore it!"

Hearing the instruction, even from my own mouth, works. I decide to retreat to my bedroom, where I can escape most of the parental memories still lingering in all the other rooms. They're both now dead, and I don't want either of them cluttering my mind. I need to focus on my meeting.

Switching the computer on, I reference the notes I compiled yesterday and put them into a legible format, organised in order of merit and supplemented with my own opinions to the validity of each. That done, I print two copies and place them in a document folder. I check the time, and there's still too much of it to fill, so I open up the vehicle data spreadsheet and spend an hour tinkering with various formulas and listing statistical conclusions.

Five minutes before the taxi is due, I close the computer down and triple-check I have everything I need. I'm still in the process of tying my shoelaces when a horn blares from outside. I glance at my watch — two minutes early. I'd typically make the driver wait, but an unexplainable eagerness to leave the house nudges me towards the front door. Perhaps *They* are the cause.

Sixteen seconds later, I'm in the back seat of the taxi. The driver, a male with no hair, confirms our destination.

The journey takes twenty-seven minutes, and by the time I exit the taxi, I am close to changing my mind and asking the driver to take me back to Durrington. I cast the thoughts aside; the nausea is likely just travel sickness. With time to spare, I find a quiet patch of pavement at the far end of the road and lean up against the exterior wall of the station. There, I close my eyes and inhale long, deep breaths to a count of one hundred. It helps, to a degree, until I check my watch: fourteen minutes. That knowledge elevates my heart rate to the point I can hear it thumping at the back of my ears.

Why is my body reacting like this?

I am approaching a seminal moment as two true Starseeds meet for the first time. There is no reason I should feel so flushed with negative emotions. Then, perhaps this is normal. Could it be that our inner energies are so powerful, they exert an electromagnetic force when in close proximity, and the human bodies we occupy cannot cope with the additional stresses?

That makes sense.

It's only a theory, but knowing the discomfort is probably normal helps to minimise the effects. My heart rate drops. After two minutes, I walk back along the pavement to the station entrance, where I come to a standstill.

The time is now.

I enter the main station building, which houses the ticket counters. Our rendezvous point is on platform one, but my research confirmed it is possible to purchase a ticket just for the sole purpose of accessing the station platforms. I acquire a ticket and pass through the automated barriers.

The platform is relatively quiet, with only eight humans waiting for a train. I turn left and walk for ten metres until I reach the cafe. Through the window it's possible to determine nearly all the tables are empty, bar two, which are occupied by couples: one pair young, and the other elderly.

I enter and scan all four corners of the cafe for The Shepherd. In hindsight, we should have confirmed what we were both wearing so identification would be easier. We didn't, but I theorised two true Starseeds would instinctively recognise one another. As it is, there are no individuals at any of the tables, but I am early.

I purchase a bottle of water from the counter and secure a table in the far corner of the room, at least six metres from the nearest human but still ideally placed to surveil the entrance. None of the humans pay any attention to me as I sip from the plastic bottle. I check the time again: 9:52 am.

Keen to avoid a repeat of the negative symptoms I experienced outside, I split my time between watching the door for twenty seconds and counting the tiles in the ceiling. There are ninety-six. I reach the end of the third count and check the door again. No one leaves and no one enters, so I start a fourth count of the ceiling tiles and then a fifth.

Another time check: 10:01 am.

I focus on the entrance again and begin a count towards twenty. On the fourteenth of those seconds, the door opens, and a lone male enters. He is of stocky build and perhaps a similar age to Mr Choudhary, but his facial skin is milk pale and blotchy — a model of poor health. He cannot be The Shepherd. I look up toward the ceiling and begin another count.

As I pass the seventy-first tile, I become aware of a nearby presence. My eyes slowly fall from the ceiling to the table, and the figure stood three metres away with a polystyrene cup in hand. He is looking directly at me.

"Um, sorry to trouble you, mate," he says in a thick Wiltshire accent.

"What?"

"Are you Epsilon?"

The very mention of my code name steals a breath. How could this excuse for a human know it?

"How do you know the name Epsilon?" I hiss.

"Long story. You mind if I take a seat."

"Yes, I do. Who are you?"

"I'm … I suppose you could say I'm here representing The Shepherd. Sorry, my friend, but he won't be meeting you today."

"I don't believe you. The Shepherd would not send an advocate in his place."

"I'm not an advocate. I'm his dad."

"Prove it."

"Alright."

The last time I witnessed a human concentrate so intently was in the early days of Mother's condition when she couldn't remember Father's middle name.

"Ĝojan … novaĵon … frato … Epsilon," he painstakingly says. "That's right, isn't it?"

Despite his accent and poor diction, there is no mistaking the security phrase The Shepherd and I created.

"Where is he?" I demand.

Without asking again, the male pulls out a chair and sits down. I'm struck by the stench of cigarettes and peppermint as he places a tatty rucksack on the adjacent chair.

"My name is Gordon … Gordon Searle. Can I ask your name?"

"Epsilon."

"I mean, the name your parents gave you."

There seems little point in not telling him; being my name is so common.

"Simon."

"It's nice to meet you, Simon. I know you and Gary have been chatting a long time, which is the only reason I came along today."

"Who is Gary?"

"The person you know as The Shepherd is my son, Gary."

Patently, The Shepherd must use a human name, as do I, and he's mentioned his Earth parents numerous times, always with a level of disdain. Even so, the name Gary does not sound worthy of a prominent Starseed.

"Why are you here?"

"You can blame my wife, Julie. This was her idea."

"You are making no sense. Why is The Shepherd not here?"

"I said it was a long story. Do you want the short version?"

Whatever fate has befallen The Shepherd, it is unlikely this human possesses the intellect to understand what he's involved in. Nevertheless, it would be prudent to ascertain how much he knows.

"Just tell me."

He slurps from the cup and then smacks his lips together. I should kill him now.

"How much do you know about Gary?"

"That is between him and me."

"I'm just asking, mate," he replies, rolling his eyes. "If you really did know Gary, you probably wouldn't be here."

"I know enough."

"Really? Do you know where he lives?"

"In Wiltshire."

"Yeah, but where in Wiltshire?"

"He never said."

"He lives with me, his mum, and younger brother, in Devizes. You know it?"

"It is a market town in central Wiltshire."

"That's the one. Next question: do you know how old Gary is?"

I shake my head.

"He's just turned thirty-nine. What does he look like?"

"I don't know."

"See, you don't know as much as you thought you did."

Gordon Searle shakes his head and pulls a mobile telephone from his pocket. He presses the screen four times and then places it in the centre of the table, facing my chair.

"That's our Gary."

I lean forward so I can examine the photograph. It portrays a human on the spherical side of obese and so unkempt he could be feral: long, greasy hair and a straggly excuse for a beard.

"I know what you're thinking," Gordon Searle says. "Truth is, Gary spends nearly every waking hour eating or staring at a screen. He's not big on leaving the house."

Overlooking his objectionable appearance, I can understand why The Shepherd is reclusive. Why would we want to mingle with humans if avoidable?

"Must I ask again? Where is he?"

"He's at home, in bed, drugged up to his eyeballs."

Such a frank admission, and one I hadn't anticipated.

"What have you done to him?"

"I haven't done anything. It was the doctor who decided to up Gary's meds."

"Doctor? What doctor?"

The male sighs deeply.

"You don't have the first clue, do you, Simon?"

"All I know is The Shepherd should be here, and you should not."

"Do you want to know why I'm here, or am I wasting my time? I didn't have to come, you know."

I do want to know, but only so I can determine this male's true motives.

"I am listening."

"Well, Julie was in Gary's room on Sunday evening, and she noticed he'd left his computer on, which is unusual as he's paranoid about us seeing what he's up to. So, she went to turn it off, and that's when she noticed your messages."

My pulse quickens.

"Those messages are highly confidential."

"That's as maybe, but experience tells us we need to be wary of Gary's internet use. Anyway, she called me in, and we spent over an hour going through all your messages. I've gotta say we were both taken aback. Six years is a bloody long time to play a game."

"A game?"

"Yeah. You and Gary are involved in some kind of role-playing game, right?"

I don't correct him. If that's what he believes, it suits my agenda.

"Yes. A game."

"So, that's why I'm here. Julie was going to reply to your last message, but … oh, yeah, is it true, you know, about you losing your mum?"

I nod.

"I'm sorry to hear that."

"Thank you."

"Anyway, Julie was going to reply to your message and explain about Gary, but the bloody computer began an automatic update before she got a chance. When it rebooted, we realised Gary had set up a password, and we ain't got a clue what it is. She's got a good heart, my wife, and she didn't think it was fair to leave you sitting here, not after you've been friends with Gary all that time."

"You still haven't explained why he is not here?"

"Yes, I have. I said he's in bed, sedated."

"But why is he sedated?"

"Not that I'm blaming you or anything, but we reckon the stress of meeting you pushed him over the edge. He had one of his episodes on Sunday, and that's why Julie was in his room after the doctor left."

"Episodes?"

"Gary has complex mental health issues … suffered since he was a kid, really. It'd be quicker for me to tell you what he ain't suffering from, but the headline condition is schizophrenia, and with that, paranoid delusions. Most of the time, he lives in his own little fantasy world."

I'm tempted to leave. It is not The Shepherd who is living in a fantasy world but this delusional human.

"When will he be better?" I ask. "We must meet."

"He'll never be better. He has good days and bad, but his condition isn't like a broken bone — it won't heal in time. I guess another reason for turning up today is to ask you a favour. We think it would be best if you don't message Gary for a while."

Finally, the human reveals his hand. As The Shepherd predicted, they are trying to undermine our mission.

"Your request is noted but declined."

"It wasn't a request."

"You don't intimidate me. I know what you're trying to do here, and it won't work."

"Oh, Jesus," he groans. "You sci-fi nerds are all the same, but this ain't a game, sunshine."

"No, I know it isn't, and if you know what's good for you, I'd suggest you keep your nose out of our business."

He appears agitated.

"Listen to me. I don't want you contacting my lad again, understood? I came here as a courtesy, and I thought you'd have your head screwed on. Clearly, you're not the full ticket. This fantasy you've been playing out with my lad ends here, okay?"

I meet his agitation with my own.

"It is no fantasy, and you will not prevent me from contacting The Shepherd. If you try, the consequences will be grave."

"Are you threatening me?"

"I'm stating a fact."

"Mate, you wouldn't know a fact if it bit you on the arse, and his name is Gary — The Shepherd is just some stupid name he borrowed from a sci-fi show."

"I will not listen to any more of your lies."

"Lies?" he snorts. "You're the one kidding yourself."

Rather than get up and skulk away, the fat male shoves his arm inside the rucksack and pulls out what looks like a hardback book. He places it on the table in front of me.

"Read the back cover," he demands.

On closer inspection, the object is not a hardback book but a DVD case with the words *The Powers of Matthew Star* on the front.

"What is this?" I demand.

"Just read it."

I turn the box over and read the premise …

"Matthew Star is a seemingly normal teenage boy whose true identity is E'Hawke, an exiled alien prince from Quadris. Together with his guardian, The Shepherd, they must survive many threats and protect their true identities from humans in the hope they might one day return to their home planet."

Unable to comprehend what I'm looking at, I read it twice more.

"For some reason, it's Gary's favourite sci-fi show," Gordon Searle remarks. "I'd never heard of it, but he found the DVD on eBay years ago. The show was a one-season flop from the '80s."

"The Shepherd," I mumble, my eyes still locked on the DVD cover.

"I've only seen a few episodes, but whatever game you've been playing, Gary has been enacting much of what he saw in that show … it's make-believe. In his head, he thinks you're really aliens, and *They* are real, the poor deluded sod. It's not good for him, and that's why I'm asking … no, telling you not to contact him again, got it?"

I don't respond, and Gordon Searle snatches the DVD away. When I look up, he's on his feet.

"A bit of friendly advice," he says. "Grow up and get yourself a life, eh?"

He throws the rucksack over his shoulder, shakes his head, and strides towards the door.

The furnace ignites.

Chapter 24

It was a china plate, roughly the same size as a dinner plate. On the front was a hand-painted scene of a stag in a wooded glen. Mother thought a lot of that plate and displayed it on the dresser in the kitchen. One day, she shut a drawer with too much force, and the plate fell to the floor where it shattered. Having just finished my dinner, I watched on as Mother gathered up the pieces and carefully laid them out on the table.

After ten minutes, it was possible to get a sense of the picture that previously adorned the plate, but there were too many pieces out of place or missing to determine the complete picture. I don't recall seeing the plate again, so Mother must have given up and thrown it away.

Here, now, I too, am missing a lot of pieces, and I'm struggling to arrange my fragmented memories.

I recall sitting in a chair in a cafe. Then rage, an upturned table, and the feel of hot skin as my hands tightened around Gordon Searle's throat. There are gaps, but I remember the bite of steel on my wrists and blue lights. More gaps, and then I recall the pungent odour of disinfectant and a disjointed voice talking at length. After that, nothing.

Now, I'm in a room, alone, on a concrete bench. The walls are a grimy shade of grey, and above my head, thirty glass bricks allow light in but offer no view of the world outside. There's a stainless-steel toilet in the corner and a door-sized slab of metal painted blue and etched with crude graffiti.

My watch, wallet, and mobile phone are all missing, as are my shoes. I get the sense I'm missing something else, but I don't know what.

There's a dull ache across my skull. I'm dehydrated. Further assessment confirms I'm in a state not dissimilar to that I endured in those final hours on Primrose Hill.

"Primrose Hill."

Like dominoes, the first memory tumbles into the next until a name brings the tumbling to an abrupt halt: The Shepherd.

Liar.

Liar.

"LIAR!"

My voice bounces back from all four corners of the room, like a jury in agreement. There is no judge here, though. No one to mete out a sentence; not that there's a punishment harsh enough — gross deceit of the highest order.

I lean back against the wall. I'm in no fit state to think clearly, but I must. There are questions to answer … so many questions. Where am I? How long have I been here? Why have *They* not come to my rescue?

Further questions arrive in quick succession. Such is their number, I feel compelled to stand up and pace the tiled floor as a distraction. Minutes tick by until a conclusion dawns — there will be no escaping the throng of questions as long as I remain trapped in this room. I must leave.

I approach the door and bang my fist against it three times.

"Let me out!"

I wait and listen. There are muffled sounds on the other side of the door, but they're distant. I bang the door three times again, pause for five seconds, and then bang a third set.

Footsteps.

Wary of who might be approaching, I take two steps back from the door. The footsteps come to a stop, and an aperture suddenly appears. Behind it, a pair of brown eyes ringed with dark circles.

"I thought you'd calmed down," a male voice says.

"Who are you? Where am I?"

"I'm Sergeant Cansfield, and you're at Salisbury Police Station."

"Why?"

"You don't remember?"

"No."

"Alright, listen. If you give me five minutes, I'll fetch the arresting officer. You're due an interview."

"Am I? For what purpose?"

"He'll explain everything, but in the meantime, just try and stay calm, okay?"

"I need water and my watch."

"I'll get you some water, but you can't have your watch until you're released."

"What time is it?"

"Just gone one in the afternoon."

Before I can ask another question, the metal flap snaps shut.

I return to my pacing while processing the last of the policeman's answers. Approximately three hours have passed since the meeting with Gordon Searle — three hours of missing memories.

The metal slat opens, and an outstretched hand appears, holding a white paper cup.

"You can have another one in the interview."

I step over to the door and take the cup. The water is tepid, and it carries a metallic tang, but I empty the cup in one gulp. I'm still thirsty, but the slat snaps shut again. I look down at the stainless-steel toilet and, for one fleeting moment, contemplate refilling the cup from the bowl. I will wait.

Ninety-three seconds later, the footsteps return and end with a mechanical clunk. The door swings open.

"How are you doing, Simon?"

A male stands in the doorway. I'd estimate his age to be similar to mine, although he is shorter by some ten centimetres.

He is dressed head-to-toe in black.

"Who are you?"

"You don't remember me?"

"No. Should I?"

"We met … well, kind of met in the cafe at Salisbury station. I'm Constable Rees Doyle."

"You are lying. We've never met."

"I'm not surprised you don't remember; you were in a bit of a daze when I arrived. To be honest, I thought you'd taken something."

"You locked me up because you think I'm a thief?"

"Err, no. I don't mean taken, as in removed. I thought you were high on something: drugs or drink."

"I have not taken drugs of any kind."

"I know that now."

"Good. I want to leave."

"It's not as simple as that. We need to have a chat first."

"About what?"

"If you come with me, we'll pop down to an interview room."

He steps aside and beckons me to exit the room. Still wary, I step through the doorway to a corridor. A strong disinfectant scent hits me, answering one question at least. I didn't imagine it.

"This way."

I follow the police officer through a door and along another corridor to a windowless room. Inside, there's a table with a pair of plastic chairs on either side.

"Grab a seat, Simon."

I do as instructed. Constable Doyle sits opposite, resting his forearms on the table.

"Can I get you anything before we begin?" he asks.

"Anything?"

"I mean, a drink."

"Water, please. Two cups."

"No problem."

He gets up and leaves, closing the door behind him. He returns with two white paper cups, which he places on the table in front of me. I empty both immediately.

"Better?"

"Slightly."

"Good. Are you feeling okay, otherwise?"

"I am ... confused."

"Would you like me to explain how you got here?"

I nod.

"We received a call from the cafe at the station to say there had been a disturbance. I arrived to find you in a chair, pretty much out of it. From the witness statements, you turned a table upside down and then jumped on top of a ..."

He stops to check a notebook.

"Ah, that's it — I couldn't remember his surname. You jumped on top of Gordon Searle as he was leaving the premises. You then put your hands around his throat. Fortunately, you didn't apply enough pressure to do any real harm, and one of the other customers managed to pull you away."

"I have no recollection of that event."

"You may not, but Mr Searle certainly does. He was quite shaken."

"Is he injured?"

"Thankfully not, otherwise this would be a very different conversation."

"Have I broken any laws?"

"Technically, yes, but thanks to divine intervention, you're not being charged. Your friend explained the situation."

"What friend?"

He checks his notebook again.

"Father Paul McCready."

"What? How ... why?"

"When you arrived, you were walking and cooperating, but we couldn't get much sense out of you. Our medical examiner checked you over, but he couldn't find anything wrong, at least not physically. We wanted to have a word with your next of kin, so the custody sergeant had a nose through the contact list on your phone, and Father McCready's number was one of only three listed. We gave him a call, and he rushed over to … add some context, shall we say."

"You should not have called him," I snap. "He cannot be trusted."

The policeman appears surprised.

"He's a priest. If you can't trust a priest, who can you trust?"

"Is that question rhetorical?"

"It is, and you need to calm yourself down, fella. If it wasn't for Father McCready, you'd likely be facing a charge of common assault. It was him who convinced Gordon Searle not to press charges. He told us you've suffered a recent bereavement, and you've not been yourself of late."

"Who else would I be if not myself? As I said: he cannot be trusted."

"I think you're doing him a disservice. He's only looking out for you."

"I have nothing further to say about Father Paul, but I do have an appointment at two o'clock, so I would like to leave now."

"You can leave when we're done," the policeman says forcibly. "Mr Searle won't press charges on the condition you keep clear of his son. Do you understand?"

"Yes."

"And, if you want to avoid getting into any more bother, I'd strongly suggest you listen to Father McCready. He's waiting out in reception for you."

"The priest is here?"

"He is."

"I don't want to see him."

"Did you just hear what I said?"

"I heard you."

"Then take my advice. He's going to drive you home, and I would think long and hard about what he's got to say."

"If I agree, can I go?"

"Yes."

I stand up.

"Not so fast. You need to sign this first."

He slides a form across the table.

"It's an official caution. It doesn't mean you'll have a criminal record, but what happened this morning will be taken into consideration if you get into trouble again. You need to keep that temper of yours in check, okay?"

"Where do I sign?"

He points to a box. I sign my name, and the policeman hands me a copy.

"Now that's done, you're free to go. I'll show you the way out."

I want to ask if we can bypass the priest, but not so much I'm willing to risk my liberty. The need to leave this place takes precedence.

We pass through a set of double doors and then continue along another stretch of featureless corridor until we reach yet another door.

"It's just through here," the policeman says, as he enters a code on a keypad.

I follow him through to a reception area almost as uninviting as that at the Elmwood Care Home. I'm then guided to a desk where my possessions are returned, and a different policeman asks if I've understood the significance of my caution. I confirm I understand.

"Simon."

I turn in the direction of the voice. Father Paul approaches.

"Thanks for your understanding," the priest says to the policeman. "I'm sure Simon is more than sorry."

They both turn to me. I look at the floor.

"Aren't you, Simon?"

"Yes."

"Let's hope our paths don't cross again."

I nod. The two males shake hands and bid each other goodbye. I don't participate.

"Let's get you out of here," the priest says.

We walk silently across the reception area and out to a car park. The sky is peppered with white clouds, sprinting across the sky in the strong wind, with the sun making intermittent appearances. I recognise Father Paul's car before we reach it, being it's the colour of pondweed. He unlocks it remotely and opens the passenger door.

"In you get."

I don't respond, but I do get into the car. It smells of boiled sweets and dust. The priest steps around the front and gets in. I lean hard against the inside of the passenger's door to maximise the distance between us.

Once seated, Father Paul presses a button, and all four doors make a clunking sound.

"You and I are long overdue a conversation," he says, staring out towards the main road and parkland beyond.

I check the time.

"It would be a more efficient use of time if you talked while driving back to Durrington."

"We're going nowhere until I say so."

"That is unacceptable."

"I don't care if it's unacceptable or not. You're going to sit there and listen to what I have to say, and we're not leaving until I'm satisfied you've understood."

"You cannot tell me …"

"Enough!"

I cannot remember him ever raising his voice or displaying such obvious agitation.

"Lord knows I've been patient with you, Simon," he says, breathing hard. "But even I have limits. Your behaviour … your attitude is unacceptable."

"I never asked for your opinion."

"No, but you're bloody well going to get it because I swore to your mother I'd keep you on the straight and narrow, and I will not break that promise. Do you hear me?"

"It would be hard not to hear you, trapped in here."

"Well, here is where you're staying until I've said my piece."

"Can you please say it quickly? I need to get back to Durrington."

"It'll take as long as it takes. I'm going to ask you some questions, and you're going to answer them honestly. Understood?"

"Fine. Just hurry up."

"Firstly, what in God's name have you been up to with that poor chap's son?"

"Who?"

"Mr Searle, the man you attacked. I had a long chat with him, and if I hadn't begged for his forgiveness, you'd still be in that cell. So, tell me: what have you been up to with his son?"

"That is none of your business."

"You made it my business, Simon, the moment I received a phone call from a police officer. This game of yours has clearly got out of hand, and it must stop."

"It is not a game."

"Mr Searle told me all about the messages you've been sending. What is it if not a game?"

"You would not understand."

"Try me."

"I can only repeat what I just said. You would not understand."

"Good grief, don't be so stubborn. For pity's sake, it's not as though you're an actual alien, is it?"

I don't respond to his mocking tone.

"Wait … please don't tell me …"

"I am saying nothing."

"Sweet Jesus," he groans, shaking his head. "Suddenly, your behaviour makes a lot more sense."

Silence looms for twelve seconds.

"Okay, let me ask you another question: is Mr Searle's son an alien?"

"You'd have to ask him."

"I'm asking you."

"And I decline to answer."

"Suit yourself, but I can tell you categorically that Gary Searle — your esteemed Shepherd — was born in a hospital in Swindon. I know that because his father told me, and he was present at the birth. How many aliens are born in Swindon, do you think?"

"Is that a serious question?"

"No less serious than the charade you and your internet buddy cooked up together. And, what were you thinking … Gary has various mental health issues and you've stoked his delusions to the point he can barely function. You've acted recklessly, Simon, and to top it all, when Gary's father tried to do the right thing and explain the truth, you tried to throttle the poor man."

"I do not want to talk about him."

"Why? Are you ashamed of your actions? You should be."

I choose not to answer but fold my arms and stare into the footwell.

"Let me ask you another question," the priest continues. "Why were you asking me about your adoption … ohh, hold on."

The priest makes a strange noise somewhere between a tut and a snort.

"This is my fault, isn't it?"

"What?"

"You were reading *War of The Worlds*, and that's when you asked me about Primrose Hill. Is that what you're basing your theories on?"

"I … I don't wish to comment. I want to go home."

"Oh, Simon," he sighs. "You're no more alien than I am."

"I said I want to go home. Now!"

The priest places his right hand on the steering wheel, but he doesn't start the engine.

"One more question, and then we'll go. If, for whatever reason, you've got it into your head you're an extra-terrestrial being, what if you're wrong? What if you really are human?"

It's unanswerable because I cannot even contemplate the notion. I remain silent.

"Promise me you'll think long and hard about an answer, and I'll start the engine. And, I won't say another word until we're back in Durrington."

I don't want to think about his question at all, but it's almost as if it's now locked in my brain, and it can't escape. I can already sense it running around, banging the walls of my skull, and screaming in my ear.

What if you really are a human?

"I'll think about it."

"You promise?"

The Shepherd is a human. Do you accept that?

"Yes."

"Thank you."

He starts the car.

If you are human, what is the point of this life?

Chapter 25

I exit Father Paul's car at 1:39 pm. He reminds me of my promise before driving away.

The priest kept his word and remained silent for the entire journey back to Durrington. My mind, on the other hand, was anything but silent. I drew up a mental checklist of the factors which would determine the validity of my argument. I concluded there are plenty of reasons to assume I am not human. At the top of that list of reasons lay the most pertinent factor — I may not have met many humans, but I don't share any of their traits. How can I be human when we are nothing alike? Yes, we share some physical similarities, but that's it. I have more in common with Merle, a cat, than I do with any human I know.

I'd like to hear Father Paul explain that anomaly.

Three minutes is long enough to enter the house, put the document folder back in my desk drawer, and consume a large glass of water. I desperately want a shower and a bowl of muesli, but I don't have time.

I depart at 1:46 pm and arrive at Elmwood Care Home on schedule. Elaine buzzes me in. Again, she appears surprised to see me.

"Did you speak to Nurse Clifford?" she asks.

"No."

"You really must."

"Why?"

"I, um … let me call her down. One minute."

She snatches up a phone and prods three numbers on the keypad.

"Diane, it's Elaine. Simon Armstrong is here."

After four seconds of silence, she hangs up.

"She'll be down in a tick."

"I don't want to talk to Nurse Clifford. I want a visitor's pass, please."

"I'm afraid I can't issue one."

"Why not?"

"Because … oh, here she is."

My question remains unanswered as Nurse Clifford strides over to the reception desk.

"Are you okay, Simon?"

"Yes."

"Can we go up to my office for a chat, please?"

"What about?"

"Primarily, about you being here."

"I've already suffered far too many chats today. Can it wait?"

"No, it most definitely cannot."

I turn back to Elaine. She is distracted by her pen rather than preparing a visitor's card.

"Simon?"

"Very well."

With much reluctance, I follow Nurse Clifton up to her office. Unlike my last visit, she sits behind her desk and insists I sit in a chair opposite.

"How are you doing?" she asks. "It must be difficult for you."

"Nothing is difficult for me."

"But you've just lost your mum. How do you feel about that?"

"I don't know. I haven't given it much thought."

"It's not typically a thought process, Simon. I was referring to your emotional state."

"My emotions are under control."

"Are you sure?"

"Yes."

"Then, why are you here?"

"Because it's two o'clock."

Nurse Clifford closes her eyes a second longer than a blink.

"I know you're keen on maintaining routines, but this is one you'll have to break. You can't keep dropping by."

"Why not?"

"Because … because your mum has gone. There's no reason for you to be here."

"Do I need a reason?"

"Yes, you do. If the management found out we were letting you in for no valid reason, we'd be in deep trouble. Do you understand?"

"It's not ideal, but I could stand outside the lounge window. I wouldn't be inside the building, so there would be no reason for anyone to get in trouble, would there?"

Her mouth opens, but no words follow.

"If there's nothing else, I'll be on my way."

"No, wait."

I remain in my seat, poised to depart.

"I'm going to ask you a question, Simon, and if you don't feel comfortable answering, just tell me. Okay?"

"Okay."

"When was the last time you saw a doctor?"

"I don't recall ever seeing a doctor. I keep myself in peak physical condition."

"Are you saying you've never seen a doctor, or you just can't remember?"

"Why are you asking? Do I look ill?"

"No, not physically."

"So?"

"There are lots of illnesses that don't have outward symptoms, especially when it comes to the mind."

"You think my brain is ill?"

"I'm not saying that, no, and I'm not qualified to diagnose mental health issues. However, I am worried you're not displaying any of the typical behaviours associated with grief. Coupled with your need to keep visiting Elmwood, I think you might benefit from a session or two with a bereavement counsellor."

I consider her suggestion.

"What benefit would I derive from such a meeting?"

"A counsellor can help you process your feelings. Even if you think you're coping, chances are you're just suppressing your emotions, and that isn't healthy."

"I am coping."

"But are you? Are you *really*?"

"I do not wish to meet with a bereavement counsellor."

"Alright," she says in a huffy tone. "But you should talk to your doctor."

"Why are you so obsessed I seek medical help?"

"Because I worry about you, Simon … we all do."

"Your worry is misplaced. I have my emotions under control, thank you."

"Today, maybe, but what happens when you can't control them, eh? You're not a robot — you're a human being, and at some point, you'll need to confront your feelings."

Her statement catches me off guard.

"Can you repeat what you just said?"

"You're not a robot, and you need to confront your feelings."

"You also said I'm a human being."

"Well, yes."

"How can you tell?"

"Eh? How can I tell what?"

"That I'm human."

"I'm a nurse, not a vet, so I guess that's as good a qualifier as any."

"You are qualified to determine I am human?"

"Err, you've lost me. Is that a serious question?"

"Yes. Would a medical practitioner, like you, be able to determine my origins?"

"Are we talking biologically or psychologically?"

"Both."

"Um, I think you'd be better off asking your doctor. In fact, if you're not willing to see a bereavement counsellor, I'd strongly advise you book an appointment with your doctor as soon as possible."

"And they will be able to determine my origins?"

"Err, yes."

"Interesting."

I consider the nurse's revelation. Unsurprisingly, she feels compelled to fill the silence.

"There's nothing to worry about. Lots of people see their doctor because they need a bit of help."

"Can they be trusted?"

"One-hundred per cent. Anything you tell a doctor will be treated in complete confidence."

"Anything?"

"We're all morally obligated to maintain patient confidentiality. Say, for example, you were married to a friend of mine, and I had to treat you for a sexually transmitted infection you picked up on a one-night stand; I couldn't tell your wife."

"But you would want to?"

"Of course, but if I did, it'd be the end of my career."

"Your advice is duly noted."

"You'll book an appointment with your doctor, then?"

"Possibly. I need to consider the ramifications."

"You do that, and we're clear on the situation with you turning up here every day?"

"I understand I am not allowed to access the building."

"Yes, but you really shouldn't be anywhere on the premises, and I don't think it would be a good idea to stand at the lounge window. You'll scare the residents."

"What about the gates?"

"What about them?"

"If I stand outside the gates, I'm not on the premises at all."

"I … um, true. Why would you, though?"

I get to my feet.

"Goodbye, Nurse Clifford."

"Wait … will you let me know how you get on with your doctor?"

"How would I do that if I'm not allowed on the premises?"

"Call me."

She grabs a pen from a pot and scribbles a number on a piece of paper.

"Here. This goes way beyond my job description, but if you need any help or you just want to talk, please call me."

I take the scrap of paper and tuck it into my pocket.

"Thank you."

"And, one other thing, Simon. When are you going to collect your mum's things?"

"What things?"

"Her clothes and personal possessions."

"Do I have to collect them? They're of no use to me."

"Yes, you do."

"Can you contact Mother's friend, Father Paul? He has a motor car, and I do not."

"Okay. What's his number?"

After furnishing Nurse Clifford with the requested number, I depart before she can recommence her lecture. I make my way back down the stairs and straight through the reception area to the exit. Then, for twenty-three minutes, I stand at the gates and count the vehicles arriving and departing. There are four more arrivals than there are departures. At 2:30 pm, I begin the journey back to Bulford Hill.

I arrive home and glance at my watch as I open the front door. Why did the journey take two minutes longer than usual? I hurry through to the kitchen and check the clock. It confirms my wristwatch is accurate — further evidence of bodily deterioration, perhaps.

Merle pokes his head through the cat flap. I sit down and invite him onto my lap. He accepts the invitation.

"This has not been a good day, Merle," I say, stroking the fur on his head. "Between you and me, my concerns are mounting."

I close my eyes and focus on his purring.

"This morning, I discovered The Shepherd is a human and a dysfunctional one at that. He is not who I thought he was, and I honestly don't know where I go from here."

No suggestions are forthcoming, but Merle's presence is enough to subdue the chaos in my head. I sense sleep approaching, and I'm too weak to fight it.

"So tired, Merle."

I'm within seconds of slipping away when I sit up with such a start, Merle raises his objection by digging his claws into my thigh. The cause is a mobile telephone, trilling away in my pocket. I scramble to answer it.

"Hello."

"Hi, Simon?"

"Yes."

"It's Rosie."

"Yes … right."

"Are you okay? You sound a bit dazed."

"I, err … yes, I'm fine."

"I was just wondering how you're doing and if you fancied some company later? No drama if you don't."

With no time to think, I have a binary decision to make. My instinct is to say no, but I cannot deny Rosie's last visit proved a welcome distraction. Perhaps today, more than before, I need distracting.

"Yes."

"Yes, you do want some company?"

"Yes. I would like to watch another science-fiction movie."

"Sure. Shall I come over at seven?"

"Seven is good. Should I prepare refreshments?"

"I'll, um, bring popcorn."

"Right. I will see you at seven o'clock."

"Yes, you will. Bye, Simon."

She ends the call.

"Did you hear that, Merle? That friendly female human is coming over again."

Still irked by his lap slumber being disturbed, he slinks off to the lounge. I assume he's off for a nap, which isn't such a terrible idea, come to think of it. To quote my late mother, I could do with resting my eyelids for an hour. Heavy-legged, I trudge up to my bedroom and set the alarm clock for 4:30 pm. I want to collapse on the bed, but I also want to sit down in front of my computer.

There is no logic in what I feel compelled to do, but I do it anyway.

Message 2817

Priority Level 1 | Encrypted @ 15:22

From: Epsilon30

To: TheShepherd82

Message Begins ...

Why did you lie to me? I thought you were my friend.

...

System Message ...

COMMUNICATION REJECTED - No such user as TheShepherd82

Chapter 26

After one hour of sleep and a meal, I would like to say I feel human again, but such a statement would surely be inappropriate? A week ago, I'd have scoffed at the notion I am human, but I cannot deny the revelations about The Shepherd and Father Paul's interference may have sewn a few doubts.

I need to restore certainty.

Now, with my energy levels at optimum and forty-one minutes at my disposal before Rosie arrives, there is time to weigh up Nurse Clifton's suggestion I see a doctor. Can a certified medical professional determine my alien origins, and if so, is there a risk they might reveal my identity to the greater world? Conversely, what is the risk if I do nothing? My existence has become increasingly destabilised of late, and I cannot let that continue. A doctor determining my true origins would provide a sense of stability, a metaphoric anchor.

I am torn, and the only way to tip the decision one way or another is to garner facts.

The fact-finding process begins with an internet search on patient confidentiality. The first link is for the General Medical Council: the body that governs medical practitioners in the United Kingdom. The page lists six links to guidance notes: situations where there might be grounds to breach patient confidentiality. Unsurprisingly, none of the situations specifically relate to the discovery of an alien being. I read each set of notes twice.

Am I suffering from a communicable disease? No.

Is my condition relevant to employment, insurance, or similar? No.

Am I suffering from a condition that might affect my ability to drive? No.

Do I have a knife or gunshot wound? No, but if I did, it seems unlikely I'd be browsing the internet whilst bleeding to death.

The final two sets of notes relate to criticism in the media, which isn't relevant, and disclosure for education and training purposes, which is worthy of further investigation. I click through to the relevant page of notes to find a reassuring statement at the top: *you'll require a patient's explicit consent.*

I sit back in my chair. As Nurse Clifton suggested, it seems medical practitioners are bound by strict rules regarding patient confidentiality, and not one of their permitted reasons for breaching those rules applies to my circumstance. And, even if a doctor did feel inclined to break the rules, I'm certain *They* would intervene.

Facts gathered and assessed, I conclude the potential benefits of visiting a doctor outweigh the risks.

That settled, there is one other issue to surmount. Nurse Clifford said I should see *my* doctor, but I don't have a doctor, nor do I know how I get one. Whenever Mother was unwell, which wasn't often until she became seriously ill, she would visit a practice in Bulford Road. Being it's the nearest doctor's surgery, logic dictates it's the first place I should visit to find my doctor. I will telephone them in the morning after I return from Amesbury.

With a plan in place, I use the remaining time to vacuum the carpets and shower.

The doorbell rings at 7:01 pm.

I cease stroking Merle in the kitchen and hurry along the hallway to the door. Opening it, Rosie once again is dressed in attire most different from her work uniform: denim jeans which look so tight they must be the wrong size, and an off-white pullover.

"Good evening, Rosie."

"Hey, Simon."

There is perhaps a sombre undercurrent to her tone — respect for Mother's passing, presumably.

"Please, enter."

I turn ninety degrees and press my shoulder blades against the hallway wall, allowing Rosie to enter unimpeded. She does so and then slips off her coat.

"Would you like me to store that?"

"Please."

I invite her into the kitchen, and Merle keeps her entertained while I hang the coat in the understairs cupboard. When I return to the kitchen, I'm met by silence, and for the first time in my life, I feel compelled to fill it.

"Are you … um, have you had an agreeable day?"

"Not bad, thanks. How are you doing, or is that a dumb question?"

"I have suffered the most disagreeable of days."

"Oh dear," she responds, followed by a heavy sigh.

"My apologies. I know it is customary to reply with a token platitude. I don't know why I didn't."

"Do you want to talk about your disagreeable day?"

"I don't know."

She steps across the kitchen and comes to a stop one metre away.

"Tell you what, why don't we watch the movie and see how you feel afterwards. If you're in the mood to talk, we can. If not, we can chat about the movie. Does that sound like a plan?"

"Yes, it does. Would you like refreshments before we begin?"

"I'd love a cup of tea if you're offering."

"That can be arranged."

I'm about to turn and fill the kettle, but I'd rather the silence didn't return.

"Will you tell me about your day?" I ask.

"I can, but it wasn't exactly exciting."

"I don't mind. Please."

As Rosie enthusiastically regales a tale about a mix-up with a neighbour's parcel delivery, I prepare the cups. The situation, I soon realise, is not too dissimilar to when Mother was here and in good health. While preparing dinner, she would chatter incessantly about her day while I listened, rarely ever passing comment. The imbalance suited us both, and perhaps that's why I'm now content with my part in this one-sided conversation, the sense of familiarity like stroking Merle's fur.

"And then," she continued. "I received a call from Elaine, asking if I'd work this evening."

"It is your evening off-duty, is it not?"

"Yeah, but because I'm the new girl, they think I'll drop everything whenever they ask me to work extra hours. If you say yes all the time, they'll forever take the piss."

"Do you not want to work all the time?"

"I love the job but not so much I'm willing to give up my social life … not that I have much of a social life."

"Why not? Are you anti-social?"

"Not really, but I'm new to the area, and I find it hard making new friends. I have trust issues."

"People are untrustworthy, on the whole. Mother used to say trust is like money: it can only be earned with toil and time."

"That's so true."

I pass Rosie her cup of tea. She takes it and smiles.

"Speaking of your mother, did you want to talk about what happened yesterday at Elmwood?"

"What happened yesterday, specifically?"

"As I said, I overheard Elaine talking to Nurse Clifford."

"If you're referring to my visit, I returned to Elmwood Care Home this afternoon, and Nurse Clifford informed me I am no longer allowed on the premises."

"Shit. Really?"

"She said I have no reason to be there."

"Forgive me for saying, but she does have a point. Why did you go back?"

I do not want to answer Rosie's question.

"Shall we watch the movie?" I suggest.

"Sure."

We retire to the lounge with a bowl of popcorn.

"So, do you fancy the next Star Trek Movie? I've brought *The Wrath of Khan* along."

"I would like to watch it, yes."

She hands over the DVD case. One minute later, we are sitting on the sofa with the bowl between us. The opening credits begin.

"Oh, I nearly forgot," Rosie then says while rummaging in her handbag. "Would you like to try an M&M?"

"What is an M&M?"

"Chocolate in a crispy shell. You do like chocolate, right?"

"I can't remember. It has been many years since I last consumed it."

"Wow! Why?"

"Because it is unhealthy."

"Newsflash, Simon. So is popcorn, but you tucked into that last time."

She makes a valid point. I had no intention of eating any of the popcorn, but Rosie insisted, and in my role as host, I felt compelled to concede. I cannot deny the popcorn was moreish.

"Go on. One won't hurt you."

Hesitantly, I pluck a red M&M from the bowl and drop it into my mouth.

"It tastes of nothing but sugar."

"Bite it."

I crunch down on the shell, and it shatters. The soft chocolate inside melts on contact with my tongue, triggering a long-forgotten memory.

"Well?" Rosie urges.

"Coins."

"Coins?"

"Yes, at Christmas. When I was a child, Mother would give me a bag of chocolate coins on Christmas Eve."

"Are you telling me you haven't eaten chocolate since you were a child?"

"I think so. I … don't remember. My father forbade me from eating confectionery, but he agreed on an exception at Christmas."

"You dad sounds like a bit of a tyrant."

"I would rather not talk about him."

"Sorry. I'll shut up now."

True to her word, Rosie remains quiet for one hour and fifty-two minutes until the movie comes to an end. I would have preferred it to be longer.

"What did you think?" Rosie asks.

"It was most enjoyable."

"You sound surprised."

"A … an acquaintance always spoke unfavourably about science-fiction movies, and I believed him."

"And now?"

"Referring to our earlier conversation, I gave my trust to someone who had not earned it. He was wrong, and I was wrong to believe him."

"Is that something you want to talk about? I can hear the bitterness in your voice."

"No, I do not."

"Fair enough," she responds. "I'm glad you enjoyed the movie, though. It was one of my granddad's favourites … he loved a good sci-fi movie. You know, he actually asked for the Star Wars theme to be played at his funeral, the crazy old sod."

"I don't know what music Mother requested for her funeral, but I doubt it'll be from a movie."

"Oh, God," she gasps. "Me and my big mouth. I'm so sorry, Simon."

"Why are you apologising?"

"Insensitive timing. I should have stopped to think."

"It matters not to me. Helen Armstrong is dead and skirting around that truth benefits no one."

My remark triggers a quizzical stare.

"You are allowed to feel hurt, Simon. She was your mum."

"Legally, but not biologically."

"You're adopted?"

Rather than respond verbally, I nod. It is probably because my mind is busy trying to understand how I became embroiled in this topic of conversation. I had no good reason to disclose my adoption to Rosie, any more than I've ever had reason to disclose it to any human.

"Do you know anything about your birth parents?" she asks. "But, please tell me to mind my own business if I'm overstepping the mark."

Is there any harm in answering her question? Unlikely.

"I recently discovered I was left in the Accident and Emergency department of a hospital in Epsom, Surrey. The authorities have no record of my biological parents."

As she did in the reception area of Elmwood Care Home, Rosie reaches over and places her hand on my arm.

"How long have you known that you were adopted?" she asks.

"Since I was sixteen."

Rosie doesn't respond immediately, but when she does, it's with another question.

"Aren't you the teeniest bit curious who left you there?"

"Curious, yes, but there is no way of knowing. The police investigated at the time but to no avail."

"Have you checked The Adoption Contact Register?"

"The what?"

She adjusts her position on the sofa, so she's seated cross-legged, facing me.

"It's like a database you can join if you're an adopted adult or you gave a child up for adoption. If both parties sign-up, they act as an intermediary to put you in touch with one another. A guy I used to work with found his birth mother that way."

"I doubt those responsible for my abandonment are signed-up."

"They might be."

"I highly doubt *They* are."

"You say that with some certainty, Simon, as if you know."

Not that I would willingly share my concerns with Rosie, but my reserves of certainty are now close to depleted.

"I was left at that hospital," I reply. "And relative to my parentage, that is all the certainty I have or require."

"Have you never discussed this with your adoptive parents?"

"I tried, but all conversation relating to my adoption upset Mother."

"I can understand that. What I can't understand is the depth of desperation a mother must be at to abandon their baby."

"Desperation may not have been their motive."

"Maybe not, but it's heart-breaking whichever way you look at it."

"I've never understood the term, heart-breaking. You cannot break a heart."

"I take it you've never had yours broken? If you did, you'd think differently — it literally does feel like your heart is breaking into pieces."

"You have experienced it?"

"Twice. I was a teenager the first time, and I found out my boyfriend had slept with my best pal."

"Why would that be heart-breaking?"

Rosie's eyebrows elevate.

"They slept together, Simon."

"Merle occasionally sleeps at the end of my bed. I wouldn't say I found it emotionally challenging."

"No, I mean they had sex together."

"And a partner indulging in intercourse with a third party is unacceptable, correct?"

"Too bloody right it is."

"Yet most other mammals have no such qualms about infidelity. Before Merle, we owned another cat called Hank, and he impregnated many female cats in the neighbourhood — sometimes on consecutive nights. Mother had him castrated in the end."

Rosie reacts to my statement with a chuckle.

"You crack me up; you know that?"

"It really isn't a laughing matter. Hank had to wear a plastic cone for a week, and he was most displeased about it."

My observation fuels Rosie's mirth.

"The cone of shame," she splutters, her chuckles developing into a full-blown fit of laughter. "Poor Hank."

Rarely does my human body surprise me these days. After puberty, development stabilised, and the only bodily issue still unresolved involves randomly waking with an erect penis. I do not understand why. Here and now, it is not an erect penis I'm surprised by, but a series of uncontrollable convulsions emanating from my stomach.

The cause is Rosie's laughter. Inexplicably, it appears contagious.

"Stop it," I gasp. "I cannot breathe."

My plight only fuels Rosie's hysterics, and every time I try to regain composure, she looks at me, and the cycle begins again

— it is as if we are reinfecting one another on a constant loop. Not even the ache in my stomach or the sting in my eyes is enough to break the cycle.

"I'm going to piss my knickers in a minute," she cries. "Can I use the loo?"

"No," I respond. Why, I do not know, but it sets off another cycle of laughter.

"Oh, God," Rosie finally shrieks. "I'm going to the loo."

She hurries off, and I'm finally able to wipe the tears from my eyes and calm the convulsions. On paper, the symptoms of laughter have always struck me as profoundly unappealing. However, despite the discomfort, the overall sensation is positive. It is also, perhaps, welcome.

Rosie returns a minute later.

"I'm so sorry," she says. "I don't know what came over me. I haven't laughed like that in ages."

"I have never laughed like that at all."

"Are you kidding me?"

"No. I have smiled and occasionally sniggered, but I have never lost control."

"I think we both needed a good laugh, don't you?"

"I cannot deny it had a positive effect, although it is disconcerting not being able to control your own body, don't you find?"

"Sometimes it's good just to let loose, go a bit crazy. We all need it from time to time."

"Do we?"

"Of course, but it probably wasn't the most appropriate time to lose it. I've no idea how we went from discussing your adoption to your dead cat's bollocks."

I avoid eye contact, but on this occasion, it's not for the usual reason.

"Please … don't … mention … Hank's …"

I can't finish the sentence as another convulsion strikes. I catch Rosie's eye. The cycle begins again.

Chapter 27

I am on the bus to Amesbury. No one is laughing, and no one is smiling — a contrast to my evening with Rosie yesterday.

She stayed until 10:00 pm, and by 10:02 pm, I concluded laughter is the most peculiar condition. It seems just as involuntary as a cough or a sneeze or a yawn, and yet it serves no obvious physiological function. That isn't to say laughter serves no purpose because without it, most of my day yesterday would have been marred by negativity.

How today unfolds remains to be seen. It could prove decimating if … no, I simply cannot consider any alternative to the truth I've held for so long.

The bus comes to a stop, and I disembark, thanking the driver for the near-punctual service. There is a slight mist of rain in the air this morning, so I am wearing full waterproof clothing. The jacket and trousers are effective, but they also make the most irritating noise as I walk, like the rustling of crisp packets. The waterproof cap makes no noise.

Once I arrive at Mr Choudhary's former business premises, I sit on the wall and remove the notepad and Thermos flask from my satchel. At precisely 8:00 am, the vehicle tallying begins. The air temperature feels close to single digits, and I am grateful for the warming tea.

After the first hour, I use a break in the traffic to compare the numbers to Monday's. The difference is marginal, but I still have two hours of data collection to complete, so that may change.

"Oi!" a male voice yells, somewhere behind me.

The interruption is unwelcome. I ignore it.

"I'm talking to you, mate."

The voice is accompanied by heavy footsteps. Still, I remain focused on my task until a male steps around the wall and approaches. Tall, with an angular face and stubbled chin, he stops two metres away and folds his arms.

"Did you not hear me?"

"Yes," I reply, keeping my eyes on the road.

"Why didn't you answer?"

"I'm busy."

"Busy doing what, exactly?"

"I am trying to collect traffic data, but your presence is a distraction."

"You're counting cars? For who?"

"For my own purpose."

"You're on my property."

"You own this wall?"

"That's right."

"Are you the person who purchased Mr Choudhary's business?"

"I am, as it happens. How do you know?"

"I used to work for Mr Choudhary, in his office. Data entry."

"Is your name Simon?"

"Correct."

"Ahh, right," he responds, his mouth curved into a sneer. "You're the number-crunching weirdo he tried to lumber me with."

I click the pen. One click, nib out. One click, nib in. I count each click: ten, eleven, twelve.

"Are you gonna jog on, or are you just gonna sit there clicking your pen like an idiot?"

"I would rather you leave me alone."

"This is my land and my wall, and I don't want you hanging around out here, making my staff uncomfortable. So, piss off and don't come back."

One click, nib out. One click, nib in. The male takes a step forward.

"Did you hear me?"

"Yes."

I stand up and take four steps to my left, then two steps backwards until I'm on the pavement, on the other side of the low wall.

"I am no longer on your property."

The male then mirrors my steps until he is standing directly in front of me. Without warning, he suddenly snatches the notebook from my hand. My reactions are dulled by the cold, so I can only watch as he hurls the notebook into the road, directly into the path of an oncoming bus.

"Fetch, retard," he sneers.

The cruel act and unkind words ignite my internal furnace.

As the heat begins to build, I cannot move, nor can I shift my eyes from his face. There is familiarity in his facial features: the twisted smile, the cold eyes, and stained teeth. This male is not Dylan Metcalfe, but his behaviour is no different. It triggers a return of the same negative emotions I have tried hard to forget.

I want to kill the male, but he scuttles away and jumps into a black car before I can break my emotional paralysis. I stand inert and watch as he pulls away from the rear of the building, waving his hand in a crude gesture as he passes. With the engine revving hard, I watch the car tear up the road. The wake catches my notebook, causing it to tumble and spin across the tarmac until it finally settles in the gutter, the pages flapping like the wings of a dying bird.

I wait for a break in the traffic and cross the road to retrieve the notebook. As I feared, it is ruined – there will be no more tallying today. I stand for a moment and appraise my options. The rain has moved from a mist to a steady downpour, and I am cold.

One hour and forty-four minutes ahead of schedule, I decide to return home.

Despite listening to static on the bus journey back to Durrington, I cannot expunge the meeting with the odious male from my thoughts. His behaviour only reinforces my lowly opinion of humans, and their ability to plumb the depths of incivility never ceases to amaze me. With Mother now gone, I feel more exposed to that incivility than ever, and the thought of spending the rest of my days on this planet is too grotesque even to consider.

My day began with such positivity, but already it is following the same downward spiral as yesterday. Alas, there will be no meeting with Rosie later to offset the negativity, so I am now reliant on a positive outcome after contacting the doctor's surgery. This sense of ill-feeling must be addressed before it crushes my alien spirit. But, if Mother's mantra is to be believed, good luck always follows bad. Saying that, I don't recall there being much in the way of good luck after her dementia diagnosis.

Arriving home, I venture into the kitchen to put the kettle on just as Merle comes crashing through the cat flap. He slides to a halt in the centre of the kitchen and glares intently back at the still-swinging flap.

"Problem with a fellow feline?" I enquire.

His focus remains fixed on the door.

"What is troubling you?"

I approach the window which overlooks the rear garden. There, at the far end, lurking in Mother's prized Photinia bush, stands a mangy-looking fox. I rap my knuckle on the glass, and it disappears.

"He is gone now," I confirm, squatting down in front of Merle. "But rest assured I'll be on close guard should he return. I know how much you despise foxes."

Settled by my words, Merle pads over and rubs his forehead against my knee. He then realises my trousers are still splattered with raindrops and quickly retreats. He does not like water unless he's lapping it from the kitchen tap.

With Merle settled, I hurry upstairs, strip off the waterproofs, and hang them in the airing cupboard to dry. It is a relief to move without a constant rustle. In my bedroom, I use a search engine to confirm the telephone number for the doctor's surgery. I then call it.

It rings and rings. Losing patience, I begin watching the second hand on my alarm clock as it journeys around the face. It makes one entire revolution before my call is answered.

"Good morning, Avon Valley Practice."

"Hello. I wish to see a doctor."

"No problem. Can I take your name, address, and date of birth, please?"

I quote the requested information. The sound of a tapping keyboard follows.

"Have you registered with us before, Mr Armstrong?"

"No. I didn't know I had to be registered."

"Don't worry. I can register you now if you have five minutes."

The female then asks many questions, using all but nineteen seconds of the predicted five minutes.

"So, I can see a doctor now?" I ask.

"It's your lucky day. We were fully booked today but I've just had a cancellation for this afternoon at four with Dr Jarvis. Alternatively, you can see Dr Raham tomorrow morning at eleven. Which would you prefer?"

"Which doctor is better qualified?"

"They're both fully qualified, experienced doctors, Mr Armstrong. It doesn't matter which one you see."

"In which case, I will see Dr Jarvis at four."

More key tapping ensues.

"That's all booked for you. We'll see you at four o'clock this afternoon."

I end the call and sit back in the chair. In less than five hours, I will be visiting a doctor for the first time. That knowledge sets off a disagreeable jittering sensation in my stomach, not dissimilar to how I felt in the minutes before my supposed meeting with The Shepherd. I do not like it.

If I'm to banish the jittering, I need to keep busy. I could spend a few hours poring over the notes I compiled for the meeting that never happened. Those notes, I fear, might only serve to enhance my stress levels. I have researched so much and concluded so little. What is to be gained by checking the same information over and over again? As Albert Einstein said: the definition of insanity is doing the same thing over and over and expecting different results. Einstein was a wise human, and insanity is not a place I wish to visit.

My options exhausted, the only remaining method of distraction is manual work. I need to be doing because doing stops the thinking. With that, a deep clean of the kitchen feels appropriate.

I visit the understairs cupboard for the mop and bucket and waste twenty-one seconds inhaling the still present scent from Rosie's coat. I don't know why but it eases the jitters.

After a break for lunch, I complete the kitchen clean and take a shower. The rain is still present, so I don my waterproofs and make my way to Elmwood Care Home. On arrival, I take up position by the front gates, careful not to step across the boundary line, and begin tracking vehicle movements in and out of the car park. There are so few I don't require a notebook, which is just as well as the rain is unforgiving for the entire thirty-minute duration of my stay.

Despite the rain, I decide to take a longer route home simply to kill time. Walking helps to quieten the nagging doubts, but I feel less inclined to visit the doctor with every passing minute. I know I must.

By the time I arrive back at Bulford Hill, the rain has ceased, and the clouds have shifted to reveal patches of bright blue sky. Some humans would consider the change of weather a good omen. I do not.

Twenty-seven minutes after opening the front door, I close it again and depart for the doctor's practice.

I arrive six minutes later with almost no recollection of the journey. Continuing on auto-pilot, I enter the building and approach the reception desk.

"Simon Armstrong," I say to the female smiling up at me. "For my four o'clock appointment."

There's a slight husk in my voice which indicates a potential plumbing issue with this human body — dry mouth, excessively moist palms.

"Dr Jarvis will see you soon," the receptionist says. "Take a seat, and we'll call you when he's free."

I would rather not sit down. Mother says I tend to fidget when I'm out of my comfort zone.

"Mother *said*," I mumble.

"Pardon?"

"Um, nothing."

I hurry away from the reception desk and secure a five-metre stretch of floor to pace. 4:00 pm arrives, but there is no call. I allow a minute to pass, but still, there's no call. The lack of punctuality stokes my agitation. After five minutes, I am close to leaving when finally, the receptionist calls my name. I approach the desk and seek directions to the doctor's room.

"It's just through that archway," she says, pointing over my shoulder. "Second door on the left."

I turn and check the route. The exit is four metres to the right of the archway.

Putting one foot in front of the other, I slowly cross the chequered carpet tiles towards the far side of the waiting area. With only three metres of carpet to cover, I must decide: left through the archway or right to the exit.

One metre remaining, I reach a decision.

Chapter 28

As I knock on the second door on the left, I note the odour in the corridor is similar to that in Elmwood Care Home, albeit there is no underlying aroma of boiled vegetables here. I suppose the two buildings serve a similar function: the maintenance of broken humans.

"Come in," a stern male voice orders.

I push open the door. The room is smaller than I imagined.

"Simon Armstrong?"

"Yes."

"I'm Dr Jarvis. Come take a seat."

In a chair, the doctor is also smaller than I imagined and older. His hair is neatly cut and shaded like storm clouds; his face lined with deep grooves. A desk abuts the right-hand wall, and the chair I'm expected to take is positioned to the right. I sit down, but the doctor appears preoccupied with his computer monitor.

"And what brings you here today?"

"I require an assessment to see if there are any anomalies with this body."

"You mean a check-up?"

"Yes, I suppose."

"Is there any reason you need a check-up? Any specific health concerns?"

"No, and no."

"Basically, you just want an MOT?" he chirps.

"A what?"

"It's an annual test on a car where all the vital components are checked to ensure they're functioning properly. That's pretty much what we do in a check-up — we ensure your body is functioning as it should."

"And this will detect anomalies?"

"We take a sample of blood to test for anything serious. Are you sure there's nothing you need to tell me about?"

"Quite sure."

"If there is, there's no reason to feel embarrassed or ashamed. Whatever the problem. I promise you I've seen it all before."

"To the best of my knowledge, I am in fine health."

"But, you're in a doctor's surgery."

"My origins are a concern."

"Your origins? Are you referring to a history of health issues in your family … like heart disease?"

"I don't know. I've never met any member of my biological family."

"Um, can you expand on that?"

"I was adopted."

"Right, I see."

His brow furrows as he turns back to the computer monitor.

"Well, seeing as you've just turned thirty, and your biological family's medical history is unknown, I guess a quick check-up is probably a good idea."

Finally, the doctor is in agreement.

"Let's start by taking your blood pressure. Can you roll up your sleeve, please?"

My discomfort level increases. I knew an examination would involve physical contact with a human, but as necessary as the contact is, it is no less welcome. As I'm prodded and poked, and various devices are attached to my body, I count the eyelets in my shoes: twelve on the left, twelve on the right. There is little in the way of conversation besides several lifestyle questions, which I answer succinctly.

"Nearly done," the doctor then announces. "I just need to take a blood sample."

He gets up, roots around in a drawer, and returns with a needle.

"You might feel a small prick."

I turn my head as he draws the needle towards my upper arm. The promised prick soon follows. It hurts but only for a second.

"All done."

I turn back as the doctor dabs my arm with a blob of cotton wool.

"You might want to hold it in place for a minute," he suggests. "Until the blood clots."

He returns to his chair and clicks the mouse three times.

"Is the examination complete?" I enquire.

"It is."

"What are you doing?"

"I'm inputting the details to your medical record."

"Those details are confidential?"

"Yes, completely."

His tone is level, verging on disinterested.

"Did you find any anomalies?"

"None at all. You're in fine fettle, Simon."

"What is fine fettle?"

He taps the keyboard five times before answering.

"Physically, you're one of the healthiest patients I've seen in a long, long time."

"I am a rare specimen?"

"Kind of," he replies. "And by that, I mean all your metrics are exactly where they should be. You're perfectly healthy, but most people I see are not, which is why they come to see me, obviously."

"I don't understand."

He stops typing and turns to face me.

"Put simply, you're a model human in terms of your body composition, blood pressure, heart rate, and repository response.

And, I'd be amazed if we find anything untoward in your blood sample."

"Are you saying I am … not abnormal?"

"No, Simon. You're a perfectly normal, healthy young man. You've absolutely nothing to worry about."

He smiles and then turns his head back towards the monitor. As he strikes the keys, I replay his words in my head. He must be mistaken, or perhaps his advanced years have compromised his abilities.

"I am not like other humans," I remark. "Surely you can tell that from your tests?"

"No, you're not like most humans," he says in a jovial tone. "I wish all my other patients took such good care of themselves."

"You misunderstand. That's not …"

"Sorry," he interjects, his brow now bearing a remarkably deep furrow. "Bear with me a second."

The doctor leans forward and runs his forefinger vertically across the monitor, his right hand clasped on the mouse. Silent seconds pass. I begin a count in my head but when I pass fifteen, the pressure becomes too much.

"What is it?" I question. "Have you found an anomaly?"

"Um, in a manner of speaking, yes."

"What? Tell me."

"Do you remember the last time you visited a doctor?"

"I don't recall ever visiting a doctor."

"Ever?"

"No."

"How strange."

He clicks the mouse again.

"How long have you lived in Durrington, Simon?"

"Approximately twenty years."

"And before that?"

"We lived in Surbiton, in Surrey."

"That makes sense but, to be clear, you've no recollection of visiting a doctor in all the time you've lived here?"

"No."

"Hmm, we might have a problem, then."

"What kind of problem?"

He spins his chair around.

"We seem to be missing some of your medical records. There's a list of entries covering your early childhood, but you were only ten on the date of the last entry, and there's nothing from your time in Durrington."

"I was ten years of age when we moved here. Patently, I was a healthy child and never required medical attention."

"What about your booster vaccinations?"

"My what?"

"The booster for tetanus, diphtheria and polio. It's administered to children in secondary school."

"I never attended secondary school. After we moved here, Mother took responsibility for my education."

"Even so, you should have still received that booster jab, and there should be a record of it. Do you remember having the jab, perhaps fifteen or sixteen years ago?"

"No."

"This is a puzzle," he says, sitting back in his chair and pressing his fingers together.

"Perhaps my mother forgot about the booster vaccination."

"Possibly, but there should still be entries after the last one from Surbiton."

"Why?"

"You really don't know?"

"If I did, I wouldn't have asked."

"Please try and remain calm. I only want to be sure because, in that last appointment, your doctor referred you to a specialist. Unless there's been an admin error with your records, not only have you missed a critical vaccination booster, but your parents neglected to follow-up on that referral."

"I was referred to a specialist, you say?"

"Yes."

My heart rate increases. Has the doctor finally found the anomaly which would prove my true origins?

"What kind of specialist?"

"Behavioural."

His reply is not what I expected.

"Are you certain that's what it says? Could this be another admin error?"

"I don't see why it would be."

Doctor Jarvis leans forward and stares at the monitor again.

"The notes state you were examined by a Dr Caron McKinlay, in Surbiton, and she referred you to a behavioural specialist. It's all here in black and white pixels."

"Why would I need to see a behavioural specialist?"

"It doesn't specifically say. Only that you were involved in an incident and the school deemed your behaviour a cause for concern."

"I … what incident?"

"I'm sorry, Simon. There's nothing else here."

"I did not see this specialist?"

"There's no follow-up note to suggest you did, but you'll have to ask your parents if they can remember what happened."

"They're dead. Father fourteen years ago and Mother last week."

"You've only just lost your mother?" the doctor confirms.

"That is correct. Your colleague, Dr Nash, diagnosed her dementia early last year. Don't you talk to one another?"

"Not about patients, no. I'm sorry for your loss."

"I don't care about platitudes, but I do care about why I was referred to a behavioural specialist. At the moment, that is my primary concern."

The doctor adjusts his position in an attempt to make direct eye contact.

"Most children experience behavioural issues of some kind, Simon, and unless you're still exhibiting such issues, I really wouldn't worry too much."

"I am worrying. What if my behaviour is still … unusual?"

"In what way unusual?"

"Unlike other humans."

"In my experience, there's no such thing as typical behaviour. Humans are complex animals, and I've yet to meet two the same."

"Are you … I eat the same food at the same time every day."

"Lots of people do that."

"They do?"

"Yes. Anything else?"

"I … I live by routines."

"Again, that's not uncommon. On the whole, people prefer the structure of routines to the chaotic alternative."

"But, I hate humans. I detest being near them and their mindless chatter, and … I hate everything about them."

"Do you *honestly* hate everything about every person you know?"

The doctor's question, and indeed his voice, carry enough gravity I take a moment to consider it thoroughly. Of all the humans in my life, how many do I really *hate*? I tolerate a few, dislike a couple, and, if I'm entirely honest, I have enjoyed spending time with one or two. Then, there is Mother — I never did, nor ever could, hate her.

"I concede I don't hate every human."

"There you are, then. Any other concerns about your mental wellbeing?"

"I don't know what would constitute concern."

"Do you ever have thoughts about harming yourself?"

"No."

"Any problems with excessive alcohol consumption, or drug use, or any other form of addiction?"

"Absolutely not."

"Do you ever feel depressed or down for prolonged periods?"

"Not particularly."

"In which case, whatever issue you experienced as a child, there's nothing in what you've told me to suggest it's an issue today."

"You think I'm normal?"

"As normal as any of us, which is to say you're not abnormal."

"No, that can't be right."

"Why can't it?"

"Because … because … can't you see it?"

"See what?"

I scour my mind for an answer, but in truth, the doctor has already unpicked every strand of my alien existence and justified his reasoning.

"One final question," I say, my voice low and hoarse. "And I would rather you answer it with complete honesty."

"Go ahead."

"Am I as human as you?"

"Interesting question," he says with a thin smile. "But it's an easy one to answer. We might be completely different in myriad ways, but once you strip away our individual personalities, yes, you and I are both run-of-the-mill human beings: flesh and blood, skin and bone."

"And this is your professional opinion?"

"It's not an opinion, Simon; it's a fact."

"A fact beyond all doubt?"

Rather than reply, he pulls a pen out of a breast pocket. He then scribbles a line on a piece of paper on his desk and holds the pen up.

"What is this?" he asks.

"A pen."

"You're one-hundred per cent certain of that?"

"Yes, I'm certain. What is the point of this question?"

"See, you're certain this is a pen because it looks exactly like a pen and functions exactly like a pen. It might be different from your pen, or the pen my colleague next door uses, or every other pen in the world perhaps, but it's still a pen."

His point delivered and received, the doctor returns the pen to his pocket.

"I *am* human," I unintentionally mumble.

"Yes, young man, you are."

The walls of the room suddenly shift, closing in as the doctor's form loses definition. In my chest, pressure builds until it feels like my heart and lungs are fit to burst. If I didn't know better, I'd say I was drowning.

I can't find a breath. The entire room begins to spin.

"Simon?"

The doctor's voice is distant like he's calling my name from the far end of the corridor outside.

"Simon … can you hear me?"

The lights go out.

Silence.

Chapter 29

The world slowly returns to focus, or at least a tiny corner of the world.

"Are you okay, Simon?"

I am sitting on the floor with my back up against a wall. Dr Jarvis's voice breaks through the murk. Blinking hard, I assess my surroundings.

"What ... what happened?"

"You experienced a panic attack and passed out momentarily."

I rarely dream, but when I do, my dreams are often strange, verging on eerie. I am now suffering the same dazed confusion that lingers after I awake.

"I must go," I croak.

"Not so fast."

The doctor helps me to my feet.

"How are you feeling?" he asks.

"Groggy."

Is that a word? It doesn't sound right.

"Here, drink this."

He passes me a plastic cup containing water. I gulp it back. Thirst quenched, my thoughts clear a little.

"You said there's nothing wrong with me. If that is the case, what just happened?"

"I said there was nothing physically wrong with you. A panic attack is a feeling of sudden and intense anxiety."

"Emotions?"

"Yes, heightened emotions."

"I have never experienced a feeling like it before … or at least I don't think I have."

"They're fairly common, and whilst the attacks themselves won't do you any harm, you shouldn't ignore whatever underlying problem is behind them."

I nod.

"Any idea what might have sparked the attack?"

I have several ideas, but none I wish to share with the doctor.

"I'd like to leave. I need some air, and … I must think."

"Okay, but I want you to book a follow-up consultation."

"For what reason?"

"Because I'm concerned about your mental wellbeing."

"I am sick?"

"That's not what I'm saying. Everyone faces challenges with their mental health, and sometimes we don't even know we need help. You've just lost your mother, and I want to ensure you have support if you need it."

"Noted."

"Please, Simon. Make that appointment."

Perhaps my mind is still not fully functioning as the doctor's voice sounds a lot like Father Paul's.

"Yes. I will."

"Good man. Are you feeling fit enough to get yourself home?"

"I am capable."

I exit the room before Dr Jarvis poses any further questions, but it isn't the doctor's questions that harangue my every step along Bulford Road. One, in particular, is so loud no amount of counting will silence it: was I wrong?

I was wrong about The Shepherd.

I was wrong about Primrose Hill.

Was I wrong to believe *They* exist? All the evidence over the last forty-eight hours suggests I was.

It horrifies me even to entertain the idea, but I might … I might be human. Worse than even that, I might be a defective human.

More questions pile in. What was so wrong with my childhood behaviour I required the attention of a behavioural specialist? And, why did I never see that specialist? What kind of parent would deny their child crucial medical attention? That is one question I can answer — Father. I can't, however, answer to his motives. Nor can I understand why Mother allowed it to happen. She has never once failed in her duty of care to me. Not once.

I stop walking.

I'm only six minutes from home – nowhere near long enough to process this flash flood of questions or the associated emotions.

Seven minutes after leaving the doctor's surgery, I stagger into the kitchen at home.

"Merle."

I count to ten, unlock the back door, and open it wide.

"Merle! Merle!"

Another count to ten, but there's no sign of him. Where is he?

I check my bedroom and the lounge, but Merle, like the answers I desperately need, is nowhere to be found.

"Calm down, Simon."

I heed my own advice and return to the kitchen with a notepad and pen. Two glasses of water dampen the furnace, but it continues to smoulder. It is, I acknowledge, anger, rooted in one broad conclusion — I cannot bear this inability to understand. Nothing makes sense. Nothing.

In the months leading up to Mother's final journey to Elmwood Care Home, I saw first-hand what a lack of understanding did to her. She struggled to recall names and places, times and events. Whenever I asked a simple question, her face would shrink and pucker as she strained to find the answer. With every passing second, her frustration would mount, and inevitably, it would lead to an outburst of negative emotions, and sometimes she would sob uncontrollably. At one point, I must have made the conscious decision never to ask her another question for fear of her reaction.

At the time, I found Mother's confusion almost as frustrating as she did. I am not ill, but I am ill-informed, and the only two people who can answer my questions are both dead: one a skeleton buried in the ground, and the other lying cold on a mortuary slab somewhere. Now, if I were to look in a mirror, I would see a different shrunken, puckered face looking back at me.

I need answers, but to what questions?

With an unsteady hand, I grip the pen and scrawl three questions on the notepad.

Question 1: Who am I?

Question 2: What is wrong with me?

Question 3: Can anyone answer questions 1 and 2?

I stare at the blank page for an indeterminable time, but to no avail. Then, my eyes are drawn to a rectangular object shrouded in red gingham at the opposite end of the table: Father's old filing box. The fortitude required to move it back up to Mother's room has proven elusive, but now circumstances have changed. I push the chair back and stand up.

My heart rate elevated, I edge around the table until I am standing directly over the filing box. I then whip the tablecloth away and let it fall to the floor — the ease of the first step not befitting the difficulty of the next. There before me is the same battered box, imprinted with the same faded words, exactly how I remember it. There is no need to remember the negative emotions as they are already making their presence felt once more.

Try as I might, I can't stop myself reading the warning message over and over again, each time the voice in my head moving a tone further away from mine and closer to Father's. By the eighth repetition, he might as well be standing behind me, hissing the words in my ear.

Property of Martin Armstrong — Strictly Private & Confidential.

How can I still recall the voice of a long-dead human with such clarity? Is this macabre illusion a symptom of the condition I suffered as a child?

Before I can stop myself, both fists slam down on the table. Still hunched forward, all the symptoms of strenuous exercise then descend: shortness of breath, dizziness, and excessive perspiration. I can only conclude this body is failing at an unprecedented rate.

Then, a wave of nausea strikes.

I swallow back saliva just as my diaphragm contracts. This is what being sick is, and it is a deeply unpleasant sensation. Worst still, if I am but seconds away from emptying the contents of my stomach, clearing that up will double the punishment.

I scan my surroundings and dash towards the bin. My diaphragm contracts again, and this time caustic bile burns its way up from my oesophagus like magma venting from a volcano. Mercifully, no solids follow, and I'm able to swallow much of the bile back. Still hunched over the bin, I wait in expectation of a third wave.

After a series of shallow breaths, the nausea begins to ease. I'm about to close the bin lid when a partial address on the corner of a crumpled letter snares my attention. I reach in and remove the letter from Cindy Akinyemi. Treating it with care this time, I carefully lay it out on the kitchen table. Barely forty-eight hours have passed since the first time I read it, but how my circumstances have changed since Monday. Six words are now pertinent to the third question on my notepad: *located another document relating to your adoption.*

It is not a telephone call I want to make, but I am willing to tolerate a conversation with Cindy Akinyemi if there's even a remote chance it might aid my quest for answers.

I locate my mobile telephone and dial the eleven digits from the letter.

It rings six times. Seven, eight, nine, ten. I will terminate the call on the fifteenth ring if there is no answer.

Eleven rings. Twelve, thirteen.

"Cindy Akinyemi," a breathless voice pants down the line.

"Hello. This is Simon Armstrong."

There a long pause before Cindy Akinyemi speaks again.

"Ahh, Simon. You're a lucky man ... I was just leaving the office for the day. You received my letter?"

"Correct."

"Just give me a mo. I need to grab your file."

The line falls silent bar the two digital tones that chime in quick succession every five seconds. They chime seven times before the line reconnects.

"Sorry about that."

"You have additional information?" I confirm. "Relating to my adoption."

"Kind of."

"Either you have or you haven't. Which is it?"

"It's not relative to your adoption per se, but there might be some link to your parentage, and I stress *might*."

"Go on."

"Okay, but I should begin with an explanation. Twenty-odd years ago, our department transitioned from paper-based filing to a fully computerised system. This was before my time, but I understand it was a long and troublesome process, not helped when senior management decided to move to an entirely different computer system halfway through."

"Is there a point to your explanation?"

"What I'm trying to say, Simon, is that somewhere along the line, a record relating to your adoption was mis-filed, and I only stumbled across it by chance after our meeting. I was unsure whether to even contact you about it, considering your … circumstances, but I discussed it with one of my colleagues during lunch last—"

"Enough," I interject. "I have neither the time nor the inclination to discuss the inefficiencies in your organisation. What have you found?"

"Um, sorry. Yes … let me find it in your file."

The sound of paper shuffling replaces Cindy Akinyemi's voice.

"Got it."

"And?"

"I know you're keen to know what I've unearthed, but once again, I'm duty-bound to manage your expectations."

"What does that even mean?"

"It means, I … let me just explain what I found."

"I wish you would."

She clears her throat without moving the phone away from her mouth. I look across at the bin and wonder if I might need it again.

"Twenty years ago," she belatedly begins. "Helen Armstrong contacted us to report an incident."

"My mother?"

"Yes."

"What kind of incident?"

"She spoke to a member of the team, Suzanne, who no longer works here so I've only got her notes to go by, but it seems your parents received a letter from a woman by the name of Lillian Tatlow. In that letter, Mrs Tatlow made certain claims that upset your mother enough that she contacted us."

"Claims?"

"Mrs Tatlow claimed to be your biological mother, and she wanted to meet you."

Cindy Akinyemi does not expand on her statement, and I am too preoccupied fending off a barrage of supplementary questions to fill the dead air between us.

"Simon?"

"What?"

"Did you understand what I just said?"

"Yes … no … I don't know."

"Before we get too carried away, there's more. Suzanne wrote to Mrs Tatlow and warned her against ever contacting your parents again and made it clear that access to an adopted child can only be granted in certain circumstances. Furthermore, Suzanne told Mrs Tatlow that any form of access would also require the consent of the adoptive parents."

"And … as I've never heard of Lillian Tatlow, let alone met her, I assume my parents did not grant access?"

"That's the thing, Simon — they never had to make that decision. We never heard back from Mrs Tatlow, and nine weeks after your mother first contacted us, she called again to say the matter had been resolved."

"Resolved how?"

"I don't know. There's nothing in Suzanne's notes and no other communication, so I guess the matter was considered closed. As I stressed, there could be nothing in this at all."

Months before her official diagnosis, I noticed a change in Mother's appetite for certain television programmes. She had always favoured quizzes and game shows but as her mental faculties deteriorated, understanding the questions proved more difficult than returning a correct answer.

Standing mute with a mobile telephone pressed to my ear, Mother's challenge is now mine.

"Simon?"

"I am here."

"Are you okay?"

"Define okay?"

"I understand it's not the news you wanted to hear, but I couldn't not tell you."

"It is not news of any kind. News should be fact-based, and the only fact you have presented relates to a single letter sent by a woman who, for all we know, could be mentally unhinged. Gossip would be a more befitting description."

"Have I made a mistake, telling you?"

It's a reasonable question. In my heightened emotional state, I'd say Cindy Akinyemi had made a mistake. However, a five-second pause is long enough to let logic back into play.

Emotions stabilised, I have a question of my own.

"What did you think I might gain from knowing?"

"If I were in your shoes, I'd much rather know a little of something over all of nothing. What you choose to do with the little is up to you, but at least you have that option now."

Far from profound, it is still unquestionably the most sensible statement to pass Cindy Akinyemi's lips in all our conversations.

"Is there anything else you can tell me?"

"I've got Lillian Tatlow's date of birth: 13th March 1974, and an address in Croydon."

As natural as breathing, my mind crunches the data without conscious thought.

"That proves it then," I scoff. "This woman cannot be my biological mother. She would have only been fifteen years of age when I was conceived, and it is illegal for a fifteen-year-old to engage in sexual intercourse, is it not?"

"Illegal, yes, but all too common, I'm afraid. It might explain how you ended up at that hospital."

"I cannot see how."

"If, and it's still a significant if, Lillian Tatlow is your biological mother, she might have kept the pregnancy from her parents. And, rather than go through the usual adoption channels, perhaps she decided it would be easier to leave her baby at a hospital and walk away without any questions."

"No questions for her, but I have plenty."

"I'm sure you have, but I must stress that this is all theory, Simon. There's nothing in Suzanne's notes to suggest Lillian Tatlow was lying, but that doesn't necessarily mean she was telling the truth."

"But she might?"

"Who knows? What I do know is that I shouldn't really be giving you this information, and I'm only doing so because of your circumstances. As I said, it's up to you what happens next. Is there anything else you want to ask?"

"This woman's address. What is it?"

"I'll text it to you. If there's anything else I can help you with, you have my number."

Cindy Akinyemi ends the call by wishing me well for however long I have left. I don't understand her point of reference, and my thoughts are too distracted to ask.

I slap the mobile telephone on the table and put my head in my hands. The notepad is directly in my line of sight, and on it, the three questions I could not answer.

Am I any better placed to answer them now?

I conclude I am not, but there are now different questions to answer, anyway.

Chapter 30

Seated in complete silence at the kitchen table; minute after minute passes by, duration unknown. Contrary to popular belief, time is not eternal. At some point, trillions and trillions of years into the future, the universe will cease to exist, and with it, time. However, I only know of one species that are slaves to time, and humans will be gone long before their master.

My thoughts are ambling, but they do eventually lead to a stark realisation. For most of my adult life, I have become a greater slave to time than any human I know, and only now can I see what I couldn't before. I still can't definitively answer the question, but I now have more information than I did before my conversation with Cindy Akinyemi. If I can establish I was abandoned as a child by a mother so young she was barely out of childhood herself, it would prove I am not what I have always believed myself to be, beyond all doubt.

There are further ramifications.

If there is any semblance of truth in my first assumption, perhaps I am cursed with faulty genes. Lillian Tatlow became pregnant whilst still at school and then decided the best course of action was to abandon her newborn child. Even for a naive adolescent, her judgement was woefully flawed. Further evidence of her poor judgement could be tied to her actions. Why did she write to my parents rather than the authorities, and why did she never follow through with her request?

I sit forward and reach for the pen. There are questions to be answered, and I need to commit each one to paper before the next one cascades in.

My hand freezes mid-air.

"Irrelevant."

Rather than posing questions, I should be considering the implications of this new information. It doesn't matter why Lillian Tatlow abandoned me, if indeed she did, and it doesn't matter why she sought to reconnect a decade later. No, the only question worth asking is: is Lillian Tatlow my biological mother? If she is, it will decimate any lingering doubts about my true origins. Born of a human, I can be nothing other than human.

I pick up the pen and jot down the only question that now matters, underlining it twice: how do I establish if Lillian Tatlow is my biological mother? There is scant information to go on, bar her full name and date of birth, and an address in Croydon, South London. On cue, my mobile telephone chimes to signal an incoming message. I snatch it up and check the screen. It is the promised address.

Croydon is not an area I am familiar with, so I need to use my personal computer to conduct research.

I get to my feet, and at some point halfway up the stairs, yet another question comes to mind: what if my parents had told me about the letter from Lillian Tatlow when I was young? I might have met her, and if I'd established back then what I need to establish now, would I have ever looked to the stars and questioned my origins? My outlook on this life and the person I am today would likely not be the same if I'd known the truth.

By the time I sit down in front of the personal computer, I can already sense a knot of resentment tightening in my chest. Wherever my research takes me, it will not result in a satisfactory ending. Lies have been told, without doubt, and the best I can hope for is to establish who spun the worst of those lies. Only then can I decide if I want to continue with this life — a life I did not ask for.

As I reach for the power button, the trill of a mobile telephone echoes up from the kitchen. My instinct is to ignore it, but I can't ignore the possibility it might be Cindy Akinyemi calling again, having unearthed further information.

I hurry downstairs and answer it on the ninth ring.

"Yes."

"Hi, Simon. How are you doing?" Father Paul asks.

"I've never understood that question. How am I doing what?"

"I mean, are you okay after yesterday?"

"You're referring to my visit to the police station?"

"Specifically, our conversation afterwards."

"I am still considering it, but I've yet to reach a definitive conclusion."

"I understand. You're okay, though, in yourself?"

"I suppose."

"Have you eaten yet?"

"No. My schedule has gone awry this afternoon."

I decide against mentioning it, but so has my appetite.

"Would you like to come over for tea? I'm happy to sit and listen if you feel like talking."

"I ... no, thank you."

"Sure?"

"Certain."

"Can we catch up later in the week, then?"

"I'll see."

"Right ... as you wish."

I remain silent in expectation of a goodbye.

"Oh, I almost forgot," the priest continues. "Nurse Clifford called me yesterday about Helen's possessions."

"What about them?"

"She wanted me to collect them."

"As I said to her, I do not have a motor car, but you do."

"Not for the remainder of this week, I don't. That journey to Salisbury finished off the clutch, and I can't get it replaced until

Friday. Fortunately, Rosie stepped into the breach, bless her, and offered to do it."

"Why would you ask her to deal with Mother's possessions?"

"I didn't. She kindly volunteered when I mentioned it last night."

This is news I hadn't anticipated. Bar the priest telling Rosie about my birthday, I wasn't aware they had interacted to any degree.

"Last night? Have you coerced her into attending one of your religious services?"

"We don't hold services on a Tuesday. Rosie attended a fundraising meeting which I happened to mention over a cup of tea at Elmwood. We're raising funds to support vulnerable pensioners in the parish, and Rosie clearly has empathy with old folks."

My mind drifts back to the afternoon when she played music for Mother. It was a thoughtful gesture.

"So, you did coerce her?"

"Not at all — she was keen to get involved. Rosie was particularly close to her grandfather, judging by the number of photos on her phone. And, as it happens, she's also a Christian, albeit one who might have strayed from the path in recent years. Her words, not mine."

"She's a religious type?"

"Yes."

I don't know what to make of the priest's revelation. I thought I felt a connection with Rosie, but now I must ask myself if she was treating me as the priest himself does — like a vulnerable oddball, to be pitied and pandered and eventually brainwashed into joining the cult.

"When does Rosie intend to return Mother's possessions?"

"She didn't say, but she did mention the two of you had planned to watch another movie together, so it made sense for her to kill two birds, so to speak."

"She told you about her visits to my house?"

"Why wouldn't she? To be frank, Simon, I'm relieved you're finally making friends. It's been a long time coming."

Already simmering with negative emotions, I can't help but vent.

"Listen to me," I snap. "Do not discuss me with Rosie again, and if you speak to her before I do, you can tell her I no longer have any interest in watching her puerile movies."

"Don't be like that, Rosie is a good person, and you need good people in your life."

"Do I? Good people like Mother, eh?"

"Yes, like your mother."

"You've just proven what a poor judge of character you are. Mother was a liar, and good people don't lie, do they?"

"I … sorry? What do you mean?"

"You'll find out in time, as I did. Goodbye."

I terminate the call and switch the mobile telephone off. If only I could turn off these cursed emotions so easily.

I read about a rare and scientifically unproven condition as a child, called spontaneous human combustion. Even now, I can remember how unsettled I felt, knowing I might suddenly burst into flames whilst sitting quietly on the sofa watching television. Later in life — after my alien awakening — I concluded it was a condition limited to humans, so I had nothing to worry about.

Here and now, I'm radiating enough emotional heat for the worry to return. I snatch a glass from the cupboard and fill it from the tap three times, gulping back the cooling liquid before each refill.

Hydration provides temporary respite, or at least the distraction of activity does. I feel compelled to remain standing at the kitchen sink and look out across the garden. There are twenty-two paving slabs that snake left across the lawn to form a path. Whoever designed the path patently did not understand that the shortest distance between two points is a straight line, and the haphazardly laid slabs have always irritated me. They still do today, but the familiar irritation acts like a beacon, guiding me back to safer waters.

Calmness finally prevails. Father Paul, Rosie, and every human I know are inconsequential — it is the human I don't know who matters now. I must focus on finding Lillian Tatlow, and the truth.

I return to my bedroom and switch the computer on. Once it boots up, I open an internet browser and enter the address provided by Cindy Akinyemi. A map pops up. With another click of the mouse, I access a pedestrian's view of a street densely packed with properties of negligible architectural merit. At first glance, Granville Close is not somewhere I would care to reside.

I click the mouse again, moving towards the head of the close. The view is different but the same. Another click and the following picture shows a female figure walking on the pavement. Her face is pixelated but not her clothing: a fawn-coloured coat and denim jeans. The odds of the female being Lillian Tatlow must be close to zero, but not zero. My attention lingers on the figure. I then lean forward and study her in closer detail.

"Are you my mother?"

I've never known Merle to shake his head, but if he were here, lying on my bed, he might. My behaviour, I concede, is not becoming of the creature he knows so well.

I sit back and click the mouse again. The figure disappears from view. Now positioned at the head of the close, there are properties to the left, right, and directly ahead. I scroll left and zoom in on the aluminium plate fixed to the wall of a three-storey building: Flats 86-92, it reads. Not the address I am looking for. I scroll to the right, and the view of a near-identical three-storey building directly opposite. Again, I zoom in on the aluminium plate: Flats 105-111. The address supplied by Cindy

Akinyemi is 111 Granville Close — I am looking at the exact building where Lillian Tatlow penned her letter twenty years ago.

Having established the location, I zoom in on the building itself. Beyond the austere brickwork, I can just make out graffiti on an adjacent wall and scraps of litter strewn in the gutter. I had no preconceived idea of the kind of property Lillian Tatlow might reside in, but a flat in a cheerless block never crossed my mind. Does that say more about her or me?

I close the map, having learnt all there is to learn. Opening a new browser window, I enter the name Lillian Tatlow into the search field and press the enter key. Quite what I hoped to find, I do not know, but I had hoped to find something. Instead, I'm offered one solitary reference to the exact name I searched for, and it relates to an entry from an ancestry website. The Lillian Tatlow in question was born in West Virginia in 1893, and died in the same American state in 1954.

With the internet of no help, I am left with just one option remaining if I'm to find Lillian Tatlow, and that is to visit the address. She might not live there anymore, but where else can I begin the search? It is a question worthy of consideration, and I invest an entire hour weighing up my options. I conclude there are none.

If I'm to unearth the truth about my origins, I must journey to Croydon.

Chapter 31

I am not prone to making miscalculations but wracked with apprehension, I made a timing error when planning my journey yesterday evening. Consequently, I arrived at Salisbury train station twenty-three minutes earlier than necessary. To compound my mistake, I decided to wait on the platform rather than outside the station. As a result, I am now standing uncomfortably close to the scene of Tuesday's humiliation. If there is any consolation, I won't be departing in a police car today.

As I wait for the train, and despite my efforts to distract it, my mind decides it would like to dwell on Tuesday's event. There's not much to remember about the latter stages of my meeting with Gordon Searle, but even if there were, it's those pivotal few minutes in the middle of our conversation that my mind wants to toil over.

The moment The Shepherd died.

"Gary," I mumble, correcting my own thoughts.

His name doesn't catch in my throat as it might have yesterday. Upon learning the truth about Gary Searle, raw emotion tainted my reaction, but time and logic have tempered that initial stance. As I consider why that might be, a cold shiver runs up my spine. I quickly conclude now is not the time for such scrutiny. Instead, I begin counting the words in a poster about planned network improvements.

The train arrives, and I embark, taking my pre-booked seat with my satchel next to me.

Upon departure, I extract my pocket radio and insert the earbuds. The sound of static and the gentle rocking motion of the train will aid the passing of time. I close my eyes. When I open them again, the scene beyond the window is one of urban chaos. The one hour and fifteen-minute journey to Clapham Junction is almost over.

I prepare myself.

As I researched my journey last night, I unearthed a troubling fact. An online article stated that Clapham Junction is the busiest railway station in Europe. Upon learning this, I almost cancelled my plans. My Waterloo experience was overwhelming enough, but the prospect of spending just ten minutes in a station even more crowded would have been a step too far. Fortunately, I am nothing if not thorough with my research, and further reading confirmed the supposed fact to be a misdirection. Clapham Junction is the busiest station in Europe based upon train movements, but not the volume of passengers. I have no issue with trains.

Barely eleven minutes after arriving in Clapham Junction, I have already left. Now I am but sixteen minutes away from Granville Close, crowded station platforms are no longer my greatest concern, nor is the disgusting state of my carriage or the two boisterous males seated behind me. In many ways, the anxiety is far worse than when I waited on Primrose Hill. There, even when I awoke in that awful toilet cubicle, I still maintained some level of belief. Now, I no longer know what I believe.

The journey to East Croydon is brief, but even when it's over, there is no sense of relief.

I make my way from the platform out to the street. Having memorised the directions, all I have to do is put one foot in front of another and take five turns: left, right, left, right, left. It's a four-minute walk, five at the most.

It begins with the first left turn.

As I walk, I go over what I plan to say should Lillian Tatlow answer the door to 111 Granville Close. Deciding on my opening statement proved simple enough whilst seated at the kitchen table last night, but I hadn't considered how a dry mouth and frazzled mind might complicate matters. I've also had time to consider the one great unknown — how she might react to my visit. Humans are unpredictable creatures, particularly when they're taken by surprise.

Maybe this was a bad idea.

I turn right, then left, concluding that yes, it might be a bad idea, but I'll only know once the theoretical consequences become a reality.

The last left turn leads me off the main road, away from the noise and pollution of the passing traffic, and along a footpath. At the end, the view becomes familiar as I enter the head of Granville Close. On the day Google captured the imagery for their online map, the sun was high and the sky blue. Today, it's grey and overcast. There's also the background noise: traffic, barking dogs, and the repetitive thump of music coming from one of the flats just up the road. The noise only adds to my growing unease.

Following the path, it leads me directly to the block where flat 111 is situated. To the front, there's a scrubby patch of grass bordered by a hedge long overdue a prune. The utilitarian design of the building blends in well with the monotone sky. It strikes me as a home for humans with no other choice because I cannot understand why anyone would willingly choose to live here.

I steel myself and walk up the path to the front door.

Much like Elmwood Care Home, there's an intercom device fixed to the wall, but with buttons numbered for each of the flats. The button for flat 111 is at the bottom. Once I press it, there is no going back.

I raise my right hand towards the intercom and press the button. The truth is all that matters now.

After six seconds, a crackle pops from the speaker.

"Yes?"

The voice is male.

"Hello. I'm looking for Lillian Tatlow."

My statement is met with silence. I'm about to repeat it when the speaker crackles again.

"Who are you?"

"My name is Simon Armstrong. I must speak with Lillian Tatlow."

Again, there is no immediate reaction, like there is a delay on the line.

"Come up," the male then orders. "Second floor."

A buzzer sounds, and the door lock disengages. I pull it open and enter the communal entrance hall. The comparison with Elmwood Care Home does not end at the intercom as I'm struck by a stench akin to standing downwind of a bin lorry on a warm day. Undeterred, I cross the tiled floor and proceed up the stairs, the stench following me all the way to the second-floor landing. The flaking paint on the walls and filthy floor tiles are in keeping with the door to flat 111. It opens, and a male roughly my height but at least twenty years older and several kilos heavier appears. He eyes me up and down.

"Jesus," he says, rubbing his bristled chin. "It's actually you."

"I am not Jesus. As I've already said, my name is Simon Armstrong."

The male responds with a wide grin.

"I didn't think you were Jesus. I know exactly who you are, lad."

"How? Have we met?"

"Briefly, a long, long time ago."

"I don't know who you are, but I assume you're not Lillian Tatlow."

"Well spotted. I'm Shane Tatlow."

"You are related?"

"Lillian's husband."

"I see. Is it possible I might speak to her?"

"It's possible, but the situation is a bit complex."

"Complex how?"

He pauses for a moment, using the time to scratch his chin again.

"Do your parents know you're here?"

"They're dead."

"Oh. I'm sorry to hear that."

"Why would you be sorry? Did you ever meet them?"

Rather than reply, he studies the mat on which I'm standing. In turn, I use the break in the conversation to appraise his attire: grey jogging pants and an ill-fitting black vest with a faded logo on the breast. If I had to describe his appearance in a single word, that word would be unkempt, but I am not here to judge this stranger.

"Did you ever meet my parents?" I ask again.

"I'm not sure I'm ready to open up old wounds, lad."

"What wounds?"

"I'd really … listen, you've caught me at an inopportune moment. If you can give me forty minutes, we could meet up, and I'll answer your questions."

"Can you not answer them now?"

"With respect, you're asking a bit much, turning up unannounced and demanding answers. Give me a chance to sort out what I've got to sort out, and then I'm all yours for as long as you need. Is that fair enough?"

"What am I supposed to do for forty minutes?"

"I don't know, lad. Buy a paper and read it in a coffee shop."

"Where?"

"There's one of those fancy places opposite the station. I can meet you there at … say, eleven-thirty?"

"And you'll answer my questions?"

"Every last one of them. You have my word."

Reluctantly, I agree. Shane Tatlow bids me goodbye and closes the door while I'm still standing on his doormat. I turn around and retrace my steps back down the stairs. My frustration at a lack of answers is tempered by relief as I leave the building, and the foul smell, behind me.

As I wander back the way I came, I consider what just occurred. When I decided to take this course of action, I envisaged a number of possible scenarios. Nothing I considered came close to the one I encountered. Now, my mind is buzzing with a swarm of new possibilities and far too many questions. The wait, even if it is only forty minutes, is likely to be tortuous.

The walk is over before I know it as I locate the coffee shop called Costa. Although it is moderately busy, I am able to secure a table in a quieter corner where I open a bottle of mineral water. Shane Tatlow didn't specify where I might purchase a newspaper, not that I would be able to focus on it, so all I can do is stare out of the window and count the passing vehicles. I reach a hundred in barely a minute and decide to count just the vans in the nearest lane.

It is difficult to concentrate.

The reason I am unable to concentrate, I conclude, is because my mind wants to explore without a map. I must resist the urge because the information I currently have at my disposal is woefully inadequate. Judgement will have to wait.

I continue the count.

At 11:36 am, Shane Tatlow finally enters the coffee shop. He scans the room and then raises his arm in my direction before ordering a beverage. Eventually, he saunters over to my table.

"Sorry I'm a bit late."

I acknowledge his apology with a faint nod. He sits down opposite and sips from a cup containing a brown liquid — coffee, I assume. I notice he has shaved and combed his hair, the shabby vest replaced by a plain navy sweater and leather jacket. He no longer looks like a vagrant.

"You are ready to answer my questions now?" I ask.

He sits back in his chair, keeping one hand on the cup.

"Yes, but would you mind if I asked you a few questions first?"

"If you must."

"Where to begin?" he says, puffing his cheeks.

Another sip of coffee seems to lubricate his thoughts.

"Why are you looking for Lil?"

"Lillian?"

"Yes."

"Do you need to know? The information I seek is sensitive. It's not a topic of conversation I'd divulge to a stranger."

"Alright, answer me this instead: how did you end up at my door then?"

"A woman working for Social Services told me about a letter, sent to my adoptive mother by Lillian Tatlow, from the address in Granville Close."

"That's the letter where she asked Helen Armstrong if she could see you."

His statement is unexpected.

"How do you know?"

"Because I helped Lil write it. Have you read it?"

"No, but that is not relevant. I am only interested in provable facts, which is why I must speak to Lillian Tatlow."

"You and me both."

"I do not understand. You are her husband, are you not?"

"Estranged husband. I haven't seen Lil since Christmas."

"Then, I am wasting my time. Where can I find her?"

"I've got a few ideas where she might be, but just sit tight for a minute. I know you're keen to find her, but there are things you don't know, lad … things you really ought to know."

"Such as?"

He reaches a hand into his jacket pocket and pulls out a rectangular piece of white card. Turning it over, he then lays it on the table in front of me.

"Recognise him?" he asks, pointing at the photograph.

"It is an infant. They all look the same."

"This photo was taken a few days after this lad was born … after *you* were born."

I lean forward to inspect the photograph. It is an infant, young, wrapped in a white crochet blanket and lying in a cot.

"Are you saying this infant is me?"

"I am, 'cos it is."

"How did you get it?"

"Lil gave it to me, must be twenty years ago now. It's the only photo she had of you."

"If what you're saying is to be believed, why would she give you her only photograph?"

"Because …"

Shane Tatlow closes his eyes for three long seconds.

"Because, Simon, Lil wanted to show me a photo of my boy."

"Your boy?"

"Yeah," he says, staring across at me intently. "There's no easy way to say this, so I'll just spit it out — I'm your dad, Simon."

Chapter 32

The world's fastest supercomputer is in Japan. Named Fagaku, it can process 442,010 teraflops of information per second, roughly the same computing power as every personal computer in Greater London combined.

As I sit here in a coffee shop in East Croydon, stunned, I would welcome an additional 442,010 teraflops of processing power. As it is, my comparatively feeble mind is in the process of rebooting, so I'm unable to respond in any meaningful way to Shane Tatlow's statement.

"Simon? You okay, lad?"

"No."

"I'm sorry. I shouldn't have just blurted it out like that."

I've always favoured concise and accurate delivery when it comes to communication, so I can hardly criticise him. However, I can only attest to his conciseness because his accuracy is yet to be determined.

Composure returns.

"Prove it."

"I'll try my best, but you have to understand one thing — for the first ten years of your life, I didn't even know you existed."

"I don't understand."

"Do you want to understand?"

"No, but I must."

"Alright," he replies, settling back in his chair. "I'll try and keep it brief."

"Go on."

"You obviously suspect that Lil … Lillian is your mum, or you wouldn't be here."

I don't recognise his statement as a question and remain mute.

"Me and Lillian first met at school, and we started dating when we were both fifteen. It got pretty intense real quick, and we both thought we'd be together forever. Anyway, six or seven months later, my old man ends up getting himself banged up for a stretch, so we had to move sharpish as the selfish bastard grassed-up some proper nasty toerags to get a lighter sentence. Before I knew it, me, my mum, and my kid sister were in a van with everything we owned, heading to some shithole of a flat in Essex, on the opposite side of London. Might as well have been the opposite side of the world back then 'cos there weren't no internet or mobile phones."

"There was public transport."

"Sure, but Mum said I'd be signing my own death warrant if I went back home. Best I could do was write to Lil and call her whenever I had a quid spare."

"Could she not visit you?"

"Maybe, but then I'd have known."

"Known what?"

"She was pregnant."

"Are you saying you didn't know?"

"That's exactly what I'm saying, lad. In the end, her folks must have moved on 'cos my letters went unanswered, and their phone was cut off. I gave up after about six months and got myself a job … tried to get on with my life, not knowing you existed."

"And yet, you say you're now married to Lillian Tatlow."

"Fast forward seven years, and I was living in Hounslow, but I happened to be travelling through Croydon one day, a few miles from here … where me and Lil grew up. I stopped off at a petrol station to grab a drink, and as I left, I held the door open for a bird coming down the aisle. At first, I didn't pay much attention to her, but as she got closer, I ... you could have knocked me over with a feather when Lil called my name. Four weeks later, we'd moved in together, and we were married within the year."

"And that is when she confesses to the pregnancy?"

"Nope. I didn't find out until one September evening a few years later. We were supposed to be going out for drinks, but Lil was acting up, proper moody. I thought it was just her time of the month but she sat on her own in our kitchen and drank half a bottle of vodka. That's when she broke down and told me. I'll never forget that moment ... still haunts me."

"Explain."

"The reason she was so moody ... well, it was your tenth birthday. It must have pushed her over the edge 'cos she broke down and confessed what she'd done."

"And what precisely had she done?"

"Given birth to a baby boy ... our baby boy, and then left him at a hospital in Epsom."

The conversation falters as Shane Tatlow tries to stem his emotions. He clears his throat and then rubs his eyes with a napkin, seemingly upset, not that I'm any judge. I'm also inept when it comes to administering sympathy.

"Are you able to continue?" I ask, attempting to mimic the tone of voice Father Paul regularly deploys.

"Yeah, I think so," he replies with a sniffle. "Sorry."

"No apology required."

"Where was I? Oh, yeah ... so, we sat up all night and talked about what we could do, you know, to put things right. We thought about contacting the adoption people but Lil thought it would be better to find out who'd taken you and appeal to their better nature. That's when she had the idea of writing to the Armstrongs."

"How did you establish who adopted me?"

"Weren't easy, I can tell you. But, as luck would have it, I knew a bloke who knew a bloke who was a whizz with computers. It didn't take him long to hack into the adoption agency's network, and he gave us your records in return for a monkey."

"What? You traded information for a primate?"

"Nah," he chuckles. "Five hundred quid."

"Oh. I see. You paid someone to gain information illegally?"

"I know what you're thinking."

"I doubt that."

"Lil was in bits, and I'm not gonna sugar-coat it; if I hadn't done something, she might have topped herself. I was desperate … we were desperate. If we'd gone through the proper channels, it would have taken months, years maybe, and we still stood bugger all chance of getting access to our boy."

He emphasises the term 'our boy' while looking directly at me. Until I know more, I'd rather assume he's talking about a third person.

"So, once you established who adopted me, you decided to write them a letter. Correct?"

"That's about the strength of it, yeah. We didn't want to cause the Armstrongs any bother, and we weren't trying to be unreasonable. We didn't even ask them to tell you who we were — we just wanted the chance to see you now and then."

"And yet, they declined."

"Nah, they didn't."

"What? You're saying they agreed you could meet me?"

"They were willing to grant access on one condition … that we pay them for it."

His revelation does not compute, and my taut frown undoubtedly confirms as much.

"They asked for money?"

"Yep. Fifty grand."

"This makes no sense. We were financially comfortable, and my parents purchased our current home with no mortgage. Why would they need your money?"

"You're thinking back to front, lad. The reason why they were able to buy a new house is because we helped them to the tune of fifty grand."

"If that is the case, why have I never met you or Lillian Tatlow?"

He takes a long slow sip of coffee before responding.

"Do you really wanna know?"

"Of course."

"Even if it completely changes your opinion of the couple who raised you?"

"I came looking for the truth. That is all I am interested in."

"Alright, I'll tell you. We desperately wanted to buy our own house but I was self-employed with a chequered credit history, so the banks would only lend us half the money we needed. All we could do is work like dogs and save like crazy until eventually, we got within a few grand of our target. That's when we started viewing houses. But, it coincided with your tenth birthday, and looking around all those family homes didn't help Lil. I guess it triggered her maternal instincts … she wanted a family home, but one with you in it."

"This was when you decided to track me down and write the letter?"

"Yeah, and a few days after we sent the letter, your old man … Martin, ain't it?"

"Yes."

"Martin called us and agreed to meet. Lil was chuffed to bits, and the following weekend we drove to some pub in Twickenham. They seemed pleasant enough for the first fifteen minutes, but then Martin's mood changed like the wind. He got all uppity and told us we'd broken all the rules contacting them directly. Then, he starts laying into Lil about abandoning you in the first place. I was about to give him a slap when he changes tack and tells us he has a proposal."

"And my mother said nothing during this meeting?"

"Not really. Looking back, I think she was scared of him, so he did all the talking. He's the one who put forward the proposal."

"Go on."

"He said, if we paid them fifty grand, they'd let you spend every other weekend with us. And, once you were old enough, they'd tell you who we really were. If we disagreed, Martin said he'd contact Social Services and tell them we'd been in touch, and we were causing them problems. Just to rub salt in, he told Lil he'd let the police know where we lived."

"For what purpose?"

"Abandoning a kid is a criminal offence. Lil was desperate at the time and just wanted the best for you, but the law is the law, and Martin bloody Armstrong knew it. I don't wish to speak ill of the dead, lad, but your old man was a nasty bastard."

Much of what Shane Tatlow has said cannot be directly corroborated, but he is factually correct on this subject. Our mutual resentment of Martin Armstrong is perhaps the first tenuous bond between us.

"We never got on," I confess. "I don't think he liked me."

"Probably because he only made fifty grand out of you. For someone like him, no amount of money would have been enough."

"But it was enough for his proposal?"

"Yeah, and he had us by the short and curlies. Either we paid him the money and accepted his terms, or he'd have destroyed any chance of us gaining access, legally. It came down to a straightforward question: were we willing to hand over every penny we'd saved, and then some, just to see our boy for a few days each month, or risk never seeing you again and Lil ending up in court? It didn't take long for us to decide, and a few days later, we transferred the money to Martin Armstrong's bank account."

"But you never did see me."

"No, and God knows we tried. We pestered and pestered, but they kept stalling, saying you were having troubles in school, and the time wasn't quite right. They eventually agreed to a date to spend the day with you, but it was three weeks down the line. I wasn't happy, but Lil said she'd waited ten long years to see you, and a few more weeks wouldn't kill us. Finally, the day came, and we travelled over to Surbiton to meet as agreed in a park. We turned up, waited and waited, and after an hour or so, we'd had enough. We hopped in the car and drove over to your parents' house, only to find it wasn't your parents' house anymore — the bastards had moved out earlier that week."

"You are certain this was not a communication breakdown?"

"No, lad. It was a con, and we were the suckers. Your old man knew we'd do anything to see you, and he exploited our desperation. We spent months trying to find out where they'd gone, but those months finally turned into a year and …"

"And?"

"It weren't just the money they took — bad as that was — it was our hopes for the future. Lil was never the same, and we sorta drifted through life for the best part of twenty years. We were stuck in a shithole of a flat and money was a constant problem … it's hard to find the motivation to earn when you've lost it all once. Then, Lil just upped and left one night before Christmas last year. Once you've had your dreams smashed, it's the hardest thing in the world to pick yourself up and go again. I'm afraid we weren't strong enough, lad."

With nothing left to add, he stares forlornly at the half-empty coffee cup.

At this point, it would be appropriate for me to feign a sympathetic expression; however, as I marry up Shane Tatlow's information with the facts already known, the need to feign an emotional response withers away. If he is to be believed, my father destroyed his and Lillian Tatlow's lives.

"You said you might know where Lillian is."

"I've got a vague idea."

"Why haven't you tried to find her?"

"I thought about it; course I have. But what would I say? Would she like to come back to the miserable life we were living?"

"You make a valid point."

"I can't even think about tracking her down until I've got my act together."

"You don't have to. I will find her."

"I don't think that'd be sensible."

"Why not?"

"Think about it, lad. She's given up all hope of ever seeing her little boy again, so what do you reckon would happen if some hulking bloke turns up out of the blue claiming to be her long lost son? She's a broken woman, and if I'm being honest, her mental health ain't too good. If this ain't handled properly, it could backfire, and you'll blow the only chance you'll ever have of getting to know your mum."

"My *alleged* mother."

"You're her boy, make no mistake. You're our boy."

"Do you have proof?"

"Happen, I might."

He returns a hand to his jacket pocket, this time pulling out two envelopes: one small and tan in colour, the other larger and bright yellow.

"This ain't proof as such, but I thought you'd like to see it," he says, opening the yellow envelope.

"What is it?"

He hands me another photograph. It features a youthful female smiling at the camera.

"That's your mum, a week or so before we were supposed to meet you in that park."

I study the photograph but being the subject is female, and I am not, it is difficult to see any obvious likeness. That said, the sharpness of her cheekbones and the slight dimpling in her chin are not unfamiliar. Her green eyes and bronze-coloured hair are slightly different shades to mine, but definitely of the same colour palette. The more I look at the female, the more I see of myself: subtle similarities, but similarities.

"In case you're wondering," Shane Tatlow then says. "You inherited more of your mum's genes than mine. You've got my build, though. Shame I've let myself go a bit, but when I was your age, I was just as fit as you are now."

We are indeed of a similar height, and despite his excessive blubber, we share the same broad shoulders and thick neck.

"A physical resemblance is not proof."

I hand the photograph back.

"You keep it," he insists. "But, if that ain't proof, this might be."

He opens the second envelope and extracts a silver locket on a chain, which he lays out on the table.

"Have a look inside, lad."

I carefully pick the locket up and use my thumbnail to prise the lozenge-shaped case open. The content is not what I expected.

"Hair?"

"Yeah ... your hair. Lil snipped a small amount from your head before she ... you know."

"Abandoned me?"

He lowers his head and nods once.

It would be impossible to ascertain the origins of the thin strands curled into a loop simply by looking at them. I suspect it's not the reason why Shane Tatlow considers this item proof of my origins.

"I've seen it on crime shows," he says. "They can use a single hair to match DNA, can't they?"

"I believe so."

"So, get it tested if the photo of Lil ain't proof enough for you. No one else could have cut that strand of hair but the woman who gave birth to you ... my Lil. And, it follows that she wouldn't let that locket out of her sight for anyone other than the man who fathered her child — me."

"And yet, it is here, but she is not."

"As I said, lad, she left in a hurry and her mind was all over the place. If she'd been thinking straight, she'd never have left it behind. Saying that, maybe she left it 'cos she didn't trust herself with it, or because she wanted to remind me of the one good thing we achieved together. Perhaps one day soon, we'll be able to ask her ... you and me together."

I close the locket and place it back on the table. It might be small, but its very existence could be of huge significance. It is, I conclude, a crucial piece of the jigsaw puzzle that constitutes my origins. Not definitive proof, but if I were to apply the rules of the justice system, everything I have seen and heard in this coffee shop would lead a juror to a verdict with minimal grounds for doubt. All the facts fit, except the one I have yet to disclose.

"I have one question. If you can satisfactorily answer it, I'd be more inclined to believe your version of events."

"I'm listening."

"What is the significance of Primrose Hill?"

"Eh?"

"You don't know?"

"Err, no idea," he replies, scratching his chin. "I know it's a posh part of London, but that's about it."

"Lillian Tatlow didn't tell you about a slip of paper left in the Moses basket in which I was found?"

"I don't think so. What did it say?"

"Primrose Hill 29/09."

"That's it?"

"Yes."

More chin-scratching ensues.

"Maybe it don't mean anything," he finally suggests. "You ever considered that?"

"Why write it down, then?"

"You ever scribble down a place and date on a slip of paper for an appointment or the like? And who's to say Lil even wrote it?"

"It was in the Moses basket she allegedly used."

"She was a teenage kid. She didn't buy it new ... most likely, she picked it up from a charity shop, or someone took pity and gave it to her. That note could have been in that basket for years before Lil ever set eyes on it."

His words lead me to an uncomfortable truth: whatever the relevance of that slip of paper, Shane Tatlow's explanation, vague as it might be, is significantly more plausible than the one I concocted.

It's my turn to stare silently at the coffee cup.

If I were to lean forward and smash my forehead against the table, the pain would be preferable to this. Foolishness is a hideous feeling, and so too is the accompanying sense of shame.

Right now, I would quite like to die.

Chapter 33

Caught in the headlights of my own stupidity, I instinctively want to run — the most primitive of human instincts when cornered. In this case, there is no escape because the threat is within me.

"You've gone very quiet, lad. You okay?"

"I don't feel ... this is all too much."

Shane Tatlow reaches across the table and nudges the bottle of water towards my hand.

"Have a drink of water and see if that helps. If it don't, there's a park nearby ... maybe we can get some fresh air?"

I follow his advice and empty the bottle.

"Can I get you another one?"

"No, thank you."

"I know this is a lot to take in, but you did the right thing coming here."

"Did I?"

"Course you did. Doing nothing is the easiest thing in the world ... take it from someone who knows. You could have ignored what you found out and just got on with your life, but you didn't, did you?"

"I suppose."

"You made a tough decision and followed through, without fear of the consequences. That takes real guts, and even though I've no right to say this, I'm proud of you. I'm proud that you're my boy."

For a few seconds, an unfamiliar but welcome sensation temporarily eclipses the shame. It is a sensation that Martin

Armstrong summarily failed to ignite in me for sixteen years, and yet, it has taken Shane Tatlow only minutes.

"Thank you."

"It should be me thanking you. I've been at rock bottom for too long now, but you turning up is a miracle, ain't it?"

"You mean miracle in the biblical sense?"

"Nah, not really. I ain't into all that religious mumbo jumbo."

Yet another topic where our views are aligned.

"What I mean," he continues, "is that you being here seems too good to be true. I never thought I'd ever get to meet you."

"I … it does seem like a good thing, but you'll have to bear with me. I am still struggling to manage my emotions."

"I get you, and take all the time you need. You've done the hard part now."

"Have I? I am still to meet the woman who you say is my mother."

"She *is* your mother, one-hundred per cent. And, you've got me now, to help you."

"Yes. That is true."

"You and me, together, we'll find her … as soon as I get back from Newcastle."

"That is … what? Newcastle?"

"I'm heading up there next week. An old mate of mine has sorted me out with a driving job."

"For how long?"

"Only six months," he replies with a nonchalant shrug. "But I promise we'll start searching for Lil the moment I get back."

One metaphorical step forward, two back.

"I cannot wait six months. I need answers."

"Haven't I given them to you?"

"No, not all of them. I want to speak with Lillian Tatlow — that was the whole purpose of travelling here."

"You'll get that chance, lad, but your timing isn't great. I wish I didn't have to go, but we can't always have what we want in life."

"If you don't want to go, don't."

"I've no choice. I'm skint, and besides, I've already agreed to sub-let the flat. A young couple are moving in on Monday."

"There has to be an alternative solution. With fear of repeating myself, I cannot wait six months."

"I don't know what to suggest, lad. I need this job because it's been months since I was last able to work, and being self-employed, I don't get any sick pay."

"You've survived thus far."

"Yeah, just. I've had no choice since Martin Armstrong robbed me of everything, but it ain't surviving; it's scraping by. I can't do it no more. This job is my only hope of putting food on the table."

He emits a heavy sigh. We have reached an impasse, and I need to find a way around it. For that, I need to think.

"May I have that bottle of water now?"

"Yeah, sure."

He smiles at me and then stands up.

"I'll be back in a minute."

I nod, but my mind is already racing ahead. With one minute at my disposal, I must banish all distractions, all emotions, and harness logic once more.

I'm so focused on finding a solution, I have no spare capacity to determine how long Shane Tatlow is away from the table. It is long enough, I think.

"There you go," he says, placing the bottle of water on the table.

"Thank you."

He sits down and checks his wristwatch.

"Do you wish to terminate our conversation?" I ask.

"No, not at all. I'm just conscious of time because I've got a lot to sort out before I leave."

"I have a solution which might negate your need to sort."

"Do you now? Let's hear it, then."

I sit forward, shoulders straight.

"I will pay you not to go to Newcastle."

He pauses, presumably to consider his answer.

"That's good of you to offer, but I can't take your money."

"Why not?"

"Because it wouldn't be right, and besides, you don't even know how much I need."

"Tell me."

"I dunno … to pay off the rent arrears and give myself enough to live on for a month or two, we're probably looking at four grand."

"I have more than four thousand pounds in my savings account."

"Yeah, but it's your money, lad. You can't just give it to me."

"I would treat it as an investment. If I help you financially, you will help me find Lillian Tatlow, and I can secure the answers I need."

"Right, but it doesn't solve the problem of where I'll live. As I said, I've already agreed to sub-let the flat."

"You could stay with me. I have plenty of room and a reliable internet connection so we can conduct research. I have money for travel, too, wherever we need to go."

"I'm not comfortable living at your expense, lad."

"Why not? I have plenty."

"Do you?"

"Yes. More than enough."

"Right," he says, thoughtfully.

Even with my limited skills in reading body language, I can tell that Shane Tatlow is seriously considering my proposal. To allow him time to think, and avoid an uncomfortable silence, I excuse myself on the pretence of needing the lavatory. As it transpires, my mobile telephone rings just as I enter.

"Hello."

"Hi, Simon. It's Rosie."

"Yes?"

"Have you spoken to Father Paul about your mother's possessions?"

"I have."

"Um, I just wondered if it's convenient to drop by shortly. I've just finished my shift, and I'll be passing your road."

"I'm in East Croydon, so no, I won't be at home for …"

"Sorry?" she interjects. "You're where?"

"East Croydon. It's in South London."

"I … yes, I know where it is. What are you doing there?"

"I'm busy. I don't have time for a conversation."

"Right … what about your mother's things?"

"Burn them for all I care. Goodbye."

I terminate the call and switch the telephone off. Perhaps I could have handled the conversation with Rosie a little less abruptly, but it wouldn't have changed my core message. Besides, if Shane Tatlow agrees to my proposal, I won't have time for entertaining guests, particularly those of a cultish disposition.

I wash my hands and return to the table.

"Have you given my proposal sufficient thought?" I ask, taking my seat.

"I have."

"And?"

He nods at a slip of paper on the table.

"My bank details," he confirms with a broad smile. "What kind of dad doesn't help his son when he needs it?"

"You agree to my solution?"

"As long as I've got the money to keep the wolves from my door, I'm all yours."

"This is good. Do you need to collect any belongings before we travel to Wiltshire?"

"Wiltshire," he splutters. "Christ, lad. I thought you lived local."

"What made you think that?"

"I dunno, but I don't suppose it matters. What does matter is that I can't come with you for a few days."

"Why not?"

"Because I've got stuff to sort out, plans to make. For starters, I need to call my mate and explain why I won't be starting work next week, and I need to pack up the flat before the new tenants move in."

"So, you can come down at the weekend?"

"Yeah, I reckon so. Give me your address and phone number."

I dictate both while he scrawls the details on a small notepad.

"I'll give you a bell once I've sorted everything, and I'll let you know when to expect me."

"How will you get to Wiltshire?"

"I'll drive."

"Very good. A vehicle will prove useful in our search for Lillian Tatlow."

"That's what I thought. I can't wait to get started."

"Is there anything you can tell me in advance?"

"There's not much, really, but I'll use the next few days to ask around. By the time I see you next, hopefully, I'll have a few solid leads."

"Understood."

"And you'll sort out that money as soon as you get home, right?"

He nods at the note containing his bank details.

"Yes," I reply, tucking the note into my pocket. "I will make it a priority."

"Good lad."

For the next hour and eight minutes, Shane Tatlow asks many questions about my life in Wiltshire. Ordinarily, I would resist such an interrogation, but if his assertion is true and he is my biological father, his curiosity is justified. Perhaps that is why I find his interest stimulating rather than irritating.

"Right, lad," he says, checking his wristwatch again. "As much as I'd love to sit and chat all afternoon, I really need to get on."

"Understood."

"We'll have plenty of time to get to know one another once I'm down at your place, right?"

"Yes, of course. I would like that."

"Me too."

He stands up, as do I.

"Something tells me you're not the huggy type," he chuckles, thrusting his hand in my direction. "But I've waited a long time to shake my son's hand."

Notwithstanding my hygiene concerns, handshaking is the most bizarre of practices. I don't understand it, and I've never wanted to do it, but for the first time in my life, I feel compelled to do it.

"It was nice to meet you," I remark, as our hands interlock.

"You're not wrong … son. One day, I think we'll both look back and reflect on what a life-changing moment this is, for both of us."

"I hope you're right."

He releases my hand but maintains his smile.

"Trust me — I am."

Chapter 34

So much has changed in the last twenty-four hours. That is the world, though; it never stops changing. Saying that, there is one tiny corner of the world that has not changed in twenty years, and that's the third bedroom in a house in Bulford Hill.

I open the door and sniff the musty air.

The bedroom is small and houses just a single bed with a table next to it, a wardrobe, and a chest of drawers. The walls are covered with floral-patterned paper, and the carpet is the colour of wet soil. I only vacuum and dust in here once a month because the room is redundant. It's a guest bedroom which, to the best of my knowledge, has never been occupied by a guest. That will change tomorrow.

I open the window and then dress the bed in fresh linen. The fresh air is welcome. I did not sleep well last night.

There is an expression I've heard many times throughout my life: the truth hurts. I never understood it because lying has a notable track record when it comes to causing pain.

As I lay in bed last night, my mind dwelt on the truth about Martin and Helen Armstrong. It did indeed hurt, though not in a way I could easily explain if someone were to ask, other than to say my internal organs felt like they'd doubled in weight. Given a choice, I would have preferred physical pain because there's usually a remedy. I discovered there's no pill or lotion to ease the discomfort of truth-induced pain.

When I finally fell into a fitful sleep, my brain must have worked on establishing the cause because I woke up this morning with a single word at the forefront of my mind —

betrayal. There can be no doubt that Martin Armstrong was the chief antagonist in the plot to defraud my biological parents, but it's Helen Armstrong's betrayal I cannot comprehend. For almost my entire life, she acted like a mother should. Indeed, she did such a good job that right up until I discovered the truth about my adoption, I had no clue. Was she a spectacular actress, or was I spectacularly naive?

Standing in the shower this morning, I concluded that Helen Armstrong's betrayal had to be the root cause of my pain. The truth does indeed hurt. Unwilling to suffer it indefinitely, I devised a treatment plan over breakfast.

I then spent an hour transferring all the framed photographs from the walls to cardboard boxes. I had intended to burn them in the garden, but it hasn't stopped raining all morning. They'll keep. At some point soon, I plan to hire a company to clear everything from my pseudo parents' bedroom, along with all their other clutter. If I am to rid myself of this intolerable curse, I must eliminate every link to the couple who inflicted it.

Much like my original mission, my life as the son of Martin and Helen Armstrong is now over. I now need a new life and a new mission to serve as a distraction. It is the only way.

Firstly, I will establish if Shane and Lillian Tatlow are my true biological parents. If — as all evidence suggests — they are, I will appraise their suitability for an ongoing parent-son relationship.

From the brief time I spent with Shane Tatlow yesterday, I found him to be friendly and supportive, which is more than can be said for Martin Armstrong. As for Lillian Tatlow, I need to understand why she abandoned me at that hospital. If her motives were genuine and she is of good character, there is a chance we might be able to move forward. She made a mistake, but she also attempted to make amends. There is no denying the mistake happened, and to pretend otherwise is illogical, but she and Shane Tatlow sacrificed everything they had to rectify it.

Humans often claim they'd willingly do anything to fix a mistake, but very few possess the fortitude to follow through on that claim. Shane and Lillian Tatlow were willing to give up all they had to be part of my life — that tells me all I need to know.

With the bed made, I vacuum the carpet and close the door. I have one more task to complete before lunch.

For my new mission to begin, I must first appraise what resources I have at my disposal. On the dresser in the kitchen sits an envelope, put there by Father Paul and subsequently ignored by me. It contains the details of Helen Armstrong's assets: her last will and testament. I've never had much interest in money, on account I had no long-term plans on Earth, but now it matters.

I locate the envelope and sit down at the table to read the contents. My mobile telephone rings, and Father Paul's name flashes up on the screen.

"Yes?"

"Have you got a minute, Simon?"

"One minute, yes."

"Good. I've got a date for your mother's funeral. It's a week Thursday."

"It is no longer of any consequence to me."

"Pardon?"

"I will not be attending."

"Heaven help me," he groans. "What's upset you now?"

"Upset me? Oh, just the lifetime of lies, deceit, and betrayal orchestrated by Martin and Helen Armstrong."

"What are you on about?"

"I don't have the time or patience to go over it, but know this: I never want to hear their names again, and there is zero chance I'll be attending that funeral. Is that clear enough for you?"

"No, it's not. What's happened to spark this … attitude?"

This is not a conversation I want, not that I ever want a conversation with Father Paul, but it is a chance to vent. It could also be an ideal opportunity to terminate our relationship — a minor milestone in my new mission.

"Why did my parents decide to move to Wiltshire?" I ask.

"I'm not sure Helen ever said much on the subject, but think it was something to do with your father's job."

"He secured a better job?"

"I don't know, but I suppose he must have. Why else would you uproot your family if not for a better job?"

"You really don't know?"

"Can you imagine how many conversations I've had in the last twenty years? You can't expect me to remember the details of every one of them, can you?"

"It matters not because I know why they dragged me here."

"You do?"

"Yes, and …"

I manage to stop myself from revealing what I know about the Armstrongs' misdeeds or who told me. Knowing Father Paul as I do, he'll either defend the indefensible or use the information as further reason to interfere with my affairs. However, the need to vent is still strong.

"Do you think they always had my best interest at heart?" I ask.

"Always."

"That's interesting because on Wednesday I had an appointment with Dr Jarvis at the surgery. He revealed an anomaly in my medical records."

"What kind of anomaly?"

"It relates to a doctor's appointment in Surbiton, shortly before we moved to Durrington. That doctor referred me to a behavioural specialist."

The priest's silence is telling.

"I never did see that behavioural specialist," I continue. "Why do you think that was?"

"I've no idea, but your parents loved you, Simon."

"There was a time, not too long ago, I might have believed in Mother's love, but that man never loved me. Ever."

"Perhaps your father wasn't equipped to show you, but he did."

"He never even wanted me — I know that much. Therefore. it isn't too great a leap to assume he neglected his parental duties, much to my detriment."

"That's not … listen, we need to talk properly. My car will be back from the garage in an hour or two, so I can come over then."

"No. There is nothing more to be said on the matter."

"There's plenty still to be said, Simon."

"Your minute is up. Goodbye, Father Paul."

I terminate the call, and with it, hopefully, my relationship with the interfering priest.

My hackles raised like Merle's when he spots a fox in the garden, I take a moment to compose myself. A glass of water helps. Then, I return to the table and Helen Armstrong's last will and testament.

I carefully peel the envelope open. Inside, there's a typed letter dated April 4th last year, when Helen Armstrong would have known about her illness. At the top, there's information about her chosen solicitor and executor.

I continue reading, and the part of most interest: a list of her assets.

The first item is the freehold property known as 30 Bulford Hill, Durrington, bequeathed to Simon Armstrong, along with all the chattels within.

As their only heir, I expected to be the new owner of this house. However, the shadow of a betrayal still looms large, and I cannot deny a sense of relief seeing it in writing.

The next two items on the list relate to bank accounts: a current account with a balance of £4,193.60, and a savings account containing £19,311.27. There are two beneficiaries, each bequeathed fifty per cent of the total: Simon Armstrong and St. Jude's Church in Durrington. I wonder what Father Paul would say if he knew the provenance of Helen Armstrong's money.

The following items on the list are as unexpected as they are puzzling: two freehold properties known as Unit 5 and Unit 6, Garratt Business Park, Wandsworth, and all associated income. Below the addresses are the contact details of a managing agent.

I sit back in the chair, perplexed. How did these properties come into Helen Armstrong's ownership, and why have they never been mentioned before? Rather than trek upstairs, I use my mobile telephone to search the addresses on a map. I discover the location of the business park is only seven miles from our former home in Surbiton. Logic suggests both properties were therefore acquired when Martin Armstrong was still alive.

With nothing else to learn from the map, I decide to call the managing agent. It rings four times before a female answers.

"I would like to speak with Roger Thomas, please."

"Who may I ask is calling?"

"Simon Armstrong."

"And can I ask the nature of your call, Mr Armstrong?"

"It relates to Units 5 and 6, Garratt Business Park, in Wandsworth."

"I'll put you through."

I'm left listening to a piano concerto for twenty-two seconds.

"Good morning. Mr Armstrong?" a thinly-accented voice then bellows. Welsh, I think.

"Yes. Mr Thomas?"

"That's right, but please call me Roger."

"I will. Did your colleague inform you of the reason for my call?"

"Yes, she did. You're Helen's son, right?"

"Legally, yes."

"Is she okay? I haven't spoken to her in person since … when was it? The summer of last year, I believe."

"She is dead."

"Oh, that's … I'm so sorry. She was a lovely woman."

I don't correct him because it would be a fundamental waste of my time.

"I'm not calling to discuss Helen Armstrong. I'm calling to discuss the properties she bequeathed to me in her will."

"I see. You now own them, do you?"

"I'm sure there are some legal formalities to be completed, but in time I will own them, yes."

"And what is it I can do for you?"

"I have questions relating to the properties. Are you able to answer them?"

"I'll do my best. Fire away."

"How long did Helen Armstrong own them?"

"I don't know off the top of my head, but I know Mr Armstrong purchased both units some twenty years ago. When he passed, Mrs Armstrong became our client."

The timing of the acquisition is interesting. Although approximate, it would have been around the time Martin Armstrong defrauded my biological parents. I wonder if their money helped fund the purchase.

"The will mentions associated income. Do you know what that refers to?"

"The rental income, I presume. Both units are on long leases."

"My knowledge of property-related matters is limited. What is a lease?"

"It's a formal rental agreement between the owner of a property and the tenant. In this case, your mother was the landlord, and the tenant is a distribution company. They pay a fixed annual rent, paid monthly, to use the buildings for their business."

"I see. How much do they pay?"

"Let me just check."

I can hear the repeated click of a mouse down the line.

"Both units are on the same terms," Roger Thomas confirms. "£36,000 per annum on a ten year, full-repairing lease, renewed two years ago."

I do the maths.

"That equates to £6,000 per month, correct."

"Yes."

"And that amount is paid to Helen Armstrong every month?"

"Yes, although we haven't heard anything from her solicitor yet. Until we do, the rent will keep rolling into her account until we're instructed otherwise."

Roger Thomas has just answered a long-standing question — who paid for Helen Armstrong's care at Elmwood House?

"Thank you, Mr … Roger. You have been most helpful."

"You're welcome, and if you don't mind me asking, what do you intend to do with the properties?"

"Do with them?"

"Are you intending to keep them or sell them?"

"I haven't decided. If I were to sell them, how much are they worth?"

"As a ballpark, they'd probably achieve £500,000 each in today's market."

I don't know much about money, but I do know that a million of anything is a lot.

"I will let you know as soon as I've made a decision."

"Righto. If there's anything you need in the interim, or you'd like a formal valuation, feel free to call me. And again, I'm sorry for your loss."

"Yes. Goodbye."

I end the call, but I keep the mobile telephone in my hand. I had no idea properties were so valuable, which begs the question: how much is this house worth?

Using the search facility, I pull up a list of local property agents and call the first number on that list. A male promptly answers.

A seven-minute conversation ensues, during which I learn that 30 Bulford Hill is worth approximately £400,000. On three separate occasions, the male asks if he can visit the house to conduct a free valuation. I decline and make a note never to speak to him again, even if I do sell the house. Some humans are too persistent for their own good.

After terminating the call to the agent, I sit back in my chair and reflect on both telephone calls. I now own assets worth approximately £1.4 million; a meaningless sum to someone who does not covet material possessions. Still, I understand that money offers opportunities, and the more of it you have, the greater those opportunities.

My new mission is more than adequately funded. I am ready to go.

Chapter 35

If I had to draw up a list of things I do not like, it would likely take an entire day to compile. At the top of that list, certainly in the top-twenty, would be waiting and vague timescales.

I arose at my usual time of 6:44 am after another restless night of sleep. I completed my ablutions, consumed breakfast with Merle, and then vacuumed the entire house twice. At 8:51 am, I still had no idea when to expect Shane Tatlow. The thought of doing nothing while I waited held no appeal, which is why I ended up on the pavement outside the house, tallying the traffic. I soon discovered that Saturday mornings are not a good time to tally traffic in a village.

By 10:22 am, I had tallied just nineteen vehicles: thirteen motor cars, and six vans. Then, my mobile telephone rang.

The conversation with Shane Tatlow was brief, and I could barely hear him due to a poor connection. He did, however, manage to confirm his estimated time of arrival. Unfortunately, he specified lunchtime. I lost the connection before I could press for a specific time.

When is lunchtime? Surely it varies from individual to individual. Shane Tatlow might arrive around noon at the earliest, but it could be as late as two o'clock.

This is why I detest vague timescales.

11:00 am comes, and I return inside. With nothing else better to do, I sit at the kitchen table with the photograph of Lillian Tatlow laid out before me.

In reality, it's just a piece of card printed with hundreds of dots in myriad colours. It is also a snapshot of a past I wasn't part of and features a female I wouldn't recognise if she sat next to me on the bus. And yet, she is my mother.

"Mother?"

Just saying the word in such an unfamiliar context produces a rush of hormones, like stepping into an ice-cold shower. When I finally get to meet Lillian Tatlow, I cannot use Helen Armstrong's moniker any more than I could live with a different cat named Merle. The associations are too numerous, the accompanying emotions too painful.

"Mum?"

There is a clash of senses. The word sounds right, but it doesn't compute with the image before me. That's probably because I'm not looking at Lillian Tatlow as she is today, but how she looked twenty years ago. She is younger in the photograph than I am today. She is mum to a ten-year-old boy who had no idea he had a mum. He had a mother, and he shared a home with a male he called father, but he never had a mum.

Is that just semantics? Perhaps I'll find out; perhaps I won't.

I pick the photograph off the table and place it on the dresser next to the envelope containing Helen Armstrong's will. Someone with imagination might suggest the positioning is symbolic, but to me, it is just a coincidence. Both items are tenuous links to two females: one I don't know, and one I didn't know as well as I thought I did.

My introspection is interrupted as the cat flap swings open. Merle then strolls across the floor and leaps up onto the table.

"I presumed you were asleep in the lounge."

I stroke the fur behind his ear, which triggers his reassuring purr.

"You're damp. Have you been in the bushes?"

Prior to my visit to Primrose Hill, I struggled to determine what I might miss about this existence. Merle, and Merle only, came to mind. And yet, I left. I abandoned him much in the same way Lillian Tatlow abandoned me. At least she left me safe in the knowledge I would be cared for, whereas I left Merle at the mercy of an unreliable priest. Who knows what might have happened to my feline companion had I not returned.

"I am sorry, Merle."

He pads nearer until our faces are close.

"If you can forgive, I can too."

Whatever he was up to in the garden, his long yawn suggests it was tiring. Moving slowly, he moves to the edge of the table and jumps down. Within three seconds, he's through the door to the hallway, heading to the lounge where he'll sleep in the armchair for the rest of the day. Merle is reliable. Merle is predictable. Merle is important. That is why I must plan my new mission around his needs.

As much as it goes against my principles, I consume lunch thirty minutes ahead of schedule. It helps to fill the time, and I don't want to be eating when Shane Tatlow arrives.

I manage half a bowl of muesli before my stomach flatly refuses to accept another morsel.

The doorbell rings.

It's not even noon yet, so it's unlikely to be Shane Tatlow. It's most likely the postman. I hurry to the front door and open it.

"Alright, lad."

Shane Tatlow stands before me, a suitcase by his side.

"You are early. It isn't quite lunchtime."

"I managed to get away a bit earlier, and the traffic was kind."

I glance over his shoulder to a silver motor car parked on the driveway. It is old and in poor cosmetic condition.

"She ain't much to look at," Shane Tatlow remarks, following my gaze. "But as reliable as rain in March."

"I guess reliability is all that matters with a motor vehicle."

"Course it is. What do you drive?"

"I don't drive. I've never had the need."

"Just as well I do, then, if we're gonna find Lil."

"Indeed. Have there been any developments since we met?"

"Uh, possibly, but aren't you gonna invite me in?"

"Right, yes. Please, come in."

I guide my guest through to the kitchen. He then stands and surveys the surroundings.

"Nice," he comments. "This is bigger than my lounge."

"Like your motor vehicle, it is old but reliably practical."

Without replying, his attention switches to the view of the garden and the open fields beyond.

"We're really out in the sticks here. You're a lucky lad having all this on your doorstep."

"Luck played no part in my being here. It was a calculated property transaction conducted by Martin and Helen Armstrong."

"Yeah," he huffs. "Don't I know it."

I hadn't intended to discuss the first stage of my new mission so soon after Shane Tatlow's arrival, but his resentment towards the couple who purchased this house must be resolved. We cannot move forward if he is distracted by negative emotions.

"We should talk. Would you like a hot beverage?"

"Cup of tea would be smashing. Milk and one sugar, ta."

"I will put the kettle on. Take a seat."

He continues his survey of the kitchen as I make the tea. This is the kind of situation where my inability to make small talk is most greatly exposed.

"How was the weather in East Croydon?" I ask.

"Miserable, like the place itself."

"You do not like living there?"

"No, I bleeding don't. Would you?"

"Highly unlikely. It is noisy and over-populated."

"You're not wrong, which is why I'm glad to be here … with my boy, obviously."

The kettle boils, and I complete my tea-making task without another word. Then, I transfer the cups to the table and take a seat opposite Shane Tatlow.

"I have given much thought to our conversation on Thursday," I announce.

"Have you now?"

"Yes, and in particular, the troubling issue of Martin and Helen Armstrong's fraud. Their actions were despicable."

"That's one way of putting it, lad."

"I'm sure there are many, but discussing them would not be productive. We should not dwell on what we cannot change."

"Easier said than done. I've spent twenty-odd years trying to get over it, but it ain't easy."

"I have a solution. Reparations."

"Err, you'll have to enlighten me. I dunno what that means, exactly."

"The dictionary defines reparations as the action of making amends for a wrong one has done, by providing payment or other assistance to those wronged."

Shane Tatlow leans forward and rests his elbows on the table, hands clamped together.

"Are you talking about money?"

"Yes, I am. I must repay the £50,000 Martin and Helen Armstrong took from you under false pretences."

His eyes widen.

"I'm lost for words. Are you willing to do that?"

"It is the right thing to do, but there is one caveat."

"I see," he says with a frown. "I should have known there would be a catch."

"My request is simple: if I repay the money, you will refrain from mentioning what occurred ever again. Your bitterness, whilst understandable, will not change anything."

"Don't you think I have every right to be bitter?"

"Yes, but Helen and Martin Armstrong are dead so your negative feelings towards them are illogical, and it also threatens to undermine our … relationship."

"I don't see how it could."

"The only course of action open to me is repaying the money, which I have offered to do. However, I cannot undo the past. Do you understand?"

"Yeah, I understand. You've repaid the debt, and you don't want me banging on about what those bastards did to us?"

"Precisely."

"I can live with that, lad. Thank you."

"Your gratitude is unnecessary. As soon as I'm in possession of the funds, I will transfer £46,000 to your bank account."

"£46,000? I thought you said you were going to repay fifty."

"I've already paid you £4,000."

"Yeah, you have. Fair enough."

Our arrangement agreed, there is a brief pause in the conversation until Shane Tatlow poses another question.

"I hope you don't think I'm being pushy, but when do you think you'll be able to pay the money?"

"That is a difficult question to answer."

"I'll take a guess if that helps."

"Your money is a modest fraction of what I stand to inherit once Helen Armstrong's will is formally executed."

"When did she pass away?"

"Six days ago."

"Bloody hell," he coughs. "I didn't realise you'd only just lost her."

"Six days or six months — it matters not. What was hers will soon be mine, and then I can repay you."

"Has her solicitor told you when they intend to sort out the will?"

"I've not spoken to her solicitor."

He shakes his head whilst sucking air across his teeth.

"You wanna get on to them ASAP, lad," he says. "Solicitors are like locusts — you let them feed on your money unchecked, and they'll strip you clean."

"I don't understand your reference."

"They charge a small fortune for every hour of work, so they stretch out even the simplest of jobs to rack up huge bills. Take it from me — I've had more than my fair share of run-ins with solicitors."

"I see."

"And then there's the taxman. If you leave assets sitting idle, he'll find a way to have his unfair cut."

"Who is the taxman?"

"It's not a person as such, it's HMRC … Her Majesty's Revenue and Customs. If you don't wrestle control of what's rightfully yours from that solicitor, you risk HMRC snooping around."

"And that is bad?"

"Bloody bad. A mate of mine lost almost half of what his old man left him once those bastards got their snouts into the trough. If you want my advice, lad, get hold of that money as soon as you possibly can, and hide it where no one but you can touch it."

Shane Tatlow has unwittingly highlighted my lack of knowledge on financial matters, particularly those pertaining to taxation and planning. It would be unwise to ignore his advice.

"I will arrange to see the solicitor first thing Monday morning."

"A sensible move. Would you like me to come with you for a bit of moral support and to make sure they don't try and fob you off?"

"You would be willing to do that?"

"Yeah, course I would," he replies enthusiastically. "Anything for my boy."

"I am grateful."

I am not naive enough to assume Shane Tatlow's motives are entirely selfless. From what I have seen of his life, it is clear he needs that money sooner rather than later. Nevertheless, it is a shared motive as I would like to move forward with my new mission as soon as possible.

"I know you're grateful, but it should be me thanking you."

"There is no need."

"That's as may be, but thank you."

Perhaps it is a sign of an already forged understanding that Shane Tatlow doesn't indulge in excessive gratitude: a mere thank you, accompanied by a smile and a nod. Anything more I'd find awkward.

"Now you've given me some good news," he then says after a sip of tea. "I'd like to share some of my news."

"You have good news regarding Lillian Tatlow?"

"I don't know if I'd call it good news as such, but it's a good start."

"Explain."

"So, I told you I'd ask around a bit, see if anyone had heard from Lil recently. I made a few calls yesterday, spreading the word that I urgently needed to speak to Lil on a life-or-death matter, and word must have got around as a woman called Donna gave me a bell late afternoon. She waited tables in a West End restaurant and got pally with one of the other waitresses, called Lillian Tatlow."

"The west end of where?"

"London."

"This is good. We know where she is employed."

"No, 'cos according to this Donna, Lil left that job in July."

"But, that's four months ago. She could be anywhere now."

"True, but Donna said Lil came in late for a shift one day and told her she'd just had an interview at some swanky hotel in Knightsbridge. She assumed Lil must have got the job because she never came back to the restaurant after that shift."

"Then we know where to start. What is the name of that hotel?"

"This is the kicker, lad — Lil never told Donna the name. I checked last night and there are over a dozen high-end hotels in Knightsbridge."

"Should we go to Knightsbridge and investigate?"

"No point. I spent an hour of my evening ringing them all, but no one would confirm if they employed someone named Lillian Tatlow. Something to do with privacy laws or something."

"Bureaucrats."

"Yeah, exactly, but your old man is good at thinking on his feet. I gave them a sob story, saying we'd split up and I hadn't seen Lil since Christmas."

"That is the truth, is it not?"

"That bit is, yeah, but I spun a white lie into it. I told them there'd been a death in the family, and I desperately needed to get hold of Lil."

"You lied."

"Just a small white lie, lad, and technically it isn't even a white lie, is it? You're our son, and you've just lost your adoptive mother."

"I suppose that is true."

"Well, it worked. Not one of them was willing to confirm if Lil worked there, but they all said they'd pass on my message if she did."

"And?"

"And nothing. That's it."

"Lillian Tatlow has not called you?"

"Give her a chance. She might not be working this weekend."

"Or she might have moved on to another job."

"Possibly, but what you've gotta understand is that me and Lil weren't in a good place when she left. Even if she believes someone in the family has snuffed it, she might still be reluctant to call. We've gotta give her a bit of time."

"And what are we supposed to do while we wait?"

"I thought we might get to know each other."

"What do you want to know about me?"

"I mean, spend some time together. I've missed out on so much of your life, and I hoped you might welcome the chance to, you know ... bond."

"Oh."

"I wasn't thinking about a trip to the swings, lad," he says with a grin. "Maybe a pint in your local and a game or two of pool."

"Visit a public house?"

"Yeah, but if that ain't your thing, we could go to the movies, have a stroll and take in some of this country air. Whatever you like."

What can two strangers who, on the face of it have nothing in common, do together?

"What did Martin do with you?" Shane Tatlow asks as if he'd internally posed the same question.

"Nothing."

"Nothing?"

"If he did, I don't remember."

"He must have ... I dunno, taught you how to ride a bike."

"No."

"A kickabout in the park? A trip to the funfair?"

"I refer to my previous answer. We did nothing together."

"Sounds like a shitty kind of childhood."

"I have nothing to compare it to."

He shakes his head.

"I'm sorry I wasn't there for you."

"No apology is necessary. You are here now."

"That, I am. For as long as you need me."

"Thank you, and I am in agreement — it would be good to get to know you too."

"That's settled then," Shane Tatlow declares, holding out his hand. "Within a week, we'll know everything there is to know about one another ... agreed?"

Almost instinctively, I reach out and shake his hand.

"Agreed."

Chapter 36

After years of studying humans, there was one particular trait I couldn't fully comprehend: empathy. Was it innate, like fear, or a skill to be learnt and developed? I figured the ability to understand and appreciate the feelings of others should be innate until one encounter suggested otherwise.

On a visit to the Post Office, I waited in the queue behind a male of late teenage years. An elderly female was at the counter, and being the Post Office is small, it was impossible not to overhear her conversation with the cashier. The elderly female was attempting to pay the modest charge for mailing a package, but she couldn't find her purse. Consequently, she was rummaging around in her handbag for loose change.

After a minute or so, she confessed to being forty-five pence short. The disinterested cashier merely shrugged his shoulders whilst the male in front of me tutted and returned his attention to the screen of a mobile telephone.

Every time I visit the post office, I always ensure I have the exact money required for my purchase plus a significant contingency to avoid the situation the elderly female faced. I would imagine it embarrassing, perhaps humiliating, and certainly to be avoided at all costs.

Sensing the elderly female's discomfort, I stepped forward and gave her the forty-five pence she required. The youth in front of me just huffed as if my intervention was somehow delaying him further. He displayed no empathy whatsoever, nor did the cashier, for that matter. At that point, I understood —

empathy was most certainly not innate or as common as it should be.

After our conversation at the kitchen table yesterday lunchtime, Shane Tatlow went to great lengths to demonstrate his empathy. Initially, we discussed what we might do together in the afternoon, and I mentioned Stonehenge being nearby. Having never visited the prehistoric monument before, he leapt at the opportunity.

We spent two hours and nine minutes at Stonehenge, and for much of that time, Shane Tatlow lavished praise about the depth of my knowledge as I answered his numerous questions. Helen Armstrong never held back when it came to giving praise, even when it wasn't due, but Martin Armstrong never had a good word to say about anything I achieved.

From Stonehenge, we drove to Amesbury, and I showed Shane Tatlow where I used to work, plus other landmarks relevant to my life, such as the library and bus stop. On the way back to Durrington we detoured to a Chinese takeaway — not my suggestion, knowing nothing of Chinese cuisine. We returned to the house with crispy seaweed, which looked nothing like the seaweed I've seen on the beaches of Bournemouth, vegetable chop suey, and duck in plum sauce. I enjoyed the seaweed and chop suey, but I couldn't contemplate eating anything that once had a bill.

After dinner, we retired to the lounge and watched a movie on Channel Four called *Ghostbusters*. Shane Tatlow seemed to enjoy it, but I preferred the Star Trek movies. Still, it was a pleasant way to spend the evening and, by the time I retired to bed, I'd reached a conclusion — Shane Tatlow was more befitting of the father title than Martin Armstrong ever was.

This morning, I am alone in the kitchen, and all is quiet. It is Sunday, and I know some humans prefer to stay in bed later than necessary, so I have gone about my usual routine as silently as possible to avoid waking my guest.

With little else to do, I decided to continue reading *War of The Worlds*. As I turn the page to chapter fourteen, I'm interrupted by a creak on the stairs. Shane Tatlow then enters the kitchen.

"Morning, lad."

"Good morning. Would you like a cup of tea?"

"I could murder one, ta."

I get up and put the kettle on.

"I don't suppose you could stretch to a bit of breakfast too," he adds, taking a seat at the table.

"I can offer you toasted brown bread or muesli. Both, if you're hungry."

"I'm more a bacon and eggs man, as you can tell."

He rubs his plump stomach as if it's worthy of pride.

"Sorry, but I have neither bacon nor eggs, but I could go to Tesco Express and purchase some. It's only a short walk away, so I can be back within eighteen minutes."

"No, I'll go. I could do with stretching my legs a bit."

"Are you sure? I am the host, after all."

"And a very good one you are too, but I want to pull my weight while I'm here."

"Understood."

I make the tea and join Shane Tatlow at the table.

"Any plans for the day, lad?"

"Nothing specific."

"Seeing as the sun's out, we could go for a walk later?"

"Yes, I would like that."

"That's settled then. I'll finish my tea and pop to Tesco. Just make sure you've got a frying pan ready when I return."

"I will."

Twenty minutes later, and armed with the simplest of directions, Shane Tatlow departs. He did say he intended to pull his weight, but I notice his cup is still on the table. I try to swallow back the irritation.

"It's just a cup, Simon."

I've only ever lived with two humans, one for the last fourteen years. Although Helen Armstrong tended to accumulate clutter, she was fastidious when it came to domestic chores and always kept the house spotlessly tidy. On a subconscious level, her forensic attitude to cleaning must have influenced her adopted son because I cannot tolerate a mess of any kind.

I'm about to wash up the cup when the doorbell rings. Perhaps Shane Tatlow has forgotten his wallet.

I hurry up the hallway and open the front door.

"Oh, it's you."

"Yes, it's me."

Dressed in his priestly attire, Father Paul stands with his hands on his hips.

"What are you doing here?"

"I've got three boxes in the boot of my car … your mother's things."

"I told Rosie I don't want them."

"Yes, you did, and you really upset her in the process, which is why I'm now lumbered with the job. If you don't want any of Helen's possessions, you can throw them away yourself."

"Fine," I mumble.

"I had to park on the road. Whose car is that?"

He turns and nods towards Shane Tatlow's motor car, occupying the driveway.

"It belongs to a guest."

Father Paul doesn't respond; his attention suddenly fixed on a sticker in the rear window.

"Whoever it belongs to, they're a long way from home," he comments.

"How do you know where their home is?"

"The Crystal Palace sticker."

"What is a Crystal Palace?"

"They're a football team based in South London, near Croydon."

I detect the merest hint of negativity in his tone as if I am duty-bound to explain myself. Perhaps he is jealous because I have a guest who isn't him.

"Who I invite into my home is none of your business."

"Who is it, Simon?"

I cross my arms, indicating how little I want this conversation to continue.

"I thought we were friends," he says, his tone softer. "I'm not prying. I'm just looking out for you."

"I am perfectly fine, thank you. Now, show me to your motor car, and I'll remove Moth ... I'll remove the boxes."

He checks the time, and his shoulders slump.

"This way."

I follow Father Paul out to the road, and he opens the boot. Keen for the priest to leave before Shane Tatlow returns, I quickly transfer the three boxes from the boot to the pavement.

"Thank you. You may go now."

"What are you doing later?" he enquires. "I've got a service in forty minutes, but I thought we might get together afterwards to talk."

"There is nothing for us to discuss."

"Really?" he snorts. "There's the small matter of you refusing to attend your mother's funeral, for starters."

"I will not change my mind. Besides, I have plans later."

"Tomorrow?"

"Again, I have plans."

"What are you up to, Simon?" he asks, his usually bulbous eyes narrow.

"None of your business."

Another frown and another check of the watch.

"I'm running late," the priest snaps. "But we'll talk again ... soon."

I don't correct him because it would only delay his departure. I pick up one of the boxes, and by the time I return to the pavement for the second, Father Paul's car is gone.

Once all three boxes are in the garage, I drape a tarpaulin over them. They will join the boxes of photographs on a pyre when time and weather allow.

I return to the kitchen table and my book.

So compelling is the story I am ignorant to the time slipping past. When the doorbell rings, I instinctively glance at the clock — Shane Tatlow has been gone for fifty-six minutes. I let him in.

"Did you get lost?" I ask.

He steps into the hallway but doesn't wipe his feet.

"Sorry, lad. I got stuck on a phone call for the best part of half an hour."

"Was it …?"

"Nah, I'm afraid it weren't Lil. It was the bloke who set me up with that driving job in Newcastle. He was trying to change my mind."

"And did he?"

"Course he didn't," he says, handing me a carrier bag. "But I'm desperate for a pony. Can you make a start on breakfast whilst I nip up to the bog?"

He hurries away before I can question the relevance of ponies and bogs. Perhaps some things are best left unknown.

I decant the packet of bacon and carton of eggs from the carrier bag and light the hob. I'm sure I ate bacon as a child, but I've never cooked it. As for eggs, I was eight years of age when I learnt they are a bi-product of a hen's reproductive system — a cluster of developing ova. I haven't eaten one since, and I cannot understand why anyone would.

I open the bacon packet and place three slices in the pan. I then turn my attention to the eggs, holding one between my thumb and forefinger.

"Sunnyside up, lad," Shane Tatlow announces, as he wanders back into the kitchen.

"I don't know what that means. I've never cooked eggs before."

"Are you kidding me?"

"I don't think eggs are humorous in any way whatsoever."

He steps up to the hob.

"Here, let me show you."

I am relieved of cooking duties but not of a lesson. Timing is everything when cooking eggs and bacon, apparently: the former must be runny, the latter crispy, and, best I can tell, both must be dripping with grease.

"That should do us, lad."

Shane Tatlow turns off the hob. The contents of the pan look highly unappetising, but that doesn't seem to dent my guest's eagerness as he slides the food onto a plate and hurries over to the table.

"Got any ketchup?" he asks, taking a seat.

"I'm afraid not."

"Brown sauce?"

"No. I have salt, pepper, and I think there's some malt vinegar in the larder."

"Never mind. Come and talk to your old man while I polish this off."

I do as instructed, taking the chair opposite, but before I have a chance to instigate the requested talk, Shane Tatlow poses a question.

"Can I ask you something, lad?"

"Yes."

"I know we talked quite a lot yesterday, but you never said what your plans are."

"Plans?"

"Yeah, for the future ... now you're on your own."

"My plans depend on what happens with Lillian Tatlow, but I am currently keeping an open mind."

"And what if we never find her?"

"Do you believe that to be a possibility?"

"I hope not, but anything is possible, ain't it?"

"No, not anything, but I take your point. And, in answer to your question, I have given much thought to my future."

"Care to share it?"

"I will continue living here until Merle dies. He is not a young cat, and it would be unfair to uproot him."

"He's just a cat."

"Yes, he is, but he's also a good companion. I cannot overlook his needs again."

"Okay, so then what?" Shane Tatlow asks whilst noisily chewing a mouthful of food.

"Do you know what a Dark Sky site is?"

"Not the foggiest."

"They are areas in the United Kingdom with the lowest levels of light pollution. I would like to move close to one of those sites so I can continue my interest in astronomy."

"Why can't you do that here? It's pretty bloody dark at night."

"I don't wish to stay in this house long term. Besides, I'd like an observatory in the loft, and that is not possible in this house due to the angle of the roof pitch."

"Where's the nearest of these dark sky places then?"

"The closest is near Bodmin, in Cornwall."

"That's a long way from Croydon."

"Yes, but you'll be able to visit. I will purchase a property with enough bedrooms."

Shane Tatlow forks half a slice of bacon into his mouth but keeps it shut this time. I wait for him to respond.

"Sounds like you've got everything in hand, lad."

"It's only a provisional plan at the moment. As I said, a lot will depend on what happens when I meet Lillian Tatlow."

"Let's hope that's soon then, eh?"

"Indeed."

After finishing his breakfast and supervising the washing up, Shane Tatlow suggests we watch television for an hour and then go for a walk. I sit with him but choose to read while he watches a programme about World War II. There is minimal conversation but no awkwardness in the periods of silence. After forty-nine minutes, he switches the television off.

"Are you ready to walk now?" I ask.

He doesn't respond but leans forward and presses his fingertips against both temples.

"Sorry, lad," he grunts. "I think I'm getting one of my migraines."

Helen Armstrong occasionally complained of migraines, and in her case, the cure was to lay in a dark room.

"You should go to your room and close the curtains."

"That only takes the edge off for me. I need painkillers … you got any?"

"Yes, I believe so. Bear with me."

I hurry to the kitchen and return with a packet of ibuprofen.

"Here we are."

"Thanks, but they don't work with the migraines I get. You got any paracetamol, or codeine?"

"No."

"Dammit," he hisses, closing his eyes again. "This is gonna be a bad one, too — I can feel it."

"I would offer to purchase alternative painkillers, but the chemist is closed on a Sunday."

"They sell them in Tesco, I'm sure."

"Would you like me to go and see what they stock?"

"If you don't mind, lad. You'd be doing—"

His words are cut short by a sudden wince.

"Will you be okay for approximately eighteen minutes?"

"I think so."

"In which case, I will leave now."

After quickly putting on my shoes, I depart.

There is no queue at Tesco Express, and true to my word, I am back within eighteen minutes with a packet of paracetamol. The instructions state the tablets should be taken with water, so I head straight for the kitchen. Merle is sitting on the floor by the dresser, next to a white envelope.

"Have you been chasing insects again?" I ask, snatching the envelope from the floor. "I've told you before not to jump up onto the dresser."

I return Helen Armstrong's will to the dresser and pour a glass of water for Shane Tatlow.

When I enter the lounge, my guest is lying on the sofa, his eyes shut. I clear my throat, and he stirs.

"I have your painkillers."

Slowly, he sits up and takes the glass of water and two pills.

"Thanks, lad," he says in a scratchy voice before swallowing the pills and emptying the glass.

"I think I might head upstairs for a lie-down."

It seems we will not be going for a walk after all.

"I hope you feel better soon."

He waves his hand in the air while shuffling through the doorway to the hall. Eleven seconds later, the bedroom door clicks shut.

I continue reading for the next three hours, and the only time I'm aware of Shane Tatlow's presence is when I visit the bathroom. As I creep across the landing, I'm sure I catch the sound of his voice from the spare bedroom. I stop and listen more intently, but all I can hear is the clock ticking down in the hallway. I continue to the bathroom.

Ninety-three further minutes pass before Shane Tatlow exits the bedroom. From the lounge, I hear the toilet flush, followed by footsteps on the stairs.

He appears in the doorway.

"How are you feeling?" I enquire.

"Much better, ta."

He shoos Merle from the armchair and flops down.

"What are we having for dinner?" he asks. "I could eat a horse."

"Unlikely. The average horse weighs seven-hundred kilogrammes."

"For crying out loud," he mutters. "Do you take everything so literally?"

I apologise. Silence ensues for six seconds.

"Ignore me. I'm always a bit cranky when I first wake up."

"Noted. As for dinner, I had baked potatoes planned."

"With?"

"With sunflower spread?"

"Ain't you got nothing else?"

"I'm afraid not."

"Don't worry, I'll nip to Tesco and get a few bits in. I should have thought about it when I went this morning."

"Would you like me to come with you?"

"Nah, you're okay. I'll go now."

He turns to walk away but stalls momentarily.

"Before I forget," he says, turning back to face me. "Something crossed my mind earlier regarding wills."

"Something?"

"Yeah, all this talk of Helen Armstrong's will got me thinking. I ain't ever had much to leave or anyone to leave it to, besides Lil, but now you've agreed to repay that fifty grand, I should get a will sorted, don't you think?"

"It would seem prudent, yes."

"I'm glad you agree because whatever I have left when I check out, I'd like to leave it to you."

"Me?"

"Yeah, who else? I ain't got no other family, so why wouldn't I leave it to my son?"

"What about Lillian Tatlow?"

"Half that money is rightfully hers, so when we find her, I'll give it to her. That still leaves twenty-five grand, and I ain't got no plans to drop dead anytime soon, but you just don't know, do you?"

He is correct — Martin Armstrong certainly didn't know his life force would end so prematurely.

"So?" he says. "What do you say?"

I have no need for his money, now or in the future, but I think declining his offer would be considered rude. I'd likely donate his money to a cat's home anyway, but Shane Tatlow will be dead, so he'll never know.

"Yes, I would be willing to be a beneficiary."

"Nice one," he responds enthusiastically. "It'll put my mind at rest, knowing the money won't end up in the Government's coffers."

"Will you arrange this will when we meet with the solicitor tomorrow?"

"Nah, I'll do it myself. It don't cost nothing to download a will template from the internet, and then all I need to do is fill it in."

"I have a computer and a printer in my bedroom."

"Perfect. Maybe you can help me later on, and then all you've gotta do is sign it."

"Does a will require a signature?"

"Yeah, a witness. If it ain't signed by a witness, it ain't legal, you see?"

"Understood. I will sign the will."

"Good lad," he says with a broad smile. "You know it makes sense."

I nod in confirmation. In this new and uncertain existence of mine, I'll take sense wherever I can find it.

Whistling to himself, Shane Tatlow then departs.

Chapter 37

Looking out of the kitchen window at the garden, it seems unlikely I will be preparing a bonfire today. It's only 7:12 am, but the sky is full of dark clouds as far as the eye can see. Rain is a near-certainty.

Despite the gloomy view, my emotional state is better than yesterday and the days before that. I slept well last night.

After Shane Tatlow departed for Tesco Express yesterday, I analysed our conversation. Although it is hard to accept anything Helen Armstrong said as truthful, I did consider her advice regarding trust. I deemed Shane Tatlow's actions as a strong indicator of his trustworthiness. Firstly, the fact he intends to pay half the reparations to Lillian Tatlow indicates he is a man of principle. Secondly, he was true to his word regarding his will.

Accordingly, we spent an hour in my bedroom yesterday evening and eventually located a suitable template on a legal website. Once I printed two copies, Shane Tatlow carefully filled out each one, signed it, and I duly witnessed both documents, one of which he gave to me. He was so thorough, he even asked for copies of my identification to avoid any potential for fraud. A reassuringly prudent approach, I figured.

This morning, we have another will to deal with — Helen Armstrong's.

The kitchen remains quiet for over an hour, and I spend the time reading. I'm about to start a new chapter when Shane Tatlow wanders in.

"Morning, lad."

"Good morning. Tea?"

"You're a diamond. Please."

We swap positions as I get up to put the kettle on, and my guest sits down at the table.

"What time are you gonna call those solicitors?" he asks.

"I checked, and their office doesn't open until 9:00 am."

He glances at his wristwatch.

"Half hour or so, then. Make sure you call on the dot of nine; before they get too busy and start making excuses."

"Do you think they'll agree to see us this morning?"

"You're the client, lad, so don't ask — demand. And, don't take no for an answer. This is important, ain't it?"

"Yes. I will try."

He smiles.

Once I've made the tea, Shane Tatlow drinks it quickly and then rushes off to deal with his mythical pony again. He returns one minute before 9:00 am.

"All set, lad?"

I nod and begin typing the solicitor's number on my mobile telephone. Then, I watch the second hand on the kitchen clock, pressing the call icon when it reaches twelve. It rings seven times.

"Good morning," a female then chirps. "Dadson, Dodd, and Mayhew."

"Hello. I wish to speak with Leslie Dodd, please. This is Simon Armstrong."

"Will he know what you're calling about?"

"Highly unlikely, considering we've never spoken before. I am calling about Helen Armstrong."

"I'll put you through to his office."

Seventeen seconds pass before I'm connected.

"Hello. Leslie Dodd's office."

"This is Simon Armstrong. I would like an appointment with Mr Dodd this morning."

"What's it regarding, Mr Armstrong?"

"Helen Armstrong's last will and testament. I understand Mr Dodd is the executor, and I need to speak with him as a matter of urgency."

"And what relation are you to Helen Armstrong?"

"I was her son, but she is now dead."

"Um, right. Let me just check Mr Dodd's diary. Please hold."

I glance across the kitchen at Shane Tatlow. He returns a thumbs-up gesture.

"Sorry about that, Mr Armstrong," the female says. "I'm afraid the earliest appointment I can offer you is tomorrow morning."

"Tomorrow is unacceptable. I must see Mr Dodd this morning."

"Is there any reason you need to see him so urgently?"

"Yes."

The line falls silent.

"Would you like to tell me the reason, Mr Armstrong?"

"No."

The female breathes a heavy sigh.

"I'll tell you what I can do. Mr Dodd has a brief gap between his appointments at ten and eleven. If you get here for quarter-to-eleven, you can see him for ten minutes. That's the best I can offer."

Covering the mouthpiece, I relay the basic facts to Shane Tatlow.

"Take the appointment," he replies.

I return to the call.

"10:45 am will suffice. Thank you."

"I'll let Mr Dodd know, and please be punctual."

"I'm always punctual."

I bid the female goodbye and end the call.

"Nice work, lad. See what happens when you show 'em who's boss."

"She did comply in the end, so yes."

"Shall we have a spot of breakfast and then head into town?"

"I've had breakfast."

"I haven't. Do you want to practise your sunnyside eggs?"

I do not, but I feel compelled to try considering the support Shane Tatlow has given me. I switch on the gas hob.

An hour later, having served a breakfast I wouldn't wish upon my worst enemy, we are ready to depart. We leave the house and get into the dilapidated silver motor car. The inside reminds me of the trains in London, minus the boisterous youths.

"I've been thinking, lad," Shane Tatlow remarks, as he starts the engine. "About Lil."

"I take it you haven't heard from her?"

"Nah, nothing, but as I said, she might not have worked the weekend. I'm thinking about what we do if we ain't heard from her within a week or so."

"And what have you concluded?"

He moves the gearstick forward, and the car lurches off the driveway.

"I ain't concluded nothing," he replies, turning the steering wheel. "But, I did have an idea. We could hire a private detective."

"Do you think it would prove beneficial?"

"Better one professional than two amateurs who don't have the first clue. They'd likely find out more in a few days than we would in a few months."

"In which case, I am in agreement."

"Good lad. Let's see how things pan out over the rest of the week, and if we've heard nothing, I'll make some enquiries."

"Very well."

Shane Tatlow then turns up the volume of the radio, which is preferable to making small talk. Some of his traits I dislike, but he has redeeming qualities too.

The journey to Amesbury passes by in eleven minutes — eight minutes quicker than the bus. The time saving is primarily down to not picking up passengers, but the driver's inability to stick to the speed limit also contributes.

We arrive at a car park at 10:33 am.

"You got any change for the ticket machine, lad?"

"Yes."

"Do the honours then."

When I was a child in Surbiton, Helen Armstrong let me put the coins in the ticket machine and press the big green button. The novelty wore off when I became an adolescent, but I'm willing to oblige on this occasion.

From the car park, it's only a two-minute walk to the offices of Dadson, Dodd, and Mayhew. One minute into that walk, my mobile telephone rings. I don't recognise the number.

"Hello."

"Simon, it's me."

Father Paul. I come to a halt.

"This is not your usual number."

"No, I'm using a colleague's phone because the mobile reception here is dreadful."

"What do you want?"

"Half-an-hour ago, I received a scrambled voicemail from Leslie Dodd … about Helen's will."

"So?"

"You're on your way to see him, I understand?"

"He had no right to tell you that. It is my business."

"Our church is a beneficiary of that will, so that's why he called me. He wanted to know if there was a problem — Leslie happens to be one of my parishioners, so he knew Helen well."

"There is no problem. You were the one who insisted I read the will, and now I simply want to ensure it is executed efficiently."

"Why the urgency, though? I'll be back from Winchester this afternoon so we could see Leslie together."

Before I can reply, Shane Tatlow steps directly into my field of vision and taps the face of his wristwatch twice.

"We ain't got long, lad," he remarks with a frown. "Tell whoever that is to call back."

"Who's that?" Father Paul barks. "Who are you with, Simon?"

"Someone who wants to help me rather than interfere."

"Simon! Who is that?"

"It is none of your business, and I don't have time to waste on a pointless conversation. Goodbye."

I terminate the call and switch the mobile telephone off.

"Who was that, lad?"

"Father Paul McCready. He was a friend of Helen Armstrong's."

"What did he want?"

"He suggested I see Mr Dodd this afternoon with him."

"Did he now?" Shane Tatlow replies, rubbing his chin. "What's it gotta do with him?"

"His church stands to inherit a sum from the will."

"He can make his own appointment, and you did the right thing hanging up on him … you can't trust religious types."

"I concur. Father Paul thinks it's his job to interfere in my life now Helen Armstrong is dead."

"You don't have to worry about him now I'm around. If he turns up and tries sticking his beak in, he'll get short shrift from me."

"It's unlikely he'll turn up. He's thirty miles away, in Winchester."

"Good to know, lad," he replies whilst checking his wristwatch again. "We'd better get going."

Forty seconds later, we enter the main reception area of Dadson, Dodd, and Mayhew. I confirm our appointment with a female behind the desk, and she asks us to take a seat and wait. We are two minutes early, so her request is fair. We comply.

"When we get in there, lad," Shane Tatlow says in a hushed voice. "Let me do the talking, eh?"

"Can I say anything?"

"Yeah, course you can, but keep your answers short and to the point. The more information you give these bastard solicitors, the more they chat … and the clock will be ticking every second we're in there."

"But we only have ten minutes."

"That's long enough for what we want."

"Understood."

A silent minute passes.

"Before we go in," I say. "I have thought about your idea to hire a private detective. I am keen to find Lillian Tatlow, so can we instigate the plan earlier than you suggested?"

"If you like. I know a few people who can put us in touch with a decent one. It'll probably cost a few quid, mind."

"A few quid is not much."

"I mean, probably thousands."

"I would consider it money well spent if the detective locates Lillian Tatlow."

"You leave it with me. I'll get on to it later."

The receptionist calls over. We may see Mr Dodd.

Shane Tatlow takes the lead as we pass through a door and along a short corridor to an anteroom where another female is at a desk.

"Mr Armstrong?" she enquires.

"Yes."

"You can go on through," she says, nodding towards the door to, presumably, Mr Dodd's office.

We do as instructed.

The office is of a decent size, but it's untidy: piles of folders and reams of paper stacked on almost every flat surface. A white-haired male of advanced years is seated behind the desk. He slowly gets to his feet.

"Mr Armstrong?" he says.

"I am Simon Armstrong."

I decline his hand shake.

"I'm Mr Tatlow," Shane Tatlow confirms, shaking Mr Dodd's hand. "I'm here as Simon's guardian … and father."

The old male looks puzzled as he sits back into his chair.

"Father?"

"Yeah. We've just reconnected after Simon tracked me down. Martin and Helen Armstrong weren't his … what's the word?"

"Biological parents," I suggest.

"That's it."

"Oh, I see," Mr Dodd says, turning to face me. "I did wonder as I knew your mother well. She was a lovely woman, and her passing is a sad loss for our church. My sincerest condolences."

I nod.

"So, what is it you needed to discuss with me so urgently?"

"The will," Shane Tatlow answers. "I'm here to make sure you don't mess my boy around. We wanna know when he's gonna get what's rightfully his?"

"With respect Mr …"

"Tatlow."

"Sorry, yes. With respect, Mr Tatlow, Mrs Armstrong only passed away last week."

"So?"

Mr Dodd looks at me as if I should react. I look at his tie, and it reminds me of an old set of curtains that once hung in the lounge.

He turns back to Shane Tatlow.

"Even with a will, the probate process can take many months. It's unlikely Mr Armstrong will see the proceeds of Mrs Armstrong's estate this side of Christmas."

"That ain't good enough. My boy has plans, and he needs that money within four weeks. Right, son?"

It really doesn't make any difference to me, but now Mr Dodd has mentioned Christmas, I would like the opportunity to bring the dusty boxes down from the loft one final time.

"I …"

"He's got his heart set on a place in Bodmin, you see," Shane Tatlow continues. "And with the property market the way it is, any delay could cost him a small fortune. Do you wanna cover that loss, Mr Dodd, just because you're a bit lazy with your admin?"

"It has nothing to do with our admin, Mr Tatlow. There's the land registry to consider, and they …"

"Don't give me excuses. If you can't sort it out within four weeks, you can whistle for all that other legal work we were gonna give your firm. Probably the best part of ten grand's worth."

Shane Tatlow turns to me.

"I know this firm of solicitors in Wandsworth. They wouldn't mess you around like this."

"Let's not be too hasty," Mr Dodd interjects, suddenly finding a smile. "I can't promise we'll be able to hit your four-week target, but I'm sure we can expedite the case, seeing as Mrs Armstrong was such a good and loyal client."

"That's what I like to hear," Shane Tatlow replies, finding a smile of his own.

"Was that all you wanted to discuss?"

"No. Simon wants me to handle all his financial affairs, so we also want power of attorney granted … and before you respond, we want it done pronto."

"Well, that's a whole …"

The telephone on Mr Dodd's desk suddenly trills. He presses a button next to the handset and leans forward.

"Janet. I'm with a client."

"I know, and I'm sorry, Mr Dodd. It's just … there's a woman in reception who wants to see you."

"Tell her to come back at lunchtime. As I said, I'm with a client."

"I did tell her, but she's quite insistent she sees you now. It's an emergency, apparently."

"Janet!" Mr Dodd replies, his tone agitated. "I said, lunchtime."

With that, he jabs a button on the telephone and sits back in his seat.

"My apologies, gentlemen. Where were we?"

Shane Tatlow opens his mouth, but in the same instant, the sounds of raised voices echo from beyond the office door. A female voice shouts something I don't quite catch.

The door swings open.

"I'm so sorry, Mr Dodd," the female from the main reception says breathlessly. "She just barged past me."

The *she* in question is another female, standing just inside the doorway and staring at Shane Tatlow.

That female is Rosie.

Chapter 38

Despite the generous proportions of Leslie Dodd's office, it suddenly feels cramped. At least one of the five people here should not be, and the second is here only because the first one is.

"What is this?" Mr Dodd demands to know. "I said I didn't want to be disturbed."

He didn't use those exact words, but I'm not inclined to correct him because I'm too busy trying to work out why Rosie is here. She is still staring at Shane Tatlow, and he is now looking at her, eyes wide. I cannot determine the expression on his face, but I wouldn't associate it with positive emotions.

"Are you okay, Simon?" Rosie asks, turning to me.

Before I can answer, Shane Tatlow leaps out of his chair and confronts Rosie.

"I don't know who you are," he growls. "But you're interrupting an important meeting. Now, piss off."

"Don't you dare …"

Shane Tatlow shoves Rosie towards the door, yelling profanities over her objections. She stumbles back but just about manages to maintain her balance by grabbing hold of the door frame.

"Get out!" he shouts over and over, adding to the chaos of the scene.

"Simon," Rosie manages to shout before Shane Tatlow shoves her again, with significantly more aggression.

She tumbles back through the doorway and lands on her backside. Not satisfied with his work, Shane Tatlow then leaps on top of Rosie, pressing his forearm up against her throat. He then leans in and spits a mouthful of words in her ear. I didn't catch what he said due to the thrumming of a heartbeat in my ears, but what is clear is that Rosie is distressed, and Shane Tatlow's extreme reaction to her arrival is clearly the cause.

I stand up and step towards the doorway.

"Desist," I demand. "You're hurting her."

"I've got this, son," he says, glancing up over his shoulder. "Go and wait outside while I deal with this ... woman."

"I said desist."

Rather than comply, he applies more pressure to Rosie's throat. Her right arm flails out, fingernails clawing at the carpet.

"Go and wait outside!"

The furnace ignites.

Almost of its own volition, my hand snaps forward and snatches the collar of Shane Tatlow's jacket. I couldn't begin to estimate his weight, but it is akin to dragging a sack of coal up a steep incline. Fortunately, my strength is greater than the weight, and I'm able to free Rosie. Coughing and spluttering, she then scrambles to her feet. I release my grip on Shane Tatlow's collar.

"What ... what has he told you?" she gasps.

"Told me?"

Shane Tatlow clambers up and lunges towards Rosie. She sidesteps his move, and he clatters into the side of a filing cabinet with another outpouring of profanities.

"Do you ... do you know who he is?" Rosie pants.

"Shut your mouth!" Shane Tatlow gasps while trying to get to his feet. "I'll swing for you!"

"He says he is my biological father," I reply.

"He's lying. When you were born, he was halfway through a two-year prison sentence for fraud."

My mind attempts to process Rosie's accusation, but it lacks sufficient information.

"How do you know who he is?"

"Because this worthless, lying scumbag used to be my stepfather."

This new information doesn't help. If anything, my thoughts are even more confused.

"I don't understand. He is helping me find my biological mother — Lillian Tatlow."

"Simon," Rosie pleads. "Lillian died fifteen years ago."

"What? This cannot be."

I turn to Shane Tatlow.

"Only one person is lying here, lad," he says. "And it ain't me. This bitch is shit-stirring."

"Go to hell, Shane," Rosie spits before turning to me.

"Listen, Simon. I don't know what lies he's been spinning, but Lillian died fifteen years ago … and I can prove it."

She pulls out her mobile telephone and frantically taps the screen.

"See, look."

I stare at the image of a simple headstone engraved *Lillian Rosemary Tatlow (née Hill)*. Below that name are two dates: the day she was born, which coincides with the date Cindy Akinyemi gave to me, and the day Lillian Rosemary Tatlow died. The latter is, as Rosie stated, fifteen years ago.

It is as good as proof. Lillian Tatlow is dead.

I turn to face the man who told me otherwise.

"You lied. You told me Lillian Tatlow left you at Christmas last year, and she was working in a hotel in Knightsbridge."

"Eh … I, err, I didn't know she was dead."

"He's a liar!" Rosie spits. "He was arrested six days after she died, trying to cash-in her benefit cheque. He got a suspended sentence for it. You can check, Simon, on the internet. Everything I've told you is the truth, I swear."

I take three steps towards Shane Tatlow.

"Why did you lie to me?"

"Alright," he huffs, backing away. "No hard feelings. I just needed the money."

He then turns to Rosie.

"You're gonna pay for this. Mark my words."

"We'll see what the police have to say about it first, shall we?"

Rosie returns her attention to the screen of her mobile phone. Shane Tatlow doesn't wait to see who she's calling.

"Fuck this, and fuck you all," he snarls before turning on his heels and barging his way back through the door towards the reception.

Silence.

"Would someone care to explain what on earth is going on here?" Mr Dodd says, now standing in the doorway.

He is not the only one with no idea what is going on.

"What was Shane doing here with you?" Rosie asks me.

"He was helping me with Helen Armstrong's will."

"Helping how exactly?"

"By looking after my finances. He said he'd take care of everything, so I didn't have to."

"Have you given him any money?"

"Four thousand pounds."

"Oh, Simon," she says with a pained sigh. "I'm so sorry, but Shane Tatlow is a con man. He's spent time in prison for defrauding people … lots of people. Whatever he was up to, he wouldn't have stopped until he'd pilfered everything your mother left to you. That man is a parasite."

"He said he was my father, and he had proof."

Mr Dodd coughs.

"Should I call the police?" he asks.

Rosie turns to me.

"We should talk, and I'll try to explain everything. You can then decide if you want the police involved."

Negative emotions pepper my thoughts, clouding the path away from this confusion.

"I ... yes. I don't understand."

"Come on. Let's get some fresh air."

Rosie apologises to Mr Dodd and then gently guides me out of the door. All I can do is put one foot in front of the other until we reach the pavement outside the building.

We walk perhaps sixty or seventy metres in silence until we come to a bench. The grey clouds are still heavy in the sky, but they've yet to release their load.

"Let's grab a seat here," Rosie says.

Drone-like, I comply and sit down. Of the many, many questions I want to ask, one is by far the most pertinent.

"How do you know ... how did you know?"

Rosie closes her eyes for two seconds and draws a long, deep breath.

"I'm sure there's a lot you want to know, but can you answer a question for me?"

I nod.

"How did Shane find you?"

"He didn't — I found him."

"I'm not with you. What do you mean?"

"I found out that Lillian Tatlow wrote to Helen Armstrong some twenty years ago, claiming to be my biological mother and asking if she could see me. A woman at Social Services gave me the address, so I went there last week. That's how I first met Shane Tatlow."

"And he lied to you about Lillian?"

"So it seems. Now, I need to know what you know."

"Yes," she replies with a puff of the cheeks. "You probably do."

Seven seconds pass before Rosie speaks again.

"What I'm about to tell you is difficult, Simon, and if it were down to me, we wouldn't be having this conversation at all. But, I owe you an explanation."

"Then, explain."

"Okay. I haven't seen Shane Tatlow in years, thank God, but I knew he still lived in East Croydon. When I called you the other day, and you said that's where you were, I presumed it was just a coincidence. Then, yesterday, Father Paul asked for a word after the service, and he mentioned the car on your driveway with the Crystal Palace sticker in the rear window. Again, I thought it was probably just a coincidence as Shane was a massive Crystal Palace fan, but I had this bad feeling in the pit of my stomach … I can't explain why."

"Wind?"

"Probably," she snorts. "I didn't sleep much last night, worrying about it, and then Father Paul called me this morning in a bit of a tizz. Whatever you think of him, he cares about you. Anyway, he told me you were on your way to the solicitors to sort out your mother's will, but you weren't alone … he didn't hear much, but he said you were with someone with a strong South London accent. I was in two minds whether to gatecrash your meeting or not, but I couldn't take the risk."

I take a moment to digest the information. That processing only incites another raft of questions.

"That evening, after we watched a movie, you said your stepfather kicked you out when you were fifteen. Was that Shane Tatlow?"

Rosie nods.

"Your mother died some months prior. Correct?"

Another nod. She then retrieves her mobile telephone from a pocket and swipes the screen several times, stopping on a photograph.

"This is her."

I lean forward to inspect the image of a woman with green eyes and bronze-coloured hair. She looks uncannily similar to the woman in the photograph Shane Tatlow gave me. Confusion mounts.

"This is Lillian Tatlow?" I ask.

"Yes, but she was only Lillian Tatlow for six years. I was in primary school when she first met Shane Tatlow, and they married a year later."

"First met? He said they were together as teenagers."

"That's not true. Lillian must have been about twenty-four when that scumbag wheedled his way into her life. Before that, her name was Lillian Hill."

"I don't understand. This Lillian woman who wrote to Social Services, claiming to be *my* mother. Or, was that another of Shane Tatlow's lies?"

"No, that part was the truth. Lillian was your biological mother."

"But … you said she was *your* mother. And, how …"

I pause for a period and recalibrate my thoughts.

"I can't trust you or anything you say. For all I know, you and Shane Tatlow are part of the same conspiracy to defraud me."

"No, Simon," Rosie replies, eyes pleading. "With God as my witness, I would never harm you in any way."

"Words are meaningless, not that yours make any sense. I am sick of lies … that's all you people do. Lie. Lie. Lie."

I'm about to stand up and depart, but Rosie places her hand on my forearm.

"I know this must be so confusing, but please, let me show you something before you walk off."

Without waiting for my reply, she delves into her handbag and pulls out a slip of cream paper.

"Look at this," she says, handing the paper to me.

"What is it?"

"It's my birth certificate, and it proves who I am."

I unfold the slip of paper. At the top, there's a crest and the words *Certificate Copy of an Entry of Birth*, both in red. Below is a table of information, written in black pen, and the header of the first column reads: when and where born. In this specific document, the *when* is the 29th September 1991 — one day before I was born — and the *where* is Croydon University Hospital.

Rosie leans across and points at the fifth column along.

"See," she says. "Name, surname, and maiden name of mother — Lillian Rosemary Hill."

I don't know if it is the same woman who wrote a letter to Helen Armstrong, but before I can question Rosie further, my eyes drift left to the second column.

"How can this certificate be yours?" I ask. "It does not say Rosie."

"No, because Rosie wasn't the name I was given at birth. When I was a little girl, I couldn't pronounce my name properly … I kept saying *Pimtoes*, so Mum suggested Rosie as it was easier to say."

I stare down at the certificate — one word hits me like a sudden jolt of electricity.

"Your name is … Primrose?"

"Yes. Born to Lillian Hill at Croydon University Hospital."

"On the 29th … Primrose Hill 29/09."

"That's right. I was born the same day as you, at the same hospital, to the same mother."

Her declaration somehow sucks the oxygen from my lungs. I cannot breathe.

"You … what? I don't …"

She grabs my hand with a grip so tight I can feel the pulse throbbing in her fingertips.

"I didn't want you to find out like this … I swear. I wasn't going to tell you until … I don't know. I just wanted to meet you, get to know my brother."

Her words come fast, as do the tears that are now rolling down her cheeks.

"I didn't even know I had a twin until last year," she continues. "When granddad died, I found an old suitcase full of Mum's possessions in his attic. I don't think he'd ever opened it

… he can't have … he'd have told me the truth. I know he would."

Despite Rosie's heightened emotions, it is impossible not to look at her revelations in any other way than with cold logic. I turn to face her.

"You are my sister?"

She nods, biting her bottom lip.

"Born to Lillian Hill on the 29th September?"

"Yes."

"But you were not abandoned, were you?"

My question is met with the slightest shake of her head.

"What kind of person decides to keep one child and abandons the other?" I ask. "Unless that person knows one of their offspring is defective."

Rosie's demeanour hardens in an instant.

"No, Simon," she says forcibly. "It wasn't like that."

"How was it then? You clearly know."

"Mum never told me about you, but knowing her I can make some assumptions. She was a sixteen-year-old runaway who'd just given birth to twins. I'm not condoning what she did or pretending I understand, but perhaps she gave you away because she thought a boy would fare better than a girl. Perhaps that was as basic and as complex as her thinking was at the time. Mum made a terrible, terrible decision, but she was just a vulnerable, naive child herself."

"You don't know, then?"

"Well, um, no. I'm just speculating because I can't begin to understand how a mother could abandon one twin baby and keep the other."

I wrench my hand from Rosie's and stand up.

"You are no better than she was, or Shane Tatlow for that matter." I counter. "You infiltrated my life under false pretences, and now you expect me to believe this … this concoction of half-truths and speculation?"

"I understand why you're upset, but …"

"Do you?"

"Of course I do. And I swear I only got the job at Elmwood so I could spend some time with you. I thought … I thought I could get to know you, and we could be friends. That's as much as I could have hoped for."

"Or, you were after my inheritance, like Shane Tatlow."

"Now you're being ridiculous. I don't want a penny of your money."

"No? Don't tell me you're not after your share of the reparations."

"Reparations? What reparations?"

"The £50,000 Martin and Helen Armstrong blackmailed from the Tatlows twenty years ago."

Her expression implies she is aghast.

"I don't know what you're on about, Simon, but I can tell you something for nothing — Shane Tatlow is far more likely to be the perpetrator of a blackmail plot than the victim. Whatever he told you, I'd bet my last fiver it's the polar opposite of the truth."

"The truth," I scoff. "You people don't know the meaning of that word."

"I can help you understand if …"

"No, you will not."

"Please, Simon."

It is now clear my entire existence is just a wall of lies, and every single individual who has passed through that existence has layered another row of lies on top of the last. That wall is now so high, there is no hope of me ever seeing the truth. Ever.

Rosie attempts to place her hand on my arm.

"Don't you dare touch me. In fact, don't you dare come anywhere near me again."

"Simon," she pleads. "Talk to me."

I have nothing further to say, and walk away. The promised rain begins to fall.

Chapter 39

I arrive home soaked to the skin, but no amount of rainfall could douse the heat building within me. Never have I known the furnace to burn with such intensity, such ferocity.

"Merle! Merle!"

My companion is not in the lounge or on my bed. I change out of the sodden clothes and hurry down to the kitchen. He is not asleep on the table or hiding in the bushes outside — no surprise, considering the rain.

"Merle! Merle!"

My calls are met with stony silence. If it were not for the occasional patter of raindrops on the window sill, that silence would be absolute. It is a stark contrast to the screaming in my head. It began within seconds of leaving Rosie on that bench, and now it feels like a coven of banshees has taken occupation of my skull.

It is intolerable.

I drink four glasses of water, one after another, and then sit at the table. There are six coasters, each patterned like a chequerboard with thirty-six yellow and blue squares.

"One, two, three …"

The screaming continues.

"Five, six, seven, eight, nine …"

Louder. Louder.

I count all thirty-six squares, but the screaming is relentless. There has to be another way. Frantic, I get up. Food? Will that distract my mind? I hurry to the cupboard and open it. As I reach for a packet of muesli, my hand stops in mid-air. On the shelf above the muesli are the four bottles Helen Armstrong kept for the purposes of entertaining: Port, Sherry, Brandy, and Vodka.

"Alcohol."

Many years ago, perhaps when I was a young adolescent, I asked Helen Armstrong why Martin Armstrong spent so much time at the public house. She said he enjoyed drinking alcohol. I wondered why, and she said some people liked to drink because it helped them cope with the stresses of life. Years later, I discovered some humans do indeed use alcohol as a mental anaesthetic.

I reach up and grab the nearest and fullest bottle: vodka.

It looks as benign as water, but the label confirms the fluid inside is forty per cent alcohol. There's no indication of what the contents might taste like. Undeterred, I twist the cap, remove it, and sniff the neck. I imagined the liquid might have a fruity scent, but the only odour I can detect is similar to hand sanitiser. The lack of any obvious scent suggests the clear liquid will be near tasteless. Perhaps no bad thing.

After half-filling a small glass, I pull a breath and take my first ever gulp of an alcoholic beverage.

"Cuuughraa!"

There is no taste, but the burning sensation at the back of my throat is shock enough. No one would be stupid enough to gargle battery acid, but I can't imagine it being any less unpleasant. That thought begs the question: why do people drink this fluid voluntarily? I wait for the burning to ease, and the answer comes to me: humans don't consume alcohol for the taste.

The screaming continues.

I refill the glass and raise it to my lips, but reluctance causes me to hesitate for a second. At that second, the familiarity of the scene triggers a long-forgotten childhood memory. It wasn't in this house, I'm sure, but I remember suffering from a stomach ache. Helen Armstrong then forced me to drink a pink-coloured medicine. From previous experience, I knew it tasted foul, but she urged me to gulp it back, saying that as nasty as the medicine was, it'd take away all the pain in a heartbeat.

On that occasion, she did not lie. Vodka is now my medicine. I empty the glass in one swift gulp and then fill it for the third time. By the sixth refill, I'm beginning to wonder if I have some level of immunity to alcohol as the screaming continues.

Lies. Lies. Lies.

Checking the clock, I realise it's only been eleven minutes since I opened the bottle. Does the process of intoxication require more time or more vodka? I cover both bases by knocking back a seventh refill and waiting.

Then, the screaming relents by a fraction. I wait another six minutes and take an eighth shot.

I feel peculiar. It is not a pleasant sensation, like standing in a hot shower after a walk on a cold day, but it is not unpleasant either. More importantly, though, it appears to have dulled the raging inferno within me. Ironic, considering the flammability of alcohol.

Peculiar, I conclude, is a preferable state of mind. With that, I dispense with the glass and gulp back vodka straight from the bottle. Two-thirds remain.

From nowhere, some kind of peace descends. It is not the same peace as pre-sleep, but a muted sense of reality, of not being in the present. I sit back in the chair and wallow in the sensation. Looking everywhere and nowhere, my attention then settles on a battered old document box hidden beneath a tea towel.

"Private and condif ... confed ..." I stammer, unable to coordinate my mouth and brain.

I already suspected this body might be failing, but now it's utterly broken.

"You, like all the others, are dead now, Martin Armstrong ... what are you going to do?"

The screams return, but I now have two weapons at my disposal: vodka, and rage.

I take another swig from the bottle and stand up. On unsteady legs, I move around the table until I'm positioned directly over the filing box. I then remove the tea towel.

"Damn you … Father!"

I pick the box up and raise it above my head. With every sinew twitching, I slam the box towards the tiled floor as if trying to break through the Earth's crust. It explodes in a flurry of dust and shattered metal and paperwork.

The release is overwhelming.

My legs buckle, and I fall to my knees. I thought the release of rage would help, but I fear it was acting like a bung. Convulsions build in my chest, and within seconds, the first escapes as a sob. Another soon follows, and another. I can no more stop them coming than I can stop waves crashing on a beach. Tears sting my eyes whilst a searing pain threatens to rip open my chest.

This … this hell, is inhuman. I would rather be dead.

The kitchen is no longer silent. The banshees must have escaped as their pained cries are now echoing around me, from every direction. I want it to stop … all of it.

But, it doesn't stop.

I curl into a foetal position and cover my ears, but I can no longer differentiate between the sounds of reality and those in my head. It is just one continuous cacophony of noise. Closing my eyes does not help. All I can see is a picture of Rosie Hill at the moment she unleashed her turmoil. To look at her face, you would assume moral purity, but she is no different from the others. The humans lie, the humans deceive, the humans manipulate. The humans inflict pain — all of them.

I no longer want to live amongst them.

My mind allows a seed of a thought to germinate. There is a way to end this, all of this. It would be permanent, too.

I must terminate my life force.

It started as just a thought, but now I have something to focus on — a problem to solve, and I'm good at solving problems. It is a project of sorts, and all successful projects rely upon effective methodology. Speed will be critical as I would not want to endure a slow death or a painful one. I do not like pain. I should also consider the efficiency of the method. There can be no margin for error.

Decision made, I allow my thoughts to hone in on a specific method of self-execution. It is a pity I cannot visit a vet and ask to be put down.

Drowning would be too haphazard, and I do not like the idea of being starved of oxygen. An overdose of medication is a possibility, but I would need to research which kind of medication is most effective, and then there is a question of sourcing it. I could cut my wrists and bleed to death. There would be some pain involved in the initial cut, but I could mitigate the worst of it by consuming more vodka. There's also the benefit of expediency. I could do it now, in this kitchen, with just a bread knife.

Something brushes against my cheek. I open my eyes.

"Merle," I rasp.

He sits down only fifteen centimetres from my face and stares at me. His inquisitive eyes are as wide and green as I've ever seen them, his fur as black and sleek as the day he first entered this house.

Why is he here, now, before me?

"Do you know?"

His eyes narrow.

I have suffered so many obnoxious emotions of late; all inflicted upon me. It is, therefore, strange that the emotion I am now suffering is self-inflicted. That is not to say the guilt is unwelcome because at least I understand it. It dampens the noise in my head, and I wonder if perhaps emotions are like elements:

some cancelling others in the same way water cancels fire. I do not know.

"I'm sorry. I promised I would not leave you again."

Helen Armstrong once said it is the most human thing of all to put the needs of others before your own. In that sense, I am human because I cannot leave Merle alone. His needs outweigh mine.

"I will not terminate my life force, Merle," I sigh. "At least, not until you have expired."

Satisfied with his intervention, he yawns and gets to his feet. I watch on as he then pads slowly across the strewn paperwork. To my surprise, he stops after covering one metre and looks back in my direction. It's no more than a glance, but it's as if he is checking on me. Task complete, he then bounds off towards the hallway while my eyes remain fixed on the spot he just vacated. The reason: an envelope with my name on it, laying on top of the paper chaos.

I sit up and reach for the envelope. The handwriting is unmistakably Helen Armstrong's.

Do I want to read it? No. Should I read it? Possibly.

I open the envelope and extract two pieces of paper, inked with the same handwriting.

My Dearest Simon,

I've written hundreds of letters over the years but none so difficult as this one. I'm on my sixth attempt now, and I hope it's the last because I need to prepare dinner soon.

There comes a point in our lives when we must face the inevitable, rather than pretend it is a problem for another day. For that reason, I've spent the last few weeks getting my affairs in order — I believe that is the term people like to use. I've prepared a will and, in time, I will confirm the plans I'd like instigated when I pass. Don't worry though; I'll ask Father Paul to handle everything.

On the subject of worry, I want you to know your father made provisions for us both in his will, so you should never have to worry about money. That isn't to say you shouldn't continue working for Mr Choudhary because it is good for you to have a purpose in life, a reason to get out of bed in the morning. We all need that, sweetheart, and for every year I've been lucky enough to call you my son, you have been mine.

Whilst I know you will never suffer from a lack of money, what does concern me is your lack of family. I would be lying if I said I'd never wished for more children, but it was not meant to be. I am sorry I failed you in that respect, and it breaks my heart to think of you being alone, when I'm gone.

The primary reason for writing this letter is because of family. It may cross your mind at some point that you have a family somewhere, or at least a group of people biologically connected to you. You may decide you'd like to find them, and you may hope they are good people who will take you to their hearts and love you like your Father and I did.

I'm so sorry to say this, my darling son, but that path will only lead to disappointment. Let me explain why.

The name of the woman who gave birth to you is Lillian Tatlow. I haven't had reason to think of her for some years, but when we last communicated, she was married to a man by the name of Shane Tatlow, and they were living in South London. I know this because they somehow discovered our address in Surbiton and wrote us a letter. They then turned up at our door a few days later, unannounced.

I will not burden you with full details of what ensued after that first meeting, but I will tell you that they levied threats to take you away from us, unless we paid them a substantial amount of money. They were not good people, and they certainly did not have your best interests at heart. Perhaps foolishly, we paid them to leave us alone. For five months, they did.

I can only assume they squandered the money on alcohol and drugs and other vices, because they came back for more. We could have paid them, but they would never have stopped. And, God forbid, if they had launched a claim for custody, even only partial, they would have made your life an intolerable misery. Shane Tatlow didn't have a paternal bone in his body, and Lillian was clearly not of sound mind. If I were being charitable, I would say she was a weak-minded woman, easily manipulated.

The reason why I'm now writing this letter in Durrington, rather than Surbiton, is because we had no choice but to disappear, to ensure those people could never find us. We gave up the lives we'd built in Surrey to do what was right for you, and I'd do it again in a heartbeat. Truth be told, I love it here now, so something good came of something awful.

Whilst we have built a good life in Wiltshire, it did come at a price. I don't know how those people discovered our address, but I couldn't risk the same thing happening, so we had to make certain sacrifices — your schooling being one of them. I should say, however, it was your father who made the greatest sacrifice. I know he could be a difficult man but he himself had a difficult upbringing. No one taught him how be a father and I'm afraid he struggled with the role. He loved you enough to give up his own dreams, though, and I never want you to forget that.

The second reason I decided to write this letter is to impart one last crumb of advice. It might be the final crumb, but it is by far the most important — embrace difference, sweetheart. I'm no philosopher, but I've learnt that difference is at the very core of what makes us human. Unlike animals, our lives are not dictated by the rising of the sun or the changing of seasons. It is human to seek different experiences, visit different places, and to learn from those who lead lives different to our own. When I am gone, I hope you can find the strength to experience what this world has to offer.

In short, don't be afraid of difference, and be proud of what makes you different. Remember, there is only one Simon Armstrong, and he is beautiful and kind and thoughtful and brave. Above all though, he is my son, and I love him more than words could ever convey.

That's all I have to say. Hopefully, you won't get to read this letter for many years, God willing.

Look after yourself, my little star man.

Love always — Mum xxxx

TEN DAYS LATER ...

Chapter 40

"Well? What do you think?"

Merle takes one look at my new suit and darts through the cat flap.

"Rude feline."

A courier delivered the suit yesterday, and I must admit it looked different in the photographs on the website where I purchased it. It is too late now. I cannot attend a funeral in denim jeans and a sweatshirt.

I check the time.

The service is due to start in fifty-four minutes, at 10:00 am, but I agreed to be there before the masses descend. It is better to be early than late, especially when attending a funeral. I leave the house.

If there is a God, he decided today's weather would be Helen Armstrong's favourite kind of weather. It is a crisp autumnal morning with the bluest of skies and a gentle breeze. Yes, Mother would have approved.

St Luke's Church is only a four-minute walk from Bulford Hill, and I spend each of those four minutes going over what I need to say when the time arrives. I am nervous, but I am also determined. The latter emotion outweighs the former.

Another emotion joins the fray as I pass through the lychgates: trepidation. This will be the first time I have stepped foot in a church in fourteen years, with the only prior visit for Father's funeral. I make my way up the path to the vestibule, the two enormous oak doors already wide open. A figure emerges from the shadows as I approach.

"Wow," he says. "That suit is quite a statement, Simon."

"Good morning, Father Paul."

"Come in," he beckons, waving his hand.

I step past the oak doors, and the temperature drops by several degrees.

"Mother loved tartan," I remark, as Father Paul invites me to sit on the nearest pew. "She had a dog as a child: a West Highland Terrier called Jock, who she used to talk to in a Scottish accent so he'd understand her better. Illogical, but I suppose Mother was very young. She was also partial to Scottish shortbread and Dundee cake. Even the curtains in her bedroom are a tartan design."

Father Paul smiles.

"Are you nervous?" he asks.

"What makes you think that?"

"You don't usually talk so much."

"I'm … anxious."

"That's why I wanted to talk to you before anyone else arrives. A bit of a pep talk, if you like."

I nod.

"Oh, I spoke to Mr Choudhary yesterday," Father Paul says brightly. "He wanted to confirm the arrangements for flowers. He also mentioned you've accepted a job with his cousin."

"That is correct. I start next week."

"I'm pleased for you. Mr Choudhary strikes me as a decent man."

"He was fond of Mother. He told me often enough."

"Most people were, Simon."

The conversation feels stilted, and I don't feel inclined to keep it going.

"Did you know your mother's side of the family all hailed from Ayrshire?"

"Possibly. She might have mentioned it."

"Well, Helen was very proud of her Scottish roots, and I think she'd be chuffed to see you in such a striking suit. I must admit it's growing on me."

We are making small talk, and I now realise that it sometimes serves a purpose. In this case, it is because I feel uncomfortable. In all honesty, I have felt uncomfortable around Father Paul since he witnessed the tail end of my emotional breakdown ten days ago.

After he returned from Winchester, he came straight to the house and let himself in. The grief I'd been warned about arrived with Mother's letter, and coming off the back of my conversation with Rosie, my mind imploded. As Father Paul knelt beside me and tried to offer comfort, I denied the situation required his involvement, but my tear-stained face and the mess in the kitchen were clear evidence I'd hit rock bottom. Admitting you need help is uncomfortable.

The small talk over, Father Paul casts his gaze across the rows of empty pews.

"I don't think there will be many empty seats today," he remarks. "Helen was a popular member of the church and the local community."

"And yet, I will be the only member of her family in attendance."

"I think we both know that family is more than just a biological connection."

I nod.

"You know, Simon," he continues, "I don't have any family … not in the traditional sense."

"They are all dead?"

"No, my Dad is still alive, and I have an elder brother, but we haven't talked in years."

"Why not?"

"Let's just say they didn't approve of my calling."

"They do not believe in religion?"

"Quite the opposite. Dad is a staunch Catholic which is why he was so against my joining the church."

"I am confused."

"Can I let you into a little secret?" he asks in a low voice.

"You can rely upon my discretion."

He leans a little closer.

"I know how it feels to be an outsider, to think of yourself as different from everyone else. I've felt the loneliness, the confusion, and I've spent too many lonely days living in denial. It's not easy coming to terms with who you really are, especially when you're on your own. Fortunately, I have all the family I need in this community, and they couldn't be more loving or supportive. Your mother was my rock, Simon … she truly was."

I'm not sure I understand the priest's confession, but I do understand he is trying to be empathetic.

"So," he continues. "I think family is simply a group of people who support one another unconditionally. A place where you belong."

"Like a tribe?"

"Yes, like a tribe, but without the tribalism. It's a small but crucial distinction."

"I would concur."

"Glad to hear it," he replies with a faint smile, although it quickly withers. "And, seeing as you brought up the subject of family, I should warn you — Rosie will be coming along to pay her respects."

"Right."

"I know she didn't break the news to you in the way she wanted, but it's been ten days. Are you going to talk to her?"

My skin prickles.

I'm about to chastise the priest, having already told him I do not welcome his conversations with Rosie in which I am the subject. However, if it were not for one such conversation, I might have fallen for Shane Tatlow's con.

"I don't think I can."

"But, the poor girl has no one else to turn to. She's your sister and as much a victim in all of this as you."

"Rosie was not abandoned as an infant."

"True, but in many ways, her life was much tougher than yours. She spent too much time in foster care, and that excuse for a step-father kicked her out when she was still a child."

"She told you about her upbringing?"

"Yes, and when I think about the life you had with Helen, you got the better deal."

"Perhaps, but there is no denying Rosie lied to me."

"Not quite. She just didn't tell you the truth."

"Withholding the truth is deception, and therefore a lie."

"Logically, I can't argue with that, but some lies inflict damage whilst others protect. Rosie didn't tell you the truth because she was trying to protect you."

"That assumes she is telling the truth about our relationship."

"If you'd spoken to her, you'd know she's telling the truth."

"She has proof?"

"She has a photo of you and her together as babies that she found in her late mother's possessions."

"That is not proof. Shane Tatlow has a photograph, and he used it to deceive me."

"The truth always comes out, Simon, as that Tatlow character discovered. When the police catch up with him, he'll get his just rewards. Rosie, on the other hand, is willing to do a DNA test … she's that confident."

"She told you that?"

"Yes, and she told me in this very church, four days ago. For a Christian, lying in God's house is a sin. She truly believes you are brother and sister."

"Believing and knowing are not the same thing. I believed I was … it doesn't matter."

"Even without a DNA test, you should look at Rosie and then look in the mirror. I can't believe I never saw it, but now I have, there's no denying you're siblings."

"There are undoubtedly physical similarities between us, but I cannot take that as proof."

"Agree to a DNA test, then, but you need to talk to her. Rosie is leaving in three days when her notice period at Elmwood is up. I'm telling you this because she doesn't want to go, and you shouldn't want her to go."

Behind us, a sudden cough breaks the silence. We both turn around. An elderly couple are standing inside the vestibule.

"Seems you're not the only early bird," Father Paul says to me in a low voice. "I'd better say hello to our first mourners."

"Okay."

"Do you want to come with me?" he asks. "I thought it would be nice for you to meet some of Helen's friends."

"Perhaps afterwards. For now, I would like time to think."

"Fair enough. Why don't you go sit at the front and use the time to reflect."

"I will."

"You could always say a quiet prayer for your mother while you're waiting," he suggests with a wry smile. "If you were so inclined."

I don't respond, but it doesn't matter. Father Paul gets up and heads towards the elderly couple, welcoming them in a suitably sombre tone.

Taking the priest's advice, I get up and move to the front pew. It won't be long until Mother's coffin is brought in and placed in front of the altar. Father Paul came to the house the day after my breakdown and spent a couple of hours talking to me about what the funeral service would entail. Better to be prepared for the tougher moments, he suggested.

I cannot deny my view on Father Paul has shifted over the last ten days. He wants to help, but as he succinctly put it, he can only do so if the recipient of his help is willing. Instead of accepting support from a man with honest intentions, I willingly took help from a charlatan. Accepting my mistake does not make me feel any better. I have been foolish, and that is why I now feel uncomfortable in Father Paul's company. If he has noticed, he hasn't mentioned it.

As much as I'd like to offer a prayer for Mother, the growing tightness in my chest is a constant distraction. I count the panes of coloured glass in each of the seven windows instead.

Slowly, quietly, the pews begin to fill.

Besides the low murmur of voices, piped music fills the still air, specifically Merle Haggard's music. It was part of Mother's wishlist, and I'm glad she chose it. It is a comforting reminder of the many times she prepared lunch while singing away to herself.

I bask in that memory for a period until I feel compelled to view the scene over my left shoulder. Father Paul was right — every pew is occupied, from front to back. Some of the faces I recognise, many I don't. These people knew Mother, though, and thought enough of her to dress up and attend this service. Knowing how little I want to be here, I have to admire their loyalty. That is what family do, I suppose. They show loyalty even when that loyalty offers no reward.

A sudden hush falls across the church, and everyone stands. I know why but I wish I didn't. I close my eyes and count to ten, and when I open them, six pallbearers are moving slowly up the aisle to my left, carrying Mother's coffin. The knot in my chest tightens.

The pallbearers carefully place the coffin on a raised platform, then turn and bow towards it. They depart, and Father Paul takes up position at the pulpit. He clears his throat.

"We gather here today to celebrate the life of Helen Armstrong, who has now returned to her home with our God, the Father."

I cannot shift my gaze from the walnut casket only four metres away, and as Father Paul says a prayer and then asks everyone to stand for a hymn, I only half hear what is said. The hymn begins, and people sing. I still don't know if I can, but I try.

The organ plays a final note, and the congregation sits down as one.

"We will now be hearing a few words from Helen's son, Simon," Father Paul confirms.

I knew this moment would come, and we've practised what I am to do at least eight times. On each occasion, I didn't have to contend with jelly-like legs or a bone-dry mouth. I swallow hard and shuffle the five metres towards the pulpit, taking Father Paul's place behind it.

He had warned me it could be overwhelming talking in front of a crowd, but he also offered some helpful advice. Rather than focus on the sea of faces staring up at me, I pick a spot on the rear wall and keep my eyes locked upon it. I can still sense the expectation, though, as if it had a physical presence.

"My name is …"

My voice is harsh, croaky. Father Paul promised to leave a large glass of water on a shelf inside the pulpit. I reach for the promised glass and take a long sip of water. I try again.

"My name is Simon Armstrong, and this is …"

Also on the shelf is a caricature of a bear with beige fur and large almond-shaped eyes. I reach for the bear and carefully sit him on the pulpit in front of me.

"This is Oscar."

I pause and count to five in order to slow the frantic beat of my heart.

"There was a time," I continue, "when I thought Oscar was my only friend. He was given to me by the woman you've all come to mourn — Helen Armstrong — my … my wonderful mother."

Another gulp of water is required.

"What I didn't realise is that Oscar was not my only friend. Like so many of you, Helen Armstrong was always there for me ... to soothe my ills, calm my soul, and keep me from harm. She was ... no, she *is*, my guardian angel."

I glance across at the priest. He replies with a reassuring smile.

"I have never made a wish before because I've never believed in wishes, but I'm willing to try one now. I wish with all my heart that Mother was still here, and I could tell her what I should have told her before it was too late."

A few deep breaths.

"Sad as it is, I don't think my wish will come true, but that doesn't mean she can't hear me."

I turn to face the walnut casket.

"So, Mum, thank you, and ... and ... I love you."

The knot is so tight I can barely breathe. Still, I have said what I had to say, which is just as well as I can feel the tears welling in my eyes, and there appears to be a small turnip lodged in my throat.

I return to the front pew.

Father Paul reads a prayer, and another hymn follows that. There's a reading, with the continuous sound of muted sobbing throughout. I don't know how long the service goes on for but I spent the remaining minutes gripping the edge of the pew so tightly, my fingernails leave an indent in the wood. I have never wanted something to end so desperately. And yet, I somehow manage to remain seated until the pallbearers return. It is my cue to stand.

As I follow Mother's coffin down the aisle, I use the same coping mechanism I employed during the eulogy. Head high, shoulders back, I keep my eyes locked on a patch of brickwork in the rear wall. To anyone looking on, it might appear Helen

Armstrong's son is a brave, stoic soul. They have no idea how close I am to another meltdown.

We emerge into the sunlight, and I can finally breathe again. It is not over yet, but the fresh air is a welcome relief.

The burial element of the service is no less challenging than the part inside the church. It is blessedly shorter, though. Once the coffin is committed to the earth, Father Paul invites me to sprinkle soil into the open grave. There was a time, not so long ago, I'd have poured scorn over such an act. I'd have called it illogical, verging on ridiculous. Now, I understand the point of it and, to a broader degree, Mother's religious values.

A final prayer is delivered, and slowly, the mourners filter away. I cannot take my eyes away from the grave and the thought that my mother is in a wooden box at the bottom.

Father Paul approaches.

"How are you holding up, Simon?"

I'm more inclined to ask a question of my own than answer the priest's.

"How do you do this?"

"This?"

"You must conduct many funerals every month. How do you cope with all the ... grief?"

"It's a good question," he replies, placing his hand on my shoulder. I flinch, but not as much as I usually would. "You're into astronomy, right?"

"I was, and hope to be again, yes."

"So, you might appreciate a quote from the Russian novelist, Fyodor Dostoevsky. He said: 'the darker the night, the brighter the stars — the deeper the grief, the closer is God.'"

I ponder his answer for eight seconds.

"I understand the reference about the stars, but the rest of that quote makes no sense to me."

"One day it might ... or it might not. What I can tell you is that it made a lot of sense to your mother, and you should take great comfort in that."

Almost instinctively, my mind begins to pick at the priest's statement. I stop the analysis within a few seconds. Here and now, I would much rather be comforted than right.

"Shall I walk you back to the vicarage?" Father Paul asks. "I know you're not keen on meeting people, but a wake is a good opportunity to celebrate rather than mourn a life."

"I will, but I'd like five minutes alone with Mother to say my last goodbye."

"Of course. Take all the time you need."

He pats me on the back and departs.

For the first time since I arrived at St Luke's, I am alone. I step towards the edge of the grave and look down.

"Hello, Mother."

There is nothing to count nearby, not that I'm inclined to count. I would much rather think about Christmas conifers and Buzz Lightyear and homemade cakes and chess and Hank Williams, and the countless other warm memories I can attribute to Helen Armstrong.

"Merle is in good health. He sends his regards."

I close my eyes and picture Mother's face. If I try really hard, I can almost hear her reply.

"And, thank you for the letter. It meant a lot."

The letter meant so much; I've kept it on my person since I first read it. I'm about to read it for the twenty-fourth time when the slightest hint of a floral scent drifts past my nose: floral but too synthetic to be from the sprays surrounding Mother's grave.

I turn around.

Chapter 41

"Hi. I'm sorry to interrupt."

Wearing a black dress and clutching a small handbag, Rosie bows her head slightly.

Her presence here threatens to ignite the furnace. I must remain calm.

"That is more or less what you said the first time we met."

"Was it?"

"I'm surprised you don't remember, being it was the moment your deceit began."

"I'm not here to defend my actions, Simon. I did what I thought was right and I'd do it again."

"You thought lying was the right thing to do?"

"Right, wrong ... what does it matter? You know the truth now, and it's clear I've already burned my bridges. To me, that's all that matters."

From a nearby tree, a lone crow caws loudly.

"I tried calling you dozens of times," she continues. "And I came round the house twice but you ... I don't think you were in."

I was at home, but I chose not to answer the door.

"What do you want from me, Rosie ... sorry, Primrose?"

"Please don't call me that. I hate it."

"It's your name."

"But I didn't choose it, any more than the dysfunctional life I had growing up. I didn't want either but that's what I got — a shitty name to go with my shitty childhood."

Rosie's words carry obvious resentment.

"You are angry," I comment. "I should be the one who is angry, don't you think?"

"You have every right to be disappointed in me, hurt even, but not angry. I never wanted the truth to come out the way it did, but it was always my intention to tell you the truth. You have to believe that."

"How can I believe you when I don't even understand your motives?"

"You want to know why I didn't tell you right from the start?"

"Yes."

Her shoulders relax a fraction.

"If I told you everything, would it help to rebuild your trust in me?"

It is a straightforward question, but I cannot compute the implications.

"Well? Will it make any difference?" Rosie urges.

I remain mute. She takes four steps towards me, stopping two metres away.

"I'm your sister, Simon … your twin sister. If that means nothing to you, just say so. I'll leave you in peace, and you'll never see me again."

I look down into the grave and then up towards the tree where the crow has ceased cawing. Rosie moves closer, but only by centimetres.

"Would it help if I told you how *I'm* feeling?"

"I don't know."

"Well, I feel angry and sad and … and, most of all, I feel cheated. I've felt lonely for as long as I can remember, and yet, all the time, I had a brother I didn't even know existed. Thirty years, Simon. When I think about all we've missed out on, I can't help but feel cheated."

Her admission is not what I expected. It raises questions.

"How long have you known about me?"

"Since September last year. I was clearing out Granddad's house as the council were keen to re-let it, and I found a suitcase in the loft. I've no idea how it got there, but I managed to break the lock, and that's when I realised it contained everything Mum owned when she died. It wasn't much to show for a life. She did own a trinket box full of cheap jewellery, although that wasn't all I found in the trinket box."

"Go on."

"There were two identity bands, the kind they put on the ankle of a newborn baby in hospital. Both were from Croydon Hospital and one had my name printed on it, plus my date and time of birth. The second had the name Aaron Hill — born on the same date but twenty-one minutes earlier."

"Aaron Hill? Not Simon?"

"No."

"Then why would you assume I am that child?"

"Because there were two photos at the bottom of the trinket box. Can I show them to you?"

"If you must."

Rosie clicks open the clasp of her handbag and withdraws the photographs. She hands the first to me. It features two cribs side-by-side, each with a tiny infant inside. It is the photograph Father Paul referenced.

"Turn it over," Rosie instructs.

I do as she asks. On the back are the hand-written names Aaron and Primrose Hill.

"This proves nothing," I remark, handing the photograph back to her.

"No, but this one might," she replies, swapping the first photograph for the second.

I inspect the image. Taken from a distance, it is of a young boy in a school playground.

"Is that boy you, Simon?"

I study the photograph, and it is unmistakably me. Aged probably nine or ten, I am seated on a wall with my back straight, staring at nothing in particular.

"Yes," I mumble.

"You need to look on the back again."

I turn it over. Again, someone has scrawled a few words in black biro, although the handwriting is different from the first photograph. There are three words: *Simon Armstrong. Aaron?*

"I don't know how Mum found you," Rosie says. "But I don't think it's too much of a leap to assume you were born Aaron Hill."

"Who took this photograph?"

"I don't know."

I don't know either, but I can make an educated guess — Shane Tatlow. Having established where my parents lived, all he had to do was watch the house and follow me to school. I wouldn't be surprised if more than one copy of this photograph once existed, with the other sent to my parents with the letter as bait.

I hand it back to Rosie.

"I know this is all circumstantial," she says, placing both photographs back in her handbag. "But I think Mum gave birth to us in Croydon Hospital and two weeks later, after being discharged, the enormity of her situation must have hit hard. Can you imagine being sixteen, and trying to cope with two babies?"

"No, I cannot."

"I don't know for sure why she decided to leave you at a hospital in Epsom, but I guess it was far enough from Croydon that no one would make a connection to a set of twins born ten miles away. In her head, it probably made sense."

"If that is what happened. As you said, this is all circumstantial."

"True, but if you're not convinced, I have two suggestions."

"Namely?"

"Firstly, we can take a DNA test. That'll prove beyond all doubt that we're brother and sister. However, I think there's another test we can do here and now."

"What kind of test?"

Rosie once again delves into her handbag and pulls out a small puck-like object. She flips it open to reveal a circular mirror.

"Here," she says, handing the mirror to me. "Look at your face and then look at mine. Then, tell me we're not siblings."

I don't take the mirror — there is no need. Deliberate or otherwise, Rosie has not applied any makeup, and her hair is tied back so I can see the entire shape of her face and the lines of her bone structure. It is the same face I look at in the bathroom mirror every morning.

Not for the first time of late, a creeping acceptance moves ever closer. I must push back, test it to breaking point.

"If you really are my sister, why did you wait an entire year to find me?"

"I didn't wait — it's taken me a year to find you. All I had to go on was the name Simon Armstrong and a date of birth, but not even that was right, was it?"

"My birthday?"

"You were born on the 29th of September, but obviously they didn't know that at the hospital where you were found. Their estimation was a day out."

"How did you find me, then?"

"It was absolute luck, and seeing as you want complete honesty, I'd all but given up looking. I must have found every Simon Armstrong in the country — and there are a lot, I can attest — but not the Simon Armstrong I wanted. Then, one day I was reading an article on some random news website. At the bottom, there was a link to an archive of local news stories. So, I clicked through to the archive and searched your name. I initially found two Simons that weren't you, but then I found an old newspaper article about some kid in Wiltshire who correctly guessed the exact number of jelly beans in a jar. I clicked on the link and compared the photo on the page to the one I found in Mum's trinket box. It was the same boy — you."

"That does not explain how you ended up working in Elmwood Care Home."

"Once I knew roughly where you lived, I searched the electoral roll, but that didn't help. I then scoured every local website I could find, trying to locate any mention of the name Armstrong. That's when I found St Luke's website, and there was a Helen Armstrong listed as treasurer. It was the longest of long shots, but I travelled to Durrington one weekend and asked around. The thing about living in a village is that everyone knows everyone, and an old guy in the Post Office said Helen Armstrong lived with her son, Simon, on Bulford Hill. I can't tell you what a moment that was … excitement, fear, trepidation all wrapped up in relief."

"When was this?"

"Five weeks ago. But then I found out about your mother being in Elmwood. I promise you, I thought long and hard about how I would approach you, and I decided it would be better to go slowly. Almost every care home in the land is desperate for staff. I've got experience of working in care, and I thought it would be the ideal way to meet my brother, without the risk of …"

Rosie looks at her shoes as if they're the most fascinating sight in the churchyard.

"Risk of?"

"Rejection," she replies in barely a whisper.

As difficult as it is, I maintain direct eye contact. The eyes are the mirror to the soul, Mother used to say.

"You thought I would reject you as my sibling?"

"In a word, yes. I've had nothing but rejection all my life, Simon, and the only person who has stood by me was Granddad.

I wanted to meet you more than I've wanted anything, but I was terrified you wouldn't want anything to do with me. That's why I didn't tell you up front. I thought … I hoped you'd get to know me, and we might become friends, and I could earn your trust."

In a situation lacking cast-iron facts, I am forced to consider matters beyond this moment and this churchyard to formulate a reaction. I'm reminded of a male who spent many years living a delusion. A male who denied his origins to such an extent he could not and would not forge any connections. That male is now alone, and he knows better than most how the sharp end of rejection feels.

The silence is heavy. I feel compelled to say something.

"What has Father Paul told you about my early life?"

"Listen, Simon, I don't want to cause any trouble between you, so maybe …"

"Your defence is not necessary," I interject. "I know his intentions are honourable. Did he tell you about the note?"

"What note?"

"When the hospital staff found me, they also found a note in the Moses basket. It read: Primrose Hill 29/09."

"Seriously?" Rosie gasps.

"Yes. Why did you think Lillian left that note with me?"

Rosie looks up to the sky and smiles. She then mouths a thank you.

"Well?"

"I didn't know about the note," she says. "And I certainly don't know why Mum left it with you. But, I'd like to think that she did something good, and that she hoped one day you'd realise the significance, and you'd look for Primrose Hill."

"I did, but it transpires that Primrose Hill is also a borough in London."

The edges of Rosie's lips curl upward again.

"Do you see why I never use the name Primrose now?"

"Yes, I do."

"I don't know what Lillian was thinking when she named me, but then again, she didn't think a lot, that woman."

"She was not a good mother?"

"I wish I could say yes to the question, Simon, but I can't lie. Her life was chaotic, and she spent most of it veering from one self-inflicted crisis to another, dragging me along in her wake."

I look down at the walnut casket.

"My mother was the complete opposite."

"You were lucky."

"Yes, I was, but my luck ran out when Mother died. I will never be able to replace her."

"No, but having a little sister in your life might go someway to banishing the loneliness, don't you think? You and I are all the family we have now."

Rosie extends her arm, offering me her hand. It's not a handshake.

"Give me a chance," she pleads. "Let me be your family."

It is true to say that Helen Armstrong and I were strangers when we met. That is not unsurprising, as I was an infant with no understanding of reality, or anything really. And yet, over the months and years, she earned the right to call herself my mother. Would it therefore be such a leap to assume I might forge a bond with another female, one who shares my genes?

Cautiously, I raise my arm.

"I can try to be your brother," I comment. "But, I am not like you."

Rosie takes my hand and squeezes it tight.

"You're not like anyone, Simon Armstrong, and don't you ever try to be."

I look into my sister's eyes once more.

"I am perhaps the most alien of humans, but I am who I am."

"Yes, you are, and there's no need to change."

"That is good, because I have come to realise that change is like vodka."

"How so?"

"A small amount is tolerable, but too much is a very bad idea."

THE END

Afterword

Thank you so much for reading *Waiting in The Sky* — I genuinely hope you enjoyed Simon's adventure.

To truly understand the tale, you probably need to understand a little about the author — well, me. Many of Simon's life experiences, and his quirks, were drawn from my fifty years on this planet.

My friends and family think it's odd that I eat the exact same thing for breakfast and lunch, and that I shower three times a day. They also can't understand why I get irrationally angry if I'm kept waiting beyond an agreed time, or why I prefer working alone rather than with other people. They don't understand why I deplore the idea of eating in restaurants, or why certain everyday sounds cause my anxiety levels to spike. They don't understand but they don't judge me.

It has been suggested that I should get myself checked out for whatever condition is behind my long list of quirks but I've resisted thus far. I ask myself if knowing why I'm wired differently would make any difference to my life, and I don't think it would, least not in a positive sense.

The reason you've just read this book is because I penned it, and the only reason I penned it is because my daily routine includes five hours of sitting at a desk and typing. It is now as much a compulsion as it is a routine.

In short, I've learned how to constructively channel my obsession with routines.

There are two other reasons why I've no desire to be tested: I don't want to live with a label, and my quirks are who I am.

Thankfully, my friends and family understand my reasoning.

With regards to Simon, I never wanted to label him either, and neither did Helen. It could be argued that she neglected her maternal duties when she decided not to book that appointment with a behavioural counsellor, but what can't be argued is how much she loved her son.

As the man responsible for Helen's behaviour, I wouldn't condone it but I know why she made the decision. It is the most human of instincts to want to protect those we love, and sometimes that involves making decisions not with the head, but the heart.

Ultimately, she gave Simon her unwavering support, and the best life she could. As a parent myself, I try to live up to those same standards.

Anyway, that's enough of my witterings for now. Thanks again for reading, and *ĝojan novaĵon al vi* (glad tidings to you).

Before You Go ...

If you enjoyed this book, and have a few minutes spare, I would be eternally grateful if you could leave a (hopefully positive) review on Amazon. If you're feeling particularly generous, a mention on Facebook or a Tweet would be equally appreciated. I know it's a pain, but it's the only way us indie authors can compete with the big publishing houses.

Stay in touch ...

For more information about me and to receive updates on my new releases, please visit my website - www.keithapearson.co.uk

If you have any questions or general feedback, you can follow me, on social media ...

Facebook: www.facebook.com/pearson.author

Twitter: www.twitter.com/keithapearson

Acknowledgments

I'd like to offer a massive thank you to my diligent beta readers who helped clean up the draft manuscript: Adrian Cousins, Kay Dadson, Adam Eccles, Vicky Emsley, Tracy Fisher, Lisa Gresty, Zoe Muse, Graham Nicholson, Greg Nicholson, Trevor Oldroyd, Sharon O'Neill, Andy Papanicolaou, Kellie Rae, Kirsty Scutter, and Paul Underdown. I can't emphasise enough how much your feedback helped.

And last but not least, an equally massive thank you to my editor, Sian Phillips. If anyone spots a grammatical error in this section of the book, it's entirely my fault as Sian had no involvement. :o)

Printed in Great Britain
by Amazon